CASTLE OF LIES

KIERSI BURKHART

carolrhoda LAB

MINNEAPOLIS

Carolrhoda Lab™ is a trademark of Lerner Publishing Group, Inc.

Carolrhoda Lab™
An imprint of Carolrhoda Books
A division of Lerner Publishing Group, Inc.
241 First Avenue North
Minneapolis, MN 55401 USA

For reading levels and more information, look up this title at
www.lernerbooks.com.

Image credits: Castle: Calavision/Shutterstock.com; Gleb Guralnyk/Shutterstock.
com (border); ElenaG177/Shutterstock.com (gold); Imagine Photographer/
Shutterstock.com (marble); Ozz Design/Shutterstock.com (swirl); Nata Kuprova/
Shutterstock.com (font); Gordan/Shutterstock.com (grunge).

Main body text set in Janson Text LT Std 10.5/15.
Typeface provided by Linotype AG.

Library of Congress Cataloging-in-Publication Data

Names: Burkhart, Kiersi, author.
Title: Castle of lies / Kiersi Burkhart.
Description: Minneapolis : Carolrhoda Lab, [2019] | Summary: Thelia has spent her
    whole life scheming to get on the throne, but when her kingdom is invaded by an
    army of elves and a dangerous well of magic is discovered under the royal castle,
    her plans change drastically.
Identifiers: LCCN 2018031556 (print) | LCCN 2018041433 (ebook) | ISBN
    9781541541856 (eb pdf) | ISBN 9781512429978 (th : alk. paper)
Subjects: | CYAC: Fantasy.
Classification: LCC PZ7.1.B88 (ebook) | LCC PZ7.1.B88 Cas 2019 (print) | DDC
    [Fic]—dc23

LC record available at https://lccn.loc.gov/2018031556

Manufactured in the United States of America
1-41597-23504-11/12/2018

FOR DANNY

I WOULDN'T HAVE MADE IT WITHOUT YOU.

CHAPTER 1

THELIA

Corene isn't made of queen material—never has been. And illustrating my point: she can't even hold her liquor. She worms across her bed in her silk nightgown, spilling wine across the blankets. Weak, inside and out.

"Thelia, I don't know what to do." My cousin settles her head on my lap and sips what's left in her glass. I play my usual part. Rubbing her shoulders so she won't guess the fury still boiling inside me. Touching her hair so she won't know how much I want to tangle my hand in it and pull until she screams.

I peel my lips back in a smile. "What do you mean? Do what you've always done."

She rolls her head around on my lap in denial. "It's more than that with Bayled. It's . . ." She lets out a frustrated puff of wine breath. "It's more complicated now."

As if things haven't always been complicated between Princess Corene and that lucky foreigner. Yes, *lucky*. Corene can pity Bayled all she wants for losing his parents when he was barely ten, but look where it landed him—in line for the throne.

So maybe his parents were unlucky. Still, they should've known leaving out a candle to welcome Magic into their house was a bad idea, especially here in the Holy Kingdom. People have been hanged for less. And always preaching how women should be allowed in politics didn't make them popular either. I've never been convinced that fire was a mere accident.

"Why would it be complicated?" I ask Corene gently. "He's the King's ward and heir. You're the Princess, the people's favorite. You two are supposed to end up together." If the King were smart—which is always a matter of suspending your disbelief—he'd be angling for the union. With Bayled on the throne, we'll get access to the Northern Republic's trade routes, their luxury market, their technology.

"We *were*." Corene empties her glass. "But I think a mistake was made."

My whole chest goes warm and bubbly, like the wine in my glass. I've been waiting for these words since the spring, when she buried that dagger in my back and she ruined my one chance at happiness.

"What happened?" I ask, keeping the eagerness out of my voice as much as I can.

Corene slides off my lap and buries her face in a pillow. Her empty glass rolls away. "I shouldn't say more."

"You know you can trust me." I take her hand and squeeze. "What's happened, Corene?"

She sniffles into the pillow. "Bayled asked me to marry him. He asked me, not Dad."

Engaged, without the King's permission. Behind his back. I hold in a wicked smile. Praise be the grace of Melidia! I know exactly how I'll repay Corene for what she did to me.

"Congratulations. I'm sure the King will approve." I take her glass and refill it. "Another?"

Corene sighs languorously. "Thank you."

I hand the full glass back, watching as she takes a long gulp. Tomorrow's banquet day, when everyone who's anyone comes to Four Halls to dine with the King, and I already have a battle plan. Mother always said that everyone needs an edge, a bit more knowledge than anyone else, so you always have a bit more power.

I've found my edge, and I know just how to use it.

I'm walking into the banquet hall when Parsifal stumbles up to me. His cheeks are bright red—he's gotten into the wine cellar with Derk again. "My dearest Thelia Finegarden. You're looking fabulous tonight."

I roll my eyes at my pig-faced cousin. He's been a flatterer ever since he arrived in the Holy Kingdom and realized certain people were laughing not only at his jokes, but also at his irregular face. It works surprisingly well for him—with most people. "I've worn this dress a dozen times, Percy." And I've re-stitched it another half-dozen times or dyed it a different color to make it look new. That's been my routine ever since the King's senseless war bankrupted us along with every other noble family. Daddy found out the hard way that just being the Queen's brother didn't protect our fortune.

"Doesn't negate my statement in the least." Parsifal's flattened nose and mouth curl into themselves as he smiles.

We take our seats next to each other at the long banquet table. I sit across from Daddy, who ignores me even though he hasn't seen me all week. That never gets easier, but at least my brother Morgaun didn't join him tonight. He's probably back at the manor performing bloody penance to the Goddess. Eating roast pig at a banquet would undoubtedly interfere with all his gratuitous self-sacrifice in Melidia's name.

I'm not interested in Parsifal's gobble tonight. I have something important to do. *Dearest uncle*, I'll say as I help the King out of his chair at the end of the banquet. He'll be drunk and grateful for my assistance. *I hate to bear this sort of news, but I believe your daughter has betrayed you.*

"I heard something that might interest you," Parsifal says, and I snap out of my private rehearsal. "Some visitors arrived at the castle earlier today."

I narrow my eyes. "Visitors?"

He holds up one finger. "You first. You must have something for me."

We've played this game for years—trading a secret for a secret. An insight for an eavesdrop. Now that our families have no coin, we only respect one kind of currency: information.

I had integrity, once upon a time. But then my brother tried to break my legs, I got this scar down the side of my face, and Mother ran off. Since then, I haven't had much patience for the hard and honest way.

So I lean over and tell Parsifal what I know, and his dark eyebrows rise up into his bounteous curls. This should be enough to buy me the gossip he promised.

"I suppose it was inevitable." Parsifal cocks his eyebrow. "You must be disappointed." He's the only one—well, besides Mother—who knows what I want more than anything: to push Corene out of the way, marry Bayled myself, and the moment the old King kicks off . . . become the Queen.

My mother clawed her way to the title of Duchess with her teeth and nails, tolerating every violation and humiliation for one fistful of power. As she always said, "What Corene was born with, you'll have to fight for." While my silly cousin was mooning over a boy, Mother taught me to cripple a man without messing up my braid.

"I'm not disappointed." I smirk at him. "I'm going to tell the King."

Parsifal sits up straight, unable to hide a curling grin. "How absolutely cruel of you."

I smile. "Did you expect anything less?"

"Never."

Nobody else would understand. Nobody else knows what Corene did to me. "Maybe he'll even be so insulted that he'll insist the two of them part ways," I say. Making Bayled available for me.

Parsifal's brows furrow. "And keep Bayled as his heir? He wouldn't choose Bayled over his own daughter."

"That's your foreign upbringing showing." He hates when I rib him about growing up in Frefois. "Bayled's not royal blood, but he's a man. That counts for more." Mother always said when you're a woman in this land, working twice as hard won't get what you want; maybe wanting it ten times as much will.

Parsifal grimaces at me. I smile back and ask, "Now what do you have for me about these visitors?"

He sighs. "They're from the South."

"The Lord of the Willows?" My eyebrows rise, and a hopeful note fills my voice. " . . . or the Baron?"

"Farther south."

There's only one place past the edge of the Kingdom—the Klissen. A sunlit land of hills, sheep, and people who are utter doorknobs. "What could those cratertooths be doing here?" I ask. "They've refused to speak to us since the war." Ten cycles ago, their scattered tribes united and elected their first head chief to repel our foolish invasion.

"Do you blame them?" Parsifal snorts. "We tried to invade and conquer, completely unprovoked. Kind of a shit move."

"So why are they here *now*?"

"I'm sure we'll find out soon."

A horn blows—the royals are entering the banquet hall. We all rise. The King walks in first under the guards' crossed spears, carrying a full goblet of wine. Behind him comes Corene, strawberry ringlets spilling down the front of her ocean-blue gown. Then Bayled enters, dressed in his favorite long red coat. The fabric makes his deep brown skin glow in the lamplight, and I can't help smiling. Supreme Ass-Kisser of the Kingdom though he is, he has a certain boyish charm.

But Bayled doesn't take his usual seat at the King's right— he settles one chair down. And he looks like he's swallowed a particularly unsavory beetle.

We're all about to return to our seats when another horn blows. A pretty young blond man I've never seen strides into the banquet hall, wide-open collar flapping across his chest. Is that the Chief? He's so much younger than I expected. He's flanked by three rough-looking bodyguards—two men and one woman, all of them armed. So it's normal in the South for women to use swords? For a second I feel foolish about setting my ambitions here, on the Holy Kingdom—but the taste of victory will be even greater when I become Queen and wield *my* sword from the King's balcony. Everything will change under my rule.

The blond man takes Bayled's seat and casts Corene a sideways look with his ocean-blue eyes. His bodyguards stand against the wall, watchful. Parsifal shoots me a look that says, *Things are getting exciting, aren't they?*

We all sit down, and a parade of servants enters the banquet hall with carts and trays full of food. I've only gotten one bite of ham when the King staggers to his feet, goblet held aloft. "Everyone!" Wine sloshes over the side of his goblet. "I have an announcement." He gestures to the blond Southerner. "Welcome to Melidihan, Nul se Lan, son of Chief Lan, and formidable leader of the Klissen. I'm sure all the noblewomen here appreciate your presence." A ripple of laughter travels down the banquet table.

Parsifal whispers, "As if only noble*women* appreciate a blond with impeccable chest definition."

"I've invited our friend from the beautiful hill country of the Klissen for a good reason," the King drones. "We've finally reached terms for annexation."

My head jolts up. Annexation would mean the Klissen becoming one of the Holy Kingdom's docile territories, like Frefois. It's all the King's ever wanted. We'll have all the sheep, iron, and potatoes the Kingdom will ever need. But what did we trade away for it?

Nul se Lan rises beside the King, goblet held up. "Very glad of this invitation I am. Honor it brings to my country to be asked by the King, and join blessed Holy Kingdom."

I turn to Parsifal, his face a reflection of how I feel, like we're missing an essential piece of the picture. Why would the cratertooths be this eager to reconcile with us? Unless . . .

I snap my gaze to Corene, sitting at the other end of the table with her eyes focused on her lap. The Princess. The key to keeping the royal bloodline going—and the perfect glue for building an alliance.

"To secure our bonds of brotherhood," the King says, voice slurring, "I am pleased to announce that in one moon, my daughter, the Princess Corene, will wed Nul se Lan of the Klissen. Our kingdoms will at last unite!"

Praise Melidia—I knew it. Everyone claps. I join in, but I'm focused on someone else. Poor, sweet, handsome, guileless Bayled, gripping his goblet so tight his knuckles strain.

"I can see the spindles turning in your head, Theels." Parsifal leans closer. "What are you plotting?"

"I'm not plotting. I hope you get crotch rot for suggesting it." He won't get more from me until he can offer me something for it.

"I could help. I'd rather see you on the throne than *that* big oaf."

Daddy has noticed we're whispering, so I raise my voice a little and say, "I'm happy for Corene, Percy. Unification will surely return the Kingdom to its former glory." Daddy gives an approving nod, and I commit it to memory.

"Absolutely," Parsifal says. "And annexing the Klissen into the Kingdom will give us a strategic barrier against . . ." He pauses for dramatic effect. "The *elven armies*." He laughs like it's all a good jape, but every muscle in my body goes tight.

"I'll stitch your lips closed with chickenthread," I hiss.

"Parsifal Bellisare." Daddy sets down his fork. "Elves are a real threat, not a punchline." My father doesn't have a shred of patience for the Bellisares. In-laws or not, they're my mother's relatives, so as far as he's concerned they're poison. "You should be spending your mental energy on what you're going to say to

Nul se Lan when you meet him. Your father could use the connection to a plentiful land like the Klissen."

Parsifal's cheeks go a fierce red. I could laugh—if I weren't too busy wondering if he's right. Maybe this deal happened not only because the King bought the Chief off with his beautiful daughter, but because they're both afraid of the same thing.

Them.

PARSIFAL

Thelia refuses to look at me. Fine, so maybe I shouldn't have brought up elves, but I thought it was all so long ago that she'd reward me with a laugh.

No point staying now—the drama's passed. Bayled and Corene have excused themselves, leaving the nobles whispering. This would be the perfect opportunity to put in a good word for Dad with Nul se Lan. Not that any amount of ass-kissing could rebuild everything our family lost when the Kingdom conquered Frefois.

I leave the banquet room without a word. Four Halls is so quiet that the heels of my light shoes echo on the stone as I head to the courtyard to reclaim my carriage. The painted faces of long-dead nobles watch me go by, judging me for being such a craggon.

Back when Thelia's chest was flat and I hadn't yet begun longing for her, we stayed particularly late at Four Halls one night, playing games with Bayled and the Princess that usually devolved into teasing Bayled and Corene defending him. We gave the Queen such a headache that she put us in the royal sitting room with the dogs so Corene could get her beauty rest. We fell asleep in front of the fire—but I leapt awake to Thelia's screams.

She clawed the air, and I pulled her to my chest so she couldn't hurt herself. When she became lucid again, I asked with a trembling voice, "What was that?"

"Them."

"Who?"

"Elves." Her voice turned to sobs. "With those awful eyes, shiny and beady—no whites. Too far apart, too big for their wrinkly gray heads." She shuddered. "Their teeth were sharpened to points."

I'd never seen an elf—no one in the Holy Kingdom has. But even in the old stories, they're nothing like Thelia's dreams. Our tutors taught us the basics: the long ears live on Magic; they maintain a small armed force to keep giants out of their glass city; they rarely breed and rarely die. And before the Split, they rained terrible destruction on humans who had overstepped their bounds.

This Kingdom has always feared the elves, even though centuries have passed since we last saw them. And for years they came to Thelia in her nightmares.

I only said it because of my recent dalliance with the indomitable Derk, who let slip that the usual nebulous chatter about the long ears has intensified. Lords from the southern parts of the Holy Kingdom have quietly traveled to Melidihan with their court wizards, requiring extra bread and cakes and scones that Derk bakes and delivers. While he lays out trays of pastry, they talk in quiet tones about "peculiar Magical frequencies"—whatever that means. Something is happening behind the curtains, and tonight's announcement has everything to do with it.

We need the Klissen, and they need us.

I don't realize I'm drunk until I reach the courtyard and the night sky swims overhead. Demons, it's chilly. The dreaded snow is soon to appear. I pull the cuffed sleeves of my coat tighter around me and scowl. I don't want to face Dad back at the mansion—he'll be in a foul mood when he learns I left the banquet early. Maybe if he weren't so bitter at the King and came himself, the Bellisare fortune wouldn't depend solely on me. Every time I see our estate out the carriage window, I'm reminded it's all we have left of Dad's once vast riches. If only I could live here in Four Halls like Thelia does, in my own suite. She has no idea how good she's got it.

Though I don't have an older brother who's so far rung up the parapets that he's gone over the other side and driven her out of her own house. There's that.

But the sun could be coming out with Corene getting married off. Now Thelia has the chance to scoop up Bayled and become queen, like my dear horrible aunt always wanted for her. Now I only worry that her resentment of Corene has consumed her. If she's too careless, if she botches this, then I'm done here. I've pinned my hopes on Thelia winning over Bayled. I can't take another decade of living under stupid Hindermarks.

I whirl around and run back into the castle. Maybe I can make amends for my tasteless elf joke and keep her focused on the real end game.

As I'm heading toward her suite in South Hall, I notice red ringlets whip around a corner. Only one person here has hair like that. I thought Corene would be in her quarters now, sobbing on her gossamer curtains. Following the flourish of her skirt down the halls, I think I've only seen her move this quickly once before—when she heard the white flu had come for her mother.

Corene stops on the bottom step of the small, winding staircase that leads to North Hall. "It's you," she says in a breathy voice.

Behind her, I duck out of sight and peer around a pillar. I can't see who stands above her.

"How feel you, Princess?" Nul se Lan's accent gives him away. "You look . . . pale. Announcement a surprise?"

Nul se Lan reaches down to Corene's face, but the pillar blocks my view. All I can make out is a disembodied hand cupping the Princess's rosy cheek. Their touch is familiar, almost casual. I lean out as far as I dare.

Corene smiles at him—a real smile that crinkles her eyes. "I'm fine." Her hand goes to his, their fingers intertwining. "I knew my father had already accepted the proposal. I just wasn't prepared for him to tell everyone about it."

Especially Bayled, I bet.

"I know." Nul se Lan steps down to the bottom step, so I can finally see all six feet of him. A curl of blond hair drops over his eyes, and a delectable diamond of carved chest peeks out from his loose collar. He tips up Corene's chin so their gazes lock. "Now, I hope you are prepared," Nul se Lan says. "Soon, my most beautiful star, we be wed."

My most beautiful star? Demons, strike me dead before I vomit on the floor.

"I've never been more prepared." Corene rises onto the balls of her feet, and their lips touch.

Oh, this is much more complicated than I thought. I turn and stumble back the way I came, clutching the hem of my shirt so I don't laugh aloud. Corene, that wily squork—what's her game? I never thought I'd feel bad for that tourist Bayled, but even I didn't see this coming. Time to ponder over what I'll tell Thelia.

BAYLED

I was nearly nine when I was brought to the Holy Kingdom, but it still feels like Corene's always been a fixture in my life. Every moment that matters—whispering during our tutors' boring lessons, practicing my swordplay in the courtyard while she watched, exploring the castle's many hidden tunnels, staying up late at night to share secrets—Corene is part of them all.

I was so lost and out of place when the Prime Minister sent my family here. We came to hold the King to the terms of his surrender, but the Holy Kingdom became so much more for me. From the moment I arrived, Corene helped me understand the customs, the way people think. Well, mostly. I've never understood the hatred they have for simple Magic. In the Republic, we let brooms and mops do all the cleaning. Doing it oneself was an enormous waste.

But Corene never seemed to care where I was from. She's the only one who's ever accepted me, loved me, just as I am. When my parents died, it was her arms I fell into. And now I'm going to lose her.

My perch on the stairs behind the kitchen is the only thing that feels familiar. My stomach grumbles—I couldn't eat much of my dinner after the announcement. The moment it was over, Corene was gone. She must have needed the time alone, so I didn't follow. Instead I stumbled out here, where no one would bother me.

When I asked Corene to marry me, I should've gone straight to the King. Told him my intentions while he kept me working late one evening and he was spilling his soul over a full goblet of wine. One of those nights, silver with camaraderie, would've been the perfect chance to ask for his blessing. He would've said yes.

"No, he wouldn't," I say aloud. I know the King pities me because my parents died, but I'm under no illusions about why he made me his ward—and heir to the throne. He wanted access to the Northern Republic's trade routes and riches, and thought he'd get it by making me the next ruler.

As everyone loved to remind me growing up, I wasn't born here, and I have no claim to this land. I certainly don't deserve to marry a Princess. Every extra fencing lesson I took in view of the King's window, every meal I brought him in the middle of the night, was to try to earn that place by her side.

With someone else in my place, where will I end up?

The kitchen door opens, and I glance up to find Corene standing over me. She knew right where to look.

"How's your night going?" I regret it as it leaves my lips. What an infantile way to start this conversation.

She pulls up her skirts and sits down next to me. "I'm so sorry, Bayled. My heart is breaking."

I'm enveloped by relief. Naturally, this wasn't some

premeditated plan to escape our engagement. Corene has no feelings for this blond stranger.

"So you didn't say yes?"

"My father did. It was his idea."

Right. It's not like a princess here has any say in who she marries. I put an arm around her shoulders and squeeze. She crumples, burying her head in the crook of my neck. We're stuck like that.

"You never did answer *my* proposal," I say. "You didn't say yes or no."

"I didn't think I had to."

I smile against her hair. The answer's been yes since we were thirteen cycles into this life and I first told her in whispers that I loved her. "So what are you going to say to your father?"

Corene pulls away. "Bayled. I have to marry Nul se Lan."

"No you don't. You love me, don't you?"

"Of course, but—"

"But nothing!" I'm on my feet before a star can flicker. Corene's eyes fly wide. I've never raised my voice to her before and I wish I could take it back. I kneel so our eyes are level and grasp her hands. "Just . . . please, Corene. If you tell your father about us—about our engagement—he may change his mind."

Corene rises to her feet and clasps her hands demurely at her waist, with all the poise that comes from high breeding. "I can't," she says, sure and steady. "If I do, he *will* change his mind. And we can't afford that. We need the Klissen. This marriage is my duty, Bayled. It's what's right." She goes to the kitchen door and opens it. "This will save the Kingdom."

SAPPHIRE

I am starting to forget what battle smells like.

I pull my chest plate off the wall hook and hold it to my face, inhaling the fragrance of metal striking metal, remembering animals roaring and giants screaming. The tang of my enemies' blood clings to it. Grooves run through the metal from blades, claws, teeth. How many blows has it absorbed to keep the flaming heart of Magic safe inside me? I sigh, my breath fogging up the smooth silver. I brush it away quickly with my sleeve.

The hiss of my front door opening startles me. Returning the armor to the hook, I find Ellze standing in the glass entryway, dressed in a dark spidersilk traveling tunic with white stitching, a cheetah fur cloak, and a gold mask sitting on his green hair. His angular frame is bathed in the pink light of the wisp dozing in my lamp.

We are not leaving until tomorrow. If he is already dressed to travel, he must be excited, too. "Mahove!" he says. "I am glad to find you here, friend Sapphire."

"Mahove." I pull the drawstring of my robe tight. "Where else would I be?"

"I thought you would be saying farewell to Laian."

"We dissolved our relationship two moons ago," I tell him.

Ever since I decided to remain a soldier after my required time was served, she had been pushing me to return to civilian life. After a decade of this, I terminated it—we simply are not compatible.

Ellze's eyes flicker. "I did not know."

"I did not tell anyone." My private life is private for a reason. And Ellze has been so involved in his work since he was promoted to Jaguar that we rarely speak anymore. "What did you need?" I want to return to meditating.

"The Commander has reassigned you," Ellze says.

A reassignment on the eve of deployment? I have been with my unit since I joined at the mandatory age of fifty. All I can imagine is that Commander Valya is punishing me for something. Surely Ellze, his nephew, will tell me what I have done to upset him.

Keeping my voice steady, I ask, "What is the new assignment?"

"You will be joining the Jaguars. At the Commander's right side." A sheepish smile creeps onto his face. "With me."

I search for words but find none. How have I been granted this honor? Once upon a time, my mother had to toss my belongings out the front door so I would leave for my tenure in the armed forces. Now I will be one of Commander Valya's ten elite warriors. How many times have I watched as a Jaguar sails in to rescue another soldier from certain death? They are the ghosts that only appear when you find yourself standing in the shadow of doom.

Ellze slides his gold mask down over his face. "The Commander has called a meeting. We should go right now." I nod, and my wisp floats down from the lamp, drifting into my hip pocket. It once guided another soldier through the darkness of Arrow Mountain; I found it hovering over his speared body, all alone, and it's refused to leave my side since.

My pocket flap closes, and the pink light winks out.

The barracks are alive tonight. The blue-green glass spires of Viteos transform into prisms, scattering the sunset across our tents. Red and orange wisps in the lamps awaken, glowing brighter as they stretch and yawn. Soldiers congregate around fire pits, hauling out vegetables, hawgrain, and protein patties to cook for dinner.

"I still don't understand it," I say. "I've done nothing to earn this honor. Why would Commander Valya choose me?"

"Perhaps he saw something in you, and he wants to give you the chance to shine."

"Or he is attracted to me," I joke.

"You are quite good-looking."

We fall into a stiff silence. When we were children Ellze would always ask, "When will you declare?" Pressuring me, pushing me. I know he wanted me to declare myself female—he loves them. But only pieces of that felt right to me, even when I was decades past when most of The People declare. And neither did the idea of male sit entirely well.

In the end, I declared something else—some of this, some of that, and some of neither. I asked my chest plates be made flat with only a hint of pectoral muscle carved in. All my tunics hang loose. I cut my pants tight because I have a fantastic rear. I thought that would finally be the end of whatever fantasy Ellze had about me. But nothing changed.

At last, we reach the Commander's quarters—a reflective blue pyramid, its gold point spearing the sky. Seeing it, I remember this is bigger than me. The force is only assembled to contain the new threat on the other side of the continent. We must all focus on the goal if we are to protect Helyanda.

The other Jaguars already sit on the floor inside, ears poking up from their gold masks, fur capes trailing across the stone. "Mahove, Ellze!" The Commander rises from his pillow, unbound hair dripping down his shoulders like molten silver. "You have brought my new recruit."

He pads barefoot toward us. I am frozen in place as he brings a hand to my cheek, stilling a hair's breadth from contact. I will admit that I have fantasized more than once about how his touch would feel.

"Mahove, Sapphire," the Commander says, withdrawing. "I have watched you fight in the practice hall and on the battlefield. I am elated to bring young talent like yours into our ranks."

I fall to one knee. "Thank you for the privilege of serving under you, Commander Valya."

He laughs and pulls me to my feet. "No need for all that." He ushers me onto the dais. My hands tingle where he touched me. A black fur, dappled with faint leopard spots, hangs from the back of a chair. The Commander picks it up, caressing the fur with his long, perfect fingers. "Turn around."

I obey, and Commander Valya drapes the fur over my shoulders. I stare out at the Jaguars who sit on the floor, watching. The deep sockets of their gold masks obscure their eyes in shadow. When I turn back around to thank him, the Commander hands me my own mask.

The gold is cold and soft as I settle it on my face. The powerful Magic imbued in it tickles my cheeks.

"My companions, please welcome Sapphire to our ranks," says Commander Valya as I step off the dais into the circle of Jaguars. They pat my shoulders and back, like we have been comrades forever. I cannot tell which one is Ellze; in our masks, we have all become part of a single faceless being.

The Commander gestures to a big blue wisp snoozing in the brazier, and it rises from its ashy bed. Stretching its tiny arms, its glow surges outward, casting us in blue light and deep shadow.

"Tomorrow," the Commander says, donning his own horned gold mask, "for the first time in centuries . . . we travel east to go to war."

CHAPTER 2

BAYLED

I inhale the sharp, cool morning air, hoping it will calm me. After waking up this morning to the servants already bustling about and preparing for the wedding, I'm relieved to have escaped the castle. The sound of Halrendar's gentle hoofbeats fills the otherwise silent forest.

To watch Corene marry someone else . . . I can't imagine a worse punishment. I've labored at the King's side since I was twelve cycles into this life, helping him strategize, decide fates, dispense justice. I've watched his love of wine grow as the Kingdom's debts pile higher and I desperately try to find coin that isn't there. Ruling is grueling, thankless work, even when you have men like me refilling the goblet whenever it runs low. I knew that this was my future; it was believing I'd marry Corene someday that made it bearable.

Without her at my side, all that becomes meaningless torture. I wish she wasn't so good, so dutiful. If she were more selfish, we'd have a chance together.

I hear someone coming down the path behind me, so I rein Halrendar around to get a look.

"Bayled!" Thelia rides up in a pine-colored cloak that makes the specks of green in her dark eyes glow. Her white palfrey, Parlor Trick, looks grumpy.

"I didn't know you ever got up this early," I say. She must have some reason for leaving her suite before noon.

Thelia arches an eyebrow. "That's rude. I get up early as often as I can. Morning is my favorite time of day for a ride."

I almost laugh. Lies come so easily to Thelia Finegarden, it's as if she breathes them. When we were kids still chasing each other around the courtyard, she always had some lie prepped when we asked, "What's that bruise? How did you manage to pick up two whole hay bales?" She had stronger, firmer arms than even me, which she'd blame on "a natural disposition." The scrapes? She slipped in some gravel. The calluses on her palms? Working hard on a tapestry, or some horsefish like that. But it was an open secret that before she ran off, wild-eyed old Delia was training her daughter in the arts people here consider inappropriate for ladies.

"I go riding almost every morning and I've never seen you," I say, even though it's like approaching a mother biylar bear, hoping you won't get attacked by both heads.

"Maybe I was anxious this morning," she says. "Maybe I'm worried about my friends after that disaster of a banquet last night."

I didn't expect that, and flounder for a response.

"What's going to happen with your engagement now?" she asks.

My spine goes frigid. How does she—? Never mind. Corene and Thelia tell each other everything.

"It's over," I say.

"And you're not upset?"

"Of course I'm upset! Corene's the love of my life."

"Then why are you letting the King marry her off to that hillman? After all the ledgers you've stayed up until dawn filling out for him?" Thelia's stopped Parlor Trick right in the middle of the road. Halrendar halts and sniffs the white palfrey. "Put up a fight for once."

There's no fight to fight. It's already done. "Corene doesn't want that. She wants what's best for the Kingdom."

"My cousin has no idea what's good for anyone," Thelia snaps. "She never has. Remember when she brought that mouse inside because she felt bad for it out in the cold, and it got loose and chewed Queen Laine's favorite gown to bits?"

I bite the inside of my lip. "Yeah."

"She made a commitment to you. She promised to marry *you* before the King gave her away to someone else." As if a secret engagement means anything in the face of the Kingdom's most valuable alliance. As if she had any choice in the matter.

"I know it's hard for you to understand concepts like duty or devotion," I find myself saying. I'm angrier than I realized. "My duty and devotion are all I have left."

Thelia sneers. "I'm the one who doesn't understand devotion, when you won't fight for the girl you love? You'll just watch as she's dragged off to that wild hill country, never to return." Thelia nudges Parlor Trick and ambles off down the road ahead.

What right does she have to act like this? She's been a snot to all of us, including Corene, ever since the spring. When the Baron gave up their courtship and went home . . .

I stop myself. Baron Durnhal. Her mother. Two people who've abandoned Thelia—and now Corene's about to do the same thing. No wonder.

"Wait!" I tap Halrendar's sides with my heels, and he jumps to a trot. "Wait, Thelia. I'm just . . . sad about all this."

"And I'm not?" she retorts. Parlor Trick is slighter and faster, and Thelia surges on ahead. "After they get married, my best friend will be gone forever."

"I know!" I urge Halrendar on and finally overtake Parlor Trick. "But there's nothing we can do about it!"

Thelia slows her horse and Parlor Trick tosses her head, annoyed that she can't keep running. Thelia's gaze searches mine. "We have one moon until the wedding," she says. "One moon to change Corene's mind."

"But how—"

"Corene just doesn't realize what she has." I didn't realize she had such a high opinion of me—which turns me suspicious of this whole conversation. She rode out today for her own reasons, and I won't learn what those are unless I step into her trap.

"What do you suggest?" I ask.

Her deep red lips, like a rose crushed and pulped, twist into a smile. "Make her jealous."

"I've never wanted anyone except Corene. I can't just move on."

She sighs, as impatient with me as always. "Don't think of it like that. Think of it as . . . finding comfort in someone else in a time of hardship."

There's only one person she could mean. "You?"

"Don't look so shocked."

"I'm flattered, but—"

"For Melidia's sake, Bayled, it's not like that." Thelia brings Parlor Trick to a complete stop. Without my asking, Halrendar stops beside her. I think he has a crush on the palfrey. "If I tell you this . . ." she begins, staring down at the path to avoid looking at me. "Promise not to tell anyone else."

"Tell me what?"

Her voice drops. "I've already given my heart away. Remember Baron Durnhal's visit?"

I nod. Another bored nobleman visiting Four Halls to amuse himself. But the Baron was an interesting, thoughtful sort of man. He brought Corene strange gifts of ostrich eggs and wyvern-skin boots, told me fascinating stories from his time on the war front, and spent an inordinate amount of time with Thelia.

It wasn't improper, but they had a way of making conversation so that everything else around them disappeared. The Baron understood her harsh, unrepentant humor. He fielded her barbs and lobbed them back. I figured Thelia wanted his connections, with her father's dukedom being bankrupt.

Her eyes shine with tears. "He stole my heart like an outlaw. Then he had to go home for business."

That's not what Corene said. He'd found himself a more suitable wife elsewhere—someone with fewer masculine pursuits, and not so well-muscled from her secret nighttime kroga lessons. I'd thought the Baron was different from the rest of these shallow Holy Kingdom nobles, but I guess not.

I study Thelia. I've seen her fake distress for attention, for pity—but the way she folds in on herself now is different. I reach out to pat her shoulder, and she jerks away. I forgot how much she dislikes being touched. I fall back on words, saying, "I'm sorry. That must be difficult."

"I miss Red every day." She inhales. "The sting hasn't left. So don't worry about me falling in love with you. I have no space in my heart for someone else."

I nod. "I get it. And if you think your plan will work . . ."

"Of course it will," Thelia chirps. "I'm Corene's best friend, and best friends know these things. When she sees you moving on, she won't be able to stop herself from doing something rash." She winks. "Like asking the King *not* to make her marry Nul se Lan."

"But how will she ever forgive me for flirting with someone else? And with her cousin—her best friend?"

Thelia waves a hand like she's clearing out a bad smell. "That's something to worry about later."

PARSIFAL

I don't even knock before entering Corene's room in North Hall—an entire quarter of the castle, just for royals. She jolts upright on her bed, scattering the fabric swatches piled in front of her.

"Hello, Percy."

I don't bother with the formalities. "I saw you with him," I say, pouring myself a glass of wine from the decanter on the table. "Last night. After the banquet." I lean against the bedpost, the stem of the glass balanced between my ring and pinky fingers.

"I don't know what you're talking about."

I let loose a catlike smile—or my version of one. "You don't need to play games with me," I say. "Bayled and I aren't friends. I won't judge you for doing what's best for you. Though I have to ask: does Nul se Lan know about your secret engagement?"

She crosses her arms. "How stupid do you think I am?"

"Hmm. How's Bayled bearing up?"

"He understands that I have a duty to my country. I love him, but everything was conditional. He had to know this could happen."

I'm sickened to think she's right. The temperate Bayled Vasha probably does understand—which doesn't bode well for Thelia's plans. He could carry a torch for Corene forever, idealizing her sacrifice, instead of looking for a rebound like any sensible man who's just been jilted.

"Do either of these poor bastards know that you're playing a game of pa-chi-chi with them?" I ask.

"I am not!" Corene snatches my wine glass and downs it. "I'm just trying to make Dad happy, Percy. If he thinks I love Nul, then he won't feel bad sending me away."

I cross my arms. "So he's *Nul* now?"

"Ugh! It doesn't mean anything." She gets her own glass and fills it. It's barely noon.

I arch an eyebrow. "Sure."

Unlike Thelia, Corene's never been a good liar. She lies best when she believes she's telling the truth. I'm sure that's how she convinced the Baron to leave Four Halls—and Thelia.

She stares into the red depths of her wine. "I love Bayled, Percy. I've always loved him."

I pat her back. "I know." And yet . . . you don't make out on the stairs with a foreigner who can't keep his shirt closed if you love someone else.

It's nothing new for her feelings to oscillate like the tides. When she was eleven, she loved horses with her whole heart. The next moon she begged her father for a hunting dog. She's always loved Bayled, though. And for all the other young nobles who have come and gone from Four Halls, Thelia remains her best and closest friend.

But like the horse and the hunting dog, Corene prefers when things belong fully to her and no one else. And who wouldn't, living a life of public performance and spectacle? Even she doesn't truly belong to herself. Perhaps what I saw the other night is as simple as that. Nul se Lan is strange and new, someone she can have completely. Someone who's all hers.

"So what's the hurry to marry Prince Sheep?" I ask. "Why does duty to the Kingdom have to come at the expense of your happiness?"

Her eyes drop to her lap. "It's my role, Percy. I got to have my happiness for eighteen whole cycles. I played with you and Thelia and Bayled all I wanted. And now the time"—she swallows—"has finally come to be a Princess."

"But why *now*?" I ask, refilling my glass. Corene's not clever, but her father tells her things the rest of us don't get to hear. "Surely this wedding isn't happening in such a rush because the Southerners suddenly think annexation is a great idea."

Corene purses her lips. "We hear the same rumors."

"Rumors about the long ears?"

"See, you know as much as I do." She crosses her arms. "And you're drinking all my wine."

I take an epically long swallow, hand her the empty glass, and head out into the hall.

"Good-bye!" she calls after me, annoyed. "I had to start getting ready anyway!" I laugh as she slams the door behind me.

Our petty little plans probably won't matter. If the elves

are already on the move, it's too late. I pay more attention to our history lessons than anyone else. If there's one thing I've learned, it's that humans are stupid, small, and insignificant. Merely a temporary blip on the face of this continent, and no marriages or alliances or political posturing will save us.

THELIA

Everything is in motion.

I put on an inspired performance for Bayled the other day, pumped full of just enough real heartbreak to get through to him—a shadow of what I'd felt this spring when I found the Baron's farewell letter.

The silly trit ate it right up.

I thought he'd learned a little skepticism since Parsifal and I, at a banquet many years ago, convinced him that the Countess of Westhaven's corset was untied. We suggested he be a good lad and go stitch it back up for her. He got a full slap to the face for that one. But as usual, Corene came to his rescue. *He's from the North*, she told the Countess. *They do things differently there.*

A lifetime of coddling doesn't prepare someone to lead. You must be assertive, Mother always said—but not by barking orders. You must find the slim place where your desires and theirs align.

I've seen a lot more of Bayled since our talk. He finds ways to sit near me in every group lesson. We have meaningless conversations so Corene can overhear. We search for any excuse to be close, laugh, and exchange conspiratorial whispers—even if all we're saying is, "Now giggle like I've said something very cute. Good."

Parsifal smirks when he catches us. We all have lessons together—and not just because Parsifal's father was a prince before Frefois fell. The King insists everyone in his daughter's periphery be refined and educated.

There's one hitch: Corene's paid us no attention at all. Half the time she doesn't even come to lessons, since she's too busy getting fitted for wedding dresses or picking out centerpieces. That suits me fine. The longer she ignores my play for Bayled, the better my chance of wrapping him up for myself. When it's too late, she'll look up and see what I've done right under her nose. What I've taken from her, just like she took Red Durnhal from me.

I'm jittery this morning as the castle roars to life. Servants rush about, preparing for this gobble of a wedding. Everyone is infuriatingly thrilled, believing this unification could change the course of the Kingdom for the better.

There are more important things on my mind. If Bayled doesn't think our plan is working, he'll be done with it—and I can't have that.

My harp tutor's lesson is utterly dull, sending my mind floating far above my body. She says I have the coordination for the harp, but no passion. Maybe I'm saving it for something else.

I try not to frustrate my tutors so much that the King decides my lessons are too burdensome to fund. One cannot become a queen without an education.

My tutor has barely left when the door flies open and Parsifal strides into my suite. "I think you'll be curious about a particular buzz I heard when I arrived at the castle this morning. It's pertinent to your plan."

"What's that?"

Parsifal drapes himself over a chair and pushes a shiny black curl away from his face. He gives me a calculating look I recognize: how much is he willing to tell me now, and how much should he keep for future use as leverage? Morgaun says his expressions are impossible to read because of his disfigurement, but that's not true if one knows him at all.

"Corene's engagement to Chief Sheep isn't necessarily involuntary."

"She *likes* the cratertooth?" I can't help a shocked laugh. Parsifal shrugs. "Corene can't have spent a decade kissing Bayled in dark hallways to change horses this quickly."

"You've seen Nul se Lan. Don't act like *you* wouldn't teeter into those arms."

"No, I wouldn't." As if I've ever wanted to hurl myself into anyone's arms. Even when I spent candle-hour upon candle-hour with Red Durnhal, learning the shape of his jaw, the silver of the hair at his temple, it took me ages just to want to hold his hand.

"Anyway," Parsifal says. "This could help. If Bayled finds out she's not being forced into this—that she *likes* the Southerner—he'll be incensed, for once. And more than ready to console himself with someone else."

I'm too struck to reply. There's just no way. Of course it would be huge for my plan—if it were true. The rumor mill must be malfunctioning. I have to be absolutely sure before I try to use it to my advantage, or I'll stick myself with my own sword.

I rise from my chair and set that awful harp on the floor.

I'd like to stomp it into splinters, but then I'd have to somehow furnish another. "I have to go see Corene." I head to the door, but Parsifal clears his throat. I sigh. "What is it, pliggan?"

"Don't I get anything for bringing you this tasty information?" he asks with a grin.

I scoff. He wants a treat for bringing me lies? "My undying friendship," I say, and head out the door.

"Worst reward ever!" he calls after me.

BAYLED

I rush to the King's private suite, holding a note that says: *Urgent. Meet me in the war room.*

The war room is an unpleasant place that smells like spilled wine, old man, and urine. No one's used it for war since the King tried—and failed—to take over the world.

Inside, King Hindermark sits at the war table with Nul se Lan and the court wizard, Forgren. A draping black robe completely shrouds Forgren's arms and legs. He must be ancient and raw under there, skin dangling from bones. The jewels hanging from his turkey neck that let him channel Magic probably weigh more than he does.

Nul se Lan is already here—as are the plates that have yet to be cleared away. They were having a private breakfast. I can't help feeling wounded.

"Bayled! Just the man I needed." The King half rises from his chair, ready to slap me on the back like he always does, but stops himself. I get a whiff of wine on his breath. "Sit."

I take an empty seat. "How can I be of service, Your Majesty?"

He lets out a great sigh as he returns to his chair, the cushions stained with purple. "Priestess. Tell him what you told me."

That's when I notice Priestess Ilisa in shapeless white robes standing in the corner, blending in with the whitewashed stone. Her body's young—she must be even younger than Thelia—but her eyes are ageless. Melidia chooses each of her priestesses with her own hand, and this one emanates the Goddess's immortal light.

"Welcome, young Master Vasha," she says, as if she's years older than I am. She doesn't bow or curtsy. No king is higher than a priestess. In Melidia's eyes, they are peers.

But not in the King's eyes. He rants about the Temple at every opportunity—"The priestesses and their ineptitude are the only reason I lost that war!" Along with the night liquor I usually bring him, it helps him sleep.

"Hurry up and tell him," the King grunts.

She doesn't look ruffled. "Melidia's Eye along the Southern Pass has seen something," Ilisa begins. One of my earliest lessons in the Holy Kingdom—how the ancient priestesses traveled around the continent to build Melidia's delicate stone Eyes, each blessed with distant sight, granting the priestesses a glimpse into goings-on all over Helyanda.

"A massive elven attack force—siege elephants, orkuks loaded down with tents and gear, mages, thousands of infantry—have crossed the Great Mountains and into our lands."

I feel as if someone's hit me in the stomach with a blunt object. "Why? What have we done to piss them off?"

She opens her mouth to reply, but Forgren cuts her off. "Who knows why elves do anything? Doesn't matter. They are creatures of Magic, not logic."

Priestess Ilisa continues as if he hasn't spoken. "We must respond immediately. Send out a call to the sworn lords—"

Forgren interrupts her. "If the long ears travel the Low Road, they must cross the hills of the Klissen. They'll meet resistance there, long before they reach our border."

Ilisa's voice is placid. "The Eye of Melidia saw a force that will easily crush the Southerners."

"Why should we believe Melidia?" Forgren asks. His hood slides as he leans forward, but somehow, it still obscures his face. I've always found it odd that a Kingdom that loathes Magic employs wizards—but this place is full of hypocrisies. Unlike the Magic users of the Northern Republic, who work together to find the best path forward, the wizard and the priestesses are constantly at odds. "The goddess's guidance didn't serve us all that well in the past."

As the King tells it, Melidia came to him in a dream saying, "It is your destiny, and yours alone, to rule the human world." With her help, his army took Frefois in a single night, and took the Bellisares as hostages.

Drunk on victory and fueled by Melidia's encouragement, the King sent his fatigued force north to conquer the Northern Republic—and then south, into the Klissen. Once he was spread thin as paper across two fronts, Melidia . . . fell silent and vanished. The Northern Republic crushed the Holy Kingdom with their superior weapons, and the tribes of the Klissen tore the rest to pieces.

The Northern Republic sent my mother, a seasoned diplomat, to negotiate a permanent peace. My family remained here to ensure the Kingdom never again stepped outside its borders—that is, until the fire. For as long as I've known him, the King has blamed it all on Melidia.

The King nods at Nul se Lan. "With the people of the Klissen as our allies, we have nothing to fear."

Nul se Lan surges to his feet, bringing a hand to his chest. "I send word to the Chief, my father, to defend."

"Thank you, my future son-in-law." The King waves a hand at Forgren. "Send a smoke message for him," he says, and the court wizard nods. "We will move up the wedding to one week from today. To cement our alliance in the face of this threat."

I am made of ice. *One week.* One precious week before I lose Corene forever.

"Dispatch the city guard to join the Chief's forces in the South," the King says. "That should be enough to manage a few elves."

My mouth drops open. The city guard is Four Halls's only defense. Should anything go wrong, we'd only have a few castle guards to defend us.

"Your Majesty!" Ilisa protests. "That won't be nearly enough to—"

"I know what I'm doing." The King rises laboriously from his chair.

She isn't daunted. "May I remind you that your daughter cannot marry under Melidia's eyes without my blessing."

The King's cheeks puff out in fury, but he says nothing. I'm in awe of the priestess as she stalks out of the war room and slams the door behind her.

He turns to us. "Don't listen to the words of a child."

I say what I know is expected of me. "Of course, Your Majesty."

Nul dips his head. "Your instructions I await."

"Soon," the King says, extending a hand toward each of us, "you will both be my sons."

Both of us? Does he plan to name Nul se Lan as his heir, instead of me?

As we leave the war room side by side, in silence, I'm tempted to tell Nul se Lan, *I've never wanted to be King, you know. You can have it.*

CHAPTER 3

THELIA

When I'm standing in front of Corene's door, about to knock, I stop to study the nicks scratched into the wood—low enough that an adult couldn't have made them: C + T.

Corene and Thelia. I was eleven when I carved this into the door with the dagger Mother made me carry everywhere. Corene begged me not to damage the fine wood in case the Queen found it. We were almost sisters back then, sleeping in the same bed, sitting at the vanity together while our handmaids did our hair, eating and drinking and bathing side by side.

But Corene always had her secrets. She used to brag about a passage in the walls that the royals could use to escape an attack on the castle. I often asked to see it, but she wouldn't show me, saying that could compromise their safety.

She showed Bayled the third day he was in the Holy Kingdom.

Even after that, I thought she loved me—but I know better now. If she'd really loved me, she wouldn't have slandered me to the one man I'd ever felt anything for. If she'd really loved me, she wouldn't have ruined my one chance at happiness.

Now I just have to get what I need from her and get out. Time to put my lifetime of experience as her best friend to use. With a great inhale, I open the door.

Corene sits in the very center of her bed, wearing a crimson dress I've never seen. She's let her hair down, and the morning sunlight turns each strand shades of ruby and gold. Her eyes are rimmed in red. A future Queen shouldn't be this fragile— but it's good for me.

"Oh, Corene." I stretch my arms toward her. "What in the name of the goddess is wrong?"

Corene buries her face in my shoulder, and fresh tears soak my shirt. I pat her back. Seeing her crying like this makes a place in my chest hurt. I wrap my other arm around her without thinking.

"The wedding's been moved up. I'll be married in less than a week."

"What?" I'm so stunned, I completely forget why I'm here. Maybe the King got wind of Corene's secret engagement after all and decided to get this marriage over with before my flighty cousin changed her mind *again*.

"I know." Corene sniffles. "I would've liked more time to transition. To get to know Nul better. To plan the perfect wedding. And say good-bye."

"Is your father thinking clearly?" I ask, incredulous. "You can't plan a whole wedding in a week. Why rush it?"

"He feels we must act immediately for the security of the kingdom." She pauses to gather herself. "Thelia, we got terrible news this morning. There's an army on the move."

My fingers freeze on her shoulders. "Who? The Northerners?" Poor Bayled, torn between his loyalty to the King and to his home country.

Corene extricates herself from my embrace, and I push the stray wet hairs behind her ear. I deserve some recognition for my work today as "Princess's Best Friend."

"Don't fleg or anything." She clasps my shoulders. "But the priestesses say that . . . elves are crossing the Great Mountains, through the Southern Pass. Heading straight toward us."

She says something else, but it's lost to a ringing sound in my ears, like the high note priestesses always hit during the solstice chant.

Elves. Wrinkled, gray skin, like rotting peaches. Knobby long ears. Beady, reflective eyes that can find you anywhere, even in the darkness. Sharpened, gnashing teeth.

The monsters of my dreams that always had their claws in the edges of my childhood. They're coming, and they'll kill us all. They'll eat Parsifal and Corene right in front of me, one limb at a time, ripping muscle from the bone.

I hear a noise, high-pitched and keening. The sound isn't coming out of Corene, whose mouth is now open, her arms trying to hold me up. It's coming from me.

PARSIFAL

No one has shown up to our history lesson besides me, so there's no one here except our soggy old tutor to admire the gold tights and shoes I paired today. I do delight, however, in his lectures. Past monarchs of the Holy Kingdom have discovered delightfully unique ways to be terrible. Once there was an inquisition that resulted in a thousand hangings. One king deliberately starved a rebellious lord's peasants to death. Each was an even bigger moldy turd than the one before him.

Halfway through our lesson, the door flies open. I expect it to be Thelia or Bayled—any of my errant classmates. Instead, it's Corene's handmaid, gasping for breath. "Master Bellisare?"

I sit up. "What is it?"

"Lady Thelia," the handmaid manages. "She's collapsed. I was told to find you."

My throat constricts. My tutor heaves a sigh that feels decades old and excuses me.

I hurry out into the courtyard and up the huge spiral staircase to Corene's room in North Hall. Halfway there, I narrowly avoid a collision with Bayled. He smells like a sweaty horse.

"Where are you headed in such a rush?" His tone is derisive, when usually he forces himself to be polite.

"Corene's room." I push past him. Bayled's footsteps echo behind me up the stairs and down the hall. I throw open the second door.

Corene kneels on the floor next to her bed, rocking Thelia in her arms. My cousin keens in a way that resembles an injured dog, her face hidden under wavy black hair.

I crouch beside Corene and hold out my hands. She gratefully slides Thelia into my arms and scoots away, like we're contaminated. I dab the sweat from Thelia's forehead as she stares blankly at the ceiling.

Corene stands over us until Bayled enters and sits cross-legged on her bed. She sinks onto the blanket beside him. "I shouldn't have said anything," she whimpers, tears pooling in her eyes. She's always been wonderful at drawing attention to herself—even in the midst of someone else's crisis.

I know what to do. Drawing Thelia against my chest, I place equal pressure on her head and her back. Her limbs are stiff, curled up like a fetal chicken's. I look up at Corene. "What happened?"

"I told her the news," Corene says, more to Bayled than to me.

Bayled makes an annoyed noise. "You know she has that phobia."

Oh. *That* phobia. The hairs stand up all over my arms, up my back, to my neck. Now it makes sense. Corene looks stricken. "She asked what was going on, so I told her. I didn't think she'd . . . leave her mind like this."

I roll my eyes. Thelia's still here—she's just stuck in a loop with a cast of invisible monsters. "Let's get her onto the bed."

Bayled climbs down and kneels in front of me, and I shift Thelia into his arms. He hoists her up like she's nothing. Melidia damn his toned muscles.

While I call for Corene's handmaid and send her to fetch water, Bayled tries to communicate with Thelia—asking questions, touching her face, clasping her hands in his. If she were aware enough to witness it, she'd be in raptures.

Corene's eyes narrow as Bayled rubs Thelia's arms, trying to warm her up. She's finally noticed. I don't have the heart to tell Bayled he's not doing it right—that compression works better than repetitive motions. When we were younger and Thelia had these sorts of episodes, I'd pile heavy blankets on top of her and stay quiet until she stopped shivering.

"There aren't any elves here," Bayled tells her earnestly. "Don't worry. A whole country stands between them and you. You're safe."

It's not even a very good lie. Thelia starts keening again. I need to interfere, despite Bayled's good intentions.

I crouch down beside them and stroke her hair. I know how she secretly loves it—it reminds her of having a handmaid. "I'm sorry I even brought them up the other day," I say. "I was only trying to goad you."

Corene leans her mouth close to my ear. "The elves *are* coming," she whispers, voice trembling. "The priestesses told us this morning. That's why my wedding has been moved up— so I can secure Nul's loyalty, and the Klissen, should the long ears invade."

Of course she's managing to make this about herself. "What happens if the Klissen falls?"

Her face contorts. "Don't you dare suggest it. The Chief will defend his lands. And Dad sent our city guard to reinforce him."

I gape at her. "You're saying we're defenseless?"

She shrugs. "As the Goddess says, don't jealously guard that which you don't need."

It's never been harder not to laugh in Corene's face, so I turn back to Thelia, who appears to have calmed down. Her head is pressed against Bayled's chest. Ah—taking full advantage of her situation. I sit beside them. "How are you feeling, Theels?"

She turns her head so I can see both her eyes, but she stays close to Bayled. "I think I'll live."

"It's not worth getting upset about," says Bayled, as if Thelia's fits have the ability to logically discriminate. "The elves could be moving for any reason. We haven't done anything."

"We exist," Thelia croaks. "That's enough."

I frown at her. This was what mystified me most when we were young—why her strange little mind decided that creatures we hadn't seen in millennia were her own personal demons. Our temples in Frefois were filled with statues of demons, to honor Melidia's saving of us from their endless torture. I have to wonder if Thelia's nervous tendency has meshed them together—and if she's that far off the mark.

"What else did the priestesses say?" I ask Bayled as he hovers over Thelia. If the Goddess really does talk to her priestesses, surely she's told them something useful.

Bayled shakes his head. "The King wouldn't let Priestess Ilisa get a word in."

Typical. "He's an arrogant prick," I say.

Corene glares at me. "Dad knew her ideas were all gobble."

"Well, it's gobble to send that tiny force of city guards to the South," I retort. "We can't trust the hillmen to fight off a horde of elves. We should be gathering the whole Kingdom's army."

"Be careful," Corene says, her voice dropping. "He's your King. What you're saying sounds a lot like treason."

Thelia's eyes go wide as plates. "The King sent away the city guard?"

"Yes," Bayled admits. I could laugh. The monsters will come knocking and find nothing in their way. He hesitates before adding, "The King smelled of alcohol when he decided that."

Corene glares at him, betrayed. "He was having a glass of sweet wine with breakfast, Bayled!"

"Corene," he says quietly. "It's never just one glass." She looks aghast, and Bayled puts a hand on hers. "How can he make wise decisions for the Kingdom in that state?"

So Bayled knows that the King he's served so loyally all these years can't be trusted to rule. Even that gullible trit would be better at the job—but he'd never be willing to do the dirty deed and step over Hindermark's body to take the throne for himself. So we'll probably all die.

"He can barely find the pot when he's had a bottle," I say. "How do you expect him to win a war?"

SAPPHIRE

First we left the towering trees of Viteos behind. Then we crossed the bare, unforgiving cliffs of the Red Mountains—and survived. But as our force descends, the windy peaks shrinking to hills and rippling grass, a sense of unease grows in my throat.

I have never seen land that breathes like this as the wind blows over it. It's so distinctly *foreign* on this side of the continent. We do not belong here. We are strangers. And yet that is what makes us ideal for this work.

We are not attached or entangled. We can see with neutral eyes the threat these mere humans don't even know is lurking under their feet—and we will save all of us.

Our small reconnaissance team moves quickly, uninterrupted by forest or rocky terrain. Even my tireless legs begin to ache as we cover league after league, steering clear of small hamlets and herd animals. The smell of Magic is here, but weak. Our great mother is a sad shadow of herself, a thin dribble of water that stubbornly keeps going though all the creatures here have rejected it.

We sleep under a rock overhang, and frigid autumn rain falls during the night. Ferah, the most talented Magicker among the Jaguars, reaches for the threads of Magic that always surround us. She invites it to her, pulling her hands through the air to gather it up like yarn. And yet, nothing. The strands are so scarce and emaciated, all she can make is a ball of pale blue light the size of a thumb.

We give up on fire and lie with our bodies close together. My wisp creeps out of the pouch at my hip and tucks itself under my chin, lending this small burst of heat. Our edges are cold and wet, but the Magic burning inside our hearts keeps us warm.

We resume before the sun rises.

That evening, Ellze and I sit by the river, watching the rest of the contingent strip off their clothes and leap into the frigid water. I try not to stare at the Commander, or his perfect muscle structure, or the water dripping down his exposed hips to the silver tendrils of hair climbing up.

Zylion, another Jaguar, surfaces from his swim and joins us, pushing his wet purple hair out of his eyes. He follows my gaze to the Commander.

"I find it to be a personal affront how unbelievably attractive he is," he says.

I smile. "Honestly, it is painful."

"You should tell him to cease at once. Put that rear end away, at least."

Ellze gives us a disapproving look. "Everyone can see you ogling."

Zylion and I both turn our heads and pretend to be speaking intimately about something—instead of staring at Commander Valya's flawless construction. Shaking his head, Ellze disappears into the water like a fish.

My eyes drift back to the Commander, floating on his back beside Ferah. "Ellze keeps tossing you glances," Zylion says.

I make a gagging sound. "I would prefer to pull an eel out of the water and put my tongue down its throat."

Zylion gasps with laughter. "I do not think he is aware of that."

"Of course not. Ellze thinks everyone in the world wants to rub hills with him." I sigh. "But I am not being fair. We have known each other our whole lives. It would not be fair to call Ellze malicious—he simply lets his desires rule him."

Zylion is about to speak when the Commander's shout echoes across the riverbank. "Everyone!" He stands in all his naked glory on a rock above us, so I can ogle without reproach. "We have to move, now. Humans nearby."

We scramble out of the water, throw our clothes on, and call for the mounts. I give my sore feet a quick rub as Ellze rides up beside me, his lion sniffing the air. "Do you need a ride? You have been walking a long time."

"I am still strong," I say. I do not want to give Ellze any ideas.

Ellze smiles. "You are indomitable, friend Sapphire."

"We continue all night," Commander Valya says, climbing on his raptor. "We cannot risk being discovered before we know what awaits us."

CHAPTER 4

BAYLED

The wedding is only four days away, and nothing has changed. So I stop Thelia in the hallway after our penmanship lesson, when the others have already left.

"What is it?" she asks, leaning into me. Corene's not even here—why put on a show?

"We need to talk." Not to mention that every time her hand touches mine, I feel like I need two baths to be able to look at myself in the mirror. "Corene hasn't said anything about what we're . . ."—I gesture at her—"trying to do here. It's not working."

Thelia gives me a wolfish smile. "Are you sure?"

I suppose I'm not. I rarely see the Princess anymore. "She hasn't mentioned it. Certainly not a hint that she'll go to her father and ask to marry me instead."

"Is that how you imagine things happen in this kingdom?" She snorts. "Oh, you poor Northerner."

Every conversation with Thelia I've ever had since I came here as a little boy has been like this one—with her reflexively condescending to me. I'm wrong, I'm ignorant,

I'm a foreigner. I tried over and over to befriend her because she was so close to Corene, but it wasn't many cycles before I gave up. Thelia Finegarden is as strong and dangerous as she is unkind.

"Tell me what I should do, then." I close my eyes and take a long breath. "Everything I've tried has failed, and I'm lost. I have nowhere else to go from here."

Thelia's eyes spark. "Maybe you should say something about me to her. Rub it in her face. You're so concerned, right, about my episode the other day?"

She'll even use her own pain, her own deepest fears, as a tool. I shake my head, disappointed in myself for believing any of her underhanded games could help me. "This is pointless. I have to go." There are more pressing matters I need to handle at the moment anyway.

"Bayled." Thelia pushes dark hair back behind her ear, and my eyes drift to the pink scar down the side of her face. "There's still hope."

Maybe she wouldn't hate that scar so much if her mother hadn't despised it. Delia depended on marrying her daughter off to someone wealthy to pull the Finegardens out of debt—and restore her life to the glamour she felt she deserved.

No surprise that Thelia's a user, when that woman brought her up.

"I'm sorry, but this can't take more of my attention," I say. "Too much else is at stake." I brush past her before she can say more.

I need to speak to the King. This tedious, piddling mess with Thelia has reminded me just how much hangs in the balance—far more than Corene's wedding.

We will come up against Melidia's most ancient enemy.

I've never been sure what to make of the Temple, figuring it was mostly a stone tomb full of zealots. But maybe we should listen to the priestesses—if we raise a full army now, act fast and decisively as she suggested, we may have a chance.

I have to at least try to convince him.

The door to the King's private study is slightly ajar. He doesn't respond to my knock, so I let myself in.

A goblet tips back and forth in his hand. His head lolls to one side, drool dribbling down the side of his mouth, when he notices me. "Bayled," he says with a sigh. "I'm glad it's you. I couldn't bear to see Corene."

"Why, Your Majesty?"

He tries to sit up, but he can't find balance. I rescue the goblet of wine before it falls. "I'm sending her away," he moans, burying his face in his arms. "I already lost her mother . . ."

Poor Queen Laine—I was always fond of her. She adopted me without hesitation after my parents died, even though I was a foreigner. Everything in Four Halls is different since she passed, especially the King.

He reaches for his goblet again, and I let him have it. "Now Corene will be gone and I'll be alone."

I take the seat next to him. He immediately leans against me. "I'll still be here, Your Majesty."

"You don't have to call me that when no one's around." He laughs into his wine and spills it down his chest. I jump to get him a napkin, but he wipes off the liquid with his palm. "You've always been too good to this clumsy old drunk. I can't trust anyone around here but you. The nobles are only out for themselves, the priestesses spout poison, and that rotten old wizard—I don't even know where he's from."

Forgren did appear a bit suddenly. His predecessor died in his sleep. Shadowed and frail, Forgren presented himself at Four Halls a week later, aware we had an opening.

The King's glassy eyes clear for a moment, and he leans toward me. "You know you have nothing to worry about, don't you?"

I'm not sure what to say. "What would I worry about?"

"Even if I have to make Nul se Lan my official heir, he'll never leave the Klissen. You'll be the ruler of the Holy Kingdom in everything but name."

So he *is* going to name the Southerner as his heir. I've known it, in my heart, since the moment Nul se Lan appeared at the banquet table. I don't feel any pain. Just . . . relief. He can have the damned Kingdom. I'll never have to wear the crown, do the job, or take the blame. "I understand." I should tell him what I came here to say. Push him to summon the entire army, to start thinking about evacuation. To take this threat seriously.

He speaks before I get the chance. "There's going to be a war, Bayled. Don't think I don't know. Part of being King is that you have to stay calm and keep up the people's morale. They don't think—they *feel*. Sending men to war is unpopular. Sending loved ones off to die makes people harder to rule. But dispatching a small militia? The people are behind that. It's easy."

So he isn't playing this game to keep the Kingdom safe. He's playing to keep the people quiet and ignorant.

"Let them believe it'll be fine until it's over." He leans

against the table and closes his eyes. I worry that, right at this moment, he's finally done himself in.

"Your Majesty?" I say, touching his shoulder. "Let's get you to bed."

"Leave me here," the King says, turning his head away so he's talking into the wood table. His next few words disappear into it. I try one more time, but he pushes me away and mumbles again, "Go. Leave me alone."

This time I back away. Parsifal was right. The old drunk isn't fit to rule anymore, and there's nothing I can do about it.

THELIA

I had the dream again. The one I haven't had since before Mother left.

They came with their gray, sallow faces, their beady black eyes, their sharpened teeth. They gathered around, laughing with high, screeching voices as they tore into Parsifal's fragile flesh. He dangled from their bony arms, blood streaming down. I screamed his name.

I woke gasping. A terrible start to banquet day.

Washing and brushing and putting up my hair takes all my willpower. Sitting at my vanity, I stare into my own brown eyes as I draw dark lines like a barrier around them, holding me in. I reach for my lip stain, but like a gust of wind has swept through my room, it falls off the edge of the vanity and rolls away.

I don't bother picking it up.

No clay powder today—not worth it. I run my finger along

the raised edge of the pink scar that connects my eye to my chin. It stands out whether I try to hide it or not, so what's the point? I can dress up in all the finery and makeup I want, but I cannot erase this mark.

It was an accident. That's what Morgaun told our parents later, and I didn't contradict him.

Every day Mother and I went out for our morning exercises, then fencing practice, and a break for tutoring. At night, when no one could see us, came the kroga instruction. Morgaun seethed at how she focused on me. And he decided to do something about it.

He asked me to go on a ride. In the stable, he went for my legs first. If I couldn't walk, he figured, I'd never steal Mother's attention from him again. Even then I was stronger and faster, and when he slashed at me, I shoved him hard—so hard he fell back. But on the way, his dagger cut into the side of my face.

Mother never looked me in the eyes again. She said no lord, prince, or king would ever want a wife with a scar.

After that, she stopped pretending. She gave up being my mother and my father's wife. A few moons later, she met a visiting knight and ran off with him to his home in the Sea Kingdoms without ever saying good-bye.

The scar doesn't actually change my face too much. My nose with its high bridge, my dark-lashed eyes, my thick, pinkish-brown lips all remain.

I'm still me. I'm still beautiful. I don't know why she couldn't see that.

No, I do know why. Mother needed an excuse to escape Daddy. To escape Morgaun. To escape me.

PARSIFAL

I show up to Four Halls early for banquet, hoping to find Thelia before the party starts. I want to know if she's made any
progress with her plan.

Smoothing down the ruffles stitched into the front of my
shirt, I start up the stairs to the West Hall. The high walkway that will take me to South Hall is preferable to crossing
the crowded courtyard. It's also where the King tends to house
guests.

I spin around the banister at the top of the stairs and take a
left to the walkway—when something heavy and metallic lands
on the stone floor with a *clang!*

The sound came from down the hall. I take a few steps
toward it to investigate, and a lone silver candlestick rolls
around the corner—taking an abrupt left toward me. It continues rolling down the rug, coming to a stop right in front of
my shoes.

I stoop to pick up the candlestick. It's cold and heavy, as
expected. Clutching it, I head to where it came from to return it.

Voices float down the hall. They're loud and tense—and
speaking in the Klissen's mother tongue. The speakers sound
agitated.

I shouldn't get involved. Just put down the candlestick and
go. I have enough to worry about right now, except . . . demons,
they're really arguing.

I lean around the corner and see three people standing
hunched over, gesturing with fury at each other. I jerk back.

Nul's personal entourage, as rocky as their hills. I've seen
the three of them stalking around before, always flanking him.
I swallow and lean forward again to take another look.

There's the one that looks part troll. One has red braids so tight they pull the skin of her forehead back. She looks as if she's never smiled in her life. The skinny small one opens the lid of a trunk and gestures at it. It's filled with burlap sacks, rope, and a pile of glinting steel weapons.

I take off back downstairs, realize I'm still clutching the candlestick, and abandon it on a table. Behind the kitchen, I find Derk covered in flour out by the stone bread oven.

He tilts his head. "Surprised to see you here." Some of that irresistible faun-brown hair topples in front of his green eyes and I have to clamp my hands together so I don't try to touch him.

"Can you help me with something?"

"Is that something *pastries*? Because then, yes."

"Pastries are tangentially involved. Mostly, you'll have to fade in the background and pay attention."

His eyes shrink to slits. "What is it?"

I can't believe I'm asking one of my lovers to get involved in politics, but here I am. This feels bigger than me. "Arrange to bring some fresh bread to Nul se Lan's quarters in the West Hall."

"I can do that." A mischievous smile crosses Derk's face, and he brushes his hand across my chest.

I step back. "When you get there, look around. Listen."

"But they don't speak—"

"There's a lot you can pick up from gestures, facial expressions. Tone. They'll be careless around a servant, and you don't understand their language."

Derk nods. "I've never trusted them anyway." He opens the oven door, slides in his great wooden paddle, and fishes out a few loaves of crusty bread. "I'll tell you what I see."

CHAPTER 5

THELIA

The seats at the banquet table have changed again. Nul se Lan now sits at the King's left, with Corene beside him. Bayled's returned to the King's right side, but his mouth goes flat as Corene and her betrothed share a private laugh, foreheads close together. There's supposed to be an announcement following the banquet tonight, but I'm having trouble focusing on anything besides my horrid dream.

"Don't look too deep into it," Parsifal says when I mention it. "It's just fresh after all the bad news."

But this one felt so *real*, like when I was a girl. Wet droplets of Parsifal's blood still cling to my face; the terror fills up my limbs until they refuse to obey. "It can't be just a coincidence," I say.

Parsifal waves off the conversation like a bad smell. "Tell me this, Theels. How's Bayled responding to your advances?"

I sigh. Whenever Mother would get carried away in a training session and leave me black and blue, Parsifal always planned some mischief to steer my thoughts away—putting a beetle in the Queen's slippers, or trying get that groom who was mean to the horses dismissed.

"He isn't," I say. At this rate, I'll never wrest Bayled away from Corene. He'll spend his life on a chaise, arm slung across his eyes, moaning about the woman who left him behind.

Across the table, Daddy snaps at Morgaun. "You can't have every single thing you want. We're not made of gold." I was horrified when I saw my brother was here, but thankfully the two of them are too busy arguing to pay me any mind.

Morgaun sneers. "I could be on the way to having a rich wife if you'd let me come to last week's banquet." So that's why he wasn't here. Daddy knew it was a big night and kept him home.

I wouldn't wish Morgaun on any woman. I'd probably find her strangled within a week of the wedding.

Parsifal's parents sit across from us—his dad, Antonin, though short in stature, is a behemoth of a man. He wears an extra-tall collar bubbling over with lacy white fabric and the bright yellow coat with the wide sleeves he so loves. Then there's Percy's mom in her usual timid gray wool, nursing hot soup.

I'm surprised she made it. She rarely leaves the Bellisare estate. "How are you, Aunt Mirisa?" I ask, leaning forward because she has the voice of a cricket.

"Fine, Thelia." Another spoonful of soup. "This soup is too salty, though."

I nod solemnly. "I'll let the kitchen know for next time."

Mirisa shrugs her bony shoulders. "Don't make them fuss on my account."

Antonin beams at me. "That's just like you, Thelia. Asking after everyone's health. You're such a nice girl."

Parsifal rolls his eyes. The Bellisares' bottomless kindness toward my mother and me has always annoyed him. Mother was Aunt Mirisa's *project*. When Mirisa's parents adopted Delia—the scraggly, tainted remains of a destroyed people— they all did their best to tame her. Since Mother left, Mirisa and Antonin's attention toward me has only grown. *Poor abandoned girl*, they must think, *just like her mother.*

"Your Majesty!" Every head at the banquet table turns as a hunched figure, draped in a black cloak, barges into the banquet hall. Two guards cross spears to block his entry. "I must speak with you, Your Majesty."

What would bring the standoffish court wizard into a packed banquet hall? Only something terrible.

The King waves Forgren in. The spears lift and the court wizard scurries down the length of the table, then addresses the King in hushed tones. The forks and knives have stopped moving as we all try to listen in. As soon as they're done conversing, Forgren whisks out of the banquet hall like a shadow.

The King lifts his goblet once again. No one breathes as he takes a long gulp of his wine. Finally he says, "Please file out to the courtyard for the announcement. Something the whole kingdom must hear."

The night air is cool and refreshing as banquet guests file out into the courtyard. We don't often gather for public announcements, but the courtiers' platform is already waiting for us. Parsifal and I find two seats far from his family and mine, hoping to be spared their drama.

People stream in from the city, filling the lowest tier of the courtyard. The noise grows as Four Halls fills up, until Parsifal and I have to shout to hear each other. The usual sound of animals squawking and oinking is mysteriously absent. Every pen stands empty.

Servants venture out to light torches all across the castle walls, weaving a glimmer of flames around the courtyard. The darkest point lies at the center of the swarm, where the common people stand and wait for something to happen.

Up on the high balcony that's rimmed with wedding tassels, the King emerges from behind a curtain. The crowd erupts. They do seem to love him, even red-faced and mushy as he's become. What a waste of good subjects. I'd be a strong, decisive Queen. My people could trust me to guide them, to lead them, to protect them in a way that cowardly old man can't. They'd cry my name, call me the most beautiful Queen to ever live. My scar, a symbol of my trials, would only make me more beloved.

"My friends," the King says. "This thing we call life—it is something we all share. A journey that all of us are on together."

I roll my eyes so hard they could fall out and leave the courtyard.

"I've always done my best to earn your affection and loyalty. I don't know if I always succeed. I try to be fair and protect this wonderful kingdom we've all built together." People shout and applaud. They're so easy, eating up any bit of gobble if it comes from their royalty, even if it's just a few pretty words strung together. "I'm pleased to announce that the exquisite southern country of the Klissen will become part of the Holy Kingdom—and soon I will be passing on the title of King."

It seems as if the entire castle is holding its breath. I can't believe this is working.

"My heir will be . . . the brave, handsome Nul se Lan, soon-to-be husband of my beloved Princess Corene." The King steps aside, and my soul cracks in half. Parsifal laughs next to me, but I can't imagine what he finds so funny. Bayled was my only path for the throne. If he's no longer the heir, it's over.

The crowd screams as Corene and Nul se Lan stride onto the balcony. Corene's strawberry hair is fire in the torchlight, perfect ringlets tumbling down her chest—but her face looks drawn and ashy. Her smile is attached to her but not a part of her, like a porcelain solstice festival mask has been pasted on top of her skin.

When Corene and Nul se Lan reach the railing, they clasp hands and raise them high overhead. The crowd shrieks and cheers. After minutes of soaking up the crowd's adulation, the two retreat to the dim archway.

The King returns to the balcony and holds up his hands again for quiet. The people stop clapping and exchange perplexed glances. A torch over the King's head flickers. "But the wedding will have to wait."

Murmurs ripple across the crowd.

"My subjects, my friends." Friends. As if. "Elves have invaded our lands," he says. "They have taken Andalore, the Klissen's capital. They have butchered our new countrymen. And they have murdered their beloved Chief."

Wails echo in the courtyard, and the courtiers gasp and murmur. Many seats down, Daddy's face is drawn. Morgaun looks . . . ecstatic.

"The long ears present a grave threat," the King shouts over the escalating anguish. "So I will address it at once." The crowd starts to undulate, stretching and expanding, with fury. I find my hand in Parsifal's, our fingers clenched so hard I worry they might fall off. "Tomorrow, the greatest force ever launched by the Holy Kingdom departs for war. I have entrusted my loyal ward, Bayled Vasha, to lead our assault against the elven force." Bayled and Nul se Lan appear at the King's side. The Southerner's face is stiff and pale—how recently did he learn his father is dead? "My daughter's fiancé, Nul se Lan, will take my place among our men riding into battle. Though he is not crowned prince yet, my daughter will welcome home a hero."

A few tenuous cheers. Bayled's smile is forced and strained.

"We will meet them on the Low Road!" The King's face is so red, it looks like he may pass out. "And we will stop them!" The crowd surges, roaring like a single beast that wants only blood. "Meanwhile, I invite everyone in Melidihan to find refuge in the walls of Four Halls. Should a siege come, we must all stand together!"

This can't be possible. The castle will be overrun, with unwashed commoners filling every crevice, nook, and corner. And with the nobility of Melidihan abandoning their estates . . .

Parsifal's flesh gives under my fingernails, but he doesn't object. "Morgaun," is all I can say. I can't decide who I fear more: him, or the flesh-ripping elves.

PARSIFAL

The moment the King leaves his balcony, it's a stampede. The common people swarm the platform with a deafening noise; I can't even see my parents' faces through the mass. "Theels, we have to get inside before we're trampled."

I don't need to tell her twice. Shoving people out of the way, Thelia leads us to the edge of the platform. She leaps off without hesitation, landing in the mud a dozen feet below. I slide off after and follow her toward the main doors. When a big guy blocks our way, she punches him in the jaw and pushes past as he stumbles.

The guards have barred the doors, trying to keep the frantic populace out. "Let us in," Thelia snarls. "I'm the Princess's cousin."

"We can't. If we open these doors—"

Thelia shoves her face right in his, teeth bared, droplets of her spit landing on his nose. "Let. Me. IN."

"But we have orders to—" Her hands leap to his throat. She yanks his face down to her level and he squeals soundlessly, face lighting up like a torch.

"I will rip your head off your neck if you don't let us in right now."

The seething masses back away, forming a wary semicircle around us. The other guard rushes to open the doors, and Thelia releases her victim. He gags and collapses to his knees as we slip in through the opening, and the door slams behind us.

I lean against the cold stone wall, gasping. Done with being a brute, Thelia looks like she's about to fleg. I usher her into the banquet room and snatch a half-empty glass of wine off the table for her.

"They're coming," she mutters, mostly to herself. "It's real."

"This will be over soon." I try to sound upbeat. "In a few days we'll get a smoke message saying Bayled crushed the long ears—then back to our old lives again."

She levels a dead-eyed stare on me. "Stop lying to protect my feelings. You think I'm going to fall on the floor sobbing again."

Maybe I do. "I'm just as upset as you are." I pick up another abandoned glass and suck it down. "Trapped with the filthy horde."

"They're not the only ones. Morgaun and Daddy won't be leaving now."

"It'll be like old times," I say, trying to keep my voice light. "Before you left your father's estate. You, me, Morgaun, our parents, all cozy—"

Thelia's arm shoots out and two of her fingers strike my armpit. It lands like a bull's charge to my pectoral. I scream as a shockwave runs through me, throat to ankles. I'm disconnected from my own body, which collapses to the floor in a tangle of limbs. I can't move any of them.

"Do you know how hard I worked to escape Morgaun?" she snarls. "I will never live with him again."

I scrabble on the floor, blubbering out half-words. Every finger and toe roars with pain. Sighing, Thelia reaches down to help me back to my feet.

"What's wrong with you?" I stumble a few steps back from her, into a chair. "Melidia be damned. I didn't realize your kroga was so good." I rub my chest bitterly.

This isn't Thelia. This is the child that's still locked inside her—the anxious, restless girl whose mother made her practice her hand-to-hand until she was dead on her feet, less a child than a lump of tempered steel. I'm not angry with Thelia. I'm angry with my horrid Aunt Delia for making her daughter this way.

"Attacking me won't help," I slur, because my mouth still isn't working right. "We're in this together."

Her laugh comes out a growl. "How do you see this playing out? A happy little family hugging and laughing over honey-roasted ham?" She leans closer, trying to intimidate me like she did the guard. My pity vanishes. "The cooks already butchered all the animals for the wedding feast. I saw the empty pens. What'll we eat after these people swarm into the castle and gorge themselves?"

I hadn't thought of that. There's still time for me to ride back to my family's estate and collect supplies—but how long would they last? Not long enough.

"I know you don't care if the kingdom sticks around or not, so this is all a great joke for you." Thelia drops her empty wine glass to the table, shattering it. She makes no note of the broken glass. "Can't say I expected more of a foreigner who acts so superior, mocks us whenever possible, but still lives off our coin. Don't worry. You'll care when you start starving like everyone else."

As she leaves the banquet hall, I reach for another half-finished drink. Why did I ever feel sorry for her in the first place? She's just like her mother. Thelia Finegarden may be beautiful, but she has no heart left.

SAPPHIRE

We travel steadily northeast, the sun always beating at our backs. Tree leaves glitter yellow and orange, like a thousand tiny sunsets. Our small troop avoids the main road—we don't want anyone to get wind of our arrival until the time is right.

The frail edifices of human activity appear on the horizon. Endless hilly grassland dotted with squat domiciles, leagues upon leagues of fences marking which territory belongs to whom. What arrogance to lay down ownership of a living thing such as land, with its own needs and desires.

They cannot see the beauty that lies in front of them, so they destroy it. Their homes and fences and guard towers are built from corpses. What incredible pride does it require to grant yourself dominion over all things?

That pride is why we arrive at the front gates to a new human city, walls constructed with freshly quarried stone, guard huts of young wood, and a lit fortress at the center. The Jaguars approach the gates, Commander Valya in the lead. Guards spot us from the towers and light a fire atop the roof. I tense, placing one hand on my sword. *Do no harm*, that is what we strive for. But we have not dealt with southern humans in centuries—and I would rather be cautious than dead.

Two humans appear on the other side of the iron gate. They are frail, small, with flat faces and flat ears. They look as dull-witted as giants. The gate opens, and they step out to meet us.

First comes an ancient man with sunken eye sockets and calloused hands, larger than I expected. The woman has yellow hair mostly gone gray, but her blue eyes shine like beacons. They are both crisscrossed with scars.

"Chief Lan." It is alien and strange to hear human language out of the Commander's mouth. Like all The People, I studied every human language to basic fluency—but it's been decades since I used any of them.

The old man nods. "Commander Valya."

The Commander steps forward to greet him, and the old woman draws a sword. I reach for my weapon, and the air between our two parties turns hot.

The Commander stops mid-step and holds out his hand as an offering. It is an unusual gesture, but the Chief recognizes it immediately. He joins his hand with the Commander's.

"It is good to put a face to the missives at last," Commander Valya says. "I did not quite know what to expect."

Releasing the handshake, the Chief nods. "I understand. As instructed, we have sent a smoke message to Four Halls detailing your . . . attack."

A rare smile crosses the Commander's face. "I know how much it will please the High Seer to place a reasonable man upon the Holy Kingdom's throne."

Ferah sends a message back to the rest of our contingent: we have safe passage. It does not take them long to arrive.

Human soldiers and citizens alike stand along the sides of the road, hands around their children, as the Jaguars march past. Next come our elephants, their trunks waving to the crowd, and a few children shriek. Finally the orkuks tromp down the main road, their great footfalls shaking the roofs of the small stone houses, sending some humans fleeing.

Ellze sighs. "I almost wish the Southerners had broken our bargain. I was looking forward to getting some blood on my blade."

A sense of unease runs through me. I know what he means—I have often felt the song of blood before battle against the giants—but only because it was necessary to defend our home.

When we've left the hovels behind, Commander Valya selects two squadrons of soldiers to accompany us on our journey. We veer off the road, heading toward the distant crags, as the army behind us continues northward along the Low Road.

We will see them again soon.

BAYLED

The King's army leaves first thing in the morning. Pages are scouring Melidihan, delivering summons to every member of the province's militia. Meanwhile, the King calls me to his chambers. I'm not surprised to find Nul se Lan already there.

Perhaps we'll die together out there. Perhaps one of us will live. Whoever survives returns home to the most generous, kindhearted, beautiful woman alive.

The King rises, setting his goblet down. "Nul se Lan, I consider you my son in spirit already. Know that your position in the kingdom is safe, and we all mourn the loss of your great father."

"Thank you, Your Majesty," Nul says, bowing.

King Hindermark looks us over. "Forgren has sent smoke messages to the sworn lords to have their forces meet you along the Low Road. I expect by the time you run into the invaders, you'll be ten thousand strong. Should be plenty to crush those long ears."

I wish I'd seen what the Priestess saw through the Eye of Melidia. Ten thousand men is a massive force—perhaps even capable of taking on the Northern Republic. But what raw, ancient power are we up against?

The King settles deep in his chair, his eyes going glassy. I want him to say something kind to me. To tell me I'm more than simply a body to hurl at these invaders like so much cannon fodder. But he says nothing else to us, so we leave him to his amusements.

Tomorrow, we go to war.

The castle's alive with frantic nobles arriving from all over, carriages loaded with clothes and food and children. But when I pass into North Hall, where only royalty live, silence reigns.

I stop before the door I know so well and knock. "Corene?"

I have so many things to do before I leave, but this one's the most important. It's too late for any of Thelia's machinations now. The plan was destined to fail from the start. Corene is too pure to fall for games. She'd have been joyful to know I'd found someone else, that I was happy.

"Corene? Let me in, please." I lean my ear against the door to listen. On the other side she's sniffling, so I try the knob and the door opens.

Corene lies curled up on her bed, knees at her chest, a burgundy nightgown pooled around her like blood. She doesn't lift her head, but her eyes open. Her cheeks are stained with tears.

"What?" she demands. Shocked by her own fury, she sits up and wipes her face. "I'm sorry. I didn't mean to snap." Always trying to make me feel better, even if she's suffocating. I sit on the edge of her bed.

"Corene, I—"

"Bayled." She reaches out to me. I gather her up in my arms. Her hands find my chest, my mouth finds her lips. Her fingers slide up the back of my neck and dig into my short, dense curls. I wrap my arms around her middle, and the strap of her gown slides off her shoulder.

"Corene," I whisper into her hair. "This may be the last time we lay eyes upon each other. I will not leave tomorrow morning with a single regret in my heart."

I've never spoken like this before. Right now, I am fire.

Corene presses her face to my chest. "I'm sorry that I didn't fight for you."

It's all I've wanted to hear.

"I love you," she says, her voice fierce and strong. She puts a hand behind my neck, tugs me towards her, and kisses me.

I fall apart. My hands wrap around her—one under her feather-soft hair, the other around her perfect waist. She presses her tongue against my lips and I accept. She tastes of everything I know. Her body presses closer, even though we are already as close as we can get. I pull her up onto my lap, and she falls even farther into me to make our shape complete.

My hand darts down her leg, more daring than I've ever been before. She emits a small noise, a sound so sweet that my trousers feel much tighter. I tug the hem of her dress up, past the soft inside of her knee, until I reach the creamy curve of her thigh. She squeezes herself closer to me, her hips scraping over mine and sending sweet sparks of pleasure into my belly. I let out an undignified moan.

Corene turns around, showing me the laced-up back of her dress. "Please." Any other day, this is where it would've stopped—with kisses and touches, urgent but restrained. Tonight there's no restraint. I could die, and I love her. I could die, and she loves me. This may be our last chance.

I struggle with the laces, and then a string comes free. She turns back toward me and peels the dress down, revealing everything underneath that I've only dreamed about. Before I can spend too long marveling, she kisses me again. Her lips pull mine apart, sucking them, inflaming them, while her fingers draw patterns on my skin.

Our bodies press together in a way that makes me tingle. Gasping, Corene unties my tunic and pulls it up and over my head. For a moment, she puts distance between us so she can look at me. I take in her fingers splayed across my bare chest, her pale freckled skin in stark contrast to my deep brown. If I come home, our children will be beautiful.

Her other hand runs through my hair again, pulling at me. I know what she wants next, so I kiss her again and pull her flush against me with both arms. She disconnects just long enough remove her gown and shove it over the side of the bed. I untie my boots and fling them away. Then come the trousers, and she gasps at what's underneath. I fill with embarrassment and pleasure and pride, in one swirling mass. I don't know how long I can contain myself. I commit this moment to memory.

We start to dance together, and I am lost to Corene.

My Princess. My love.

CHAPTER 6

PARSIFAL

I've made a quick trip to our estate and returned with a dozen trunks to get us through our stay at Four Halls. When I return to South Hall, I find Derk standing outside Thelia's door. I drop the trunk.

"I went to the Southerners' quarters, like you asked." His eyes are painfully wide. "Two nights now I've brought bread and scones. Last night, nothing. But tonight, after the announcement, I heard them speaking fast and hushed. Suspicious-like. Each of Nul se Lan's bodyguards had three weapons at least—tucked in pants, inside boots, up a sleeve."

"Is that all?" I ask. It sounds suspicious, but not enough for action.

Derk exhales sharply. "Well, I don't know exactly what they're planning, since I couldn't understand them. But I kept hearing Vasha. Over and over."

Why would Nul se Lan go after Bayled? The cratertooth already has the throne. When they return from war, he'll be King.

I touch Derk's cheek. "Thank you for your help," I say, and turn to enter the suite.

"Is that it?" Derk asks.

"I said thank you."

"I risked a lot to learn this for you."

"You took someone bread and blended into the background. I appreciate you. You're helping the Kingdom, titta tatta." I shrug. "Is that what you want to hear?"

Derk narrows his eyes at me and stalks off down the hall. Oh well. He was a good lover, but not great.

When I finally open the door, I find Morgaun and Duke Finegarden unpacking their things in Thelia's bedroom. With no Thelia. She must be avoiding them—unfortunate, given what I've just learned. I may not like that gullible trit Bayled, but I don't relish the idea of those cratertooths offing him.

"That's where my shrine goes, Dad!" Morgaun roars and pushes a trunk out of his way.

"You ungrateful child." Duke Finegarden looms over his son. "You will talk to me with respect, or you'll sleep in the barn with the rats."

That's what my mother has always said about the Duke: *He has a temper and no conscience.* Morgaun's ten spades worse.

I pretend that I'm not listening, but I can feel Morgaun's gaze worm into me. His hair is dark, like Thelia's, and his bone structure is just as fine. That's where the similarity ends. Morgaun's eyes are ratlike and small, and his thin lips perpetually form a grimace.

"Where's sister?" Morgaun asks, turning to the Duke. "It's the middle of the night. She should be here already. You know how Melidia feels about women who stay out late."

The Duke glances at me. "You two are always tittering about together, Parsifal," he says. "You must know."

If Thelia were asked about my whereabouts, she'd throw *me*

to the crows. She'd tell my dad I was off serving the serving ladies in the larder, and she'd enjoy it.

"She's comforting the Princess," I say instead. "Corene's fiancé is leaving for war, you know." Thelia owes me.

Morgaun smirks. "High time for a war with the long ears. I'd like to kill one of those Magic-worshipping monsters myself, maybe strangle it with my bare hands."

"And mount its head among the rest of your collection?" I roll my eyes. I've seen the walls of his room back at the Finegarden manor, covered in toothy torture devices he calls *antiques*. "Spare us."

Morgaun purses his lips. "No. I'd kill it slowly. Make it watch me fuck its sister."

No Frefoisian would dare speak the way Morgaun does. The only crime our courts considered worse than murder was rape, and Morgaun would've long ago gotten his tongue snipped off. They do that so you can't make too much noise when the magister snips the rest of you.

The moment the Finegardens retreat back into Thelia's room, my parents poke their heads out of the opposite door. "You should stay with us in here, Percy," Dad says, flicking a nervous look at the closed door. "We'll make space for you."

I wave him off. "Thanks. I'll be in later." As far as parents go, I'm better off than Thelia. Sure, Dad sees me as a symbol of his discontent here; my lack of passion in restoring what we lost irritates him endlessly. But Mom has always been quiet and passive, and she's been in poor health as long as I remember, so there's no way to know if it's her illness or her personality.

I open up the trunk, licking my lips as I pull out one of my three bottles of black wine. One thing I'll say: my father enjoys a quality bottle as much as I do. I curl up with it on a bench in the hallway and start sipping.

A mounted torch crackles as it burns. It's the dead of night, but people still creep around the halls, looking for spare rooms. Some doze on the stairs or against the walls. I let the nearly empty bottle fall into my lap. I won't go back inside until I'm sure that everyone's asleep.

"Percy?"

I open my eyes and realize I've drifted off with my head propped against the wall. Thelia's gaze drops to my lap, and she gives me a nasty smile. "Dreaming of me?"

"No." I cross my legs. Her catlike smile grows wider. "Someone else."

She sits down next to me, the hem of her dress landing above the knee—enough that I get a hearty swallow of leg. I wince.

"I'm disappointed," she says, reaching for my bottle of wine. "But it's for the best. We're going to be living right next to each other." When I don't give up the wine, she tries to wrest it away from me.

"Stop it." I yank it back. "It's mine."

"We're family." She tries again. "Come on, share with me."

"Shut up, witch," I slur, clutching the wine to my chest. "You left me with your filthy craggon of a brother, and I protected you. You thank me by taking my one comfort?"

She looks insulted. "Percy, I—"

"That's not my damned name!" I stumble to my feet, blood rushing to my head. How have I stood her this long? She doesn't care about anyone but herself. She'll step on anyone, even me, if it means getting what she wants. Down the hall, an oil lamp flickers. "I know where you were." I sway as I stick a finger in her face. "Out looking for Bayled Vasha, right?"

"None of your business."

"Why? He has nothing to offer you now—definitely not a crown. Don't tell me you want him." I know I shouldn't. I'm lowering the match to the oil, waiting for it to explode. But nothing will matter soon, when the long ears arrive. Might as well enjoy some fireworks.

"We don't know who's coming back from this war and who's not," says Thelia. "I've picked my horse in this race."

I snort a laugh. "Still obsessed with him. It's all you care about."

"You're just jealous of my ambition," she snaps back. "At least I *want* something. You've given up. You just want to see it all burn."

More lamps flicker, up and down the hall. Thelia's eyes dart around, then back to me. "You couldn't find him, could you?" I sneer. "He's avoiding you, Theels. He can't stand you. Your plan never would've worked. Besides, I know something about him that you don't."

"I don't want to play this game right now, Percy."

"You play with *me* all the time, just like you did in the banquet hall."

"Your trews are all twisted up from a little two-finger punch?" She rolls her eyes, as if she didn't leave me on the floor in white-hot pain only a few hours ago. "You've always been a weakling."

The wine in my stomach rises up, hot as dragon's breath.

Crash. Glass shatters down the hall—like a vase was smashed. People scream as the oil lamp goes out, dumping broken glass all over them and the floor.

I stand up and lean perilously toward her in the darkness, ignoring the chaos down the hall. I'd planned on telling her what I'd learned from Derk, but why bother? In fact, why concern myself with anything that happens to any of them? They wouldn't do it for me.

"Your looks won't last forever, you know," I hiss at her. "You'll grow old and be just as bitter and alone as your mother. Unless your fearsome little elves kill us first."

Before she can say anything in response, I turn and stride back through the door to my family's suite.

I lie in bed, undo the top button of my breeches, and slip one hand in. I imagine Corene first. Then Nul se Lan. It doesn't respond, so I close my eyes and try to imagine Thelia instead. But all I see behind my eyelids is a frightened little girl, curled up in a ball in front of the fire, screaming.

The elves are coming!

THELIA

Parsifal pops another bread roll into his mouth. "We didn't see you last night, cousin."

I scowl at him across the table. After everything he said, he has the nerve to play aloof? Maybe he was so drunk that he doesn't remember. Does that mean he's forgotten his secret about Bayled, too?

Down the table, Daddy and Antonin argue over how long the war will be—and what'll happen when the food runs out. "There's a parade this morning," Morgaun says. "The army is marching out."

I spit out a quail bone in surprise, and my father eyeballs me. "When did I raise such a disgusting daughter?"

"Sorry." I figured we were beyond rules now. No reason to bother, with all the eligible bachelors gone off to war.

Morgaun laughs. "You didn't raise her," he says. "Mother did—to be a heathen, just like her. Like sow, like piglet." He carves off more ham with his knife, popping a whole piece into his mouth, and licks the blade with a wink.

I feel like flegging up that quail, but how many more meals like this will I get?

"I blame Baron Durnhal," Parsifal says, smirking at me. So he does remember last night—and he's still angry. "If the Baron had just proposed, he could've turned Thelia into a proper lady."

How dare my cousin take part in this? After all those times Daddy scolded me for being too loud, for learning kroga, for dressing in trousers for practice, and Parsifal assured me, *You'd be made a Princess in Frefois for that.* It always made me feel better. Now he's turned on me.

Morgaun laughs. "She needs a stronger antidote than marriage to fix what's wrong with her."

I set down my fork and get up. I don't need to listen to this. Morgaun's mockery follows me out of the suite—*my* suite, now stacked to the ceiling with their moldy trunks. Elves won't be the ones to kill me. Morgaun will.

Of course he had to bring up Red just when I've been moving on—patching over the holes it left in me when I woke up and I found that letter under my door.

Is it too late to flee Four Halls? I wouldn't even be here if that self-righteous trit Corene hadn't interfered. I remember thinking it perfectly normal when I passed them talking in the hallway; now I know she was poisoning Baron Durnhal against me.

If it weren't for her, I'd be Baroness of the Crimson

Woods—and nowhere near this awful castle. My head grows hot with rage remembering Red's roguish smile, the swipe of silver at his temple, his clefted chin. Now Corene is safe up in her tower while Parsifal and I are shoved into a stone box with Morgaun, the dogs, and the commoners.

I'm a cousin of the Princess. I will not go back to that room, with those horrid people.

I stamp up the stairs to North Hall. When I reach the top, two guards block my way. "No entry for non-royals."

"I'm here to see my cousin," I say calmly.

"Let her through," the first guard says, his fingers ghosting over his neck. He's the one from last night. They step aside and I march past.

I pause outside Corene's door and take a deep breath. I can't storm in there, overflowing with rage, and expect to get what I want. There are a lot of empty rooms on this hall—I can simply ask to have one.

My gaze falls on the inscription. *C + T.*

I still can't figure out why she did it. Sure, Corene and I had our little tiffs growing up. But I never hated her before the spring, and I didn't think she hated me. I remember how she smelled every time I got up on her bed, bruised and cut, and she wrapped her arms around me. "Oh, Delia just loves you too much," she'd say in a mollifying voice. "She wants the best for you." The beautiful Princess would pat my back and have a handmaid bring us cakes and maybe a jester to perform for our pleasure.

I'm standing in the hallway, thinking, when the door opens. Corene gasps, her hair in a wild tangle and her gown on backward. "Thelia?" Her frenzied expression fades into an awkward smile. "Did you come to see me?"

"I, uh . . ." I lick my lips. "No. I'm going to Bayled's quarters."

Her eyebrows furrow. "He's not here."

"I know. I'm just going to see . . . if he left a note for me."

She tilts her head. "Why would he leave you a note?" The way she says *you*, like I'm no more significant in this castle than a serving girl, brings all my hatred roaring back.

Corene's always looked down on me. Queen Laine hated my mother, always harped in front of me about how disappointed she was with her brother for stooping to marry her. I want to stick my hand in Corene's stupid orange hair, twist it into a knot, and pull as hard as I can. I want to hurt her like I hurt when I found the Baron gone.

"Oh, horsefish," I say. "Never mind." I turn and start back the way I came. I'll never get anything I want from Corene. It's all about her, always has been.

"Wait," Corene calls after me. I ignore her and slip down the arched stone hallway to the stairs. Her tiny footsteps follow me. "Theels, wait!"

I spin. "Don't you dare call me *Theels*. Don't you dare."

"What . . . ?" She has the nerve to look confused. All the fake hugs and comforting and tenderness—shit right out of a troll's ass.

I'm not going to take it anymore. "You rotten rib cage," I snap, taking a step forward. "You made him leave. *My* Red. How could you?"

His letter didn't say outright who was to blame for his decision to leave court, but it was easy to read between the lines. Someone who I trust knows your heart.

Corene's face falls. "I—I didn't mean to . . ."

Another step, and Corene presses her back to the wall. "Oh, you didn't mean to pull him aside one night and brim over with my secrets?" I ask. "You just *accidentally* told him about my mother?" I'm sure she told him every sordid detail.

"I . . . didn't realize . . ." She's clawing around the inside of her skull for what she thinks I want to hear. "How you felt about him—?"

"Too late now, isn't it?" All my coiled-up muscles release, like a trigger in a trap. I lunge at her, letting out the shriek of rage that's been building inside me for moons.

Corene tries to step out of the way but I adjust instantly and tackle her to the ground. We fall to the floor, me on top. She's so weak, it's like wrestling with a mannequin. It would be so easy, so quick, to kill her right now.

"Theels!" Corene shrieks. "I didn't mean to!" She flails like a caught fish. Of course she meant to tell him everything that was unappealing and unladylike about me—everything that made me unfit to be a Baronness. "If I'd known you loved him—"

The moment she says it, I realize: I did love him. I trusted him. He kept up with me and even seemed to relish my darker tendencies. Maybe, after a time, I could've seen him without clothes and not felt ill. Maybe I could've done the things with him that wives do.

I could've gone to the Crimson Woods and ruled the barony at his side. I could've left everything here behind—Morgaun's seething and brooding, Daddy's judging, and Mother's desperate ambitions for my future that still lingered. I could've easily given up marrying Bayled, given up becoming Queen, for *him*.

All at once, the pleasure's gone out of this. Killing Corene wouldn't get him back. And I'd live the rest of my life in a dungeon, however much of it is left to me.

I free my hand from Corene's tangles and stumble away. Her face is red where I smacked it against the floor, her cheeks covered in shining tears as she struggles up to her feet. She's accepted her punishment.

I straighten my skirts, feeling nothing now but bottomless sadness. "Why?" I ask her. "You were supposed to be my best friend."

Corene wipes her face with her sleeve. "I just . . . I thought you were only after his title. I thought you'd break his heart. I was protecting him."

"Protecting him from *me*?" The tears hurt the soft skin under my eyes as they start to pour out. I cover my face with my hands because I can't seem to stop them. I've never cried in front of her, even when Mother left. Never. "We're family. You were my best friend. That's beyond sideways, Corene."

"I know." She sniffles. "I'm sorry. He was just so much older than you." Corene takes a step toward me—testing the water. "I had no idea you actually cared about him. Like that."

"Never hurts to ask!" I shout through the tears, but I'm drained of all my venom. I wish I could sink into this floor and be sucked into the earth.

Corene's blue eyes are glassy and heavy. "I know," she whispers. "I'm sorry he went home."

She's so innocent and vacant, like a horse. The Corene-sized hole in my chest is filling up again. I sigh and take a matching step toward her. We each take one more and then we're together, and we wrap our arms around each other.

"Everything is horrible. Bayled's gone. Father keeps drinking. And now you hate me." She holds me tighter and sniffles. I don't contradict her, but I maneuver my arm around her shoulder and lead her back to her room.

Corene collapses into her bed, grabs the nearest pillow, and buries her face in it. I lie down next to her, like when the Queen was dying, like when Mother left.

Corene sniffles. "I can't believe we're just . . . cows waiting to have our heads cut off."

"They don't cut off cows' heads." Mother took me to watch once. They stick a sharp blade right through the brain. That is how you end it fast, with no noise.

"You know what I mean!" She hiccups, which certainly means she's crying into the pillow. "What if we all die?"

Melidia curse my corpse, please. "Then at least we die together." It's something out of one of our children's stories, but it seems like the right thing to say.

"What about Nul and Bayled? They'll die first, far away in battle!"

Great. Now I'm stuck comforting Corene again. "Bayled will come back for you. That—I know."

She creases the pillow with her fingernails. "Daddy sent them away without any preparation. They're doomed."

I want to strangle her all over again. "You think so little of Bayled?" Maybe I've called him stupid in front of Parsifal before, but he's truly not. "He can think for himself. He'll find a way to survive. Don't you believe in him?"

Corene pulls her face away from the pillow, eyes sprinkled with red. "I do!"

"Then what are you sitting here crying about?" I snap. "I'm trapped in my tiny room with *Morgaun*, of all people, and you're blubbering over some horsefish that hasn't even happened yet?"

Her eyes open wide, like she just woke up from a dream. "Oh, right. Morgaun's here." It's an effort not to roll my eyes.

"I couldn't be in a room with him another moment," I say. I hide the smile crossing my face. She just needs a little push to go over the edge. "I'm always scared."

Corene sits up, inspired. She is justice. She is fairness and generosity. "You shouldn't live in fear. Let me try to make up for all I've done. Come live with me in North Hall—we have plenty of room."

"Really?" I rub my face like I'm scattering tears. "Parsifal, too? Morgaun's ready to eat him alive down there."

You owe me one, Percy. The debt is paid—now he'd better make like a dragon and give up his hoard. I need to know what he knows.

"He's welcome, too." Corene smiles graciously. "It's what Mom would want. You're family."

Damn right I am.

PARSIFAL

I'm sizzling, swelling, and ready to pop. I keep saying things I shouldn't, but everything is upside-down and I don't know where to find the ground.

I'm searching the castle halls for signs of Derk, hoping we might reconcile for a day—and studiously avoiding going back to our suite—when I nearly crash into Thelia on the stairs. I cover my chest, sure she's going to two-finger slam me again.

"Just the person I was looking for." She smiles in a way that's almost convincing. "I know last night was hard—but can we forget that now? Please? I have a surprise for you."

No, I'm not ready to forget it. But my curiosity is more powerful than my resentment, so I grudgingly follow her up the stairs to North Hall. The guards posted there don't question us as we pass toward Corene's room.

Thelia stops in front of a room that hasn't been used since the long-dead King Ingoll fathered a dozen children. She throws the door open to reveal an empty suite. "This is all ours now."

Not as big as Corene's, but it has a vaulted wood ceiling with two doors, one leading into an adjoining sitting room. "Look, Percy. This could be yours!"

She's trying to bribe me, hoping to find out what I know by giving me what I want more than anything: to escape those two tiny rooms in South Hall. It works.

"I bet we could take out this sofa and get a bed in here for you," Thelia says, plopping down on the scarlet cushions. She runs a hand across their curling wood arms, brushed with gold leaf.

I could be one door away from Thelia, hearing her soft breaths through the wall between us. Her eyes touch mine, and for a moment I believe she's thinking it, too.

Guilt floods me. "Thelia." I should've told her before. I should've told everyone about my suspicions, but I was angry. Nobody in the Kingdom has ever cared about me, so why should I try to save it? But I can't keep this from Thelia. My only friend.

"I think Nul se Lan's going to betray Bayled. And if I don't send word to him, that stupid trit will fall right into whatever trap the cratertooth lays out."

War is a glorious thing for everyone but those who have to fight in it.

Every time we pass a junction on the Low Road, we find a new company of soldiers waiting, sent by their lords. Only half have armor, and even fewer are properly armed. Swords are in short supply so most men bring hatchets or hoes. Their faces are drawn and fearful, like prisoners awaiting the gallows. The lords of Melidihan have holed up in Four Halls, and I expect the rest to stay on their own distant estates. Only a few, like the battle-seasoned Baron Durnhal, will come to ride with us.

Citizens gather at the crossroads, cheering as the King's army passes. You'd think we'd already won the war the way they shake their pennants and hold out their infants. Most soldiers keep their faces straight ahead, silent as we march. But one particular company bellows and cheers as we pass.

Nul se Lan scowls. "These men make trouble again. Do something."

A hulking, red-haired man riding an enormous chestnut stallion leads the company. When we left Melidihan, his men rigged up a keg astride a donkey. The emptier it gets, the louder their hollering and cheering, as if this is all some sporting event.

I sigh. "Stone Company might act like stupid craggons, but they can win a fight. Especially their leader, Harged Halen. The King gave him a medal of accomplishment after the war."

Not that he's in fighting shape now as he sways perilously on his horse. In the years since his company of common city-folk helped conquer Frefois, gossip says Harged's spent his time dominating Melidihan's underground kroga ring—the one that meets in taverns late at night, and draws as many nobles as commoners for betting.

Lan tightens his grip on his reins. "My father died. My city destroyed. This constant celebration insult me." He spits over the side of his horse's neck.

I'm overcome by a soul-deep exhaustion. "What would you like me to do it about it?"

"Send them home. Only trouble they'll get us." Nul sets his jaw. I size him up. He's thinner than I am, but not less powerful. All lean muscle, tough and hard as his southern hills. But he's not in command here.

"I'm sorry about your father," I say. "But we have less than three thousand men at present. I will not send our best fighters home just because you don't like them."

Nul se Lan makes a *hmmph* sound. I turn around on my horse and holler, "Halen! To the front. Now."

Harged Halen rides up past Nul's three stony-faced bodyguards and wedges himself between Nul and me at the head of the troop. "Good to finally get an audience with you, Vasha." I don't miss the note of irony.

"The King sends his gratitude for your service." *And it's General Vasha*, I think, but that won't earn any respect from Halen.

Harged snorts. "Why isn't he here himself?"

"His Majesty's health is poor," I say stiffly.

"Drinking too much?" I don't reply, and Harged lets out a startling guffaw. "Can't say I expected different. Old fool has never had any self-control as long as I've known him."

"Speaking of self-control." I give him as meaningful a look as I can muster. "You need to keep your men—and yourself—in line. The keg and the donkey go at the next junction."

His eyes widen. "That keg was a hundred coin, boss!"

"This *war*," Lan interrupts him. "Not party."

Harged glances between us. "Hmm. The King's ward and the King's heir. So which one of you is leading us against the long ears?"

"I am," I say at the same time that Nul se Lan says, "Me." I turn in my saddle to find him staring back at me, his severe blue eyes like icicles.

"You two had better figure that out," Harged says with a chuckle. "Someone will need to give orders in battle."

I stare down at Halrendar's mane, clenching the reins tight. I'm the general; Lan is the heir. I thought the King made this clear. Why is he pretending otherwise?

When we finally halt in the evening to make camp, the men are tired, unused to long-distance travel. They sit quietly around their fires, eating in solemn silence as I retreat into my tent.

It's not long before the sound of singing filters in through the flap. I reemerge to find Harged and the rest of Stone Company sitting around one of the fires, belting out an old traveling song I haven't heard since I was a boy.

Our knees ache and
Our feet cry for air,
Our heads bleed and
To our hearts, it's not fair;

Out on the road
There are no friends
Only a weary comrade;
Together, we meet our ends.

I sit down in the dirt near the fire, and a soldier wordlessly brings me a bowl of soup while I listen. It's thin, mostly water, and the vegetables squeeze when I chew them. If this is what they're eating, it's what I'll eat.

Someone taps me on the shoulder. It's Sasel, a priestess-in-training the Temple sent along with us to send and receive smoke messages. "Evening."

I'm not a King, but neither is she a priestess. I guess King-in-training and priestess-in-training means neither of us gets a title. "Evening."

She crouches next to me, dressed in leather traveling clothes stitched with the Temple's colors of white and black. "I received a message for you from a priestess at Four Halls."

I glance around, searching the heads for Lan. He'll get his trews all twisted up if I don't include him.

She squeezes my shoulder, hard. I forget how strong the priestesses are, always hiding under shapeless shifts. "*Only* for you." She holds out a piece of paper. "I wrote it down."

I hold up the paper to the firelight.

Don't trust the hillman.
He has a plan.
From P & T.

Parsifal and Thelia. Why would they, of all people, send a warning like this? They don't even like me.

I remember meeting Parsifal at a party his dad threw at the Bellisare estate, out in the country. He and Thelia offered to show me his dad's collection of bizarre antiques in the basement—the "Museum." They asked me all sorts of questions about the cultures and places these strange objects came from. When I didn't know the answers, they laughed and sneered.

"Northerners," Parsifal said in a mocking voice. "Think they're so much better than us, but this one doesn't know anything!"

When Corene found us, she berated them for making a spectacle of me. *He's not some toy for you to play with*, she'd said. *He's a dignified visitor*. I fell in love with her then.

It's strange that they would try to help me now. Is this part of some other game of theirs? I fold up the piece of paper. "I wish they'd said more."

"Nevertheless," Sasel says, "you won't want anyone else to see it." She lifts her torch to the paper, and it goes up in flame.

CHAPTER 7

SAPPHIRE

When humankind first sprouted from Melidia's seeds, we tried to help them as one would help a small child learning to walk. The dwarves built them sewer systems, designed aqueducts to bring them fresh water. We taught them principle, agriculture, Magic.

It was a great mistake. The human children grew fierce and many. Everything in sight was theirs; they multiplied and expanded, more farms, more towns—more, more—swallowing everything.

So The People left, frightened. We took Magic with us and retreated to the other side of the Great Mountains, to Viteos. We said, *You remain there, and we remain here, to never cross.* The dwarves, being dwarves, dug further underground. Instead of running, they hid. I do not know how far down they have gone to escape the steady encroachment of humankind, but we didn't see a single sign of them as we hiked up the tallest peaks in the Forgotten Crags, past rockfalls and crevasses, to the place where Commander Valya knew to look. For a silver door, set in the mountain.

We have been underground for almost a week now. I thought I could tolerate these old abandoned tunnels, but the darkness grows closer each day, squeezing me, choking me.

I am grateful to rest when we stop to eat. My feet are tired and sore, and my hair is full of cobwebs.

"How do they live like this?" I ask Ellze, for the fiftieth time.

"I don't know." He runs one hand through his heavy, oily hair, and instantly regrets it. We haven't run across even one water source—an underground pool, a tiny waterfall, nothing. Our bodies can retain water for a long time, but we may reach our limit soon.

I don't dare ask the Commander when we can expect to arrive, lest I acquire the reputation of complaining. But he is the only one with a map.

Under my feet, the ground begins to tremble. I crouch down and place my hand flat on the stone floor. No, it is not the ground—the vibration is *me*, as if an electric current is running thick through me, using me as a conduit.

"Ferah." Our Magicker glances over, and I hold out my hand. "Do you feel this?"

She wraps her hand around mine. The thrumming travels through me, into her. Her eyes grow wide. "Magic."

She lifts both hands in the air. Her fingers hook and pull, hook and pull, weaving invisible threads into her palms. Drawing them into herself. "Commander Valya, look." She holds out one hand, and a small flicker of light appears in her palm. The Commander looks up from his own meal as the light expands, pulsing with blue veins. With life.

A smile teases his mouth. "We're getting close."

Ferah picks more skittering threads of Magic out of the air, gathering them up into a ball of beautiful white light. It swells until the entire cavern is awash in bright sunbeams that tickle my skin with warmth. It feels like we are standing outside in the most perfect, cloudless afternoon.

We resume our march. Even when evening arrives, we do not rest with our destination so close and Ferah's simulated sun beating our backs.

The scent of sulfur and cinnamon creeps up my nose and I sneeze. It's spicy and sweet and sour, all at once. Magic. Pressure grows inside my ears, the way it does when a big storm is rolling in. The force of it is unlike anything I have ever felt, even at our great well inside the High Seer's cavern. I have knelt before that glittering green pool that is our pulsing heart, and it was nothing compared to this.

My wisp comes to an abrupt halt. I creep forward to look at what it's found. Its mauve glow reflects off something in the ceiling, something flat and smooth and perfectly round—a pattern that doesn't occur naturally down here. A door, right overhead.

"Sapphire?" the Commander asks. "Are you ready?" I must remember what I have come here to do and keep the plan at the front of my mind.

I put on a cloak and raise the hood to hide the shape of my ears. The Commander pulls the door down, showering us with centuries of dust. Only darkness lies on the other side. My wisp chirps nervously.

"Go on." I gesture upward. "I need you to help me see."

It flies through the door, casting the tunnel above in dusky pink. This, clearly, is not the same craftsmanship or masonry as what lies behind us. The stones are smaller, more clumsily fitted. I have to jump to get my hands inside the door's frame, where I grab on and lift myself the rest of the way into the tight stone tunnel. The wisp bobs above me, urging me on.

I start up. Follow the smell of Magic.

BAYLED

We're supposed to reach the Crimson Woods tonight, but everyone's dragging. Autumn rain started falling as soon as we woke up and hasn't stopped. The soldiers are tired and our boots are soggy. Our progress will only grow slower as we add more reserves to the ranks.

My insides feel coarse in a way they never felt before Nul se Lan arrived at Four Halls. Ever since, all I knew to be certain turned to liquid slipping out through the cracks in the floor.

The King trusts Lan, or he would never have made him heir. But I can't stop thinking about Thelia and Parsifal's message. Can I even trust them? Maybe I've known them longer than this Southerner, but that only reminds me of all the games they've played with me before. Was it just skipping another stone in their endless pa-chi-chi game?

At sundown, we pause to divvy up dinner rations. "Make it quick," I holler. "We have to press on."

"Here we should camp for the night," Nul se Lan says, dismounting. "You not lead before, so you not know. But after they stop, men not go farther."

It's too early in the campaign for cutting our days short. I climb up onto a wagon to help my voice travel through the ranks of soldiers.

"We're in Crimson Woods territory," I shout. Some of the men raise their heads from their bowls. "Baron Durnhal and his men will join us at the Crossing, making us five thousand strong. We can't leave them waiting all night!"

A few of them grunt in acknowledgment as the message travels back, but Harged and his men are too busy swigging beer. I jump down from the wagon and march back to them.

"We won't leave them waiting, will we?" I kick the keg, and Stone Company all jump to attention.

"Sir!" Harged brings his arm up into a salute. The rest of the company follows. Nul se Lan stands by his horse, watching us with his arms crossed.

"Would you leave your own to stand in the rain waiting, to stare into the horizon hoping?" I demand.

"No!" one man shouts.

Harged hollers, "We'd be total pricks!"

"So are we going to stop here?"

His face turns bright red. "NO!"

The rest of the men hear his bellow and stand up at attention. "No!"

Nul se Lan scowls at me as I get back on my horse. "Get your men organized," I roar. "On to the Crossing."

By the time the moon is high over our heads, we're all sagging in our saddles, half asleep. Maybe pushing ahead was a mistake. The truth is that I wanted the Baron's counsel; he's someone who remembers the war, someone with a steady mind. What would he make of Thelia and Parsifal's warning?

"There!" one of the scouts calls back. "The Crossing!"

The three and a half towers of the Crossing appear on the moonlit horizon. The last tower was ravaged in the war, when the King's force met the unified tribes of the Klissen on the Low Road—and fell to their swords. It was an easy victory for them.

As we approach, it's clear something is wrong. The towers aren't lit. If the Baron were here, the braziers inside the high windows would be blazing. I think of the warning message and start searching the rooftops for shadowy figures. But we are painfully alone here.

I urge Halrendar into a trot. Nul follows me toward the dark Crossing, but there's no one in sight. Dust blows across the road that serpentines off into the Crimson Woods.

"General." It's Harged, charging up on his massive stallion. "The Baron's a deserter."

My chest squeezes. "We don't know for sure," I hedge. I can't imagine Baron Durnhal abandoning the Kingdom in a time of such great need. And I don't want to think about what that would mean for us.

"Pretentious trit of a lord," says Harged, spitting. "Can't be bothered to show up for war. Doesn't want to get his pretty armor dirty."

With a sigh, Nul se Lan says, "Maybe now, we camp?"

I nod. Perhaps they were held up and will arrive during the night.

Don't trust the hillman. He has a plan.

Well, it looks as if I can't trust the Baron either.

I wheel Halrendar around and hold my arm in the air. "We'll set up camp here for the night and wait for Baron Durnhal's men to arrive." I call Sasel over. "Can you send a smoke message to the Crimson Woods? We're here at the Crossing, and we're waiting."

"Of course, General." She glances at Nul se Lan before scurrying off with her smokesticks. My wrist twitches. I hope this is only a misunderstanding. Or else I'll have to kill him.

PARSIFAL

The first evening in my new room, there's a knock on my door. I get up to find the two most beautiful women in the world standing on the other side. Thelia winks as she leads Corene in, and they peer around my little space. They look bright and fresh and newly washed.

"You brought all this from home?" Thelia asks, admiring one of my paintings.

"Of course. What is life without art? If you're going to suffer, there's no reason to do it in ugliness."

Corene flops down on my sofa with a great sigh. I've decided to keep it instead of a bed. "I get it. The little comforts can give you a boost when you really need it."

Thelia sits down on the arm of the sofa. "It'll take a lot of wine and foot massages for me to forget we're all stuck in here, waiting to be killed."

"That can be arranged."

After digging around in a cupboard earlier today, I discovered some crystal wine glasses, hand-carved in the shape of the Hindermarks' coat of arms. As the girls walk around, observing the artwork I painstakingly packed in my trunks, I pour some wine for each of us and hold out the glasses. "Here you are, ladies."

My cousin snickers as I pour one for her. "Always willing and able to get everybody drunk."

"That's his job, isn't it?" Corene stretches out even further, like a cat when sunbathing. "First time I ever had a drink was at the mansion, and so were my second and third and fourth. I remember when Mom let me try her wine for the first time and I forgot to be disgusted by it. She guessed right then what we'd been up to."

A snort escapes me. "Queen Laine! It only took her, what, a year to catch on? Melidia bless her memory."

Corene raises her glass, which I fill. "Thank you, Percy." Thelia gives her a look. "I mean, Parsifal."

I smile and clink my glass against hers. "You're both perfectly welcome." It's like escaping our awful families has taken us back in time, to when everything was less complicated. When we didn't fight. I throw back my own glass and pour another.

This was the night I've needed for so long. Bayled isn't here, and while I'm sure he hovers on the edge of Corene's mind, she doesn't bring him up. I don't want to think about him out on the Low Road, cold and sleeping on the hard ground. I certainly don't want to imagine that cratertooth sneaking up on him in the night and burying a dagger in his back.

We cover every meaningless topic possible, from artwork to architecture to gossip about our history tutor. Corene's wine sloshes forward in her glass and her face is bright red. We're in the second bottle now and it's almost gone. "I swear to you, I saw him with old Madame Feroult," she says. "They were out in the courtyard, sneaking kisses in the dark right under my window."

"Had you been drinking?" Thelia asks with a bright, ringing laugh. "Your eyes make stuff up when you've had a few."

"What? You think I'm a liar?"

"I think you saw what you wanted to see. That lady is so old, her coot is probably dried as a prune."

I raise a hand. "Stop right there. Women only get better with age. There is no such thing as a dried out coot. It is all good—always good."

Corene's mouth falls open, and Thelia howls. "Melidia hold me! You have it for Madame Feroult."

My fists clench. "That's not true."

"Yes it is. You cannot tolerate the idea of her getting poked by Sir Pedrekel because you want to poke her yourself."

I know it's the wine that's getting me all warm and angry, but I still say, "No, it's you who wants to get poked by Sir Pedrekel. You like older men."

The room goes silent. Corene hunches her shoulders like she's trying to disappear and takes a long gulp of her wine.

Thelia's scowl could melt holes in iron. She gets up and puts her glass down. "Theels," I say, getting up to stop her.

"I'm hungry since I skipped dinner. I'm going to the kitchen." She's trying her hardest not to sound angry, just flat. She glances at Corene. "You want anything?" Corene shakes her head, so Thelia disappears out the door.

"I'm sorry I ruined it," Corene says into her glass. "Seems like I ruin everything lately."

I tilt my head. "To what are you referring, Princess?"

"I'm the one who messed up everything with the Baron. I hurt her so much. She truly loved him."

Even the demons could've predicted Corene would make

this about her. I gulp down the rest of my wine. "You did what you thought was right at the time."

Time to open more. Corkscrew in one hand, I reach for a fresh bottle—my last one.

"I guess." Her eyes grow misty. "I just . . . Thelia is all I have."

I lower the wine bottle. "What about Bayled?"

"It's not the same. I was almost eight when he came to the Holy Kingdom. But Thelia's always been there." She hiccups as her tears brim over. "And she was going to *leave*. If I said nothing, she'd have married the Baron and left for the Crimson Woods and never come back. I did you a favor."

I can only gape at her. The selfish little pliggan.

Corene's tears fall into the wine. "I lost Mom already." She won't look at me, won't take in the horrified look on my face. "Someday I'll lose Dad, too, and then who would I be left with—?"

My throat and chest feel hot. I can never tell Thelia this. Time for more wine. But when I go to pour it, the bottle shakes in my hand, spilling red droplets.

I stare at my hand, wondering if I'm that upset—when the bottle wobbles again.

"Do you feel that?" I ask. Corene gives me a strange look. Now even the couch is vibrating underneath me. "Is the ground shaking?" They have these in the Sand Shelves, great quakes that rip holes in the earth. But this feels like . . . a warning.

Corene starts to look angry. "Nothing is shaking, Parsifal. You're drunk." Behind me, the three-pronged candelabra on the desk topples off, falling on the ground with an immense *clang!*

I jump to my feet. "You know," I say, putting the bottle of

wine down. "I should go help Thelia bring food back. I wanted some too." The candlesticks keep trying to tell me things.

Parsifal, do you know how absolutely rung up the parapets you sound? But I'd rather be wrong and know it than be right and ignore my instincts.

I put down the bottle and run out of the room. I nearly slip on the stairs but catch myself on a windowsill. There's so much wine inside me that my limbs aren't working. "Thelia?" I hiss. She must be coming back this way. "Theels!"

When I reach the bottom of the stairs, I slide across the stone floor, tripping over the runners. I make it down the main hall, almost to the kitchens. Someone is moving around inside.

Clink, clink. It's coming from down the hall. I freeze.

They're metallic footsteps—someone in armor. I dive through the open kitchen door, landing at Thelia's feet. She's picking through the leftovers from dinner, a candle on the center island.

"Parsifal? What are you—"

"Shhh." I duck behind a counter and gesture for her to follow. She picks up her plate of food and swaggers after me.

"Playing a game?" she asks. Too loudly. "You're quite drunk, aren't—"

More clinking. I grab her arm and drag her down next to me. "Quiet," I whisper. She stares into my face and, for once in her life, she shuts up.

A shadow appears in the doorway. Maybe they'll move on—whoever *they* are. But the shadow doesn't move. Thelia's candle flickers on the counter. A head peers in, hidden in a silver helmet. Two long, pointed ears stick out the sides.

I grab Thelia's hand. *Please don't make a sound.*

Humans are so small. I have to stoop to avoid brushing the ceiling as my wisp and I traverse the tiny hallways. A few steps up. A turn. Another turn. A few steps down. I must be right back where I started—except for the thrumming, pulsing energy running through me.

I can feel Melidia's eyes boring a hole into the back of my neck. She's here, watching. The Magic flowing through this place is thick with her. If their goddess is focused this intently on them, our operation here may not go as we expect.

I shake it off. I'm a trained soldier, and no goddess will unroot me.

The bobbing wisp stops. Its arms curl in and it ducks behind me. "What is it?" I take two more steps before I can feel it too. The air is hotter, thicker, more fetid, like sweaty bodies and feces. I cover my face with my hood and gasp into it. I've never smelled anything as repugnant as this. I offer the wisp my hand and it climbs in, hiding behind my thumb.

I stop at a small wooden door bound together with crude iron rivets. It opens with a croak. The next room is just as dark, and the smell is much worse.

Wood racks rise up to the ceiling all around me, lit by the wisp's dim glow. I have to hunch to climb out the trap door, then it falls closed behind me.

Bottles fill the racks—probably wine. I've heard humans like it. We started getting it from the Northerners a few cycles ago, but most of The People don't consume. Who would enjoy losing control?

I close my eyes and feel through myself for Melidia's

unwavering gaze. It is more of a glare. But from where is she watching me?

Down a hall, I meet a dead end. Voices echo overhead and I usher the wisp into my pocket, following the sound. Light floods in through a metal grate. And the smell—humans are the foulest creatures ever created. Melidia, you ought to be ashamed of yourself.

There's splashing, and then footsteps. The voices recede. I push open the grate and peer out. I am in a small, round room—with a pool of feces right in the middle. Before I can vomit, I cover my face and race out, behind two squat women.

I follow them down the halls as Melidia's presence grows stronger. I keep myself pressed to the wall, in the shadow. "If I have to empty another one of that old, creepy wizard's chamberpots . . ." one woman says, or so I think—I'm out of practice with this language.

"It'll only get worse. Or maybe better, when the food runs out and they have nothing left to shit."

The women disappear down the hall. Following the smell of sulfur and cinnamon, I take the other fork. It is night, so most of the humans should be asleep.

It hits me like a sling to the head: Melidia is staring right at me.

I will not be intimidated out of completing my mission. I follow the force of her gaze until I am standing before tall stone doors. Drawing my sword, I push them open with a horrific creak.

The temple is silent. When I pass a pool of water, a glass globe rises to the surface, pulsing with light. There is Magic here. Deeper in the temple, I enter a vaulted atrium.

It reminds me of the High Seer's garden back in Viteos—except for the towering statue of Melidia. Her stone eyes glare down at me as I walk underneath. The smell of Magic leads me deeper, to a hall of doors. This must be where the priestesses live.

I enter the first room. The person in the bed shifts but doesn't wake up. I lean over and tap her three times on the temple. Her eyes open for a moment before they roll back in her head. She should be out until morning.

I repeat my task in each room. But in the last one, the bed is empty. I search the closet, under the bed. This isn't good—only priestesses have access to the sort of Magic that would present a problem to us. If even one of them gets away . . . "Can I help you?" I spin to find a tiny girl standing in the doorway, white-blond hair piled on top of her head. "Wow," she says, smiling at me. "You're beautiful."

It would be three steps and three taps. She wouldn't get away. She is small and human. But that smile is brilliant.

The Commander will surely dismiss me if I ruin this task. I take a step toward her—and she points a knife at my chest.

I can probably move faster than she can, and my hard skin might be able to repel a weak attack. But I don't know what powers Melidia might grant her most precious servants, and I rather like my life.

"What are you after?" the Priestess asks.

My grasp of the language is awful, but I might as well try. "To clean."

"Clean? Clean what?" She takes a step closer. I take a matching one in reverse so the backs of my legs press against the bed.

"Magic."

She tilts her head. "You want to clean Magic? That doesn't make sense." She carries smokesticks in her hand—ready to call for help.

I gesture around us, hoping I can convince her not to. "Too much Magic. Unsafe. For everyone."

The Priestess follows my eyes to the sticks in her hands, and she smiles even wider. I leap onto the bed, whipping out my sword. She raises the smokesticks in the air and, with a single word, lights them.

"Try it and I send a message," she says. "The army will turn around and come back."

"Try-y-y it." I level the sword at her: a dare.

"Melidia has chosen me to live and to die. Death matters not."

"We not here to kill." I lower my sword. "Just help. Too much Magic—dangerous."

"Dangerous? We're fine."

"No. Soo-o-oon, will be dangerous. More, more Magic." The steady burn at the end of her smokesticks suddenly leaps into flame. She drops them, surprised, and I stomp them out before she can burn down the temple. "See?" I say. "Dangerous."

We are face to face, weapons down. In her icy eyes I see the shadow of Melidia. Finally she says, "My people are what matter to me. Don't hurt them. Please."

I shake my head. "Not if yo-o-ou co-o-o-operate."

She evaluates me. Her face is expressive and intelligent—not like giants or ogres or animals. Human eyes are not supposed to look into me, to consider me like one of my own kind would. This is wrong.

"Fine," she says, putting her dagger away. "Let me tell my people why you're here. Then we'll surrender."

"Yes." I sheathe my sword. "Tell them."

I take her arm in my hand, when a scream ripples down the hall. The Priestess's face falls. "What's that?"

I do not know myself. They were supposed to wait for my signal. I hold her tighter as the sound of metal on metal echoes through the temple.

"No!" she shouts. "You lied to me!" I yank her by the arm and run toward the sound.

THELIA

We're going to die. Right here, in the kitchen, under one of the tables, among crumbs of stale bread and crusty ham.

They're here. Did they defeat Bayled and the rest of our army—or bypass them entirely?

The soldier in the doorway peers around the room, helmet built around its long ears. My eyes drop to the plate of food on the floor next to me, the plate I wouldn't abandon when Parsifal showed up. My back's pressed up against crates of apples and potatoes that will creak if I breathe. The plate's out in the open. If this . . . *thing* sees that—it sees me.

As the creature steps farther into the kitchen, armor clanking, my heart pumps so loud I can hear it. My lungs clench, desperate for new air. The candle's tiny flame flickers but the open kitchen door shields us, just barely. Should the soldier look in our direction, the whites of our eyes would give us away.

I keep my gaze on the floor as the thing pivots, walking around the center island. It stops in front of the candle, one silver boot less than a foot from my plate. The soldier reaches out and picks up the candle by the finger hook. Its flesh isn't gray or wrinkled like my nightmares. Its skin is . . . shiny. Perfectly smooth. A deep gold, like metal. The perfect hand, with its perfect fingernails, brings the candle up to its face.

No. It . . . it can't be. This is worse than anything I imagined—so much worse.

A pink tongue shoots out, licking the metal. It sets the candle back down and continues on. Four feet away from us. Five. I'm feeling dizzy from not taking a single proper breath.

The creature heads toward the other end of the kitchen, its back to us. A mane of long, flaxen hair tumbles down a silken cape from under the helmet. Flaxen hair?

Behind me, Parsifal moves. *No, no!* I want to shout at him. *You'll slip on the floor and give us away!* I grab Parsifal's arm to stop him, but he dodges. He snags a piece of hard bread off my plate and leans around the door. I don't have time to interfere.

He chucks it. The crusty bread skitters across the floor, hits the doorframe, and stops. Parsifal clenches his fists. Not far enough.

The monster spins. Its gaze slides right past us as it storms toward the bread.

They are not the beady, black eyes from my dreams. Even in the dim light I can make out small pupils in a ring of bright hazel, whites around the outside, and long lashes. Just like mine. I clamp my mouth shut, hard.

When the elf gets close, the piece of bread wobbles—then falls over. And falls over again. Soon the bread is rolling, of its own accord, into the hallway. The elf rushes out the door, following the rolling hunk of bread away from us.

The moment it's clear, Parsifal jumps up. He runs over and peers into the hall, holding up one hand, as footsteps clink away.

He gestures forward and we run, leaving behind my plate of food and that miserable candle.

The elf catches the fleeing bread the moment we leap around the nearest corner. It's not the right hallway, but we know this castle. Or we would, if we were sober.

The wine in my belly makes my steps sloppy and uncoordinated. Parsifal lags at the end of the hall. I grab his hand and yank him after me up the stairs. "Come on!"

His eyes are red and watery. "I'm trying!" He's frightened. So am I—except Mother trained the freeze of fear out of me.

We race up the stairs, two at a time. Dusty dogs sleep on the steps, children mixed in with them. "Run!" I shout as we jump over them. When we reach the next floor, I head for the open walkway that leads to North Hall. We have to get back to Corene.

"This way!" I yank Parsifal along. Halfway across the walkway, the screaming starts. Parsifal's panting and gasping, so I clutch his hand tighter. "Move," I tell him.

"Shut up, Mom."

Thank Melidia that the servants lit the torches so I can make out the door to our room. We made it. When we charge inside, Corene sits up on the couch and smiles. Until she sees our faces. "What's wrong?"

"Remember when we were little, Corene?" I ask her, keeping my voice calm. "You told me that there was a secret chamber? A hiding place?"

She stares at me blankly.

"Where is it, Corene? Tell me. Now."

"Why?"

"They're here."

I have to grab Corene to get her up, because she's drunk too. We run back into the hallway, where the sound of screaming echoes up the stairs. I look at Parsifal. "They're coming here next."

Corene whimpers as we reach the door of her suite. Inside, she tries to light a candle but I stop her. "Just bring it. The fire striker too."

By the meager light of the moon through the window, Corene finds her way to the far wall. "Here." She pulls on the side of an enormous dresser. It moves, but only an inch. "Help me."

I grab the corner and heave. It makes an awful squeaking sound as the legs drag along the floor. "That's enough," she says, reaching behind it.

The whole wall creaks. Some of the stones start to pull away from others. It's a door, big enough for us to walk through while crouched.

I don't have time to be amazed as the noise outside gets louder. "You first," I tell Corene. She bends over and slides into the damp darkness. "Now you, Parsifal. I'll close it."

Familiar clinking footsteps echo in the hallway. I shove Parsifal into the passage as the knob of the bedroom door turns. I climb in behind them. Corene lights the candle as I yank the heavy stone back into place.

The last of the moonlight disappears, and we're entombed in darkness.

CHAPTER 8

SAPPHIRE

I did not intend to lie to the Priestess. The Commander assured us our invasion would be bloodless. *Do no harm.* That is always our objective.

Whatever violence happened must have been necessary to secure the surrender.

I have tied the Priestess's hands, and she is surprisingly composed as we leave through the atrium.

But outside the temple, metal screams on stone. Children wail down the hall. "Let me go," the Priestess snarls. "I have to help them." She tries to pull away, but my grip does not relent.

Up ahead, one of our soldiers in Unit Two emerges from a hallway with a human male struggling in her grasp. She strikes him in the side of the head with her elbow and he falls to the floor.

"How dare you!" the Priestess screeches.

I heft her up onto my shoulder and run over as she pounds her fists against my back. "Where is the Commander?" I ask.

The soldier points behind her. "That way, searching out the King."

The hallway walls are smeared with human blood. Some must have died—but how? Why? Our soldiers seem to have convinced most residents of the castle to stay in their rooms, and are posted in front of each door. The serving staff are trapped in the larder, pounding the door as we pass.

My captive has finally stopped struggling. My wisp settles on her shoulder and pulls back the hairs that have fallen into her eyes.

At the top of a wide marble staircase I find Zylion leaning against his sword, his mask pulled up so it sits on his hair. "I have her."

Zylion looks weary. He gestures down a long hallway. "The Commander is down there."

I have to step over the body of what appears to be a royal guard, blood pooled on the floor underneath him. He must have fought back to end up like this.

I notice a dot of crimson on my boot, and a wave of cold washes over me. I hope this human wasn't ill. We have no immunity to human diseases, should we be exposed. We would be helpless. I will clean it off at my first opportunity.

Inside the room, the King is strapped to a chair. Commander Valya prods him with one finger, the tip bathed in angry red light. Each time the Commander touches him, the King cries out. "I don't know where they are," the greasy old man sobs. "They haven't sent a smoke message in—"

The Commander prods him once more, and the sound the King makes wrenches my stomach. "Where is your daughter?" he snarls. I have never seen him like this.

"I don't know." The King rocks forward, and his voice

slurs. "She wasn't with me." Another prod, and the man lets out a windy gasp before collapsing in his chair. The Commander looks up when he finally notices us standing there.

"Ah—Mahove, Sapphire! You have secured the temple?"

I nod. "Incapacitated all the priestesses, as instructed." I lean down, roll my captive off my shoulder, and try to help her into a sitting position on the ground. She lies there limply, but her blue eyes are riveted to the Commander in a scathing glare. "I negotiated a peaceful surrender . . ."

The Commander's gaze whips back to me. "Why would you do that?"

"I thought that was the plan, Commander."

He snorts. "Plans change. This drunk King was easier to capture than even my wildest hopes. No need for negotiation." My wisp pulses a dark purple—it is upset. "Have this priestess contact the sworn lords to demand a full surrender. The King's Magicker claims he cannot do it." The King coughs and gags.

"I won't help," the Priestess says immediately. "I'd rather die."

The Commander shrugs. "We can make that happen." Shame fills me like piss in a bucket. "Sapphire, quarantine her with the others." He returns to his work, and I am dismissed.

Unit One has rounded up the rest of the priestesses in an old cellar. When I step inside the door with my priestess, it's as if someone has clapped their hands over my ears. The room's been treated to dampen Magic—no priestesses will be calling for help in here.

I leave my priestess there. My wisp, glowing an angry red, dives into my pouch pocket and refuses to come out.

I find a stone bench in the atrium, under Melidia's hateful gaze, and allow myself a moment to rest, close my eyes, and inhale the scent of an immense blue flower planted nearby, its long petals like shards of moonlight.

"Something wrong, friend Sapphire?" Ellze's voice. I open my eyes just as he steps on the flower, snapping the stem in half.

"This—this is not what I expected," I stammer.

"What *did* you expect? We are here to do what is asked of us. You are fortunate you got this promotion. You should be happy."

Responding would be a waste. Rising from the stone bench, I walk past him and leave the Temple.

I know I have this cloak on my back only because Ellze is the Commander's nephew. And I am not fulfilling his expectations.

PARSIFAL

Corene's candle shows me what I probably would've been better off not seeing: a ceiling so low we brush our heads, and constellations of cobwebs hanging in every corner and crevice. Dust sits in a heavy white layer on the walls and floor, like fallen ash. A little shiver ripples down my back. I hate dust. I hate cobwebs. And I definitely hate spiders.

The narrow tunnel extends into nothingness in two directions. Through the walls come the muffled sounds of the long ears speaking and of furniture legs squeaking as they're moved. The elves are searching. They know we were there, but not where we went.

"Corene," I whisper, kneeling beside her. I shudder knowing how filthy my clothes are getting. "Where does this go? We need to leave before they find us." Even my whispers could lead them here.

Corene says in a tiny voice, "Dad's room."

"Excellent," I whisper. "Finding the King is a good idea. Which way?"

The clink of silver boots on stone echoes right next to us. We have to go. Corene makes a sound like a trapped animal, and Thelia twitches with irritation. "Corene. Stop squacking and talk." I don't know how effective browbeating the Princess will be when she's this upset.

The muffled voices fade. "They must be moving on," I whisper. If they haven't gotten to the King already, they're on the way.

Thelia grips Corene's arm. "We have to go now. You can just point."

Corene grimaces and points to her left. On we go.

Through stone walls come the wails of people, dogs barking, and armor clinking—all garbled. I wonder if this is what the demon plane was like, before Melidia supposedly saved us. We walk in the frigid in-between place for longer than it should take to reach another chamber in North Hall.

Abruptly, Corene stops. "Here." She holds up the candle, illuminating the faint outline of another door.

Before anyone moves, Thelia says, "Wait. They may have arrived first."

I press my ear to the wall. "I don't hear anything." But the truth is that I don't want to go out there and maybe die. What if we stay in hiding until the furor calms down?

Thelia pushes the door open enough for some torchlight to spill in and peers through the crack. "It's clear." She glances back at me. "Come on, let's take a look around. You know, for the King."

I sigh. "Fine. But you owe me."

"If we live long enough, I'll give you as many foot massages as you want."

As we slip out, I glance back at Corene, who's become a piece of furniture—not moving or speaking. "Be right back," Thelia tells her.

The King's chamber is huge. The enormous, velvet-draped platform bed is a mess, sheets halfway off like he was ripped out of it as he slept. He's gone—grabbed by long ears.

Thelia jogs to the bedroom door and slips her fingers between the door and the frame to pull it open, avoiding the creaky doorknob. It opens without a sound, a trick I'm sure she was taught by her mother. Delia Finegarden may have been a horrible person, but at this moment I'm grateful she raised my cousin.

"What in Melidia's arsehole are you planning?" I whisper. I thought we were just taking a look around the room.

She mouths, "The armory." I give her a bewildered look, and she clenches her hands into fists. "So I can get a sword."

That's what she's after—a way to fight back. Against seven-foot-tall murderous elves. What an inspired plan.

Yet, here I am, jogging down the hallway after her in my least comfortable heeled boots, wishing I'd worn absolutely anything else today.

Thelia stops at the third door. The armory.

That's when the clanking starts on the stairs. Soldiers' footsteps. Thelia glances behind us. "They're coming." She reaches for a door, pushes it open, and shoves me in.

THELIA

Glittering silver everywhere. A feast of blades, each one capable of its own select deeds. My hands itch to grab one. The truly impressive weapons—the halberds and spears—are arranged on elaborate silver stands. I could have anything I want, but first we have to hide. I only hope they don't look in this room right away.

Along the wall, four suits of armor hang on vaguely human-looking statues. Perfect. I start unlacing a set of plates and point at a statuette dressed in leather. "Put it on, Percy."

"No way."

"Just do it." It'll be easier than mine—putting this on properly could take whole candle-hours. Thankfully, I'm small enough that I can slide on the chestplate without taking it apart.

Parsifal reluctantly dons the jerkin. "Don't bother tying it," I hiss at him.

A door opens across the hallway. They're looking. I throw on the pauldrons, but the greaves will take forever. I hope the darkness will hide it. I slip the plate helmet over my head and tuck in my hair.

Parsifal's barely got the leather helm on when I pull him into line with the other statuettes. "Close your eyes," I hiss. "Don't move."

The door creaks open. Eyelids pressed shut, I stand dead still, praying that it's too dim for them to notice something is off.

Light footsteps enter the armory, then pause, looking around. The elves speak in melodic, rhythmic words utterly unlike what I know as speech. It's more of a song, with rising and falling pitches. Two voices. Two monsters I might have to gut if they catch us.

I don't breathe as they pass through the room. Then the footsteps recede, out through the open doorway.

I gasp for air as soon as the door closes. Parsifal yanks his helmet off. "It's too tight!"

"Maybe your head's too big." Still, we survived. The long ears may be bigger than we are, but they can't see any better in the dark—and they're definitely not as smart as I feared.

"Hey." I tap the jerkin strapped across Parsifal's chest. "Give me that." I need something to protect my organs. He slides off the chest piece and hands it to me. Even if it doesn't fit right, it'll still keep off glancing blows.

And now, my reward: the wall of death. It'll take time to choose the perfect weapons from such a pristine crop. A weapon is a comrade, a confidante, a partner. It should fit your hand just right, weigh neither too little nor too much, and cut through the air precisely the way you want.

But time is in short supply. I snatch a dagger and a belt, then a shortsword and a sheath—and finally a long, slender, curved scimitar, like the ones my mother's ancestors used. The people who lived in the scrubland between the Holy Kingdom and the Northern Republic—until the Hindermarks decided the iron buried in those sandy hills belonged to them. Now they're all dead, except Mother. Not sure if that bodes well for the scimitar, but it's beautifully light, and I twirl it once before sinking it into a sheath with a lovely *fooohh*.

Parsifal needs something. I lift a slender saber off the wall and offer him the pommel. "We both know how this will end," he says, slipping it into his belt. "A missing finger. Maybe a lopped-off prick."

Even a breath away from being discovered and killed by elves, Parsifal reaches for quips to feel better. I roll my eyes. "You haven't been taking fencing lessons all these years for nothing."

"Not for nothing. Those lessons are how I came by this excellent physique, thank you very much."

We've been here too long, but I still can't resist taking down a hatchet as we leave the room. "Planning to arm the entire castle?" Parsifal asks.

"Planning to kill some damned long ears." I nod. "Let's get back to Corene."

The King's bedroom is still empty.

"Corene!" Parsifal taps the wall. "Open the door. I don't know how it works from this side." Nothing.

I know she's in there, cowering in the darkness. Feeling sorry for herself. "Corene, let us in. I have swords and you won't die. I promise. No elves."

As prepared as I am to fight, my blood's still filled with wine. Which is probably how I ended up with two swords, two daggers, and a hatchet.

Slowly, the door opens. I'm so done with this creepy passage, but I crouch down and crawl back in anyway. Corene closes the door behind us. "Did you find him?"

Oh, piss. I can't have her break down, so I temper my voice. "Your dad must have hidden somewhere the long ears wouldn't find him." I have to let her believe he escaped. Corene closes her eyes and massages her temple. "But," I say brightly, "I did get into the armory." I hook the hatchet onto my belt.

"I see." She looks over my new personal arsenal.

"Does this secret place go to other parts of the castle?" Parsifal breaks in. "Like South Hall?"

Suddenly I think of Daddy, trapped somewhere. Or worse.

Corene shakes her head. "Wrong level."

"Are there any other tunnels like this?" he presses.

"Loads. Stuff from the old days. A whole set of pipes run under the castle, though most of those are sealed . . ."

She's babbling, so I cut her off. "Do you know where they are?"

Corene shrugs. "Bayled and I played in some of them when we were kids, though Mom didn't like it. We can't reach them from here." That's a great help.

"Where does this passageway end?" asks Parsifal, like he's speaking to a small child. Corene doesn't answer but starts to walk, holding the candle out in front.

Soon we reach a flat wall that marks the end. "Here." She illuminates a latch holding the door closed. We hear chaos in the room beyond.

"What's on the other side?" I ask.

"No idea. Mom and Dad only said how to get to their room

from mine." Her tone's defensive. "That's all they thought I'd need—to hide until the threat passed. I do know how to get to the old sewers, though."

"Sewers?" I ask.

"Before the Split, when we were friendly with the dwarves, they helped us build a system for disposing of our waste. After the Split, parts of it collapsed." Corene sounds like she's reading something from her memory. "That's where the Pit is now—we dump our waste in a derelict sewage drain."

"Does it leave the castle?" Parsifal asks. "Can we get out?"

"One of the pipes dumps into the moat."

Parsifal sits forward, avoiding the jeweled pommel of my shortsword. "How do we get to it?"

Corene's head swivels slowly toward him. "How do you think?"

I'm instantly nauseated. "Ugh. The Pit?" My handmaid went there for me, until Dad dismissed her because we couldn't afford the expense. I went myself once or twice, emptying my chamberpot in the pool of feces, but I flegged each time. Now I dump my chamberpot out the window, hoping nobody's down below.

"Why couldn't the door have been in the kitchen?" Parsifal moans, just as horrified.

"I'd rather fight and die," I say.

Parsifal glares at me. "I say we wait. Let everything quiet down out there, then take a look around."

"You mean, after everyone who would fight back is dead and the rest have surrendered?" An image flashes in my mind of Daddy collapsed on the floor like a puppet. "Coward."

Parsifal shrugs. "Correct."

But we need hope, even if it's false, or we'll stumble right off the cliff of despair. I know how dangerous that crevasse is. I managed to avoid it for most of my life—believing that when I was finally perfect, Mom would be finished. She would tell me I was ready. Then Morgaun sliced me open, and I went over the edge.

I clench one hand into a fist. Daddy had no part in that. He doesn't deserve . . . "We have to try," I growl. "If there *is* a way to get out of Four Halls, we can't leave them behind."

"Shouldn't we at least wait until it quiets down?" He looks like he hopes that will be *never.* "No point charging out and dying before we get anywhere near South Hall."

I hate that it comes from cowardice, but he's right. I don't know if I can take on one of those huge creatures.

"When it dies down, I go." I stare at Parsifal. "With or without you." He looks away, his face turning red.

As much as I don't want to fester in the dark, sneaking out under their noses may be our best shot.

BAYLED

By morning, the Baron still hasn't arrived. I emerge from my tent, and Sasel's downcast face tells me her smoke message went unanswered.

"Don't send word back to Four Halls," I tell Sasel. "Not yet."

Nobody needs this news now. Doubt already swirls around

my ability to lead—and that's not unfounded. I have no experience, like Nul said. The men don't even respect me.

So I need the one whose respect matters less than his loyalty, if I'm going to do something truly stupid.

I have to kick Harged's bedroll a few times before he rolls over and groans, "Just a little longer, Ma."

"I'm not your mother." I kick once more and Harged lets out a grunt. Maybe this explains the name of his company—he seems to be made of actual stone.

Once he's conscious, he peers up at me. "What is it, boss? You look upset."

"Everything's fine." I hope I sound stoic but not angry.

"Good." Harged lumbers to his feet. "It's far too soon for our general to show weakness. The men would get discouraged. They're already skeptical of a ward from the Northern Republic leading us into battle."

I'm too stunned to even be annoyed.

"So young to be leading so many. Some of the men are happy with the hillman becoming King. Everyone knows how they fight off trolls and wolves down in the Klissen."

I blink, not sure how to respond. "Trolls?"

"Those mountains are riddled with all kinds of 'em. Swamp trolls. Mountain trolls. Sometimes ogres too."

He goes on about the other differences between swamp trolls, other low-altitude trolls, and ones from the higher places in the world.

"Harged," I interrupt. "Since you know so much about hunting elusive things, what would you think of going on a little mission with me?"

While the contingent finishes saddling up, I approach Nul se Lan. "What is it, Northerner?" he snaps.

"I'm leaving with Stone Company to find the Baron—and learn whether this was simply a mistake. If it's not . . ." I leave it unsaid. We hold each other's gazes. I will not let Lan see the thinness of my resolve.

I station Sasel in one of the three functional watchtowers at the Crossing, so she'll be ready to send a smoke message to the rest of the army when I find out what's become of the Baron.

Nul se Lan and the rest of the lords are clear on their orders: resume the march south. The senior officers give me strange looks as we part ways. I think of Thelia and Parsifal's message, and hope I won't regret letting Nul se Lan out of my sight. Not that I have a choice—a crime of this magnitude cannot go ignored.

It will only take a few days. Such a small contingent of men should catch up with the rest of the army easily.

And my mission will be more than worthwhile if it turns out the Baron has remained loyal after all, and this is all just a case of a missed smoke message.

"Eyes open, feet firm," I tell the men of Stone Company, hitting my chest with one closed fist. "Be prepared for anything at the Baron's fortress." The donkey with the keg pulls up the rear. One of Harged's men hands him a full mug of beer.

I gawk. "It's first thing in the morning!"

"The only cure for the liquor shivers, you know, is more liquor." Harged takes a long sip and his face brightens like the sun. "There we go. Like new again." He passes the mug back and each of the twenty men take a gulp. "Ready, fellows?"

"Ready!" they sing back. Another mug is poured and we're on our way.

Hours pass before it's finally quiet. Corene's fallen asleep in a corner. I take out my hatchet. "You don't have to go with me, Percy."

"As if I won't." The firmness in his voice, the stern resolve, takes me by surprise.

I'm relieved. While I don't trust Parsifal to do much with his saber, his quick mind is valuable. "Fine. We should leave Corene. She's in no state to run."

I tap Corene's shoulder to wake her. "We're going."

She wobbles up to a sitting position. "What if you don't come back?"

"Don't worry about that." I can't muster anything more comforting. I need my head facing forward if we're going to survive.

I gesture for Parsifal to follow me, and he pats the pommel of his saber. Ready. We pull the lever on the door and it creaks open. I peek through the crack.

It's a stairway—and not even a hidden side stairway. This door opens onto the main stairs that lead down to the banquet hall. Just great.

"Theels," Parsifal whispers. "If everything goes wrong, let them take me. Understand? If they get you, we're bear food." He looks me straight in the eyes, and there is something strange and fierce and fearless in them. "I've never done anything in my life that really mattered, Theels. This is the one thing I can do."

I want to say something, but I don't know what. Parsifal's never spoken to me like this. I want to hit him. I just nod, and we slip out together. Corene pulls the door shut behind us.

SAPPHIRE

Melidia's gaze burns into us as we stand in a circle in the temple atrium, our sleek cloaks knitting a ring around the Commander. It feels wrong, alien, to have our briefing here, among the priestesses' brightly-colored plants.

Ferah steps forward. "Commander, I will erect the shield immediately. But the Magic spillage here is far greater than we expected. Stripping it off so many living creatures will take time."

The Commander nods. "I understand. We must establish a location for the new settlement immediately so we may begin cleaning. Meanwhile, with this much Magic everywhere, we must guard our human charges closely. Report anything strange back to me." He clears his throat. "Now, my Jaguars, we have encountered one minor complication."

Ellze is the first to break formation. "What is it, Commander?"

"While I know little about the Holy Kingdom's politics, the Chief of the Klissen informed me that the King has one child, a daughter. Once the King leaves this mortal plane, she will doubtless take command of the army that we lured southward with the Chief's message."

"Our force should encounter them any day now," Ellze says. He clenches his fists. "We will crush them." The thrill in his eyes sends a shiver down my spine.

Commander Valya tilts his head up, gazing into Melidia's hateful face. "Humans are unpredictable, nephew. And thousands of them inhabit this kingdom. The only thing we can be sure of is that they hold their royalty above everything else. Should their King command it, they would surrender at once. But the King is a useless, drunken mess."

His gaze travels across our assembly. "However, under his instruction, his daughter could command the sworn lords to lay down their arms. Unfortunately, she is missing. And if she escapes our grasp, the sworn lords may choose instead to rise up against us. We must locate the Princess, or this operation could become bloodier than we wanted."

Bloodier. My Magic heart feels cold. This was supposed to be bloodless.

"Perhaps she escaped already," I suggest.

"I do not believe she could have made it out undetected. I trust my Jaguars to capture her before daylight."

He says the word *trust* with an edge. I cannot help feeling like the Commander's eyes are on me to make up for the priestess's refusal to cooperate.

So we must search for the Princess—not that we know what she looks like.

We have scoured the entire wing meant for royalty, but she is gone like a ghost. One at a time, Ellze interrogates the nobles we have confined to their rooms. The Princess could be among them, pretending to be a mere courtier. When no one speaks up in response to his questions, he uses the Commander's technique of threatening them with one bright finger.

But after dozens of interviews, we learn little. Zylion and the others begin inspecting the rest of the prisoners—looking for young women among them with smooth, clean skin and good teeth.

The sun is coming up outside, turning the sky a subdued orange. I pause to rest, sitting at the top of the stairs and watching through the window as sunlight spills over the city's high stone walls. Off in the distance I can make out the foggy shapes of green hills.

Their country is beautiful. Not that Viteos isn't, with trees that touch the sky and glass spires—shaped out of sand and Magic—that refract the sun. The giants have always been jealous of what we have made *with* the land, rather than quarrying and contorting it.

But the landscape here is different: wide open and green, with more sky than I've ever seen. I am far from home.

Outside, a dark figure strides across the castle wall. It is Ferah, arms in the air like she is attempting to raise the dead.

A sheen of thin, blue light wafts up from the ground, like vapor rising off water. The glowing edges stitch themselves together, stretching upward one thread at a time through the conduit of her body. The glowing wall reaches toward the sky.

Her beautiful protective shield will keep the outside out, and everything within—humans, Magic, us—will stay in. It should prevent the spill from spreading any farther, but it also means the concentration of Magic inside the shield will accelerate. We are steeped in it like a thick coat of snow. The sour spicy smell of it floods everything, a tang on the back of your tongue that you can't swallow.

Voices. I stand up and look for the source. They are human, but they do not echo the way other voices echo here. Spirits, perhaps? Maybe Melidia is playing a trick on me.

Footsteps on the stairs. I race down the hall. Whispers travel across the stone walls. Sun streams in the window, turning the marble staircase bloodred.

Two humans race down the steps, casting shadows a hundred feet long.

I follow, taking the stairs two at a time. At the faint sound of my footsteps, the one with hair down to her waist spins around and I glimpse a long, thin scar burning down her cheek. Her eyes grow wide and angry. The Princess!

She shouts and charges back up the stairs toward me. I have to admit that it takes me by surprise—but I'm faster, stronger, and trained. With one leap, I cover the six steps between us. This will hurt both of us, but I need to disable her to bring her before the Commander and prove my promotion was not a mistake.

Except the Princess takes two sideways steps, out of the path of my tackle, so I fly right past. *Curl and roll.* I'm grateful for my impenetrable skin as I hit the blunt edges of the steps.

When I reach the bottom level and stop rolling, I leap back to my feet. Both humans stand five steps up, weapons drawn. Ready to fight. It's almost cute.

The Princess's companion, a man with a flattened face, charges me first with his saber. I raise an arm to block his swing, but he ducks under it. I have to admire his fast feet. He returns with the blade pointed at my exposed chest and swings. It cuts through my clothes but bounces off the hard bronze skin underneath, leaving only a dent in the surface.

His eyes turn into saucers. "Oh, gobble." Taking a delicate backward hop up to the step behind him, he points the saber at me again. He thinks I do not notice the Princess charging me from the side, her scimitar drawn.

I dodge by leaping up onto the same step as the boy—and swipe at him with one leg. My boot catches his ankle, sending him sprawling down the steps. He hits each one with a meaty *thunk*.

"Parsifal!" the Princess shouts. I expect her to go after him, but she turns on me instead. The swing of her scimitar is much faster than I expected.

I jump up one more step. She catches the toe of my boot on her blade, and the fabric tears open. She swipes again. And again. I am forced onto the defensive, backing up one step at a time to avoid the feverish slices of her scimitar, until I am almost to the second level. Someone has trained her well.

Time to end this.

On her next swipe, I seize the blade of the scimitar in my bare hand. The edge manages to slide under the skin of my palm so my purple blood oozes out. The Princess tries to yank her weapon back, but she is not strong enough. I squeeze and twist—and the blade snaps in half. The curved tip flies over the banister, crashing to the marble floor far below.

The Princess's lips tighten in fury. "I'll kill you."

I do not even think to move out of the way before she hurls herself at me. Her body smashes into mine, the point of her shoulder jabbing between my ribs. It doesn't hurt, but it sends me flying back against the banister, rattling it.

I shove her off me and, finally, reach for my own sword. *Do not damage her—just subdue her.* At the bottom of the stairs, her companion is getting up off the steps, ready to provide support. I need to disable them, fast.

"You better run," she shouts at me, just before she reaches over her head and rips another sword off her back. This one is longer, wider, meaner. I will not be able to break it in half. She points the tip at my chest and springs forward.

I deflect her sword with mine, the metal ringing. I reach for the sword pommel, trying to disarm her, but she spins around and hops up the steps so we are level. She holds the sword out to the side with one hand, like she's about to take a wide, reckless swing at me—when her other hand comes up bearing a dagger.

I hear it fly through the air before I see it. On instinct I twist my head away, but the blade catches my ear, and I feel a tiny piece of flesh come off. The knife flies on and sticks in the wall, a minuscule bit of me attached to it.

I turn back as the Princess's lips curl up in a feral smile. "Got you." She looks so proud of herself. My ear will restore itself in a week or two, but she doesn't know that.

She swings the sword again and I parry. Another swing, a step back. A swing and a step and she has me backed up against the banister. How did she manage to corner me? The only way out from here is up.

Being made for humans, the banister's not high—it's easy to jump straight up and land on top. Once I have my footing, I crouch and spring again.

The Princess's mouth falls open as I sail through the air. I land on the flat edge of her outstretched sword, and my immense weight forces her arms to collapse. Using the blade's slight buouancy as a lift, I jump again. The sword skitters down the steps and she lets out a curse.

I land on the other side of her, so we stand back to back, and drop to my knees. I swipe one foot backward and my leg connects with hers. With a spin, I catch her as she falls and deliver three small taps to her temple. Light fizzes around my finger, and she crumples into my arms.

"No!" The boy has managed to get to his feet. He races up the steps toward me, saber in his hand again.

I duck out of the way. "Sorry," I say in his language, hoisting the Princess with one arm. I grab him in my other and headbutt him.

He falls unconscious. The day has barely begun, and all my hopelessness has been swept away. Commander Valya will be thrilled.

CHAPTER 9

BAYLED

The road through the thick, scarlet trees is narrow and winding, and disappears often only to pick back up a hundred feet away. Saplings and bushy ferns grow over the path, as if no one has maintained it in many cycles. I don't know if it's autumn turning the leaves red or if they always look this way, but framing the dark tree bark, it makes me think of charred bones and flesh.

"This all seems like a bad idea," Harged mumbles as our horses push thorugh the dense brush. "Deserters ain't good people."

I sigh. "Nobody asked you, did they? You're the muscle here, not the brains." It popped out—I regret it right away.

Harged doesn't look offended. He nods thoughtfully and says, "Guess that's true."

"Sir!" one of the men calls in a whisper-shout. "There's noise out in the woods."

"What kind of noise?" I bring Halrendar to a halt while a soldier trots up on his horse.

"Rustling. I think someone's following us."

"Have you seen anything?" I drop my voice. It couldn't be Nul se Lan way out here—he's back on the Low Road with the army.

The man shakes his head. "Whoever it is, they're hiding themselves good."

"What do you think it is, boss?" asks Harged in a whisper.

"Could be the Baron's soldiers." Though we're still another day's journey from the Durnhal fortress.

Harged stiffens. "What if they attack?"

"That's why I brought you." If we have to fight for our lives, having Harged Halen on my side seemed like my best chance for survival.

We move on in silence, ears trained on the woods. Still, nothing. Whoever was tailing us must know they've been found out, and won't return until they're ready to make a move.

As the sun dips behind the tree canopy, I call a halt. "We're pitching camp for the night. Let's take the time to hunt dinner and prepare for tomorrow." I dismount and let Halrendar go sniffing around for greens to eat.

"Are you sure that's wise?" asks Harged as the men start unloading their horses. "We're squatting squorks here. Someone—such as a deserter—could storm us in the middle of the night."

I pull one of my bags off my horse and rifle through it. "That could happen anywhere we stopped."

"I don't think we should take any chances in these woods. If we keep moving, we can keep watching." Fear doesn't come naturally to his coarse face.

"I said we're stopping. We need rest."

Harged's eyes drop to his saddle. "'Course, boss."

The last few days have caught up to me, and my abdomen gives a little lurch. "Finish setting up camp," I tell the men. "I'll be back soon."

Harged frowns. "You shouldn't go off alone, boss."

I spin on him. "Stop telling your superior officer what to do. The King put me in charge of all of this, even that crater-tooth Nul se Lan. If I want to go have some privacy, that's what I'll do." Ignoring his shocked face, I head out into the trees.

THELIA

I wish whoever's talking would stop. I can't understand what they're saying, and the noise in my tender ears is ringing me up the parapets.

"Shut up." My throat is coated in sand. "Please." Incredibly, the voices do stop.

Everything aches—particularly my neck. When my eyes open it feels like dirt's been rubbed under my eyelids. I'm tied to a chair.

The elf is still here. Still absolutely beautiful. With hair like sky and eyes to match, and shining bronze skin. It makes me feel sick. There's a small bandage on one ear where I got through.

The elf's at least seven feet tall—not a giant, but like a human laid on the floor and pulled hard by the arms and feet, and then dunked in molten bronze. No wrinkled, gray, sallow flesh. No teeth sharpened to points with stones.

The elf's teeth are straight. Flat. Perfectly white and

flawless. That's so much worse. I could've had pure hatred for the demons in my nightmares, but these beautiful creatures . . .

"What do you want?" I strain forward against the straps, and they cut into me. "Why are you here?"

"She awakens." The voice is deep, masculine, undulating. The accent makes me think of a biylar bear struggling to wrap its muzzle around language.

I twist around to find another elf, silver-and-turquoise chest plate strapped tight to his broad torso, chiseled pectorals carved into the steel. Long, straight, silver hair flows over its shoulders like a waterfall, down to its hips. Like the other elf's, his skin reflects the light in a way skin shouldn't— like metal.

We're in the Temple. The walls are plain and a cot's pressed against the wall. Must have been a priestess's room before this catastrophe.

"Where's Parsifal?" I manage through a scratchy throat. What did that elf do to me?

"I'm here, Theels." My neck screams as I twist the other way to find Parsifal tied to another chair. He offers a rueful smile.

"We have captured your King," the silver elf says. "The era of the Holy Kingdom has ended."

Remember Mother's training. Give no indication of how this makes me feel. Face blank, lips tweaked on each side in a ghost of a smile as if I already know this, while I wonder, *Have they caught Corene too?*

The silver elf leans down, picks up a strand of my hair, and sniffs it. I yank my head away but he holds fast. "How did my soldier happen to find you running free, after we checked every crevice of this castle? Where have you been hiding, *Princess?*"

Princess? I've worked for that title my whole life, and it's a stupid long ear mistaking me for Corene.

It's Parsifal who barks out a laugh. "Have you been eating the rare plants in here? Some of those can make you hallucinate."

I hope my survival doesn't hinge on a mistaken identity, because he's just blown it.

The silver elf arches an eyebrow. "Sapphire, remind me, where did you find these two?" The blue one peels away from the doorway and brushes some dust from their flat, undecorated chest plate. Scars mar the metal, as if it's taken many blows.

"Stairs," Sapphire says. "North Hall. Where yo-o-ou found King." The blue elf gestures to a pile of metal—my confiscated blades. "They wield weapons from King's armory."

"We took them." I add with a glare, "To defend ourselves against certain *invaders.*"

"You robbed your own King?" The silver elf, clearly the one in charge, touches his chin. "Nobility would not do such a thing."

"What's he ever done for us?" I toss back. "We saw a chance to arm ourselves and we took it. You're the ones who seized our castle—is defending ourselves a crime?"

"Hmm. If you are not the Princess, where is she?"

"Like I'd tell *you* if I knew." I press my mouth in a stiff line and glare.

The silver elf waves a hand the way you'd clear away a bad smell, and says something to Sapphire in that rolling, musical tongue. Sapphire walks behind me and unties my ropes. Am I being set free, or have we sentenced ourselves to death? Our captor doesn't speak as we're led from the room.

But it doesn't take me long to realize we're headed to the dungeon. My knees almost buckle when the elf kicks open the heavy iron door.

Parsifal bumps my shoulder with his. "We'll survive this," he says.

We descend into darkness.

PARSIFAL

Another rock hits the bars, shaking our whole cell. More howls of laughter.

"Lee-tle royals!" the prisoner two cells down hollers at us. "Come to our party?"

"No beer, just piss!" calls his cellmate, peering through dirty strands of hair that have molded and tangled into birds' nests. "I promise, you won't get better down here than my piss."

I knew we had prisoners under Four Halls. Petty thieves, deserters, rapists—they all end up in the same place. Transgress the King's laws, drink your own piss in his dungeon.

I never imagined we'd be here with them. If I wasn't filthy from the dust and cobwebs in Corene's creepy passage, I am now. The previous prisoner remains here in the form of a full chamberpot and some rat-chewed rags. I'll never get these shit stains out of my clothes.

We haven't been fed since we were left here, either.

The prisoners all go quiet as the dungeon door creaks open. Then they go wild against the bars, like monkeys in the circus shows we had back in Frefois.

A tall being, taller than any human in the Holy Kingdom, makes its way down the row of cells toward us. Prisoners reach through the bars, grabbing at the elf's arms and clothes. The elf easily dodges.

Sapphire. This isn't just some lowly soldier, that much is obvious. The elf wears only a chest plate and a long cloak that never seems to get in the way of their delicate feet. As the creature leans down in front of our cell, the unnaturally smooth skin reflects the glow of the torches. Blue eyes with the faintest hints of gold and brown peer through the bars. To stand in wonder at the perfection and glamour of your conquerer is the most horrific punishment I could've imagined.

"Food," the elf says, opening the panel in our cell door and sliding two plates through. Leftovers from the kitchen. Real food.

Thelia grabs my arm before I can reach for it. "That could be poisoned."

I scoff at her and pick up a roll. "Why would it be poisoned?"

"*It* wants us to talk," she says, pointing at Sapphire. "Kill one of us, motivate the other to give up information."

The elf looks like she's spit in its face. "*They*," Sapphire growls. "Not *it*. *It* is for animals. Do you think I am a-a-a-a-a-nimal?" Sapphire's mouth draws out the word, like a lyric in a song.

I don't know what I think. Frefoisians don't believe Melidia is the only divine being impressing their will upon us. An elf isn't a mortal, but certainly not a god either. They could be demons, perhaps—but I've never seen evidence they exist outside the Temple's stories.

"What else should we think?" Thelia asks. "You've put us behind bars. I've seen the blood on the walls."

"I killed no one," Sapphire snarls. Are they lying? Or do

they simply need to justify it to themself? If they were human, I might be able to tell the difference. "Eat," they command us.

I pop the roll into my mouth and Thelia grips my arm. "Percy! You can't die on me."

"We all die someday," I say. The roll is chewy. "Bit stale."

Thelia sneers. "Like you?"

Sapphire's lips purse. "Commander only wants to know— where is the real Pri-i-incess?"

I spread my arms wide. "We don't know anything." I don't know how long this game will work, but I'll put in my best effort.

Thelia finally succumbs and eats a piece of dry ham. Sapphire says nothing. Their blue-brown eyes bore into mine, searching me for the truth. I wonder if it's possible to force it out of someone with Magic.

I press my face between the bars, the rusty, dirty iron biting into me. "We know nothing," I say, letting each word roll off. "So just let us out."

"I cannot."

One of the prisoners screeches, and it travels like a wave down the cells, one prisoner after another wailing for food or water. Sapphire's hand clenches. Without saying anything else, they close the food panel, turn, and leave. The dungeon door falls closed again.

"Damn it!" I drop to the floor. "Maybe we *should* tell them where to find Corene. If that's what we have to say to get out of here—"

"We couldn't do that to her." Thelia's face turns bright red. "We promised we'd come back." However much those girls tear at each other, a lifetime of loyalty is hard to break.

The tall prisoner in the cell next to ours hollers at us. "Why don't you share that food?" His face is a skull with pale skin draped across it. He smiles at Thelia and drags himself across the floor by his hands, to the bars that separate us. "What a lovely girl."

He seizes one of the bars and hauls his torso upright. He smells like a thing that's already died and begun to rot. "I know you," he says to Thelia, showing two rows of blackened teeth. "You're the Princess's cousin. I bet you have a sweet, tight hole." His tongue darts out of his mouth.

Thelia smirks. "Wouldn't you like to know."

"I'll find out soon enough," he says with a gasping laugh. I look around for something I can hit him with. Over his head, one of the cell's iron bars wobbles.

I look up just as it cracks and separates from the stone ceiling. It tips over, landing right on his skull.

Four of his teeth pop out, spinning across the ground. He doesn't even scream—just slides down to the floor of his cell. Blood drips from his face.

"What was that?" Thelia whispers.

I look between her and the ceiling. "This keeps happening to me, Theels. First it was candlesticks. Now . . ." I stick my hand through the new gap in the bars and pick up the fallen length of iron. It wobbles in my hand, almost like it's alive.

BAYLED

Finally, silence. I pick my way through the wide black tree trunks, looking for a place to squat—and be alone. When I find a good spot, I dig down a little and unbutton my trousers.

There's movement in the bushes. I jump, pulling my trousers back up, but it's only a squork rooting through the pine needles.

"Hey, git!" I kick in its direction to scare it off—I don't need an animal watching me do my business. "This is private." The squork lets out a squeak and tears off through the trees.

That's when three figures burst through the branches.

I'm too slow to pull out my sword. A big troll-like man—I recognize him as one of Nul se Lan's bodyguards—hurls himself at me. His body slam knocks me flat, and we roll across the ground, twigs and branches tearing into my back. I try to shove him away with my legs, but he's too heavy. He wraps both arms around me and rolls until I'm facedown and subdued, tree needles stabbing into my face and neck.

It must've been Nul se Lan's bodyguards following us all this time.

The troll man grabs my hands and yanks them behind me. Both my shoulder joints yowl in pain.

I wish I'd listened to Thelia and Parsifal. But then again, would I have done anything different? Maybe. I probably wouldn't have wandered off alone to take a shit.

I hear someone roar like a lion. There's an immense crash, but I can't see anything pinned to the ground. A woman hollers in fury and Harged's voice yells, "That's what you get for comin' after our general!"

The scuffle continues over my head and I wriggle around, trying to squeeze out from under the troll man's huge body. At least I can see a little now—just enough to make out one of Lan's other bodyguards, the woman with the head full of red braids, getting pummeled by a rain of Harged's fists. She absorbs most of them with the meat of her forearms, protecting her head.

The small, slender bodyguard, with three knives tucked into his belt and a hood over his head, approaches Harged from behind—ready to gut him through the back. "Harged!" I shout. "Behind you!"

He spins around as the little creeper lunges. Harged drops to his knees and rolls out of the way—he's far more agile than I'd thought a man his size could be. No wonder he's a kroga champion.

Having dodged the sneak thief's dagger, Harged throws out one huge arm and catches his attacker right in the face. The much smaller man tumbles backward to the ground, the wind knocked out of him.

Troll man must see that his comrades aren't faring that well and climbs off me. I gasp for breath and struggle up to my knees—just as the bodyguard lunges at Harged.

The two giants slam into the ground, tussling in one big ball of hair and thick arms. I get to my feet and assess my surroundings, like I was taught. I didn't do all that late-night fencing practice for nothing.

The woman with the braids is trying to get in the middle of the fight and pull Harged off her cohort. I'm about to take a step toward her, hand on the hilt of my sword, when I feel a cold, sharp point gently press into the flesh at the back of my neck.

"No. Move."

It must be the dagger-happy little creep. I wince but don't release the hilt of my sword. Why doesn't he just sink it in? Instead, he puts his dagger away, yanks my hands behind my back, and starts tying them together.

The braided woman stomps over to us and says something to him I can't understand. Something angry. If I had to guess, it would be, *Just kill him already!*

My captor yells something back at her. I hear Nul se Lan's name. Perhaps, for a split second, there's a chance for me to escape this. They must know Stone Company isn't too far away, and the moment I'm gone, word will travel. Lan saw me leave Sasel back at the Crossroads—

My heart sinks. Surely, he's killed her to prevent anyone at Four Halls from getting wind of my death.

The pressure of the rope around my wrist eases; my captor's distracted by his argument with the braided woman. Troll man roars something at them—Harged has him pinned, ready to snap his neck. The man standing behind me throws me to the ground, again, and charges over to help.

I set to loosening the rope around my wrists. The knot's badly tied. He should've killed me while he had the chance.

I finally get a grip on the handle of my sword as Harged is dog-piled by all three of Lan's bodyguards. None of them notice as I walk up behind the big one, the rope still tied around one of my hands, and I drive the tip of my sword into the base of his skull.

He falls limp, right on top of Harged. It shouldn't have hurt.

Harged lets out a groan as the other two bodyguards leap up, ready to tear me in half. I point my sword at the sneak-thief's face, and his mouth forms a perfect circle.

"No move," I say, mimicking him. His face twists in fury and he lunges at me. I copy Harged's move and step sideways, out of the way—and whip my free hand through the air. The rope still attached to me swings around and slaps him right across the face.

His skin rips open, splattering blood. The little man screeches, reeling away to cover his wound. I twist and let my sword collide with his exposed rib cage.

The woman with the braids rounds on me, her mouth set in a glare as her last ally crumples to the forest floor.

"I'm going to kill you, Northern man." She lunges, one hand reaching over her shoulder. I don't see her hand axe until it's cutting me open.

Pain tears through my side. I stumble forward, gasping, and try to keep my grip on my sword. *Don't get distracted by the pain. Keep an eye on your opponent.* I set my feet apart and turn around, just as I see her swinging the bloody blade a second time.

Instead of cleaving my face in half, her axe collides with Harged's steel bracer.

Howling with fury, the braided woman swings around in a circle and charges at him again. Harged does not move out of the way.

Instead, he drops down low, his head vanishing under her sparkling steel sword—a kroga move. His agility and strength reminds me of the way Thelia moves when she thinks no one's watching.

The redhead overshoots, and he pops back up to her immediate left like a groundhog. Then he slams down on her wrists with both arms.

She howls and crashes to the ground, her axe flying. Her hands hang limply like a pair of dead animals. Harged kicks her flat and pins her in place with his foot.

Blood's dripping from my side. But I can't worry about that yet. I kneel down by the bodyguard. "Why did Nul se Lan send you to kill me?"

She wrinkles her face up and sticks out her tongue. I crouch down, grab her tongue in my fingers, and hold it there. She squeals and yanks her head away. "Tell me." She flaps her broken wrists. I grab one and squeeze. That provokes a scream but no more words.

"Fine," I say, standing up. "Harged, let's bring her back with us. Maybe she'll think of more to say later."

He stoops to pick her up and we start the long walk back, me clutching my bleeding side.

"Glad you happened to find me," I tell him as I limp along.

Harged laughs. "I followed you. I wasn't going to let you go alone." So he disobeyed my orders just in time to save my life. Harged Halen might be a bit of a dull knob, but he has good instincts.

I clear my throat. "Thank you."

He grunts and nods. "Couldn't let General Vasha down."

I smile at him and it makes my whole face hurt. "Before we go back," I say, "I have to make a stop. I never finished what I came out here to do."

CHAPTER 10

THELIA

When I was nine cycles in this life, Mother was teaching me a new kroga move: the reverse blind throw. But I couldn't get it right. I'd aim over my shoulder and miss, aim and miss. She screamed in frustration and threw me, head over heels, to the ground.

When I sat up, wincing at the throbbing in my neck—and knowing better than to admit it hurt—she stooped down in front of me. She put her hands on either side of my face and pulled me close.

"Do you know why I'm so hard on you?"

"You want me to be Queen and have what you didn't have."

"Yes." Her eyes were so wild that I wanted to run to my bedroom and hide under the bed. "That's why I teach you to brush your hair, walk with your back straight, and listen to what people aren't saying. But that's not why I teach you kroga, why we fight with the practice foils until you're ready to fall over."

I knew there was a reason my arms and back hurt every day, but I was too afraid of her wide eyes and sunken cheeks to ask. I knew it would one day be Morgaun's job to run the dukedom, to tell the serfs what to do, to pay the taxes. But Mother wanted *me* to be Queen—and queens don't need to fight. Queens need to be clever and subtle and easy on the eyes. Her training had some other purpose, more secret than the throne.

"I teach you to protect yourself because of men like Daddy and Morgaun," she whispered. "The moment that you try for power, my little Thelia, you'll become a threat. And they'll come for you." She shook me, making the ache worse. "You must be able to fight. Never let them get you by the throat and take what they want." I couldn't stop my frightened tears, so Mother grabbed my hair. "Why are you crying? This is nothing, Thelia. I am kind. I am helping you. Them—they want to take their wet, sharp pricks and jam them into you. They relish your pain and lick it up off the floor."

I tried not to picture what she meant, but I knew. She kept on. "You fight so they can't trap you. Like your father did to me."

"Not Daddy," I sobbed. The strict old man who always petted my hair, told me I was pretty, yelled and then was always so sorry for yelling—

"Just like Daddy," Mother spat. "Now here we are. Prisoners." Her face was no longer human. She'd had her soul sucked out and all that was left was rage wrapped in skin.

She may have been awful and frightening, but she never lied to me.

In the end, I couldn't protect myself. The elf defeated me. Now I'm here in the King's dungeon, a prisoner, like Mother always feared. I could've struggled, biting and kicking when I saw where they were taking us. Mother believed in fighting until they cut off your hands, or your eyes popped from your head, or you fell over dead. My mother, the eternal fighter, the husk.

But I saw the way the elf danced along my sword like some kind of skyborne spirit. I saw the blood smears on the walls. There was no way to win.

The most awful thing is that they're *not* the creatures from my nightmares. Was what I saw with my eyes closed perhaps not their outsides, but their insides?

The moment I'm free, I'll recover my dagger and slide it under the edges of the elf's face—the blue one who captured us. Then I'll peel it off while they still breathe, tearing the skin away one fiber of muscle at a time. First the eyes, then the nose, the lips, the whole thing. When we're free, I'll hang it on my wall so I will never forget.

We must outlast them.

Parsifal and I have grown used to long stretches of silence. The other prisoners don't have the energy to shriek and rattle the bars all day, so they spend most of their time lying on their backs, eyes closed, looking dead. Just enough light spills in through the two tiny, barred windows up near the ceiling that at least I know if it's day or night. Sometimes that's worse, though—watching time pass without us. Parsifal and I sit and surmise what's become of Corene. Of Bayled. Of the King. What about Daddy and Parsifal's parents? Are they dead?

"We should've told the long ears something, anything," Parsifal grumbles. "Now they're just going to leave us down here and forget about us, like the rest of these sad bastards."

There's no crime someone could commit that deserves starving to death in the dark, wallowing in your own shit and piss. "If we had told them what we know," I say, "Corene would've been captured too."

Parsifal shrugs. "So?"

I get it. To Parsifal, Corene's fun to study, tease, and sometimes manipulate—but in the end, she's still part of the royal family who conquered his homeland and took him hostage. He truly doesn't care if she lives or dies.

But this isn't how I wanted it to end. In my fantasy, Corene married someone else. Or she was disgraced, banished from court, and ran off to live among nomads in the Sand Shelves. Those were the scenarios in which the bereft Bayled took my hand in his, and we ascended the throne together with no guilt on our hands.

It never ended with Corene held aloft between two beautiful, horrible elves, blood gurgling out her mouth and asking, *Why, Thelia?* My childhood playmate. My sister. The one person who knows everything about me.

When Bayled returns with the army, kills every last metal-skinned monstrosity, and sends that cratertooth interloper back to the Klissen—I'll have a clear path to becoming Queen. As long as he never learns how I got there.

But . . . I couldn't wear her crown knowing I was responsible for her death.

I begin to say something and Parsifal stops me with a finger. "I know. I'm not going to tell, either. No matter what they do."

This is where the stone falls—one step short of skipping the last stone on the board, because our foolish hearts are too soft.

Mother would be so disappointed in me.

Death is our constant companion here. The smell fills every crevice of this dungeon, no thanks to the inmate decomposing next to us. Parsifal and I do each other the courtesy of turning away and covering our ears when the other has to use the chamberpot—which has long overflowed into a pile in the corner of our cell. While I'm squatting over the pile, my shoes squishing in cold, wet shit, I look down to find blood smeared all over my thighs.

Parsifal turns around when I wail, covering his eyes with both hands. "What's wrong?"

I yank my dress back down and hold out one hand. He uncovers his eyes and looks down at my palms, smeared with blood. "It's everywhere," I moan, wiping at the red streaks down my clothes and legs. Parsifal moves toward me.

"Don't look. Don't come close." But he pulls me into a hug. I don't even want to shove him away. For once, the human contact feels the way everyone says it does.

When I've stopped gasping for air, I say, "Percy, we have to escape."

He lets me go. "Demon dogs we do."

"I mean, now." I gesture to the dead body in the cell next to ours. "This will only get worse. More will die."

Parsifal looks both sad and exasperated. "What do you want me to do? Go up to this cell door and say"—he leans toward the bars—"*please, my dearest, most beautiful, beloved cell door—won't you please open?*" He laughs and waves a hand at the rigid iron bars.

There's a metallic creak. We both spin around.

Click, click. The lock inside the cell door is turning. *CLICK.* The door lets out a creak as it opens.

Thelia and I gape at the lock. "How did you do that?" she whispers.

By asking nicely, apparently. I've tried that before, but it's never worked on anyone until now. "Maybe the elf just forgot to lock it."

Thelia goes first, pushing the door open. I follow her out of the cell and down the hall. The other prisoners, those with the energy left, rise up like angry spirits. "They're escaping!" one roars through yellow, bloodied teeth.

I give him a little wave. "You're just jealous."

We reach the steps that brought us down here. At the top sits an impenetrable iron door. "You first," Thelia says. "You're the sweet talker."

I march up the steps while the prisoners screech. In front of the immense door, I put my weight on one hip like I would if I were talking to Derk. "Hey," I say, giving it a coquettish look. "Maybe you could, uh, open up for us? We really need to get out."

Nothing happens. "*Sweeter*," Thelia whispers.

I clear my throat. "Dear dungeon door . . ." I feel ridiculous. "You are . . . very attractive. Quite pretty, I might say. Please, uh, won't you let us out, you handsome door, you?"

Nothing. The prisoners start howling with laughter. "Stupid lee-tle royals!" one of them roars. "Stuck here, with us—forever!"

"We'd better get back to our cell," Thelia says. "In case the elf comes back."

"Yeah. It must have just been a fluke." But it didn't feel like a fluke. There have been too many flukes.

We return to our prison cell, pulling the door closed behind us. I don't know what that elf Sapphire will do if they discover what I've done today.

The next time the elf comes, Thelia's already at the cell door, shaking the bars—careful to not shake hard enough to open it.

"Please," she says, before Sapphire can even get a bowl of food through the slot. "I'm bleeding."

The elf's face gives nothing away, but they say, "Are you i-i-injured?" Their accent is better now, though they still draw out all the vowels.

They've been studying. They want to communicate with us. Good to know.

"No, you dolt," she says. "It's normal. It happens every moon." She shows them her hands.

Fear contorts the elf's perfect face. "Where?" They back away, shoulders rising.

"It would be impolite to show you." I can tell she's getting some pleasure from this. "But it lasts a whole week. I need clean cloths every day." Thelia gestures at our Unmentionable Corner. "Please let us out of here. We're living in filth."

Sapphire's mouth opens and snaps closed. They shove the two bowls of food through the small door. "Not my-y-y decision," Sapphire says, avoiding our eyes.

"Please," I echo. "Look. This guy's dead." I point at the corpse that smells worse than our latrine. "The rats will be coming for him."

Sapphire looks at the body and shakes their head, like they can't believe it either.

"Soon," they say, and they leave as quickly as they arrived. Thelia looks like she's about to throw her food in rage.

"Don't," I say, taking the bowl. She squashes her eyes closed and I can tell she's trying not to panic again, but she's beginning to wheeze. Tentatively, I touch her shoulder, and she sinks into me. "I know."

For now, that seems to be all she needs to hear, and we remain motionless until her breathing evens out again.

We eat in silence, until the dungeon door reopens. Sapphire's back.

They head to the cell next to ours and fiddle with the lock, but it doesn't budge. They pull their sword from the sheath and slash it in one smooth motion. The noise that rings out as the blade slices through metal makes us cover our ears. What kind of steel must that sword be made of? The remnants of the lock glow a fierce orange, and the cell door falls open.

Sapphire covers their mouth and nose with one sleeve and reaches in with the other hand to grab the festering corpse by the collar. They drag it out of the cell, down the hall, and back up the stairs.

"Please let us out!" I shout. I could push this cell door open right now and try to run out the open dungeon door, but I'd be caught in a second.

Then the light at the top of the stairs vanishes. We're locked in once again.

SAPPHIRE

Magic does not gravitate to me. Being nowhere near as talented as Ferah, I can usually use only what is in my hands. But now that handful is thick and dense and powerful. I merely have to gesture for plates and bowls and food to arrange themselves.

Which is not enough to secure me any important duties. My only role now is tending to prisoners. When I am not over-seeing the two in the dungeon, I am responsible for the bedrid-den King and the priestesses down in their quarantine room: bringing them water and food, emptying their chamberpots. The King is too locked in a battle with his own body to even notice me.

But whenever I open the door to the priestesses' cellar, the pink wisp leaps from the pouch at my belt, lands on Ilisa's shoulder, and picks through pieces of her long white hair.

"What will you do with us?" she asks every day. And every day, I say nothing. The less they know, the less they will fight. If any of them knew what the cleaning entailed, there would be a riot.

After the priestesses, I visit the King's personal Magicker— a man named Forgren who hides under draping black robes. We have allowed him to remain in the West Hall only because the priestesses blocked the door to their cellar, adamantly refusing to let us place him with them.

"He's useless without those jewels anyway," Ilisa said con-temptuously. "Take those, and he's just a sad old man."

Something about the Magicker is unlike the other humans here. I wonder if he is also a foreigner. He offered no resistance as I stripped him of all his Magical items, and he even offered up others stashed away in his drawers. Even when he was brought before Commander Valya and instructed to contact the King's sworn lords, he simply said, "Believe me, I would if I could. But I cannot without the King himself present. Only he and the Princess know the code required for the lords to agree to a surrender."

I have begun to study language and history in Forgren's library while the Magicker sleeps. I am now the most well-versed among us in communicating with the humans. Sadly, this has led Commander Valya to assign me exclusively to the task of caring for important human prisoners.

Seeing these small, fragile creatures barred in their rooms, provided a minimum of food and water as one would for pets, gives me an uneasy feeling.

When I complain to Ellze about my tedious assignment, he only smiles wryly. "The Commander trusts you. You should be grateful." To Ellze, more responsibilities means you are valued. Powerful. *Be grateful.*

I cannot fathom how I ever anticipated this mission with such eagerness—especially when I find myself dragging a stinking, rotting corpse out of the dungeon.

Bits tear off as we go. First an ear. I will have to come back for that. A bit farther up the stairs, an arm snaps and flops around. A soldier on patrol stops in the hallway as I hurl the body against a wall and slam the dungeon door closed, shoving the heavy iron lock back into place. I take a gasping breath of clean air.

The soldier rushes over to help, then throws a hand across the intake vent of her helmet. "What is this?"

"Killed by a fellow prisoner." I stumble down the hall to find fresh air, but everything in this castle smells like human, Magic, and rot, all rolled up into a filthy ball.

"I know where to dispose of the corpse," she says. "Do you need assistance?"

I nod gratefully. I can carry a human body alone, but the shape is awkward. I would not reject the company, either—it is lonely in this alien land, with my duties keeping me so isolated from my comrades.

The soldier and I heft up the body together, not breathing through our noses. Outside, under the fresh sunlight, we make our way through a courtyard full of slop and mud that was probably once grass. We found humans in every part of Four Halls—including some living in squalor out in the open courtyard. Commander Valya had wood cages erected for them so they could not escape. They shout and sob as we walk by.

Surely this is not acceptable, even for animals—but what choices did we have? The humans were the ones who had crammed themselves in here and might as well have rolled around in pure Magic. They brought it on themselves. Captivity was our best option, besides killing them. And the High Seer insisted on mercy, on our directive.

The blue dome of our Magickers' shield blinks erratically in the sunlight. Outside the shield, the world is pleasantly oblivious to us: white clouds drift past, overlaid by the occasional bird.

We bank around the corner of the castle, past the empty animal pens. In the stable, horses whinny. We continue to feed them in case we need them. Our force is still some ways away—and, mysteriously, has not encountered the King's army. We cannot begin cleaning and relocating until they arrive, as we have barely the resources to keep our patrols staffed.

But this will not last forever. Once we have evacuated all the humans we can topple this awful castle, expose the beautiful well underneath, and build a new fortress here to secure it.

We will stop the reckless spread of raw Magic—and Viteos will gain a new, plentiful power source.

The humans will get used to their new condition. This is the best outcome possible for them—if we can find and capture the Princess, and prevent a Kingdom-wide rebellion.

The soldier leads me to the far back of the courtyard, where I'm assaulted by an even worse smell than the one in the dungeon. Bodies. Only a few, but far more than the High Seer would have wanted. A wave of nausea sweeps over me. They have been here rotting since the coup.

"We could do nothing with them until the barrier went up," the soldier says, seeing my horrified face. "They are covered in Magic. If we burned them, they would explode. If we bury them, they will reanimate."

We toss the corpse of the prisoner onto the pile, and I am glad to be rid of it. As we head back into the cramped castle halls, I ask, "Do you know where I can find cloth? Rags?"

"I heard they store linens in the washroom near the kitchens. What do you need them for?"

"To clean up blood." I shake my head. "Humans are . . . strange and mysterious."

The soldier laughs. "They are disgusting. Is it you who must watch the prisoners?"

"It is not as horrid as you would expect." Except when I disposed of a corpse.

The captives are waiting when I make my third visit of the day. The stench of their waste makes my stomach roll, so I cannot imagine how it feels to be locked in there every moment.

Do not fall into the trap, I remind myself. The humans created this prison for themselves.

I open the food slot and the girl human, her dark hair in wild, greasy tangles, rushes for the door. "You brought something. Oh, by Melidia's grace."

I pass her four clean rags and she grabs them like I might attempt to take them back. She turns to the other captive, the flat-faced boy, and her body shudders. A sound comes out that tells me she's sobbing. The boy hugs her.

Some cloth meant this much? They must be in misery. I have to leave before I say or do something I regret.

I step back from the cell, and the door swings wide open.

The two humans disentangle themselves, guilt written all over them. Somehow, they opened a locked iron door—and then pretended it was closed again. My Magic heart goes cold.

"He did it!" a prisoner in a different cell screeches. "I saw him. Then he tried to talk with sex voice to the dungeon door." He falls back in a tangle of limbs and howls with laughter. "Didn't work!"

The realization sets in more slowly than it should. The one named Parsifal used Magic to open this door, though not well enough to do it again. My own Magical ability has grown noticeably the longer we stay here, so it should not come as a revelation to me that humans have begun to wield it, too. But if the Commander finds out, the boy is dead. Without question.

His brown eyes look into mine. Hopeful and hopeless, at the same time. Unwitting. He did not mean to do this—he did not cut the earth open and cause Magic to come spilling out. I cannot allow him to be punished for it.

As I enter the Commander's headquarters in the temple, he rises from his desk. He has been drawing something, and I snatch a look as I pass. It is a rough sketch of a settlement, with numbered squares and circles for buildings.

"Mahove, friend Sapphire. Please, sit." He gestures at a chair. "What brings you before me today? Have the captives given up the Princess?"

I sit down, endeavoring not to let the tension I feel show on the surface of me. "The humans still claim not to know her whereabouts. Keeping them in the dungeon is not working. It is misery."

The Commander snorts. "The Princess is here somewhere, hiding. And I am certain they know where." He narrows his eyes at me. "Squeeze her location out of them—however you see fit."

I do not let my surprise show. I think of Commander Valya prodding the King with the red-hot tip of his finger, and I dislike the image of him prodding my two humans that way.

"They will not talk where they are now," I say. "But if we show them kindness, they may reciprocate." In any case, I have to get them somewhere more secure before they find a way out on their own. "Move them somewhere comfortable," I suggest. "Show them we are capable of mercy if they help us. I fear torturing them further will yield the same result we have gotten from the King."

"Hmm." I wait while the Commander riffles through papers on his desk. "Let us see if your hunch is correct, Sapphire. Move them. Earn their trust. Get what I need."

Back at camp, the men are sitting around the fire looking morose when we emerge from the trees. They leap to their feet as Harged drops Nul se Lan's bodyguard to the ground. She howls in pain.

"Sir? General? You're alive!" The men of Stone Company descend on us with embraces and claps on the back.

Harged shoves them off. "Watch out. We were ambushed by the cratertooth's peons, and the General is injured."

"Thanks for the warm welcome," I say, clutching my side. "But we need to move out. Now."

"Where are we headed, boss?" one asks.

"Back to the Crossing." If it had been anyone but Stone Company, they would've complained about their sore joints after riding all day and how much more they'll hurt after riding all night. But after one of the men ties a tourniquet around my middle, nobody says a word.

The keg is gone, so we strap our prisoner to the donkey. Soon we're mounted up and off the way we came.

The Baron is at the bottom of my list of worries now. Even worse than a deserter is a traitor. Maybe I could have stopped Nul se Lan, had I remained behind; maybe he would have simply found a different way to end my life. But I will bring him to account for what he's done.

All night we trek through the trees. My entire body aches, especially my side. By the time we spot the three and a half towers of the Crossing on the horizon, the sun is rising, turning the sky pink-gray. In the shadow of the crumbling fourth tower, I fish a candle out of my saddlebag and light it. I wave it back and forth until another candle answers from one of the dark windows.

"She's still here." I hobble to the foot of the tower, and Sasel meets me at the door. Her face is drawn, dark bags hanging under her eyes. She crumples against the stone wall.

"Are you all right?" I ask. I have some of the men bring her wine and food, and she consumes both eagerly—but only with one trembling hand. Her other arm hangs limp at her side.

"I received a smoke message from Forgren, back at Four Halls," she says. "The King is dead."

Everyone gasps. *No. That means . . .* My question comes out a whisper. "The long ears?"

She covers her face. It's all the confirmation I need. "Nul se Lan's personal wizard received the same message. Then they came back for me." She trails off and sinks further down to the ground, cradling her broken arm. "I needed to go with the army, they said, now that Nul se Lan is King. It was my duty to return with him to the Klissen, the new seat of power. But I had promised you I'd remain here—and that's when he told me you weren't coming back."

Her face, washed out and sickly, tips up to stare at me. "I ran from them to the broken tower. The old, rotten stairs collapsed under me, and this fragile bone of mine snapped." She looks down at the arm. "Only with Melidia's protection did I make it to the top, where they couldn't come after me."

I sit down next to her, numb. Nul se Lan must have known this news was coming when he tried to have me killed, so there would be no doubt as to who would wear the crown. "I'm sorry, Sasel."

"There's nothing you could have done." I look into her calm, wise eyes. "I watched them go, General. They are not taking the Low Road. Lan is taking the army far to the west, through the woods."

I glance at the bodyguard we captured. She stares back with grim satisfaction. "Fighting long ears is death," she says. "You knew, and sent soldiers anyway. But we save lives."

No, it was the King who sent them to death. But here I am, bearing the consequences. The Kingdom has fallen. Nul se Lan—the new King, as filthy as those words sound—has stolen the army.

There's nothing left for us.

CHAPTER 11

THELIA

The light's fading in our two tiny windows when the dungeon door opens again. I jump up and peer through the bars. Fourth time today.

Sapphire trots down the steps carrying rope, and my heart sinks into my feet. We've been sentenced to die by hanging, all because Parsifal used Magic. It's like I always told Bayled when he first arrived here. *Maybe Magic can clean your floors and empty the ashes from your fireplaces, but what do you have when it turns on you?*

"Hold out yo-o-o-our hands," the elf says. They no longer sound like their mouth's completely full of mothballs. We do as we're told. What choice do we have left? When our hands are tied, Sapphire pulls on our ropes. "Come."

Only a few prisoners can get up on their knees and stick their arms through the bars as we pass. The rest stay down, dead or dying. I don't breathe through my nose until we reach the stairs. At least we're leaving this horrid place.

The dungeon door opens. Bright evening light assaults us—real light. Everywhere, reddish sunset filters through the windows, and I have to shut my eyes. I've forgotten what it's like.

Instead of taking us to the courtyard, the elf leads us deeper into the castle. Parsifal and I look at each other, daring the other to guess where we're headed. When the halls get dark, a tiny pink light appears.

A stone sticks in my throat. "What's that?" I hiss, grabbing Parsifal's sleeve. A small bauble of light bobs out of a pouch at Sapphire's waist, floating up in the air in front of us.

"A wisp," Sapphire says. "Old, old friends. They go wherever Magic is."

Parsifal watches in curiosity as it circles us. "It's cute."

"If the critter likes Magic," I growl, "it's obviously evil."

Sapphire sighs. "Magic is not evil. Only those who use it."

Easy enough for them to say from where they're standing. But I know better.

We end up on the second floor of North Hall, the wisp leading the way. Is Corene still here hiding in the walls? Or are we being released because they've finally found her? Sapphire stops at a familiar door—the room that was ours before this nightmare began. They open up a pouch on their belt and usher the little glow ball in, then snap the top closed.

Inside the room, everything is upside-down, emptied out, and scattered across the floor. "You're staying here for now," Sapphire says.

"Here?" Parsifal cranes his head to look at the elf, who towers over us. "Why?"

Sapphire looks at him like he's defective. "Are you not grateful?"

Cold fear fills my bones.

"No, no," Parsifal says, giving an awkward smile. "We're *very* grateful to not be in that shithole anymore."

Sapphire makes a face and nods. Guilt. I'm sure that's what it was. Sapphire didn't want to keep us in that dungeon. I grip this new piece of information close like a dagger to use later.

Returning to the doorway, Sapphire holds up their hands, palms out. At first nothing happens, and they look intently focused. After a moment, a colorful shimmer rises from the base of the doorframe, rippling like oil on the surface of water. It flows upward, past Sapphire's hands, all the way to the top. In a moment, the doorframe around the door is filled with a nearly-invisible, shining *something*.

"Do not try to leave," Sapphire says. "It will stop you." They fiddle for a moment with the ropes binding our hands. Then we're free.

I massage the spots where the rope bit into my flesh. Parsifal and I have tracked filth all over the clean floor. It reminds me that once upon a time, I was also clean, and didn't reek of body odor and shit. I wonder how far I can push our luck today.

Pressing my mouth into a smile, I gaze up at Sapphire. "How should I get water up for a bath?"

Parsifal covers his mouth, like he's embarassed to be seen with me. But what's the worst the elf can do after our stint in the dungeon?

Sapphire heads for the fireplace, leans down toward the charred remains of the last logs, and breathes onto them. The logs burst into flame. I gasp and recoil, while Parsifal leans in.

"Fascinating," he says. I glare at him.

Then Sapphire flicks a hand. The bedroom door flies open and a bucket sails in, unimpeded by the shimmering wall. I hold in a shriek. The bucket hangs itself from the hook over the fire, wobbling back and forth until the water inside is steaming.

Parsifal's entranced. "This must be how they go about

things in the Northern Republic," he murmurs. "No wonder Bayled thought us all complete asses. Much less work."

Unhooking itself, the bucket flies into the washing room and dumps the boiling water into Corene's huge wooden wash-tub, only to depart again for more. Again and again, the bucket performs these tasks until the tub's full, and the water's still steaming. By this time it's usually tepid.

"Get in," Sapphire says, pointing to the tub. I don't need to be told twice. I barely realize Sapphire's watching as I strip. I probably look like a dirty, disgusting dog to them. I climb into the bathtub and grab the soap. Sapphire's still staring, so I slide down into the tub until my breasts vanish under the surface of the water. Squeaking and clanging echoes in the other room as Parsifal rights his furniture and returns his belongings to their proper places. I ignore it, focusing on this small moment: the scent of soap. The gentle lather and foamy bubbles. The evidence of my imprisonment sliding off me, vanishing into the hot water until my smooth, oaky skin reveals its perfect self.

I don't get out until the water's completely cold. I'm new. I'm alive. And I will never again let them make me into that weak, hopeless thing I was in the dungeon.

PARSIFAL

Once Thelia's finished, I get to indulge myself in a bath. As I scrub the dirt and shit from every wrinkle in my skin, I promise Melidia—and the demons, while I'm at it—that I'll never again take cleanliness for granted.

The sun has almost set by the time I'm dressed in fresh clothes. Sapphire's still here, watching us.

Standing under an oil lamp, I go to strike a fire starter, but the wick bursts into flame on its own. One at a time, *poof, poof, poof,* every oil lamp ignites. "That wasn't me," I say to Sapphire, holding up my hands to show I'm blameless.

"I asked the lamps to do the lighting," they say, with the faintest smile. That's what I did too. I *asked* the cell door to open, and it did. It just wanted me to be polite. Is that how Magic works?

A shimmer outside the window grabs my eye. Something's there, in the sky beyond the walls of the castle. I walk to the sill and peer out.

A glowing blue barrier surrounds Four Halls. It only becomes visible at choice moments, like when it reflects a flicker of moonlight, and the whole outer layer sparkles for a second before vanishing. Before I can ask about it, the oil-sheen barrier in the doorway dissipates with a sound like wind blowing through, and the bedroom door flies open. Thelia and I both jump in surprise as a little service cart wheels itself in, unhindered. It's covered in plates of food, probably enough to feed four people. Thelia and I advance on it, so hungry we can't restrain ourselves. I'm about to take a plate when I realize that I don't even recognize what's on it.

Sapphire anticipates my question. "Everything in the kitchens ran out. We have not been able to copy exa-a-a-actly what was here when we arrived, but I am doing my best." I take note of the way Sapphire says it, like we're going to give them a poor progress report later.

Thelia takes a bite of a misshapen, cake-like object, topped with a blackened vegetable. It looks awful. "Not bad," she says encouragingly. Sapphire's lips tweak, but they don't smile. Thelia looks even less pleased with the next cake, but once I have food moving into my mouth—as unfortunate as the collision of flavors might be—I can't stop. The texture is wrong and it tastes like someone mixed dirt with salt, but Thelia and I keep going until we can't eat any more. Feeling full for the first time in a week, I collapse into a chair in front of the fire.

The cart rolls itself back out and the door closes, the Magic barrier filling the doorframe once again. I return to my room, only to find that the broom and dustpan I'd been using to clean up broken glass are now shuffling about, completely on their own. The broom sweeps debris into the pan, then skips on to the main room, where Thelia sleeps.

"Watch out," I call through the door. "Broom incoming."

"You don't need to clean my room for me, P—oh, for Melidia's sake!" Thelia holds her chest, gasping, as the broom works past her. "Everything has a mind of its own all of the sudden."

We both look Sapphire. "This is why we-e-e are here," is all they say, not meeting our eyes.

Thelia frowns. "Because the brooms have suddenly learned self-determination?"

"It is spillage."

I repeat it. "Spillage?"

"Too much Magic. Dangerous." Sapphire gestures at the shimmering wall outside the window. "We built that to keep all the Magic in."

I'm lost. "Where's it coming from? Did you bring it with you?"

Sapphire laughs—a rare sound, like wind chimes. "You think The People bring Magic here? You understand no-o-o-othing." They flick their hand across their nose and say derisively, "Humans."

"The Magic was already here?"

"U-u-underground, yes." Sapphire spreads their arms wide. "Magic's heart lives deep in Helyanda. Beneath us all. From time to time, the surface cracks. It bubbles over."

"That doesn't explain *you* being here."

Sapphire lets out an impatient breath. "This much Magic is dangerous. In the wro-o-o-ong hands."

I know they mean human hands. "So what does keeping us all prisoner accomplish?" I ask tartly.

"We will fix," Sapphire says.

"How?"

"You would not understa-a-a-and."

"Try us." Thelia says it like a dare.

Sapphire crosses their arms. "No more. Time for sleeping." Something about the authoritative way they say it makes me wonder what other delicious things they might demand in that tone.

Sleeping on my couch instead of a hard stone floor is the most precious thing in the world. I sink into its cushions and run my face along the fur trim of my blanket. In the main room, Sapphire lies down on the floor in front of my door. I can't go by, and neither can Thelia, without stepping over them. They plan to stay and keep watch—probably to make sure I don't do more Magic. Not that I actually can on request.

The lamps all go out at once, but I'm too tired to get my trews in a twist. I'm asleep the moment I close my eyes.

BAYLED

Where do I go from here? The castle, the kingdom—gone. The army—stolen. Corene—imprisoned at best, dead at worst. I can still smell her hair in my hands, taste her lips on mine, feel what she felt like—

"What about the Baron?" asks Harged.

I'm so tired from trying to heal after Sasel used her good hand to stitch me up that I answer dryly, "What about him?"

"He's still out there in the Crimson Woods thinking he got away with deserting."

I shake my head. "We go after Nul se Lan. Fight back."

"How?" Harged presses. "We're more than two days behind them, and they're off wandering through the forest far from the Low Road. How would we find 'em?"

Sasel nods. "And the men with him are loyal to him now—not you."

It hurts to hear, but it's the truth. He's the King, however awful that feels. "Fine. We'll go find the Baron. I don't want to be out on this road any longer than we have to be." I still don't know where the full elven host is, and I don't want to find out.

Clouds drift in as we climb on our horses and start off down the same road we took yesterday. The men complain a lot more this time. Before long, the clouds darken and gather so thick that the sky vanishes, so there's no way to know when the sun finally sets.

"Gonna snow," Harged says, glancing skyward.

"It's too early in the cycle."

"Early or not, snowin' is what these clouds are here to do." Injury on top of insult on top of your king's death.

We stop to find dinner and the men hobble their horses. I step into the woods to search out branches for a fire—I need a distraction. Harged stands up. "Boss, I'm going with you."

I want to roll my eyes, but wandering off alone did go pretty poorly for me last time. "Come on, then."

Thick, fat snowflakes are falling by the time we return. I drag our prisoner under the shelter of a tree and she curses at me. By the time we get four tents up, the snow is cascading down in waves of white. The sky lights up as the moon rises, reflecting off the thick layer of clouds and casting the world in pale, eerie silver.

As we huddle together, the temperature drops. In the corner, the prisoner glares at us whenever we catch her eye. I listen to Halrendar's hooves shuffling, wishing I was back at the castle.

I should have stayed and fought.

We wake up to heavy snow cover and gray skies. As soon as it's light enough to see, we pack up our makeshift tents and ride on.

Plodding through the snow and bramble, none of us speak until our path is blocked by what looks like the rotted-out beams of an old shack, covered in snow and brush. "Hey, boss," one of the men calls. "Look."

One of the men drags away some branches that have been draped across the skeletal wooden mass. "I think it's a catapult."

"It's been camouflaged," I say. Someone hid this here. "Maybe it belongs to the Baron."

We descend deeper into the woods and pass a brush-covered wagon that I forbid the men from investigating, in case it's rigged. Harged spots a trap in the forest floor before anyone can step on it. We get off our horses and make a wide arc around it. I keep my gaze pinned on the ground, looking for more traps, until I hear one of the men shout.

My hand is on the hilt of my sword before someone strong grabs me by the back of my coat and yanks. I stumble backward, toppling into the freezing snow.

Three men in fur coats and fur-lined helmets stand above me, swords pointed at my face. I raise my hands in the air. I recognize their colors right away—the red, white, and black of the Crimson Woods. Baron Durnhal's men. Just who I was looking for.

"Don't move," one says.

"Relax." I show my empty hands. My sword never made it out of its sheath. "You're the Baron's soldiers? We've been looking for you. I want to talk to him."

They don't answer and their faces are unyielding. One drags me over to the rest of my men, who've been surrounded. The prisoner laughs hysterically, even when one of the soldiers growls at her. She flaps her broken wrists at him.

The Baron had an entire army hidden away out here. Why did I think coming to the Crimson Woods was a good idea?

We're tied up and tossed back on our horses like vegetables. There's an old saying my dad used at times like this: *Free from one jaw of a biylar bear, swallowed up by the other.*

I leave the room in North Hall before the humans awaken and head to the kitchens to make breakfast. As I step into the dark room, the wisp lighting my way, a shriek greets me. A figure darts in front of me, and reflexively, I grab it. Disgruntled pots and pans hop and float out of our way as we collide on top of the counter.

"Let me go!" she wails in her human language, blue eyes flashing with maddened fear, long red hair in messy tangles all over her head.

I know that red hair, those fearful blue eyes—just like her father, the King. "Princess?" I ask. She cowers like a starving animal and tries again to escape my grip, but her body is like a twig in the wind. She has spent too long hiding.

The door flies open and Ellze stumbles in. He must have heard us screeching. He rushes over to us, pulls a rope from his belt, and ties the Princess's wrists. She screams and sobs, the noise drawing other elves in. "I got her!" Ellze crows. "I found the Princess. Someone tell my uncle."

His green eyes flash to me, and then away. She keeps screaming.

The Commander is smiling for the first time in days, but it shows more lines on his face than there ever have been before. He walks around the Princess in circles as she kneels on the floor, crying. "I want to see my dad," she whimpers.

"I will allow it," the Commander says in her language. He kneels and lifts her chin with one hand. "*If you send a smoke* message to each of your sworn lords telling them to surrender to us." She may be starving, but she has enough spirit left to spit on his shoes. The Commander sighs and stands up. "Put her in the dungeon until she is more agreeable."

"Should my humans know we have found her?" I ask.

Ellze snickers. "*Your* humans?"

I scowl back at him—my supposed friend. He finds nothing wrong with the Commander believing it was he who found the Princess. "You know my intent."

"Say nothing to them," Commander Valya says. "We face even greater obstacles now. Our squadron leaders back with the rest of our force should have encountered the King's army by now . . . but it appears they have gone missing."

"The King must know where they are," I say.

"I doubt we will glean anything of value from him. His mind is going. And *your* humans, Sapphire." Commander Valya looks hard at me. "If the Princess refuses to talk, they are the ones who can tell us where their army has gone. Find out."

I nod, though I wish I could tell the Commander how wrong he is. And I fear what will become of Thelia and Parsifal when they cannot provide the information he demands.

THELIA

When I wake, Sapphire's gone. Parsifal and I both let out our breath.

Breakfast arrives on the cart—some kind of starchy egg mush that tastes nothing like eggs. "What is this?" I ask, choking it down. I need the nutrients, but it's agony.

"Certainly not eggs." Parsifal picks at it. "Didn't Sapphire say the castle is out of food? This wasn't laid by a chicken. It was made."

I choke down as much as I can. Now it's time to get out of here.

When the cart skitters out of the room and the door starts to swing closed, I lunge to catch it before it slams—and my outstretched arm smashes into a hard, flat surface. The air around the door ripples.

I howl, clutching my hand, and stagger back. In terms of pain, this doesn't compare to most things Mother did. But something about this hurts much more.

Parsifal helps me to one of the chairs by the fire. "So much for getting out that way."

I sit up, the pain only emboldening me. "What about the secret place? It's connected to this room, right? If we can't get out through the door, maybe we can find Corene—if she hasn't already starved to death. Then we could try again for the sewers."

Following the wall, I tap with my good hand and hope the secret place passes through here. I tap and tap, but it doesn't have the hollow sound I was hoping for. Parsifal joins me and we keep going, tapping along the wall in his room together. Nothing.

The doorknob twists in the main room. We scramble onto Parsifal's couch and pretend to be reading as Sapphire walks in. They look exhausted, and it's still morning.

"Do you want to go out?" they ask, holding up a length of rope. "Outside?"

We both glance out the window. Oh, to feel daylight on my

skin again, to feel fresh air through my hair . . . "Yes!" I jump from the couch. "Yes, please." I don't even have a plan. I just want to see the outside. I can figure it out as I go.

Sapphire winds a rope around each of us at the hip and holds the end. At the door, they wave one hand in front of the shimmering emptiness that I know from hard-earned experience is a solid, hard wall. "Open, please."

With a familiar *shhhhh* sound, the door opens. We pass through the doorway unimpeded.

The castle is empty and silent, the little pink wisp leading the way down the dark hallways. On the ground floor, Sapphire takes an abrupt turn to pass through the stable. I yank at the rope. "Parlor Trick!" I holler. "Please, Sapphire. I miss my horse."

Sapphire sighs and lets me walk over to Parlor Trick's stall. She shoves her head eagerly over the door and lips at my hands. "I'm sorry, girl. I don't have any treats." I pat her nose and she snorts, annoyed.

"Hold your hand out." Sapphire drops a whole apple into my palms.

"Where'd this come from?" Parlor Trick's perfect white ears flick forward and her huge nostrils widen.

"I made it out of hay."

I let her have it all, and she's in bliss. The other horses' heads are all bowed, and their stall doors bear chew marks. "Are you feeding them?" I ask.

"Yes."

"Exercising them?" Sapphire looks down at the ground, and I want to break Parlor Trick out of here right now. "Horses need exercise or they'll be miserable. Let them run around the courtyard, or in the paddock behind the castle at least."

"I will try," Sapphire says.

I scowl. "If you won't exercise them, then let them go. Keeping them in here is cruel."

Sapphire glances at me and then away, face full of guilt. The long ears don't know what they're doing, not at all.

I have to say good-bye to Parlor Trick, and Sapphire leads us out of the stable into the muddy courtyard. I expected we'd be alone out here—until we turn a corner.

Peasants, dozens of them, are trapped in wooden cages. They reach for us through the gaps, calling out. Some are sobbing; others lie on the cage floors, staring straight up.

Parsifal gasps and covers his mouth, then runs toward the cage dragging me with him. "Derk!"

Sapphire tries to pull him away, but Parsifal digs his feet in. On the other side of the wooden bars, at the very back, sits Derk the baker—his clothes torn, and his hair and face covered with mud. He barely lifts his head. "Parsifal?"

Parsifal sinks to his knees, reaching through the bars.

I turn to Sapphire. "What are you going to do with them?" This is no better than the dungeon—worse, since it's colder out here.

"Wash, relocate," Sapphire says, not meeting my eyes.

Parsifal stretches a hand out. "Derk, I'm so glad you're all right."

"Are you?" the thin, dirty baker asks. "I'd say you're more glad that you're not in here with me."

A fragile, elderly man rises up next to Derk. "Traitors," he snarls at us. "Working with *them*."

"What?" Parsifal stands up again, his face red. "That's not at all—"

"Then why else are you out there with one of them?" Derk

asks with a rueful laugh. "You've never cared what becomes of commoners like me. And neither do they."

I reach for Parsifal's arm and pull him away. This will do no one any good. He lets me, and Sapphire pulls us along through the muddy courtyard. I apply steady pressure to his arm through his shirt—*Derk didn't mean it.* Though I know better.

"Sapphire," I ask. "What did you mean by washing? And relocating where?" They don't answer. I refuse to move, letting the rope stretch taut in Sapphire's hand.

Sapphire lets out a frustrated sigh. "We must not be seen," they say. "Keep moving."

So they've disobeyed orders to bring us out here. Another little piece of what Sapphire's thinking.

Soon we're returning to the castle, and I say good-bye to the sky. The trip to North Hall is a blur. Wherever our parents are, I hope they're being treated better than those people in the cage.

Sapphire leaves us in our room in silence, sealing the door behind them. Parsifal and I sit in front of the empty hearth together, not speaking. I think about my lovely Parlor Trick, alone in the stable. She must be bored and lonely, like us. And all those people like Derk, crammed into wooden crates. At least I get my lunch on a sentient cart—they probably eat from a trough.

It's almost sundown, and getting cold. I turn to Parsifal. "Wouldn't a fire be nice right now?" I miss the old days—falling asleep together in front of the fire with the dogs.

Parsifal nods. "I wouldn't mind." There's a sound like a spark, and the logs in the hearth burst into flame, showering us with warmth. We're not even surprised anymore.

"This is just . . . so beyond reality," I say. "It all feels like a nightmare we can't escape." My hand finds its way into his. I've never craved someone's touch like I do now.

"At least we're here and not down in the dungeon anymore."

He's right. In a way, though, this is worse. The fire in the hearth. The walk around the courtyard. Morsels of kindness, of comfort—enough that we want to feel grateful, when really, we deserve our lives back.

"We're still prisoners," I say. "What about Daddy? And your parents? I want to see them." I get up and pace to the window. "I want to know if they're alive."

In the reflection I see Parsifal approach me. He places his hands on my shoulders, and I don't move as he sinks his fingers into my tough flesh. I didn't realize how tense my iron muscles have been, how much pain they've been waiting to release.

I don't look at his face in the window. My eyes are riveted on the castle's high walls, and the occasional shimmer of blue that keeps us all trapped here. "Patience," Parsifal says. "Every time Sapphire speaks, we learn something new. Like today— washing. Relocating. Each one is another piece of the puzzle."

But what image does the puzzle make? I'm tired of being a pa-chi-chi stone for others to use. "Percy," I say, and his hands stop. It felt so good. "I won't wait. I don't want to end up like Derk. I want to choose where I go next."

I reach out and pull the handle on the window. It doesn't budge. Locked—and frigid cold. Taking a breath, I reel my arm back and punch the glass. My fist crashes through the window, scattering glass all over the floor.

Parsifal stumbles back. "Maybe some warning next time?"

I ignore him. My hand burns from tiny cuts, but I'm setting myself free.

Reaching through the hole in the glass, I grab and pull the exposed window frame. Nothing happens, so I pull harder, with my entire body weight. It gives way and opens.

When I climb up on the sill, shards of broken glass bite through the soles of my shoes. "What are you going to do?" Parsifal asks. Not bothering to answer, I step over the side and start climbing down the stone wall. "Is your head full of mincemeat?" he calls after me.

"I'm making it up as I go." I find the next ledge with the toe of one shoe and start to bring my other foot down. I lean back and—

I can't move. A glance over my shoulder tells me there's nothing behind me, or under me.

I'm stuck in mid-air. "What's happening?" I mutter. I'm still holding onto the sill, so I try to climb back up to the window where I started—but something holds me back. I'm riveted to the spot, hanging in emptiness.

Parsifal's head appears over the sill. "Oh, demons. Why are you floating?"

"I don't know!" I let go of the sill with one hand. As I'd feared, I don't fall. I'm trapped like a bug in a spider's web. I reach back with my free hand to find out what's caught me, but all I feel is something soft and sticky, like wet sand. I try to pull my hand away but it's stuck now too, and whatever is holding me back tears the hairs out of my skin. "Percy! Help!"

CHAPTER 12

PARSIFAL

Hovering in midair, Thelia flails her arms, but they only move a little—like she's stuck on a giant, invisible spiderweb.

"Help!" she calls again. She rips one arm forward, trying to free herself, and succeeds only in peeling off her sleeve. She wriggles like a trapped fly. "I'm stuck. It's going to tear my skin right off."

This is surely the demon plane, and we're locked in a prison that looks like Four Halls.

I can't watch her flail anymore so I slide to the floor, putting my head in my hands. "Percy!" Her voice rips a hole through me, and I clutch at the opening it leaves behind. If I close my eyes, maybe I can pretend for a moment this isn't real. Maybe I can find some kind of equilibrium again, start over, and wake up ready to solve this mess.

Behind me, the door opens. I spin around to find Sapphire striding in. "What is . . .?" they start. Faster than a lightning bolt, they're at the window. "Thelia!" I've never heard Sapphire use our names before.

Without hesitating, they jump out the window. One

hand grips the windowsill as they slide down the stone wall, keeping flush against it. I lean over the side and watch. With their free hand, Sapphire grabs one of Thelia's arms and pulls.

She roars in fury. "My skin is stuck!"

"I know." Sapphire's not sympathetic. They pull her arm free and she lets out a shriek. Next they grapple with one of her legs, then the other. Even the one time I spied on horrible old Delia's sparring lessons, I've never heard Thelia make a noise of such terrible agony.

Finally, Sapphire's able to loop an arm around her waist, and with one last pull, Thelia's second arm comes free—leaving behind pieces of her clothes, strands of hair, and bloody bits of skin.

She fiercely holds in her sobs, her body limp, as Sapphire climbs back up and passes her through the window to me. I try not to touch the fresh wounds on the backs of her arms and legs as I bring her in. Her long hair sticks out everywhere, stiff and wild at the same time.

Once Sapphire's back inside, we carry Thelia to her bed and lay her on it, face down and wounds up. She lets out an anguished howl. Sapphire holds up one hand and the door flies open. In sails a bowl with a bundle of rags, landing on the table by the bed. Sapphire reaches down and taps the side of Thelia's temple. Her head falls limp and she goes silent.

"You knocked her out?" I gape at Sapphire.

"What wo-o-ould you do?" They dip a rag into the soapy water and begin cleaning off the raw spots on Thelia's arms, where beads of blood rise to the surface all along her flesh.

"Why didn't you do that earlier?" I ask. "You could've saved her a lot of pain."

Sapphire scoffs. "Then she would not have learned anything."

I take a long breath to shove my temper back down into my stomach. I peer out the window, seeing what Thelia saw: freedom.

Four Halls has become a prison beyond my worst imaginings.

BAYLED

More of the Baron's soldiers appear in the flurry of white, all dressed for winter. One raises a spear and points into the dense, snow-covered trees. Without a word, my men start walking.

I square my shoulders and dig my feet in. "Where are you taking us?" The soldier pressing his dagger into my side slides down his hood.

It's a woman—oh, it's Captain Tarkness. When the Baron first visited Four Halls, the Captain's role as his right hand was a popular topic of gossip.

"Red will be the one to talk with you." She prods my side with the point of the blade and I jump forward. She doesn't sound angry or cruel, but stern, like my mother was. The steely, measured voice of a diplomat.

The Baron's fortress is one squat tower hidden behind two fearsome wooden stakewalls, their points facing out to stop unwanted cavalry. But inside, the castle has low ceilings and thick stone and a fire blazing in the main hearth. For the first time since we left Melidihan, I feel warm. The captain calls out, "Red, come down!"

A man descends the stairs, dressed in a scarlet jacket and handsome riding boots, with wisps of silver hair at his temples. He recognizes me at once. "Bayled Vasha."

No "Master" or "Young Master" or "Ward." Just my name. I always liked that about him.

The captain salutes. "We caught them sneaking through the woods."

"We were on our way here to talk with you," I say.

The Baron quirks one of his thick, sharply-arched eyebrows. "About what?"

"About the fact that you failed to answer the King's call to arms." What audacity to feign ignorance.

"I see." He tilts his head at our prisoner. "And who's this?" She bares all her teeth at him.

"This one tried to kill General Vasha," Harged chimes in, much to my irritation. I shoot him a look to shut up, but he's oblivious. "She works for that craggon Nul se Lan."

The Baron's gaze flicks to me. "The King's heir tried to have you murdered?" He walks up to the prisoner and peers down. "Why did your master command you do this?"

She says nothing and sets her jaw. Red turns around and gestures at Captain Tarkness. "Please, Captain."

She nods and approaches the prisoner, removing her sword from its sheath. By the time I realize what she's about to do, it's too late to stop it. The Captain slides her sword through the braided woman's chest. The prisoner smiles, blood seeping through her lips.

Everyone in Stone Company, even Sasel, gasps. The prisoner falls forward to the floor, never to get up again. Harged tenses up behind me like he's ready to fight.

"Was that necessary?" I ask. "She was a prisoner. She presented no danger to anyone."

The Baron levels his gaze on me. "Not *at this moment*. But she did before and would again. You should have killed her as soon as it was clear she wouldn't talk."

I take a step forward, and the Captain seizes the rope still tied around my hands. "You're the one I should kill," I snap. "Deserting is a crime punishable by death."

This threat doesn't seem to faze him. "Captain, Bayled and I will discuss this further in my study. Get these soldiers something to eat, please." The Baron waves at Harged. "You can relax, Halen. I won't kill your general tonight—unless he tries it first."

SAPPHIRE

The Commander told us humans are stupid, slaves to their instincts, like orkuks. They will take orders if you offer them something good enough. They only learn lessons the most difficult way—through experience.

Parsifal, however. He only says a tiny fraction of the many thoughts that I see flickering behind his eyes. Always he is observing, cataloging, planning. I have to be careful what I say around him, because he could use it against me later.

He stares down at Thelia while I rub salve on her wounds and bandage them up. "What was that outside the window, Sapphire?" he asks quietly.

The more they know, the more they can scheme and manipulate me. I peel the bits of torn fabric away from Thelia's back. "A net. To keep humans from leaving."

"First that blue shield to hold in the Magic, now this invisible net? What happens if we leave, Sapphire?"

I retreat from the bed, finished with my work for now, and make my way to the hearth. With a wave of my hand over the logs, they catch fire.

Parsifal follows. "Don't avoid me."

"You are covered in Magic." I reach out and brush a finger down his shoulder, trying to indicate the thick layer of Magic draped over him like a second skin. The sensation of him under my fingers is lightning, and Parsifal jolts back. We both felt it. "That Magic makes you dangerous."

"Is that why I can do . . . things?" he asks.

"Probably." I should not be telling him anything he doesn't need to know. We will handle it, as soon as the host arrives and builds the new sanctuary. I just need these two to stop getting into trouble until then.

"That's why you've trapped us in here?" Parsifal asks. "You don't want us running around out there doing Magic."

I weigh what I want to tell him with what I *can* tell him. The language barrier keeps getting in my way. "Yes. Without control, Magic is very dangerous. But soon we will take it all off, then you can leave." They cannot know how excruciating the cleansing process will be, or they will never cooperate. But I wish I could assure them that after they are brought before the Magicker and scream until they are hoarse, they will get to leave this place whole.

That was the plan—clean, relocate, and be done with it. Simple. But in this moment, I realize it is not simple at all. We will build them a new home, of course. But their real home— this castle, the Holy Kingdom—will be gone.

Their short lives will never be the same, and they will hate us forever for it.

Parsifal's flat nose wrinkles in confusion. "Take it off us? I don't—"

"Get some rest," I interrupt, ushering him back to his room. "We can talk more later, when Thelia is well again."

I check on the King next. He writhes in his bed, not noticing when I enter. I wave my hand and a tray of food flies in, bearing bread and a bowl of soup, and lands on the bedside table. The surfeit of Magic here may not be reliable, but its omnipresence makes my work easier.

I kneel by his bed and touch his arm to get his attention. His eyes creak open, coated in a layer of yellow-green muck.

"We've captured your daughter," I tell him. "You have no reason to resist the Commander's wishes now." All he has to do is capitulate and order the surrender; then we can cease worrying that the sworn lords will come to their sovereign's rescue. The more humans who stream into Melidihan, the more we will have to subdue, sanitize and relocate—and the greater predicament it becomes.

The King's reddened eyes close again. "Corene," he whispers. "I want to see her."

I already know what the Commander would say: absolutely

not. We must keep the Princess feeling hopeless and isolated so she will do as Commander Valya asks.

"You can see your daughter once you announce the surrender," I say. He gives no response. I cannot stay longer, as I am behind in preparing meals for the rest of my charges.

I hand the King a spoon and turn to leave.

"Please," he moans after me. "My daughter." I close the door and seal it.

Now comes my worst task. Down to the dungeon, where the Princess leans against the bars of her cell, sunken eyes staring out. I've done what I can to clean up the filth down here, but there is only so much time. Now that Thelia has torn herself up, I'm afraid to leave my charges in North Hall alone for too long should some further horror befall them.

Be grateful, Ellze said. Indeed.

I push a bowl of food through the panel in the cell door, but the Princess does not respond. I walk over and press her arm through the bars.

"What?" she growls.

I step back. "Ensuring you are still alive."

Her head lolls away so she can look down at the floor. "I'd die if I could."

So dramatic. I take out her old, dirty bowl. "Your friends are fine, yo-o-ou know."

The Princess looks up. "What friends?"

"Thelia and Parsifal. I have them. They lied for you, though they knew all along where you were hiding." I am not certain that this is true, but I sense the Princess will tell me.

She snorts. "Easy not to tell when you're sleeping in a bed and eating three meals a day."

"They were kept in this same cell."

A sigh escapes her. "Whatever. My cousin's a biylar bear—one head saying how great you are, the other biting your face off. If she knew there was something in it for her she'd have turned me in."

I find myself surprised at her venom. The Princess is wrong, but I will not tell her. "Do you know where your father's army is?" I try one more time.

She scoffs. "As if I'd know. Didn't anyone tell you being the Princess makes me the least important person here?"

I do not press; I think I can get more from the two upstairs. If I feed them the right answers to their questions, something will give.

THELIA

I wake lying facedown on my bed. My whole body throbs. When I try to roll over, I understand why. The bandaged wounds down my back scream with pain, and I let out a moan, turning back onto my stomach.

The door opens and our food cart rolls in. I didn't think I'd ever describe an inanimate object as "shy," but that's how the cart seems as it inches toward my bed, trying not to let its wheels squeak.

"Parsifal," I call out. "Breakfast." I bury myself under the blankets again. Everything hurts. The cart bumps into the bed lightly and I thrash out with one foot. It wheels back to avoid getting kicked and spins in feverish circles.

"Come on," Parsifal says, peeling back my blanket. "You should eat. And you're giving the food cart anxiety."

I manage to eat a little before I give up and put the plates back. I want to sleep forever and forget this ever happened—just sleep until whatever the long ears have planned for us is done.

Long after the cart's gone comes the *zzzt* of the Magic seal unraveling, and the door opens again. "Hello." It's Sapphire's voice. I pull the blankets over my head. "Thelia? Are you well?"

I stay silent. I feel the mattress squish as Sapphire sits at the end of my bed. They must weigh a lot—I bet it's all that metal in their skin. "How are your wounds?" Sapphire asks.

"Still sting."

"That should stop soon." They peel back one of the bandages. "Loo-o-ooking better."

"What about all this?" I roll onto my side and gesture at my hair, which explodes from my head in every direction. Huge chunks stick together. Each time I've tried to peel them apart, they won't give, and I get a sticky mess on my hands. "How do I get the goop out?"

Sapphire reaches out and touches a few locks of my hair. "It has hardened." No shit. "The only way to remove it is to cut the hair off." Sapphire produces a small knife.

It feels like I've swallowed a rock. Mother always praised me for my voluminous dark locks, tumbling effortlessly to my waist. *You have the last few pieces of my people*, she'd say as she braided it before our practices. *Those dark eyes, that high nose, this beautiful black hair. Fit for a Queen.*

With my face cut open—and my beauty ruined—my hair was all I had left in her eyes. "Please," I say, but I have no energy to resist. What's one more humiliation anyway?

Sapphire pats the sides of my head. I can't tell if it's to comfort me or appraise the damage. The sensation doesn't feel . . . gross or uncomfortable, like I'd expect. I must be numb.

They start to cut. Exposing one chunk of my long hair, Sapphire finds the sticking point and chops. Lift, search, chop. Some bits of the sticky mess lie flush against my neck, and Sapphire has to go deep to cut them out. When the deed's finally done, there's enough of my hair on the floor for a rug.

I look down at it, feeling blank. No Queen of the Holy Kingdom has ever had short hair like a man. But my head feels light as a feather.

PARSIFAL

"It's hot horsefish," Thelia says, staring at herself in the mirror. Her hair now sits unevenly above her shoulders—some chunks shorter, some longer, still sticking out in every direction.

After putting the pieces of the window back and stitching it together with some kind of Magical hand-waving, Sapphire has left, again, for only demons know what. At least their salves have worked, and Thelia can move again.

"Who are you?" I ask, peering at her in the mirror. "I don't think we've met before. I'm Parsifal."

Thelia scowls at my reflection. "Stuff it, Percy."

"You've always had it long, but I think it looks better like this."

She rolls her eyes. "Flatterer. I kept it long because Mother wanted it that way. I wonder what Daddy will think when he sees. I'm worried about him." How she can think of him now, when we're trapped inside by a giant Magical spider web, mystifies me. But she's always hungered for his approval.

The broom hastens in and begins brushing up the chopped hair on the floor.

"Hey!" She kicks at it. "That's mine!" The broom just dodges her and continues its work.

"What are you planning to do with it?" I ask. "Knit something?"

"It's the principle." She gets up and hobbles around after the broom, but her injuries make it hard for her to keep up. Suddenly she freezes, staring at the wall.

A hole has opened up in it.

No, not a hole. A mouth. With teeth. And a lolling pink tongue. In one swing, the broom sweeps the pile of Thelia's raven-black hair into the open mouth. Not all the hair makes it in, but the enormous tongue shoots out, curls around the rest, and licks it up.

The floor is clean except for a very large spot of drool. We both stand there, staring, as the broom hustles away. The mouth shrinks, the stones around it flattening back out, until it's gone. The wall looks the same as before.

"What was that?" Thelia asks.

"A hallucination?" I pat the wall where the mouth was, but it's simply a wall. "I mean, neither of us really knows what's in the food the long ears have been feeding us."

She stares at the spot. "It ate my hair."

"Seemed to enjoy it too."

Thelia sinks back into the chair at her vanity, staring into the mirror like she's been struck by lightning. I find myself gazing at her wildly-chopped hair, like she woke up on the wrong side of the bed five times in a row. It gives me an idea.

I dash back to my room and open my desk drawer, looking for some way to halt what feels like a nonstop downward spiral. I root through old quills, used papers, clips, and bindings. There they are—scissors.

I return to Thelia. "Sit still. I'm going to fix this mess Sapphire made."

She doesn't say anything, but she doesn't send me away. Her injuries must have drained her of some of her fight. So I take a breath, turn her away from the mirror so she can't watch, and start snipping.

The elf hasn't left me a lot to work with. Some sections on the top of her head are cut barely longer than the length of my hand. Others hang loose down her neck. Keeping it as long as I can on the sides, I trim the back close so it won't look awful when it grows out.

Her hair is shorter than mine now. I'm surprised at how good it looks. Smiling, I turn her back around to face the mirror. "What do you think?"

She stares at herself a long time without speaking. My satisfaction vanishes. "Did I mess it up that badly?" I ask.

"No, Parsifal." She meets my eyes in the mirror, trying to smile. "It's wonderful." But she can only do it for so long before she drops her head into her hands. "They've taken everything from us."

So much for lightening the mood.

As I'd hoped, the broom comes back, drawn by the allure of another mess to clean up. It sweeps up the small pile of short, black hairs, carefully dodging Thelia's feet.

There's a *shloop!* as the stones in the wall separate and curl up into lips. Once more, the hole opens in the center, and a tongue lolls out. Thelia lets out a little gasp.

I approach the mouth, holding my hands up in a signal of peace. The tongue stops mid-lick.

"What are you?" I ask. The tongue retracts and the teeth close. "No, wait!" It's here to eat. What could I offer it?

I take a chance and toss the scissors in my hands. In a single swoop the tongue lashes out and catches the scissors. The mouth swallows them. Both sides of the mouth curl up slightly. Is it smiling?

"Thelia! Bring me more stuff." I grab an inkpot off her desk and throw that next. The mouth smashes the glass between its teeth, sucking down ink. It licks its lips, smearing black everywhere.

The tongue lolls back out again. Waiting. I can relate.

Thelia hobbles over. "Are you absolutely rung up the parapets?"

"Of course. Aren't you?" I tear one of the wood arms off the chair at her vanity, tossing it into the mouth. As it chews, the smile grows wider. The mouth has grown in size. It wants the rest of the chair.

I heave the whole thing over my head as Thelia shouts, "Parsifal!" The chair goes flying. The stones part so the mouth can open wider and wider, until it's almost as big as the wall itself. Inside the gaping maw the chair goes. The teeth slam down, chewing, scattering splinters everywhere.

Thelia and I look at each other. "What *is* it?" she asks, breathless, as the mouth shrinks, leaving behind only a plain stone wall.

I remember what Sapphire said about the Magic spillage and everything becoming coated in it—including us. "It's the castle," I say. "Magic has brought the castle to life."

BAYLED

"A drink?" Red asks, pouring a glass of dark alcohol.

"If you insist." I've never been a big drinker like Thelia and Parsifal, but even with a fire in the sitting room hearth, I wouldn't mind the warmth in my bones.

He puts the glass in my hands and sits down across from me. "Now, where were we?"

Baron Durnhal has always been a little too clever for his trousers. I frown and say, "Hm, I don't know—what about you cutting down my prisoner? Or how a cratertooth tried to have me killed? Or perhaps we could start with how you deserted us in our time of greatest need?"

The Baron gives me another inscrutable look. "Where are the others? Tell me, Bayled, where are the other lords who responded to the King's call and sent their men off to join his army? Where are they now?"

I hate rhetorical traps. It's just the sort of thing Thelia does. "I don't know," I finally admit. I hate how childish I sound. "Nul se Lan seized the army and left as soon as the elves captured Melidihan. They're gone."

"Ah," Red says, his face still betraying nothing. He sips his drink. "You have always been too trusting. I expect that's how you ended up in this situation."

"Maybe you're right. I certainly never thought you'd turn out to be a man of such poor character." I won't let him deflect the conversation from his own crimes.

He sighs. "When the command came to join up, I knew what I had to do. Not for the Kingdom, but for the Crimson Woods."

"You knew the punishment."

"I'd rather risk that than let my people be fodder for King Hindermark's harebrained plan." He sets his drink back down with a *clink*. "His tactic hasn't changed in a decade. Hurling soldiers into battle like rocks, thinking that the more of them you throw—even if your aim's shit—the more damage you'll do."

I'm reminded of the thousands of men we picked up along the Low Road, carrying nothing but pig knives or rusty swords, none of them trained for war. Pebbles in an avalanche.

"We could've won it," I say. "If I hadn't left my army to come after a deserter—"

Red shakes his head. "No human army can win against The People. The oldest living creatures on Helyanda? You're as much of a knob as the King if you believed that."

I had to believe it if I was going to lead. "You're a traitor," I say. "Why should I hear this as anything other than an excuse for betraying us?"

He shrugs. "Maybe to you I'm a traitor. To the people of the Crimson Woods, I've kept us alive." He stands up and walks to the fireplace, poking a log to scatter the ashes. "You should do the same."

Only *his* people, *his* barony, matter to him. I'm disgusted by his indifference to the rest of us.

"No." I get up and join him where he looks into the flames. "I have to get to Melidihan." And find Corene.

Red chortles, as if this is all just a game. "There's no point in playing at heroism when The People are involved. If they have truly taken Four Halls, you don't have a chance. Go home."

"That *is* my home."

"No," he says. "The Northern Republic." I shake my head. I don't know that place anymore. It's where I'm from, but it's not who I am now. "You'll be safe there."

"Safe?" What a pointless word. "And abandon everyone I care about? Go back to a country that I don't remember—that doesn't remember me—without the woman I love?" I turn to face the Baron. "I'm going to do what I can to salvage the Holy Kingdom. That's my duty."

"Stupidest idea I've ever heard," he says into his glass. "You'll die."

I shrug. "Dying was a distinct possibility when I led the Kingdom into war."

Calmly, he says, "The Holy Kingdom doesn't care about you, Bayled Vasha." It's supposed to hurt, and it does. I don't let it show. "You're a foreigner. The King never intended to actually pass the crown to you. You do realize he's just been using you this whole time? He saw you as a path to the vast riches and commerce of the Northern Republic. He made you his heir because he thought it could lead to wealth, and perhaps to annexation."

It's so hard not to laugh. "Annex the Northern Republic? The Republic crushed the Kingdom in the war."

"As if that could stop a man that greedy from scheming. You've always just been a pa-chi-chi piece on the King's board—and a much easier one to move around than Hareed and Nella Vasha."

"My parents?" I ask. "What do they have to do with—"

"Didn't you ever think it was odd?" Red asks. "After all the times your father put out a candle to make a welcoming home for Magic, it only caught fire when you were out riding with your friends?"

My mouth bobs open and closed, but I can't put the words together.

"But when Hindermark saw he could annex the Klissen much more easily," he continues, "he dropped you for Nul se Lan."

I shake my head. This is horsefish. It has to be. "He's been like a father to me," I say, but it sounds pathetic.

"Has he?" Red asks. "Making you keep the Kingdom's ledgers, solve his problems, clean up his messes?"

It hurts too much for me to go down that road now. I shut my eyes, try to tamp it down, and say, "*He* doesn't matter. *My people* are the ones who need my help."

"I've tried to tell you it's pointless, Bayled. No mortal can win this fight."

"Is that why you left Four Halls last spring?" I demand, white-hot anger coursing through me. "Because you knew the elves were coming?"

He startles. "What? Don't be ridiculous. There were rumors that The People were gathering their forces, but everyone had heard them." He turns to me, and the reflection of the flames turn his eyes red. "No, I left for . . . personal reasons."

"Corene said that you left to get away from Thelia, that you'd found a more suitable woman for marriage," I blurt.

The Baron snorts. "There are no other women, I assure you. There will never be other *women*. Thelia was my exception."

"Exception?" He raises his eyebrows meaningfully, and my face flushes. "Oh." Corene probably didn't know this about him. Why would she tell me something that wasn't true? "Then why did you really leave?"

"I was warned," he says, watching me carefully. "Someone told me I would regret marrying Thelia."

"What did they say?"

"That her mother is an orphan from the Midland Hills," he says, swishing his liquor around. "That she's descended from Magickers. That her blood is cursed, like her ancestors' was. That she's been trained in every art a woman should never be trained in—in kroga, in the sword, in manipulation and trickery."

My heart grows heavier and harder, like stone. It sinks into my stomach as he speaks. He's not wrong. He's just also not right. "That's what drove you away?" I ask. "That she can't control who her parents are, and she can protect herself?"

The Baron laughs and returns to his comfortable chair. "Is that supposed to be a joke? Everything she said only made me like Thelia more."

She?

Red digs a hand into the thick, plush fabric. "Except for the last thing. She insisted that everything Thelia ever told me was a lie so she could marry me for my title and wealth."

I can't believe it. Not after what Thelia told *me* about her feelings for the Baron. "The word of one person was enough to outweigh everything you felt?"

"I had no reason to doubt. Why would the Princess want to sabotage her own cousin's love life?"

The Princess. I try to find words, but I don't have any. Corene, sabotage Thelia? I search my memory for a reason. Could she really have thought she was protecting the Baron? From her own best friend?

"Corene said she knew Thelia didn't love me," Red says, "because Thelia loves *you*."

My mouth falls open. The idea is so preposterous that I burst into laughter.

"Are you mocking me?" Red asks quietly.

"No!" I take a deep breath to stop cackling. "It's just . . . impossible. Thelia doesn't even *like* me."

"How do you know?"

I remember the morning she told me about the Baron like it was today. "I've known Thelia since we were children. She never had one crush. She didn't like anyone touching her— certainly not me. She was in love with *you*."

He stares at me, and in his open face I see an opportunity. Thelia is a gaping sore spot for this hardened man, and I can use that, if I place my stones right.

"She told me so in confidence," I add. "And I believe it was the truth." I have him now. Thelia would be so proud.

"But how . . . how can you be certain?"

"She let you touch her, right? Kiss her?" Red's face goes, well—red.

"Many times." He stares into the flames flickering inside the fireplace. "It was always like a little thunderstorm."

I feel sick to my stomach. Red truly loved Thelia, and Corene spoiled it. She must have meant well, but—I need to finish this. "Then you left," I say, pressing him. The Baron turns away and grimaces. "You could've taken her with you, to your safe little fortress guarded by all your clever traps. But you didn't."

"You don't understand."

"You're right. I don't." I put my glass down on the table. "I won't try. Your romantic problems aren't my concern. It's time I be off to bed. If I'm going to ride back to Melidihan, I'd better get started early." I pause for effect. "So I can save the woman I love."

Red's still staring at the hearth. "Good night," I say. "Thank you for the hospitality." I let the door fall closed behind me.

CHAPTER 13

PARSIFAL

We hear the sound of the Magic barrier unsealing and opening as Sapphire appears silently in the doorway. But they stop in their tracks when they see Thelia sitting on her bed, reading a book. For once, their expression isn't guarded.

She's beautiful—I know. Her new short hair shows off a sleek neck and a proud, square jaw. Her shoulders are strength and elegance.

When Thelia looks up, Sapphire's eyes dart away. They finally notice me watching them, and I know how to get what we want.

"I'm glad you're here," I say to Sapphire, sidling up to them. They take a matching step back, eyeing me. "Last night, you know . . . it shook us up. Particularly my cousin." I walk over to Thelia, who's giving me a perplexed look. I put an arm over her shoulders, avoiding her wounds. "She desperately wants to see her family. To know that they're alive."

Sapphire glances between us, their icy-blue eyes hard to read. I think they're nervous. "Not my decision."

But it was their decision to sneak us outside, so I know

Sapphire has at least some sway—maybe not enough to bust us out of here, but enough to shuffle us around a little.

"I miss my dad," Thelia says, glancing at me. Saying what we discussed. "His health isn't great. I don't want him to die and not get to say good-bye."

Sapphire's reaction is so slight that I almost miss it—but there it is, the flash of sympathy. "They're so close. Don't you have parents, Sapphire?" I realize I don't actually know the answer. Do elves simply grow out of the ground?

Sapphire looks at me like they're trying to parse my intentions, but the cultural barrier is just thick enough. "I do." Their indifference falters for a moment, and I can see it: affection. Nostalgia.

"Wouldn't you want to know whether your own parents were alive or dead?"

The elf lets out a great sigh. "Fine. We will go, now. I can give you only minutes, so be quick."

Usually I'm not interested in thanking Melidia for things like these Holy Kingdom folks do—I mean, she's never done much for me—but right now, I do.

The castle is silent and dark and frigid. Winter has come while we've been locked inside. The tiny pink wisp leads us once again, occasionally doing loops in the air past our heads. Thelia squeaks as it gets close to her face, but I feel only a gust of fresh air as it passes, chittering like a rodent.

In South Hall, guards dressed in gleaming silver stand in front of the doorways, a pike against one shoulder. They don't look bored. Do long ears even get bored? I'd be bored.

My hand finds Thelia's. I didn't intend it but now we're holding hands, afraid of what we'll find.

Sapphire stops in front of Thelia's old suite. "I brought visitors," they tell the guard. "Authorized by Commander Valya." That's a lie, and Sapphire's telling it for us.

Wordlessly, the guard taps the pike once on the floor before stepping aside. With a *zzztttt*, the blue, oil-sheen glow around the door starts to peel off, fading and darkening, until it's gone. Sapphire twists the doorknob.

Inside, there's a fetid smell. Trunks lie open, spilling out their contents. Random objects lie scattered around. The table's covered in dirty dishes. Where's their Magic food cart?

Morgaun springs up from the table. Not the first person I'd hoped to see. Duke Finegarden staggers to his feet much more slowly. "Thelia. Parsifal." For the first time I can remember, his voice shakes.

"Daddy!" Thelia goes straight for the Duke and wraps her arms around his stiff body. At least Sapphire, who's watching this unfold, will believe the story I told to get us here.

Duke Finegarden drapes his arms over his daughter's shoulders and, after a heavy breath, squeezes back. "We thought you were dead."

"Not so much."

"Your hair," he whispers.

She ducks her head. "I know. It's a long story."

I peer around the suite, and when I don't find what I'm searching for, I step into the adjoining room. Our trunks are still here and the bed's been slept in, but it's like my parents have turned invisible.

"Where have you been?" Morgaun's asking when I return to the main room.

"We've been locked up in North Hall," Thelia says.

"Where are Mom and Dad?" My voice comes out strained. My mother, already frail, and my father, who can never keep his mouth shut. The Duke looks away, but Morgaun's lips curl up on one side like he's relishing what he's about to say.

"Oh, they were the first to go."

That smile—twitching, growing on his filthy ratlike face. I could rip it right off him, and his appending throat, and any organs thereafter. Perhaps Thelia would help me do it. I take a step forward, squeezing my hand into a fist. He's stronger than I am, but maybe I can make him hurt before I go down.

Duke Finegarden steps in front of his son and places a hand on my shoulder. I believe it's the only time he's ever touched me. "I'm sorry for your loss, Percy. I really am."

I gather myself and look up at him. "What happened?"

The Duke's shoulders fall. He can only show sympathy and humanity for my parents in their death. "Your mother wouldn't eat and died within days. When they came to collect the body . . ." He turns his head away. "Antonin wouldn't let her go. It came to blows." His gaze travels to Sapphire standing in the doorway, and his gray eyes harden into marbles. "A weakened, hungry, grieving man—they slammed him to the floor, right here. His spine snapped like a twig."

Thelia reaches out to comfort me, but I shake her off. I spin on Sapphire. "How could you let this happen?"

Before they can answer, Morgaun stomps across the room toward them. "What's this long ear still doing here?" Sapphire's gaze follows him, but they don't move. "Get out!" Morgaun shouts. "I should get to talk to my sister without your disgusting ears listening."

The elf looks startled and reaches for their sword. "I cannot—"

"If you don't leave right now, I'm going to beat those creepy eyeballs right out of your head."

Sapphire glances from Thelia to me—like they're asking, *Will you be safe if I leave?* I can't even look at them right now.

"It's fine, Sapphire," Thelia says. Morgaun's head whips to her. Sapphire makes an expression I can't decipher and leaves the room.

THELIA

"Oh, so the monster listens to you?" Morgaun snarls at me. "I bet you're fucking, huh?"

The one thing I'll say about rotting in squalor down in a dungeon—there was no Morgaun. I want to two-finger slam him right in the abdomen. Unlike the armpit slam, which shocks the nervous system into temporary paralysis, the abdomen slam bursts the organs. Your skin doesn't break, but you'll still bleed to death inside.

"Morgaun," our father snaps at him. "Sit down. Now."

Morgaun yanks a chair out from under the table and sits down hard. "I'm just saying, if she got between an elf's legs, it would come as no surprise to me."

Daddy leans forward. "If you say another word, I'll hang you out the window myself. You don't talk about my daughter that way."

He has a particular way of saying *my daughter*, like I'm a

possession. Is that all I've ever been to him? I think it's something I've always known, but pretended not to.

I don't know if Parsifal's listening as he picks through his parents' possessions. This must be how he's felt all these years living at the King's mercy—like an object with no control over his life. And now he's all that's left of the Bellisares.

"It's only a matter of time before they kill us," Morgaun says. "Like boiling and plucking chickens for dinner, except dinner is a mass sacrifice. Just like the goddess warned us."

I stare at him. Sapphire would never participate in that, would they? They just said *wash, relocate.* Nothing worse. "If they wanted us dead, why aren't we?"

"Because it's not time yet." Morgaun slams his fist into the table and a glass spills. "But I'm going to stop them before that time comes. With Melidia's blessing, I'm going to free us all."

"What's wrong with you?" I ask, stunned. "Do you know how strong they are?"

Morgaun sneers at me. "Do you?"

"Yes. I fought one. They're ten times more powerful than you, pliggan."

"Well, I have a plan." Morgaun smirks. "I won't say more in case you tattle to your elfie friend."

"They're not my friend!" I snap at him. "I'm as much a prisoner here as you. I want to escape as badly as you." I touch my impossibly short hair. "How do you think this happened? Trying to escape, and failing. It's not as easy as you think."

Morgaun scoffs. "Of course you can't get out with Magic everywhere." He grins at my surprised expression. "I know what's going on. There's so much Magic inside this castle it's practically shivering with it." Maybe Morgaun's years of zealous study in the Temple have made him more knowledgeable than I expected.

"There's an elf who goes outside to burn it off every night," he continues. "I see her through the window, siphoning Magic in bursts of flame. So that's what I'll do too." His voice drops to a whisper. "Catch it all on fire. Watch this place burn down—and them."

My hand flies instinctively to the scar down my face. I don't know what he's talking about, but if there's one thing Morgaun is good at, it's destruction.

SAPPHIRE

I don't like this. That man—the one who must be Thelia's sibling—is an awful creature. I hated leaving my humans with him, so I pace the halls, too restless to attend to other duties. The wisp hovers beside me, equally agitated. The longer I leave them, the greater chance we have of being discovered.

Without asking the guard, I barge into the room. "Time to go," I say. The humans' language is like grinding marble in my molars.

Thelia jumps up from the table, pale and grave. "I guess that's it."

Her brother sneers. "So you do what they tell you?"

Thelia ignores him and hugs her father again, fast. "I'm glad I got to see you, Daddy." The old man just nods once. Parsifal, however, is alone. Pain rolls off him in stifling waves, and he hunches over as if his shoulder has been injured.

Tying their hands together once more, I lead them out, and the soldier seals the door behind us.

Back in North Hall, I insist that Parsifal let me examine him. If he is hurt, I need to know so we can treat him. He shoves me away angrily.

"I'm fine." He unbuttons his coat, revealing a glass bottle tucked under his arm. "Since my father isn't around to enjoy this anymore, I took it."

There are no words that can soothe such a wound—nor atone for what The People have done to him. But I feel obligated to try. "I am sorry for your loss, Parsifal. And for the part my kind played in it."

His eyes are rimmed with red when he looks up at me, but there's no anger left in them. Only defeat, resignation. "I half expected it," he says, plopping down in one of the soft chairs by the fire. "Mom's never been in good health. Dad, though . . ." He peers through the glass bottle. "He's always been a stubborn fool. He survived one hostile takeover—chances were good he wouldn't make it through another, bull-headed as he is."

I stoop to look at the bottle. "What is this?"

"Wine." Oh, that. I purse my lips. "You don't approve?" Parsifal snorts.

"It perverts the mind."

Thelia laughs and reaches for the bottle. "It's harmless fun. We could all stand to relax a little." She seems happier now—I suppose the visit to South Hall worked, like Parsifal said it would.

Her eyes land on mine, and I can't look away. Her red lips, thick and full and soft as rose petals, curl up on one side.

I cross my arms. Commander Valya gave me one task: get information. "This trip was not free," I say.

"I figured it wasn't," Parsifal says. "Princess Corene is hiding in a secret tunnel with an entrance in the King's chambers."

"Percy!" Thelia gapes at him, but Parsifal rolls his eyes.

"What? Look at their face. The long ears already figured it out anyway." Parsifal squints at me, clearly reading my expressions better than I realized. I was correct in remaining suspicious of his intellect. "What else do you want to know?"

"Where is the King's army? If the sworn lords do not surrender, there will be even more bloodshed."

He shrugs. "No idea. Bayled was in charge of it."

"Bayled?"

Parsifal sighs and starts at the beginning. We were wrong about Hindermark having only a daughter. I wonder what other incomplete information the Commander received from the Chief of the Klissen.

"Right before they left for war," Parsifal says, "the King named a foreigner as his heir. He's gone with the army too."

"Heir?"

"Some good-looking craggon named Nul se Lan, from the Klissen. He becomes King if old Hindermark dies."

More kings? The Commander will be furious when he learns that the one human who could actually secure the Lords' surrender has vanished—along with the rest of the thousands of men that our host *should* have crushed on their journey north.

"Not what you wanted to hear, is it?" Thelia asks, leaning

forward. I love the way her short hair shows off her neck, her collarbone, even her earlobes.

"Not particularly." That is not their fault—but I worry Commander Valya would find a way to make it their fault.

Parsifal holds out the wine bottle to Thelia. "I think it's time to drink. You had to deal with Morgaun. I'm suddenly an orphan. There's not a more appropriate occasion for wine than this."

Thelia examines the label. "Wow, where did you find this?"

"Dad and I were saving it. So I'm drinking in his honor." Parsifal is looking at Thelia, or maybe at the wine bottle, or maybe both. Something deep in him seems to settle down. I do not know what to make of his expression. Maybe that is because of his features—they did not seem unusual until I had gotten used to the other humans. He is unique, like a piece of his art collection.

I stand up abruptly. "Are you going somewhere?" Parsifal asks. He holds out the bottle, a peace offering. One I do not deserve. "Drink with us."

I shake my head. "Sorry. Duties." The last thing I need is to get closer to them. To continue feeling sorry for them. Or worse, consume something that would make me forget myself. A clever creature like Parsifal could subvert me. Or powerful, confident Thelia—it would be easy to fall under her spell.

I escape before they can argue. I should report to Commander Valya that the real heir to the throne is still out there, and all our efforts securing a surrender from the Princess will be for nothing.

But something inside me does not want him to know. Not yet. If he decides there is no more useful information to be extracted from my humans, he may assign me other duties—and who knows what would become of them then? I may never see them again.

Instead I trek across the castle to a place I've only been once before. I plug my nose and take a deep breath before entering the shit garden. It is overflowing with waste and there is little I can do to block the smell. My wisp leaps from the pouch at my waist and squeals at me as I rush past, toward the hidden door.

Down below is the cobwebbed, dark room full of bottles that I did not realize were so valuable. "Some help?" I ask, and the wisp reluctantly flies down to show me what I need to see.

I grab the first three bottles I see and tuck them into my cloak, thinking how much Parsifal will like them. I hope it will revive his spirit.

BAYLED

After my first good night's rest in ages, Stone Company congregates in the main hall of the fortress. Warm winter gear waits by our old coats. We put it on and head out to the stables for our horses.

As we load up in the courtyard, I take one last look around. No one's here, and nobody stops us from leaving—so we set off into the woods. The snow's falling again. We're in for another cold night, but at least we have new gear to get us through.

"Boss!" one of the men calls. "Up ahead!" Through the white I can make out dozens of figures. No, hundreds.

"Long ears?" Harged snarls.

"I don't know." One ambush after another—and this one might be the end of us.

Someone with a familiar swagger emerges from the clouds of white. "Red?"

The Baron leads his enormous black stallion towards us. "My King," he says. "I pledge all the arms of the Crimson Woods to your cause. Wherever you go, may we follow. We will never serve the southern traitor."

"Hear!" his soldiers shout, thrusting their fists in the air.

I can't help smiling with relief. My lecture worked, and we won't have to go back to Melidihan alone. "Thank you, Baron. I promise we'll find Thelia."

He nods. "You're a man of your word, my King. I assume you have a plan?"

I let out a long, shivering breath. "I do."

Somehow, through all the snow cover and without a trail to follow, Captain Tarkness always knows where we are. Every so often she glances up, holds one hand over her face, nods, and turns her horse in a slightly different direction. Sasel has started riding next to her, and the two of them talk quietly until we stop to make camp.

"What's the Captain doing?" Harged asks suspiciously. Sasel and Captain Tarkness hover together over the snow, a tiny ball of glowing blue light palmed between them. "Looks like Magic."

"Because it is." Red smiles. "Captain Tarkness is my court wizard. Her family was from the Midland Hills." Like Thelia's mother.

Harged gapes at him. "You'd let a skim into your army? As your right hand? How could you trust—"

Red seizes Harged by the collar. "Say one more thing."

Harged grabs Red's wrist and twists—a classic kroga move. But Red's faster, and before Harged can finish, Red punches him squarely in the stomach. Harged doubles over, groaning. Red places his boot on top of Harged's inert body.

"Let him go," I say, trudging through the foot-deep snow toward them.

Red's face is flushed with rage. "I'm sick of this horsefish. First Thelia, then—"

"I know, Red," I say. "I'm a Northerner who's lived in the Holy Kingdom for a decade. I get it. But we don't have time for it here and now. If we live, there will be time."

This seems to get through. Red grunts and releases Harged, who moans as he rolls over. I yank him upright. He tries to shove me away, but I don't let go. "Learn to keep your mouth shut," I hiss. "While you're here complaining about a perfectly fine human helping us get through these woods, our friends and family are at the mercy of long ears. A traitor tried to murder us. Get your damned priorities right." He tries to splutter something out, but I interrupt him. "Not another word about Captain Tarkness."

Stone Company's gathered around us, but none of them move to help Harged clamber back onto his horse. He sniffles and dusts the snow off himself as we all mount up and start off again.

We've been sitting on the floor by the fire, trying to get the bottle open for most of a candlestick-hour, when the *zzztttt* sound of the seal on the door interrupts us.

Parsifal looks up, pleading, as Sapphire strides in. "Help! We have no corkscrew to get this open." The only progress we've made is shoving the cork even farther down the bottle's neck.

Sapphire takes it and begins fiddling. If we can get them to drink with us, maybe they'll open up. Tell us what the long ears are really doing, what they mean by "cleaning and relocating." Maybe, if we can worm through their defenses . . . they'll want to help us. I swallow a bit of bile thinking of the sticky, invisible net outside my window. Sapphire's affection may be the only way out of this prison.

"I have to be careful." Sapphire sticks a finger down the bottle's neck. "Magic is everywhere now. Tapping into even a small thread could end up being far more than I want. Bad results." A glow emanates from Sapphire's finger. I wonder what they mean.

Parsifal leans over to get a closer look. "What are you doing?"

"Binding the cork to my finger." Sapphire yanks, scattering a few droplets of bloodred wine.

Relief spreads through me. *Wine.* Parsifal takes the bottle and fills two glasses. "Now, take it slow," he says as I throw back most of my glass. He glares. "This is all we have."

Sapphire grins. "Oh, is it?" It's the first time I've seen them look truly delighted. It's . . . becoming. They reach into their enormous black cloak and pull out three dark, dusty bottles. Parsifal's eyes go as wide as his mouth.

"No way." He takes one and turns it over in his hands. "It's a Melidia-be-damned Bellisare-style party now!"

A laugh bursts out of me. "Where did you get this, Sapphire?"

They shrug. "Below the castle. A secret door under poop garden."

"Poop garden?" Parsifal and I exchange a look. "You mean the Pit?" I laugh again.

"Wisp was not pleased." Sapphire turns over one of the other bottles. "A room full of these down there."

"How old are they?" I ask.

"As if your palate is advanced enough to care." Parsifal sniffs the wine and winces. "I wonder if this was made by dwarves." He takes a measured, regal sip. "Didn't Corene say everything under the castle was abandoned after the Split? So this would be from before."

Corene. Is she even still alive? I swallow, ashamed at how little I've thought of her.

"Could be a few hundred cycles old," Parsifal says. "And maybe they'll taste like shit."

I smirk at Sapphire. "Guess we'll find out."

I finish off most of Parsifal's bottle myself. I get a delightful airy feeling, like I'm filled with bath steam.

"Is this what you get when you make grapes sad and then kill them?" Sapphire says, putting their glass of wine down. "Tepid grape blood, that is the name it should have."

Parsifal snorts. "Did you just make a joke?"

"Was it a good joke?" Sapphire asks.

I have to laugh at their earnestness. "It was a . . . well, it was a joke." I refill my glass from Sapphire's bottle and take a taste. "I can't tell if this is delicious or disgusting."

Parsifal sniffs it expertly. "It's . . . complex." He takes a small sip. "Not rotten. Nor faintly reminding me of taking a bad shit, like I'd feared."

When I raise my head from the glass, I find Sapphire looking at me. They quickly look away. I taste the wine again. "It has a lot of layers," I say, watching Sapphire out of the corner of my eye. Their hands keep fidgeting with the stem of the wine glass. I think they *like* me. Good. This is helpful.

"Wine that's been around since before the Hindermarks," I say, finishing off my next glass. If it's making me feel cloudy, Sapphire must be flying in the sky. "Sapphire." This time they hold my gaze. Time to give this a whirl. "My brother said he saw elves—I mean, saw one of The People up on the wall, burning something."

"Magic." Sapphire leans back and pulls their long legs up, knees to their chest. They look small and young, almost human—if they weren't sitting nearly a head above me. "Too much Magic inside castle. They burn it off." Their grasp of language has adorably deteriorated.

"Why is so much Magic bad?"

"Dangerous," they say. It makes me wonder about the mouth in the wall. How dangerous is that?

"You've said that before." Parsifal leans forward, and his eyes flick to mine for a moment. He knows how to play this game too. "But what specifically will happen?"

Sapphire struggles for the right words. "Magic infuses. Like wine. I drink wine, wine changes me." They laugh.

"See? I feel . . . different. Air. Light. Happiness. But with too much, problems happen. Vomit. Foolishness. With Magic, humans turn . . . corrupted. Maybe decay. Or catch fire. Explode."

I suppose that explains why the Holy Kingdom has feared it—but too much of any good thing can turn poisonous. Like Mother's consuming need to keep me safe.

"You said you were here to fix it, though," Parsifal says.

"Yes. We clean humans, keep world safe from you."

"How do you do that, exactly?" I ask.

Sapphire looks annoyed. "Cleansing process. It is complicated."

"We're intelligent. Try to explain it."

Their lips press together. "Cannot." They're doing it again—clamping down. Sapphire sips their wine and gazes into the fire in silence.

That's all we'll get. For now.

SAPPHIRE

I did not like my first taste of wine, or my second one. But by the third sip I started to understand. It is the not-loving that makes the wine lovable. After my fourth sip, I decided wine is the spiritual cousin to war. It is complicated and beautiful, like Laian was. Bitter and sweet.

Or maybe that is the alcohol in my veins, because after the first glass I feel loosened and wiggly, like my wisp. Everything moves more.

"Try it! Try it!" I insist to Parsifal as he pours the second bottle of the Mysterious Under-Castle Wine. I find myself staring at Parsifal's lips as he tastes the wine and swishes it around in his mouth, thinking.

"Glorious." He grins. "Like I imagine Melidia would taste, if I had the chance. My father would've started a new trade route for this." Then his smile falters, and I want to grab it out of the air and hand it back to him. But I cannot undo how we have damaged his world.

"I did good?" I ask.

Parsifal looks at me from the side of his eye, and some of the smile returns. "You did good." I let out an exultant breath and smile back. His brown eyes are glittering.

"I can't believe it doesn't taste like literal shit," Thelia says, taking another sip. "Really surprised." Her laugh is high, light, wild—a laugh she's been using since her second glass of wine, like something inside her has unbound, unwound, and stretched out on the floor for the first time in ages.

My stomach is swirling around and I do not know if it is the wine or the laugh. This liquid is nectar, composed of layers upon layers, each one extending tentacles of flavor through my nose and mouth and head. "No wonder humans enjoy drinking this," I say, marveling at the way my lips wrap around human words. "It is, what you say, fucking great?"

This time even Parsifal laughs so hard he spills some of his wine. "Oh, demons!" He bends over and starts desperately licking the droplets up off the floor, which sends me into fits of laughter.

Thelia grimaces. "Disgusting, Percy."

"Percy?" I ask, rolling the word around in my mouth.

Parsifal shoots her a nasty look. "You taught them the nickname! Why would you do that?"

"Sorry," Thelia says between giggles. "Now your secret's out. Percy."

Parsifal collapses back to the floor. "I hate that name."

I scoot forward and pat Parsifal's back. "If do not like it, I not call you it." He is not laughing anymore. I draw my hand away, afraid my touch bothered him.

"You know," Parsifal says to me, tilting his head, "you're good, Sapphire."

Thelia also stops laughing. She doesn't look happy with what he's said. The last thing I want is my two humans fighting on account of whether or not I am good. I grow more certain every moment that I am not.

"I apologize." I put down the wine glass. "Shouldn't be . . . do-o-oing this."

"Why?" Thelia's lips tighten in a line. "You're *too* good for us?"

"Not this, like you say. The other. The—" I can't think of the words. It has all fled out my head and left red mush. "Something that is bad for you. That is me."

Parsifal shoots Thelia a glare, then moves toward me. He returns my wine glass to my hand. "Have another drink."

Though he is peculiar, his beautiful face opens for me. I can see all the way to his heart—creased and hard, but strong. Seeing him so exposed I feel like an invader, so I throw back the wine and hold out the glass like a supplicant. More wine will drive all these dark thoughts out of me. "Come," I say. "There is more. Don't be cowards."

Parsifal laughs and opens the next bottle. The conversation steers away to the other elves. "Who's that guy I saw you with the first time?" Parsifal asks. "Big Silver Guy."

"Commander Valya. He . . ." I realize too late that I am hiding my face with my wine glass.

"Oh Melidia," Thelia says, covering her mouth. "You have a crush."

I squeeze in the abstract shape of a rear end. "Bathed together many times. I not look away."

Thelia howls. "You're twisted!"

We descend into the third bottle, and in a blink it vanishes. I am invincible. I talk about life back in the glass spires of Viteos and everything I say is met with laughter. We discuss the ideal shape of a behind at length. We are closer together than ever in front of the fire, knees touching.

"I know you sad about hair," I tell Thelia, finding my hand already lightly brushing her head as I say it. At first she retracts, and I freeze in place, but after a moment she leans into my palm. "You are stunning like this."

She glances up at me, suspicious. "You think I'm attractive? A human?"

"Yes. I like that I can see more of you now."

"But you're the beautiful one."

"Not . . . strange?" I have heard the humans talk about us. I know our skin appears like metal, but we are still flesh— merely not as porous. Not as delicate. I have heard them call our hair and eyes *wrong*, but it is just how we are made: we reflect the gift Magic has given each of us. My parents made me with sky and afternoons, and so that is how I am.

Thelia reaches up and brushes a lock of hair away from my face. I feel naked. Parsifal is watching us, but his face has closed up and I cannot see what he's thinking any longer. Something in me hurts.

I pull my hand back, but Thelia leans toward me, her face inches from mine. She is so close I feel her breath. She is also strange, and it is wonderful.

"Maybe the strangeness is why I like looking at you," she says, and her face enraptures me, every line, every shape. She is a warrior full of fire and power.

She closes her eyes and her face drifts closer. Her lips touch mine. Something inside me explodes.

Thelia is soft. My hands find her bare arms as her lips mold to mine. She is all around me. I taste her, I smell her—unique and wondrous like this landscape, with its rippling green hills and neverending blue sky.

Thelia's lips leave mine and instantly I want her back. When I open my eyes, she looks as surprised as I feel. Out of the corner of my eye, I see Parsifal staring at us, his gaze flat. Something unpleasant lurks behind it.

"Parsifal," I say as he stands up and turns his back. He was sitting only inches from us when Thelia's lips found mine. We did it without thinking at all.

I am the shit and piss overflowing in the poop garden.

"The wine's done anyway," Parsifal says, picking up his empty glass. "Thanks for bringing this, Sapphire. I'm going to bed." He walks into his suite and closes the door without another word.

Thelia stares down at her hands. I push away the remainder of my glass of wine. I am in too deep. These two lovely humans—eventually they will be taken away for cleaning, and then they will be gone. I will never see them again, and this moment will become like a lost dream.

I stand up. Thelia reaches for my arm but I yank it away. "Sapphire."

"I sorry," I say. "I did not intend to hurt—to get in between—"

"You didn't. We're not—"

I cannot listen. I will not be absolved. The rushing inside of me is so loud I cannot hear myself think. I *kissed a human*. If Ellze were to find out . . .

My career. My friends. My family. Gone.

I shut the door and seal it.

CHAPTER 14

SAPPHIRE

"Mahove," Ellze says brightly when I wake up the next morning on the floor of the room we share with Zylion. My guts ache. "Got a little too free with *your* humans last night?"

"Please, be quiet." My head weighs five times as much as usual. The air is dense, stifling.

"You are there all the time," Ellze says as I stand up slowly.

"It is my job."

"Not your all day, every day job."

I shove him out of the way as I head to the window, pull it open, and eject the contents of my stomach down the side of the stone castle walls. Tasting that dark red poison was a foolish idea.

When it is all out of me, I slump to the floor, wiping my face.

"It is the Magic, you know." Ellze crouches next to me. "They are so slick with it, you cannot help but be drawn to them. Their pores are filled with Magic, their hair, their mouths. It calls to you. That is our nature."

Their mouths. My eyes flick to his gold face. Does he know something? But Ellze spouts on. "You cannot be blamed for finding them so appealing. With the Magic dripping off them like sugar . . ."

"That must be it," I find myself saying, if only to end this conversation. Ellze's voice grates like an incessant tapping on my shoulder.

"Now that you know," he says, "keep your distance. Perform your duties only. Other things require your attention."

I lie back down on the bedroll. He is not the one in command, but he behaves as if he were. "My responsibility is keeping the royals alive," I say.

Ellze pulls me to my feet. Everything swims, but I remain upright. "Since the King is so close to the end, the Commander interrogated him once more and in his haze, he let slip that a Prince is still free, with the missing army. Now the Commander wants you to bring the Princess to him. Be grateful I did not tell him you were feeling unwell."

The dungeon—my least favorite place in this whole horrid castle. Its condition has only worsened. Commander Valya does not believe expending resources here will benefit us in the long term.

The air down here is filled with noise. Roaring and howling, punctuated by the Princess's screams.

I rush into the dark and find all the prisoners who used to lie on the floor—starving or dead—are now on their feet. Shaking the bars. Screeching in a way not even close to human.

"Please!" Corene wails. "Melidia, wherever you are, save me from this place!" She's backed up against the wall. The prisoners in adjacent cells reach through the bars toward her, spitting blood through gaps in their gums where teeth used to be.

"Finally!" the Princess sobs as I reach her cell door. She rushes to me, dodging an arm coming through the bars to grab at her. "Let me out at once."

Once I have tied rope around her wrists, she runs ahead so fast that I have to jerk her back. The prisoners squall and shake as we pass. Their eyes are empty, faces oozing where their mouths opened too wide and the bloodless skin tore like paper.

"They are dead," I murmur.

"You think?" The Princess charges up the stairs.

I slam the dungeon door and drag her to the Commander's chambers in the temple, my mind cycling back through everything I witnessed. The prisoners were coated in Magic like everyone else. We left them there, forgot about them, and the worst happened.

It is the first thing out of my mouth when the Commander opens his door to me. "Commander. The dead have risen."

His silver eyes look duller than I remember. Flat, like marbles, with shadows underneath that I have never seen before. He focuses on me and his lips twist down. Glancing around, he says, "Where is Ellze? If some dead are alive again, there will be others." He pushes past me, not even noticing I have the Princess.

I do not know what to do with her now, but I am tired of her incessant begging to see her father.

Inside the King's room, Corene lunges at his bed. "Dad!"

The King groans and lifts one arm. She clasps his hand as he gazes upon her, his strained, sagging face morphing into a smile.

"Sweet daughter." He reaches forward and strokes her red hair. "What have they done to you?"

She glances back at me. "I've . . . been all right."

"Have you heard news?" The King's eyes are closing. "About Bayled? Or Nul se Lan?"

The Princess slowly shakes her head. "None."

"You must get out of here." The King looks at me. Until this moment his mind has been elsewhere, disassociated from his body. Now his blue eyes are alert and piercing and I sense he has finally seen me. "This is going to go wrong. It'll all go wrong and I don't want you here when it does, daughter."

I should quiet him—the last thing I need is for the Princess to panic. But what could be worth more panic than being trapped in a cage with the vicious dead?

"I don't know what to do, Dad," Corene says, her voice breaking with tears.

"Find Forgren." The King's eyes widen for just a moment, the whites streaked with red. "He knows." With that, he falls back asleep. His rumbling, congested snores fill up the room.

Corene kneels by the side of his bed and lays her head on his lap. It would be a sorrowful scene if I cared for either of them.

A war horn tears through the air. I leave the Princess at her father's side long enough to poke my head out the door. "Was that . . . ?" I ask the soldiers there.

"The rest of the force," one says, nodding. "They have arrived."

Sapphire doesn't return that night to sleep on the floor. We've ceased to be useful, so they've abandoned us. Just like everyone else in my life.

Parsifal keeps his door closed. I knew he was attracted to me—he's never hidden that, and I've never felt guilty using it. But I didn't know he he harbored something more than lust for me. I've misunderstood.

Since I have nothing better to do, I start rearranging the room. I have to remember my injuries as I move, but I work up a little sweat after all this time in dungeons with no exercise.

I'm taking out the dresser drawers and setting them on the floor when the door opens. The cart wheels in. I didn't realize how hungry I'd gotten, and I rush over.

It's empty.

"Percy!" I shout. The cart backs away, pressing itself up against the door. Parsifal pokes his head out of his room. "Look." I point at the empty cart where it's cowering like a frightened dog.

"It looks positively ashamed." Parsifal trots in and peers down at it. "I always thought the food just . . . happened. Maybe Sapphire makes it?"

"And they decided to stop today?"

He narrows his eyes. "Maybe you shouldn't have kissed them without asking."

I snort. "They were all for it."

"Well, you did *something* to get us punished like this."

I whirl on him. "Maybe *you* did something by bringing wine in the first place. Maybe getting Sapphire so thoroughly brimmed over that they couldn't walk is a crime in their culture."

The cart slides back out of the room and the door closes behind it. Without replying, Parsifal returns to his room in a huff.

Afternoon comes and goes. I wish I had something to break, someone to fight. Starving—what a way to go out. If this is how I feel after only a day, what's next? I shake my head. I can't think about Corene suffering, hiding in the crushing dark, or it'll be too much for the widening cracks in my soul to stand. A few candlestick-hours later, Parsifal pokes his head through my door again. "Food yet?"

I throw a pillow at him but completely miss. "What do you think?"

"Still?" For the first time, worry settles over him. "Maybe they forgot."

"Maybe they're angry." But that's not like Sapphire. Or is it? I don't know them at all. I've never seen them upset before. Did I twist things up that badly with a kiss?

BWOOOOOOHHH! The blow of a war horn shakes the very walls of the castle.

I rush to the window. Down below, the gates of Four Halls are opening.

On the other side stands a horde. "Parsifal!" I duck down under the windowsill, just my eyes peering out. "Look."

He kneels next to me as the shining silver helmets of the troops pour through the gate. A parade of animals in saddles follows: a lion, a one-headed bear, rows of elephants.

"What's wrong with that bear?" Parsifal whispers.

"It's a mutant."

Then come much bigger creatures—no, monsters—I've never seen before. As big as four elephants, they have great square heads like lizards and bare brown flesh.

I sink to my knees as the elven host pours into the courtyard. It's so much more overwhelming than I could've ever imagined. I feel the size of an ant in the face of that horde. There's no defeating it. No force of humans could ever hope to win.

Which means Bayled and Nul se Lan are dead.

Cold regret slithers through me. My hopes of being Queen die with Bayled.

I shouldn't lie to myself, though. It's about more than my dreams. We were children together. So many of my moments with Corene and Parsifal were also Bayled moments. Horseback rides behind Four Halls. Swimming at the lake. Sweet, honorable, gullible Bayled . . . what an absolute waste. He didn't deserve that drunk old King sending him off to die for nothing. Now the Kingdom is over, and there'll be nothing left to rule when those monsters are finished with us. The lords will surrender, and Parsifal and I will go to the room where everyone else goes eventually, and suffer some horrible fate—if Sapphire doesn't let us starve first.

Gray, sunken faces with beady eyes, enormous ears, and sharpened teeth. My head swims. The faces flicker in my mind's eye—and then fade into Sapphire's face. Beautiful. Kind. Quiet. Perfect.

Without their help, we're definitely going to die.

My chest is collapsing. Everything hurts. "Thelia," I hear Parsifal say. "Breathe. You need to breathe." But I can't. My lungs convulse so hard with sobs that air can't get in or out. He reaches for the goblet by my bed, but it's empty. I curl up in a ball on the floor.

Parsifal leans over me. "Take deep breaths. Look at me." I open my eyes again. Parsifal, trying so hard to smile. Here for me, yet again, when the world has shifted upside-down.

He holds me until I'm able to breathe again, and I close my eyes against the sound of our heartbeats.

PARSIFAL

We can't keep out the sound. Not even the Magic seal around our window muffles the thousands of voices, nor the thunderous grumbling of the great monsters. Thelia's still shaking, but she's breathing. We sit on her bed, leaned up against the pillows.

Daylight fades into night. Thelia's eyes close and she slides lower on the bed until her head comes to rest on my chest. Flames kindle under my clothes where she's touching me. I settle my hands in her soft, short hair, which feels like rabbit fur. I start running my fingers through it.

"Your nails feel good," she whispers. "Don't stop."

I'm so hungry, and even more tired, but I won't ever stop.

The cart returns in the morning, still empty. It wheels around the middle of the room and Thelia scrambles out of bed, still awkward with her bandages, but not enough to restrain her. "Why?" she roars. The cart backs up against the door.

"Don't shout at it." I lean down in front of the cart. "You don't have any control over the food, do you?" The cart wobbles. I think that's a *no*. "So Sapphire *was* making all our meals. Maybe they're in trouble?"

The cart does one more frightened lap around the room,

then zooms back out the door, which seals back up behind it. Thelia says nothing and goes to sit in front of the fire, curling up in a chair with her arms around her knees. With frigid winter winds beating the side of the castle, the fire burns all day long now.

"I'm sorry," she says. "I did this."

I shake my head. "I should be apologizing for how I reacted. You were simply trying to get us out of here, and I threw a tantrum."

She hides her face between her knees. "Th-there was more to it, Percy. Yes, I want to escape. With all my soul I miss riding, I miss the sky, I miss grass." I hear her swallow a few times. "But that kiss was more. I needed it."

"So?" I ask. Thelia stares at me. "There's no shame in following your desire where it takes you. I feel it too, you know."

Her voice chokes up. "You?"

I squeeze her shoulder. "Me."

"But we should hate Sapphire. Once, I wanted nothing more than to kill them. But touching them felt . . . amazing." She looks disgusted. "More. I'm still thinking about more."

"Please don't berate yourself, Theels," I say. "We're prisoners here, and Sapphire is our only connection to the outside— to a hope of escaping here alive. It's all tied up together. All three of us are contorted and stretched to impossible positions to fit our roles. There are no right decisions, only decisions that we choose to make." I squeeze her shoulders and she lets me. "Perhaps someday, when we're free, we can try to untangle the damned knot this has made of us."

She nods and swallows, letting her head sink against mine.

When. I said it with a confidence I don't feel, but in this moment, I need her to feel it.

BAYLED

We're on the third day of constant snowfall when Captain Tarkness brings her horse to a halt. "We're here."

Ahead, the trees thin out into a clearing paved with untouched white snow. Sasel does a sweep with one hand for anyone who might be hiding. "There's a biylar bear," she says, pointing to the other side of the meadow. "That's all."

I visited Antonin Bellisare's brick mansion a few times when we were younger, for fancy parties with egregious amounts of imported wine. Then Antonin's money ran out and Parsifal spent all his time at Four Halls, so we had no reason to visit the estate.

The roads and carriage circle are all buried by deep snow, and it's slow going as our horses pick through it. Standing before the outer wall, Captain Tarkness raises her hand and focuses. A small ball of glittering energy forms in her hand. She peers at Sasel. "Do you feel that?" she asks.

Sasel nods. "It's thick here."

The ball swells and, after a moment, bursts into flame. The captain reels one arm back and hurls the ball of fire into the wall—tearing a massive hole through the middle.

So this is what real Magic looks like.

"That was amazing," says Harged.

We climb through the hole and into the courtyard. The mansion's front doors are locked, too, as a final annoyance. Hopefully Antonin won't discover that we blew them apart to get in.

Inside, the high-ceilinged rooms are filled with ghosts. Portraits on the walls. Granite busts. Sculptures depicting legends I never learned about. We take the hallway under the main stairs past room after room.

There it is—the inset door with the rubbed bronze knob. I twist the doorknob, but the door doesn't budge. Captain Tarkness prepares to blow it open, but Red raises a hand to stop her "Don't want to risk damaging what's inside." He pulls a hairpin out of his ponytail, jams one end into the keyhole, and fiddles with it.

The door groans as it opens, and a wave of dust greets us. We both cough before we can move forward into the darkness. I find a torch and light it to reveal stairs.

We descend into a familiar cellar, where the passage opens up into a sprawling room: the Museum. A chariot stands against one wall, propped up by fake horses made from steel and gold. Four Frefoisian nobles, their wax faces astonishingly lifelike, wear old eastern clothes—high breeches, billowing necklines, long-tailed coats, and enormous wigs. Jewelry that must be worth as much as the mansion itself hangs from their necks, wrists, and ears. I know all about the sculptures and vases and masks now, from when I desperately hoped to impress Thelia and Parsifal—not realizing it was impossible.

The Baron quirks an eyebrow as we pass. "This whole place is obscene. They wouldn't have been poor if they sold any of this."

I snort. "I wouldn't dare suggest that to Antonin's face."

The Baron stops in his tracks and laughs. "This must be what we're here for."

Another set of mannequins stands on a pedestal. They're dressed in the familiar crimson reds, deep blues, and shimmering golds the Northern Republic prefers. Behind them stands an old Northern carriage—the fancy kind studded with copper that the Prime Minister or her family would use when traveling.

I begin stripping the mannequins. First I slide the long red coat over my own shoulders. It's an older style, one that not even my father would have worn. It has quite a lot of tassels but it fits me perfectly. We have five more outfits—some brown women's trousers, a wooly gold shirt, and even more coats and hats.

"This idea of yours may work after all." Red puts on one of the short blue vests rimmed with embroidered gold, and it fits his chest snugly. He glances at one of the many mirrors hanging on the wall. "I look fantastic in this."

I chuckle. "Everyone should wear Northern fashion."

SAPPHIRE

Every time I close my eyes, I can see Parsifal's face collapsing. The memory is seared into my skin. I did not mean to come between them, to hurt them. My warm heart of Magic aches.

Jealousy. I know its name, but never before has it had a face. If only I could wish away that moment, undo the damage I did. At least apologize—but I cannot return.

Ellze was right. I should have stayed away. I said so many things I should not have, and my involvement has worsened everything.

There is so much else to do as our troops set out for the new settlement site to begin building. Others erect shelters in the nearby woods for the elephants and orkuks. The fresh wave of Magickers are put to work siphoning off the Magic flooding out of the well. With the relocation site in motion, we begin to clean. For the first time, I believe we can regain control of this spiraling disaster.

A disaster for which, I am loath to admit, we are partially responsible.

I let the horses out into the paddock and watch as they run and run, thrilled to stretch their legs. Zylion and Ferah find me there after Ferah has done her stint on the castle wall, burning off Magic—but there is more than we could ever burn. Zylion's pulled his long purple hair back in a high ponytail, and Ferah stands with her arms crossed, light from the window making her white hair look like a shimmering halo. "The Commander wants to see us," Zylion says.

With the main host's squadron leaders in attendance, there are too many of us to fit into the temple, so the Commander assembles us in the banquet hall. The newcomers are easy to spot because they refuse to sit in any chairs or touch any objects that humans might have touched. They will grow tired of the effort this takes soon enough.

Commander Valya sits in the wine-stained purple chair that once belonged to the King. He looks at home in it, hands spread out across the cushioned arms. "Our operation faces yet another hurdle," he says. His voice is unusually weak, and we all lean in to hear. "When we arrived, we severely underestimated how much Magic had pervaded the humans' bodies."

Ferah steps forward. "We must be rid of the corpses somehow. The longer we leave them in the dungeon, the more powerful they grow. Magic has animated them, and Magic can free them."

Commander Valya nods. "Indeed. We must burn them."

"But Commander," Zylion says, shaking his head, "they are so drenched in Magic that the last one we burned proceeded to explode. A jail cell is gone."

Before the Commander can respond, Ellze says, "Then take them somewhere the explosion cannot do any damage." Commander Valya does not reprimand him, as I would have expected. Instead, he nods.

At the end of the meeting, Ellze leans down to whisper something in his uncle's ear, and they both chuckle. This Ellze is different from my childhood friend. Perhaps I am jealous— perhaps not. But I do not think I like him anymore.

THELIA

Parsifal sits in front of the fire, silently reading. Neither of us has the energy to do much else. Even talking makes me tired, so I just look—mostly at Parsifal. At his soft, milky human skin. The wrinkles at the side of his mouth and nostrils that make his dimples move as he scans the page. His nose is flat, of course. The thick eyebrows high above his eyes crease as he thinks.

He's beautiful, in his way. Familiar. The one who's always been by my side. I used to think that person was Corene, but that fantasy is gone.

The elves must have found her, and that's why Sapphire doesn't need us anymore. I can't decide if I should feel relieved or angry or grateful. I'm too jumbled up, like Parsifal said. Attempting to untangle that knot might kill me.

Corene. I hope she's not still starving in the dark. Mother would be ashamed of me, pitying her—but no one deserves to die in a hole in the wall.

"What?" asks Parsifal. I didn't realize I was staring at him again. Parsifal—the only one who never betrayed me, not once. No lies stand between us.

I don't speak, just reach out to touch the side of his face. At first, he jerks away. I don't move my hand, and slowly, he lets me rest my fingers on the parts of him that have made him the subject of endless mockery. I wouldn't be here without Parsifal at my side, keeping my feet on the ground.

His brown eyes are riveted to mine. "Thelia," he whispers, and the sound of my name on his lips stirs something I've never felt before—a seeping warmth at the base of me. "Can I kiss you?"

I breathe the word "yes" before I think about it, and he presses his lips to mine.

It's something I've thought about only in my wildest, most guilty fantasies. Now that it's here, I feel . . . awake. I kissed Red, of course. Well, he kissed me. It felt nice, but it wasn't like this. I've been lit on fire.

My tongue presses at Parsifal's lips of its own accord. Wanting. Asking for more. I could eat him, and thank Melidia, he lets me in.

It's an entire new world. My arms wind around his neck, and his around my middle. I feel contained, like my unruly, escaping edges are finally tucked in and I'm no longer spilling out across the floor, *drip-drip-drip*, until there's nothing left. I'm staying right here.

I don't know what comes next, but Parsifal does. One of his hands takes mine, our fingers laced together. But the spaces between his fingers are too tight and it hurts my hand, so I pull it back.

Parsifal withdraws, his face collapsing with anguish as he

reads my reaction completely wrong. "I'm so sorry." He looks like he's been hit across the face. "I didn't . . ."

"Percy." I crawl closer. It's my turn to kiss him now. I know I'm sloppy and drooling, but he kisses me back anyway, and I can taste his relief. He takes my hands back and holds them inside his palms this time.

I press my body against his. Through my thin nightgown, I can feel everything—and he can certainly feel all of me. We pull away, both of us breathing hard. His pants are straining. "I'm sorry," he says, trying to cover it.

I'll admit the bulge in his purple trousers is frightening— I don't know what's underneath. I've heard words like *snake*, *whip*, *dragon*, *rod*. Hard things, frightening things with teeth lie between a man's legs, or so Mother said. I've never wanted anything to do with the snakes or rods.

My chest is hot as the fire in the hearth, and it burns all the way to the space between my own legs. I want to know what's in those trousers, begging to escape.

"Show me," I say, pushing the confidence into my voice.

Parsifal grins. But instead of reaching for his trousers, he lifts his shirt up over his head. Underneath, he's bare. He flinches when my cold hand touches his warm flesh, and he presses his hands to mine.

We slide across the floor closer to the fire, and he points at me with his chin. "Your turn."

Oh, I suppose it is. I slide my nightgown off my shoulders, my exposed nipples poking up like tiny caps on a tower roof. He leans forward and wraps his lips around one and it's the most wonderful feeling. I lean back and can't help the sound I make.

"Good?" he asks.

"I think so."

He laughs and goes for the other one, but I stop him. "Your turn."

The trousers, at last, are gone. Feeling first is a lot easier than seeing. He's soft—the dense, curly hair below is plush and welcoming. And below that, his erect penis is soft, too. A nice kind of soft—not awkward or wrinkled. How does it do that? Be hard and soft at the same time?

The rug underneath us is coarse against my bare skin, but Parsifal draws me into his arms, as close as he's ever been before, and I forget all about it. He licks one of his fingers, and then his hand finds its way down between my legs, where no hand has ever been but my own. I must look terrified, because Parsifal chuckles a little. "It will feel good. Promise."

I unclench the iron grip of my thighs and his wet finger dives between them. And demons, he's right. I'm biting the flesh of his neck before I can stop myself, because otherwise, who knows what I'd sound like?

"Good?" he asks, and I can feel his face smiling against my throat.

I bite harder and whisper, "Good."

I go to touch him again, but he shakes his head. "I think it would make me let off too soon." So I don't, as much as I want to feel that soft, wonderful thing under my hand again. It's not a snake. It's just Parsifal.

He nudges my knees and I let my legs open. He tries to push inside me, but immediately it feels tense and awkward. I want it, though. I can feel how ready I am, but for some reason, my body won't cooperate. My face gets flaming hot.

"Here." Parsifal shifts me around so he's lying behind me, our bodies flush together, looking into the fire. I don't like that

I can't see his face, but his arms wrap around me. He touches me again down there, lathering me up the way I do with my hair in the bath.

It takes more tries than I can count before I feel him nudge into me and it works. Finally, we're there. Together. I finally let myself make a sound. "That's a good noise," he breathes into my ear. He doesn't move for a long time, his hands stroking my flesh, playing quietly with me. Distracting me from the discomfort.

The pressure there breathes, pulses. Somehow it's so good. When I've relaxed again, he moves. Slowly. So slowly.

I stop holding my voice back.

CHAPTER 15

SAPPHIRE

I descend back into the dungeon with Ferah, Zylion, and Ellze. We open the first cell where a former human waits, covered in dried blood, howling and raking his nails against the metal.

First, Ferah binds him with threads of Magic. Once he's restrained, she taps him three times on the temple—but he doesn't collapse. Tearing his way out of his bindings, the corpse lunges at us, and Ferah leaps back.

Ellze hurls the mindless creature against the stone wall. Bones break with a *snap, crack*. Ellze laughs at Ferah's horrified face before he kicks in the creature's skull. It falls over, stunned but still functioning, even with a new concave head shape.

I have never seen him exhibit such cruelty, and I have a feeling he will not reserve it for only the undead.

We each drag a corpse up the stairs, avoiding the teeth. They recoil from the light streaming in through the windows, but only momentarily, before they strain their ropes and tear their rotting flesh.

More Jaguars appear, rolling decrepit barrels we found in the courtyard. We shove one of the risen inside each barrel, and Ferah seals the tops closed. Inside, the creatures bang and screech.

Together we roll them through the courtyard, out the front gate of the castle, through Ferah's Magic shield, and down the abandoned main road—until we reach the outer walls of the city. Off in the distance lie abandoned houses and farms; but here it's empty save for grass and mud.

Ferah kicks one of the barrels away, and the monster inside howls. The rest of us step back as she begins gathering great shining ropes of Magic, curling them and looping them and bundling them up until her arms are full of glowing, pulsing energy.

"Stand back!" she shouts, and we duck behind the high city walls. We're peering out through the gate as she hurls the sparking ball of Magic toward the first barrel.

The explosion rocks the ground. Pieces of stone crumble off the wall and fall onto our heads. Ferah slaps her hands together. "Bring me the next one."

I am ready to hurl my guts out a window again by the time we finish. Sleep does not find me easily as I remember the bleeding, skeletal faces of the inmates as we blew them to bits. In my nightmares I find Thelia and Parsifal among them.

The next day, Commander Valya hands down a new edict: no human may die from now on. The density of Magic in and around them makes them too volatile. We are expected to keep our distance, even from the living. Should they experience any powerful stimulus, any sudden upset, the results could be disastrous. If this operation goes astray, risen humans may not be the only thing that explodes in ash and dust.

I am too afraid to return to my humans. The fear is new and strange and tastes like something rotten. Even if they do not hate me now—which they surely do—I cannot see them become those *things*. I imagine Thelia stuffed into a barrel, and Parsifal's eyes rupturing as the Magic inside him ignites, unable to bear the confines of his flesh. I would rather die than watch them burst.

PARSIFAL

I've always wanted this, but long ago I resigned myself to letting her go.

Thelia Finegarden's ambitions have always ruled our relationship. The most I could ever hope for was to be one of her advisors. Never her consort, or even a secret lover. A Queen like her—a true leader—would never waste time so frivolously.

Even in my fantasies, I didn't dream it would be like this with her. That it *could* be like this, with anyone. Yet here I am, still full of the smell of her, the feel of her, the taste of her. Is she asleep? I can't see her face from behind, so I run my fingers through her short hair. She doesn't move. Asleep, then. I love her hair like this.

As I start to drift off, my bare skin chafing on the rug and the orange flames dancing in front of us, I'm reminded of when we were just children, lying with the dogs in front of the fire. When we fell asleep curled up with them, and only Thelia's nightmares broke the spell.

I'm awoken by a grinding sound, stone scraping on stone. A doorway is opening in the wall. How did we miss it before?

I leap up, throwing a blanket over Thelia, and scramble for my clothes. I'd rather nobody know that her backside has been pressed against me all night.

As I'm pulling my trousers on, a shock of orange-red hair appears in the gap. The Princess's face slides through.

"Corene?" Thelia's voice comes from behind me. She lunges across the room at Corene, wrapped only in a blanket, and throws her arms around her cousin before she can emerge all the way.

"Thelia!" Corene's crying when they finally release each other. "You're alive. I didn't think . . ." Her voice breaks into tears again. She's thinner, and her face is broken-out and pasty.

"Alive," I say. "Though we haven't had a meal in a few days."

"Percy." She's smiling through her tears. "It's so good to see you."

"You as well, Princess." I peer at the hole in the wall behind her—a place I thought we'd surely checked. "How did you find us? Have you been hiding all this time?"

She shakes her head. "No. An elf caught me trying to find food. I was tossed in the dungeon."

"Oh, no." Thelia cradles Corene's hand, as if we can undo everything that's happened since we left her in the secret place. "They put you there too?"

I can't imagine fragile, spoiled Corene confined to stone floors and an overflowing chamber pot with criminals reaching through the bars.

"Everyone was dead," she says, and I can barely understand her through the tears. "The long ears just ignored them. But that one elf kept saying, 'It's not my job. I can't do anything.' When the last prisoner finally died—you've smelled nothing like it." I have, actually. "And then the bodies started to move."

I'm listening again.

"They got up and screeched like animals, trying to tear through the bars to get to me. I thought the ones in the cell next to mine would kill me. Where there were two to a cell, they'd bite and rip at each other. I was sure I'd ended up on the demon plane."

Thelia wraps her arms around Corene again, and the Princess cries into her shoulder. I pat her back. "You made it out, though."

"The elf came for me. Took me to see my father. He looks so awful." Corene has to keep stopping to sob. "I ended up back in my old room again. Stupid long ears—they never did find the secret place."

So that's how she got here.

"I waited until I was alone and decided I'd try to escape again. But while I was finding my way around in the dark—no candles left, you know—I heard your voices."

She glances at me and I wonder what she heard. "I'm glad you're all right," I offer.

Her face crumbles. "Sure, I am. But my father . . . He's dying." Thelia and I exchange a look. "They could stop it, but they don't. We need to get out of here. Once the long ears are done with their little operation, they're going to finish what they started."

It sounds like Morgaun's grim fantasy. I grab her arm. "What do you mean?"

She pulls away in disbelief that I'd even dare. "I know how these things go. Invasions end in blood. We have to get out now and find Nul while we can, before we die and rise again and the long ears get rid of us too."

Nul, not Bayled. Very interesting.

"I agree that we need to escape," I tell Corene. "And I have an idea. Thelia, you'd better get dressed." While Thelia returns to her room, I walk over to a wall. "Hey there, friend," I say, tapping it with a knuckle. "I have something yummy for you to eat."

No response. When Thelia comes back, wearing her one remaining clean gown, I hear Corene whisper to her, "Has he gone all the way up the parapets and over the top?"

Thelia makes a shushing sound. "Wait."

I gesture again at the wall. "I know there are a lot of demands on your time." I pick up a vase, and Corene yelps as I hurl it to the floor. It shatters into a hundred pieces.

"What are you doing?" she snaps. I hold a finger to my lips as the broom against the wall sits up suddenly. Corene shrinks back when it bustles over, sweeps the broken pieces into a little pile, and brushes it toward the wall.

The stones grind and move apart to make room for the mouth. It swells up, tongue sliding out. Corene starts screaming and I pinch her arm. "You need to stop, Princess."

The broom launches the pieces of broken vase, and the tongue laps them up. The bits are smashed between the white teeth and swallowed. Before it can vanish, I say, "Wait. If I feed you more stuff, will you help us get out of this room?"

The tongue jumps back out and the corners of the mouth rise. "Is it smiling?" Corene asks. "What is happening right now?"

"Just watch and be quiet," Thelia says.

The mouth starts to move across the wall, and the stones shuffle and part to make space. Once it arrives on the far side of my room, it stops and opens wide. Wider and wider, teeth spreading apart like cobblestones on a broken city street, until it's as high as our necks. The tongue lolls out, unrolling across the floor like a rug. Then it flaps—beckoning us in.

"Absolutely not," Corene says. Thelia ignores her and goes first. Corene grabs her wrist. "It'll eat you."

"So?" Thelia shakes her off. "How is that worse than starving to death here?" Into the mouth she goes, ducking under the protruding teeth. The tongue wobbles as she walks over it, like her feet are tickling it.

I go next, my slippers squishing on the tongue. As I crest the teeth and descend into the darkness, I hear Corene shout, "Wait for me!"

I turn and offer her my hand. She seizes it, charging past me into the depths. The mouth closes behind us, and we're entombed in black.

"I can't see!" Corene shrieks. It's not wet in here, as I'd feared—nor is it warm. It's cold and dry and reminds me of the secret place. Maybe that's where we are. "What have we done?" I hear Corene ask. "We'll be eaten like that vase, Percy."

Suddenly, the tongue under our feet moves. It pushes me forward and I stumble, landing on my hands. Ahead of us, a spot of light appears, growing and growing until the tongue jolts again—and launches us forward in a tangle of limbs.

Through the opening we go. I land partially on top of Thelia, and Corene topples over both of us. Thelia yells, "Get off me!"

We all climb to our feet. I spin around just as the mouth closes up, tongue and teeth vanishing. There's a *shloop* sound as it shrinks to nothingness, and the stones around it rearrange themselves.

I look around. We're in Corene's room, right next door.

"I asked to get out of the room." I touch the wall. "It took me very literally." At least we're not out in the hall, where any passing elf could discover us.

"Well, we're alive, and only covered in a little slobber." Thelia lifts her shoes, sniffs them, and makes a face.

The mouth opened a passage through one wall, from one room to another. Maybe we can keep going, one wall at a time—pass into the hall, and then into the next room, on and on until we make our way into the belly of the castle.

I dash across Corene's room and yank a painting off the wall. "Percy! What are you doing?"

"I have to find out more." I drop the painting to the floor and smash my foot through it. There's no reason to suffer in ugliness, but what if ugliness is the end to your suffering?

"Stop!" Corene races over to stop me, but it's too late. The stones grind and groan, and the tongue darts out again, panting eagerly.

"Hold on." I hold the shards of the painting away like a tease. "Can you get us out of the castle?"

The tongue retracts and the mouth closes up, the lips pursing.

"I don't think it can," Thelia says, picking up a piece of the picture frame and kneeling in front of the mouth. "It *is* the castle, after all." The tongue whips out and she drops the piece in. It's chewed up and swallowed. "Hey friend," she says. "Can you get us down to the sewers? Then we can find our own way out."

It licks its lips, thinking. I toss it another piece of the painting, but it still frowns.

Corene stands up. She throws one of the pieces in herself and the mouth gives her a jolly grin. "If we get to the Pit on our own, can you drop us into the sewers below it?"

The mouth eats up and smiles again. "I'd take that as a yes," I say.

THELIA

"How do we get to the Pit?" Parsifal says. His energy is high and furious. With Corene's help, we can finally escape.

"When you left me . . ." Corene turns her head away. "And then never came back, I thought I was going to die."

Shame rushes through me. I should have tried harder to find her, to contact her.

"I had to leave or starve to death. I knew there was a service tunnel that the servants used to bring me hot meals straight from the kitchen—so I took it hoping I could find food. But that's when that horrid blue elf caught me." She spits.

"Sapphire," I say without thinking.

Corene throws me a sharp look. "You know its name?"

"*Their* name."

Corene rounds on me. "*They*, cousin?" she snaps. "*They* are not human. They are monsters. You've seen how they've treated us!"

Maybe some of the long ears are—especially Sapphire's commander. "But Sapphire—" I begin.

"Is no different from the rest!" Corene peers at me, suspicious now. "You've been seduced by a beautiful face."

She's wrong. Sapphire is beautiful—absolutely. But they are so much more than that: shy, curious, and sharp-witted. I may resent Sapphire—maybe hate them for abandoning us—but I can still appreciate them as someone who mattered to me. Someone I wanted. Someone I kissed, and liked kissing.

"So these service tunnels," I say, ignoring her. "You think we can use them to get to the Pit?"

"Yes," she huffs. "And good thing. I need to get you out of here before they can brainwash you. Maybe we'll find Nul out there. He'll want to stop the long ears as much as I do."

Corene stomps off into her adjoining room to get some traveling clothes and boots. The moment she's out of earshot I whisper to Parsifal, "She wants to find *Nul*, not Bayled."

He frowns. "Makes sense to me. He's heir to the throne. The Klissen has soldiers and defenses. It's the perfect place to establish a new seat of power."

A seat that won't be mine. If Nul se Lan becomes King of some new, mutant Holy Kingdom—a merging of the Klissen and the remnants of our own people—with Corene as his Queen . . .

There's no space for me in the South. Or anywhere.

"We don't know what happened to the army," Parsifal whispers. "Nul and Bayled might both be dead. Maybe we join up with one of the sworn lords. Or return to Frefois! Dad's old friends would welcome us."

Everything he says sounds so impossible. All I want is to make it out of Four Halls alive. I want to see trees and walk on dirt and feel like a human again. Where we go, what alliance we build, whether the stupid crown goes to Nul se Lan and Corene . . . I feel tired.

And poor, foolish Bayled, caught up in all of it. "Do you

really care anymore about all that, Percy?" I ask wearily. "Because I don't."

He looks me up and down, as if there's been some mistake and I've become someone else in front of his very eyes. "Are you ill?"

I shake my head. "I'm just exhausted."

Corene stomps back through the door with coats and boots. "Can't guarantee they'll fit," she says, dropping them at our feet. We change our shoes and layer up to prepare for the winter world outside Four Halls, then duck into the secret place. We don't speak as we trail along behind Corene in the darkness, each of us holding onto the other's shirt so we don't get separated. She walks with perfect confidence, even though she can't see. She must've spent a lot of time in here.

Corene stops abruptly, bends, and lifts a trap door in the floor. "Service tunnel," she says and disappears into it. I follow, feet first, feeling around with my toes to find the ladder. Down and down, what feels like a hundred rungs, and suddenly—hard ground.

The passageway is wider here, but just ahead it ends in a flat wall that I can only make out because of the faint light around the outline of a door. Corene feels along it, then pulls on something. There's a creak and it opens.

She peers through. "Clear," she whispers. We follow her out, and I don't recognize the empty room we're standing in now.

"Servants' quarters," Corene says. "The Pit is down the hall." She pushes the door closed with an awful *bang!* as the stones snap back into place. "This way," Corene says. We run, trying to keep our footfalls light, but we're still human.

The familiar odor of old shit and piss greets us in the latrine. A stone pool in the center of the room overflows with brown, steaming slop. Now that I know what I'm looking at, I can't fathom how I missed before that it was a collapsed sewer pipe—a relic of a time long gone, when the Holy Kingdom and the dwarves cooperated. We should be standing right above the sewer system.

Behind us, I hear footsteps. "Someone's coming," I whisper.

"They must be coming to empty chamberpots," Parsifal says. Our footsteps make *slap, slap* sounds through the muck. The distant footsteps stop, and the voices rise. I know that sing-song language. They've heard us.

"Parsifal." I grab his arm. "Call the castle. Now."

He looks around the room, brown eyes wide. "Nothing to feed it." He sounds frantic.

"Where's the big mouth, Percy?" Corene hisses.

Running feet echo down the hall. Parsifal hits the wall. "I'm so stupid. Why didn't I think to bring something to feed it?"

I glance backward. If they find us trying to escape, Sapphire can't possibly save us.

PARSIFAL

Spinning around, I search the Pit for anything I could offer the castle in return for letting us through, even a leftover chamberpot.

There's nothing except shit. I've never been this foolish. "Please," I whisper, as the long ears' voices echo off the walls just down the hall. "Help us get to those sewers and I promise

I'll never mistreat another stone as long as I live." I kneel down and press my palms to the floor. "Please."

Something inside me, down in a place in my chest I've never felt before, starts to vibrate. The feet are thundering. "Parsifal, they're in the room," Thelia whispers. She presses her lips to the side of my face. "I'm sorry. It's over."

I'm hot everywhere, so hot I think I'll faint. "Percy." Corene sounds horrified. "You're glowing."

The elves shout as they sprint toward us. "Well, come on then," I say to the castle, in a voice that comes from deep inside me.

The stones of the floor rise up, like a wave of ocean water. White teeth leap up over our heads, and the elves stop in their tracks on the opposite edge of the Pit. An enormous tongue thrusts out from a growing hole in the floor. In one swoop, it scoops up all three of us.

Everything goes dark. The shouting abruptly vanishes. My arms find their way around Thelia, squeezing her against me.

"Percy," Corene grunts. "Why are you hugging me?"

Before I can answer, a hole opens—below us this time—and the soft tongue under my feet releases us, shoving us all toward the chasm.

Down I fall. I land on top of Corene, who lets out a pained yelp. I look up only to find Thelia falling on top of me. Then the mouth closes, and everything disappears into darkness.

The smell that assaults me is even worse than in the Pit upstairs. I shove Corene out of the way and fleg right there. Soon I hear Thelia doing it too. Our stomachs were empty, but my abdomen contracts and forces out fluid anyway.

When I manage to stand up, I can't see my own hands. Thelia lets out a frustrated noise. "I can't believe we don't have a candle."

"If we had, all that would've been a lot easier," I say. I shut my eyes, then open them again. There's no difference in how pitch-black it is. Up above, the sound of armored boots and shouting is muffled. They can find a way down if we give them time. We can't give them time, but we can't keep moving without light.

That thing in my chest, that suffocating heat—can I find it again? I think of one word: *light.* "Won't you help one more time?" I ask out loud.

"What did you say?" Corene asks. I ignore her, thinking of a candle, of Sapphire's little bobbing Magic light.

Suddenly, Corene lets out a screech. When I open my eyes, pink light fills the yawning sewer pipe. "Melidia be damned." She sounds as if this is her last moment on Helyanda. "They found us."

Sapphire's pink wisp circles the air over our heads, chittering with excitement. I can make out a high curved ceiling made of a few huge, perfectly smooth stones that fit together as one. Behind us lie the collapsed remains of the sewage pipe that has become the Pit. Ahead, an endless tunnel, filled with human waste that could be hundreds of cycles old.

"The wisp won't hurt us," Thelia assures Corene. Overhead, the voices grow more numerous.

"Run," I say. The little pink light happily illuminates the path ahead of us, like this is all a big game.

"Do you know where we're going?" Thelia asks as we scramble over centuries-old human waste.

"This drain should lead to the moat," Corene says.

We keep going, the muck making a sucking sound with each step. I have to yank my foot up to withdraw and press hard to move forward. We trudge through darkness for what feels like the rest of my life, and I start to breathe hard—only through my mouth. I haven't heard any noises except our footfalls.

The wisp starts to bob excitedly. A pinprick of light appears far ahead. "There!" Thelia shouts.

She rushes onward. I follow, passing Corene as she slogs through the muck. "Wait!" she calls after us. But we can't be stopped. The light expands as we approach. My lungs seize, sucking in the putrid air.

Thelia comes to an abrupt halt, just a shadow surrounded by a circle of bright light. I stop inches shy of careening off the edge of the stone pipe, out into the rushing water below.

Blue sky. A few fluffy white clouds. The moat beneath us. Ahead, the rooftops and walls of the city, stretching off into the snowy hills beyond.

No more walls. A limitless expanse. "There it is," Thelia whispers. "Freedom."

I gaze down at the fifty-foot drop. From here on, I don't know what we'll do or where we'll go. But we'll survive together.

BAYLED

We follow the Bellisares' private road toward Melidihan, with Halrendar hitched to the creaky old carriage and me in the driver's seat. Before we meet the Low Road, we pass a set of tracks I don't recognize. "These feet are much bigger than a human's," the Baron says, crouching down to examine one print.

Long ears. What they're doing out here, though, I don't know.

It's a short journey up the bumping, rocky Low Road. The hilly grasslands turn flat and muddy, until over the next ridge, the high stone walls of the city appear. It's strange to see it again after all this time. It's smaller than I remember, and the construction looks cheap.

Beyond the wall and the sinking rooftops of the Lower City is Four Halls.

"Look," I whisper, pointing. I don't know how to describe what I'm seeing. A flickering blue bubble, like glass, has been erected all around the castle.

Harged freezes. "That's Magic, sir," he says. He looks at Captain Tarkness guiltily. "The bad kind this time." She acknowledges the veiled apology with a nod.

We stop in front of the city gate—no guards. It's not even locked. Nearby the ground is disturbed, and flies hover in a gray cloud. The air smells foul. The Captain climbs out of the carriage to open the city gate but stops abruptly and grimaces down at her feet. "Bits of bones."

"We shouldn't be here," Harged whispers. "We're going to die."

The Baron and I exchange a look. *We're here*, his eyes say to me. *We only have one direction to go.*

Inside.

Once we're through the gate, the Captain disappears into the carriage. She, Harged, and the Baron are obviously not Northerners, so they've agreed to stay hidden.

The city, as expected, is abandoned. Everyone took shelter inside Four Halls and tied their fates to the royals. The decision was sensible at the time—royalty will preserve themselves until the very last. But whose bones were those?

The carriage wheels echo on the cobblestone as we climb the weathered streets from the Lower City to the Upper City. Houses gape at us through broken windows and open doors. The high walls of Four Halls come into sight.

Our carriage stops in front of the bridge, which crosses a hundred feet of moat before ending at the portcullis. I look up at the two figures standing atop the wall.

"Greetings!" I call out in Keshar. It feels rusty on my tongue. "I'm an emissary from the Northern Republic. We've received word that power has changed hands in the Holy Kingdom. We would like to speak with you on matters of diplomacy."

My plan is simple. Get inside the castle peacefully, lure the elves into telling me where Corene is being kept, then have Captain Tarkness give the signal for the Baron's men to attack.

One of the elves leaps off the wall and disappears. A flicker of light down below catches my gaze. It's hair—red hair. I squint and see three people standing on a stone outcropping hanging over the moat. It's a drainage pipe, barely visible from the bridge.

One of them looks up. It's a girl with short black hair. Red lips. Big eyes. Thelia? Then the redheaded person behind her can only be—

Corene? No! They were supposed to be inside, locked up, ready to run when we got through these walls. But they're already running. They don't need me to rescue them.

Ahead of us, one of the elves calls something out loud that I can't understand. There's a great rumble, and the portcullis starts to open.

"Is that the Princess?" I hear Harged say. He's hanging out the window of the carriage, where he was supposed to be hiding. I turn around in the driver's seat and gesture with a finger to keep quiet—but he's not looking at me. He waves his arm and shouts, "Princess!"

"Shut up," the Baron hisses. The castle gate's halfway up. We're almost in. Down below, Thelia, Corene, and Parsifal duck back inside the drainage pipe. The portcullis slides all the way open—and Harged's still shouting. My eyes find the Baron's and we both know at once that our plan is ruined.

Elven soldiers in silver armor rush out onto the bridge, heads covered except for their long, pointed ears. It's not until they're on top of us that I realize how tall they are—as tall as man on horseback. Halrendar tries to rear up as dozens of them swarm around us, their faces reflecting the sun like steel, but he's attached to the carriage yoke. He thrashes uselessly.

Two elves leap off the bridge. One lands on the top of the pipe, balancing perfectly. The other lands in the water and swims. I hear Thelia yelling, but it's too late. One has grabbed her and is dragging her back out.

"Thelia!" the Baron shouts.

Harged's out of the carriage, sword drawn, face contorted in fury. "Harged!" My words are licked away by the frenzy. "Don't!" If he attacks before we get inside, they'll fight back. We would lose that fight. But we still have a chance to make it inside as prisoners if we surrender our arms.

I leap off the carriage and sprint toward Harged as more elven soldiers dive off the bridge. Corene screeches down below—I'd know the sound anywhere. Harged's sword collides with armor, and the air fills with a metallic *ringggg*. I stumble to a halt. It's too late.

An elf wearing a cheetah-print fur cloak strides toward me across the bridge, face hidden behind a gold mask. His green hair glints in the sunlight, and his metallic gold skin is blinding. He stops right behind Harged as he slashes again, and he pulls up his mask so I can see his face. The elf's grin is wicked.

"Prince," he says over the din.

I narrow my eyes. "I'm no prince." His smile only grows wider, showing rows of straight, perfect teeth.

Down below, some long ears drag Parsifal off the ledge. Corene shouts curses, her hands bound behind her back. Thelia fights off one, but another one seizes her from behind.

"Come," the elf in the cheetah cape says, gesturing me to the open gate. "We have so much to discuss." He sheathes his sword, and the others nearby lay down their arms. A peace offering.

Harged's panting, sword raised in the air to land another blow, but I hold up my hand. "Wait."

His eyes narrow. "Sir," he says. "Don't—" I glare, and he falls silent.

Taking a step toward the green-haired elf, I lower my own sword. Perhaps this can still go the way I intended. When the tip of my blade touches the ground, the side of the elf's mouth twists up in a cruel smile.

He tears his sword from its sheath and slides the blade through Harged's middle, spraying blood.

Harged stumbles to his knees. I run to him as a dozen more soldiers dive off the bridge. Captain Tarkness raises her hands, a ball of Magic at the center of them, but a blunt hit with a spear knocks her down.

I kneel by Harged's side. He smiles, blood bubbling out of his mouth. He looks defiant, satisfied. "It's been my honor to serve you, King Vasha." With that, he topples forward. I rush to grab him, but two elves seize my shoulders from behind.

The elf—no, the *demon*—with green hair ties me up. "Welcome," he sneers. Captain Tarkness and the Baron have already been tied up. Soldiers haul Corene, Thelia, and Parsifal out of the moat. The Green Demon lines us up like a crew headed to the gallows.

I can't bear to look at the others. This was our only chance, and I failed them all.

CHAPTER 16

SAPPHIRE

I'm in the kitchen trying to cook when the food cart I sent up to Thelia and Parsifal returns—with food still on it, untouched.

My humans must be starving by now. There is only one reason they would not eat any of their meal.

I run from the kitchen as fast as my legs will go. If they have escaped, the Commander will strip me of my rank. Send me back to Viteos in disgrace. And I will never see Thelia and Parsifal again. They will be out there covered in Magic, a danger to themselves and everything around them.

The door to their suite is still closed and sealed. I flick my hand angrily and the Magic seal blows off. The door flies wide, scattering splinters. I should be more careful, given how thick and volatile Magic here has become, but part of me wants to seize as much as I can and light it on fire.

A pa-chi-chi board sits in front of the hearth next to a puddle of blankets, as if someone has been sleeping here. I charge into Parsifal's room.

Empty. They are gone.

I should never have kept Parsifal's use of Magic secret; surely it is how they escaped. I was immeasurably foolish to care about him, to protect him, at my own expense.

Parsifal. Thelia. How could you do this to me?

In Commander Valya's quarters, I hold out my gold mask. The Commander looks up. His eyes are rimmed with dark circles. The sheen on his skin is dulled. "What is this, friend Sapphire?"

"My mask," I say. "I am resigning as one of your Jaguars, Commander." I let them escape. Time to meet my punishment with a strong face.

He does not take my mask. "You are not so easily released from your obligations. And I have already received the news about your prisoners. They were spotted escaping through the old dwarves' sewers, beneath the castle. They have been apprehended—along with their rescuers."

What rescuers? Not that it concerns me now. Surely I will never see them again.

His lips twist, like he has eaten something rotten. "In any case, your two little pets are the least of my worries."

"I—" I begin, but Commander Valya places a finger on my lips. He leans toward me so his face is barely an inch away from mine, as if he is either going to kiss me or eat me. I get a whiff of his breath, which smells like . . . meat. Like rot.

"Go from my sight. Attend to your duties—we have new prisoners in the dungeon. Then I will decide what becomes of your mask."

THELIA

Whoever that big red-haired man was, he's dead now. The elf with the green hair and the cloak like Sapphire's—clearly the leader of this group—put him down like an animal.

Corene was right. The long ears aren't going to let us survive this. Maybe if Parsifal had never found out he could use Magic, if we'd just stayed put, we might have lived. Not now.

At least Bayled's alive—one thing that isn't terrible. I'm surprised at the relief I feel. He may no longer be the King's heir, but there's no throne to speak of, either. I'm simply glad to see his familiar face and know our childhood companion isn't dead.

And Red. Oh, Red. Why did you come for me *now*?

The long ears march us through the courtyard—filled with strange giant animals and elven soldiers—and back into the castle. "Thelia," Red whispers, reaching for my hand with his. "I'm so sorry."

His face—square chin with the cleft in the middle, bushy eyebrows, high cheekbones, dark hair pulled back in a ponytail—is a reminder of everything I once loved. Red clearly came here for me. Even after everything Corene told him, after he fled the castle and left me that letter . . .

I thought you'd be better off pursuing your own dreams.

My fingers brush against Red's for a split second before he and Captain Tarkness are dragged away in a direction I already know. "Red!" I shout. That awful Commander Valya is going to let them rot down in the dungeon, until they die and rise again.

The green-haired elf looks Parsifal and me up and down. "Ah, Sapphire's pets," he says in a thick accent, exposing his canines. So he knows Sapphire. Where are they? By now, they must have discovered us gone. They must be furious.

I focus on my hands as Bayled, Corene, Parsifal, and I are dragged through the castle, toward the South Tower. Up the stairs, down the hall, to a familiar door. My gut twists. My own suite, where I've lived for years—free.

Our caravan of soldiers and humans and this grinning idiot of an elf, who's acting like he's received the world's greatest solstice gift, all stop. A nightmare lies behind this door that's no better than the dungeon.

Parsifal wriggles his hands so his wrist can brush mine. Just the momentary sensation sends a spark rippling up my arm. He's trying to assure me, but there's no peace at this door.

Our captors reach an agreement with the guards, and the suite opens. Morgaun sits at the table in the main room, surrounded by piles of books. When he sees us, his lips warp into a smile that never reaches his eyes.

"Hello, sister."

BAYLED

I should be thrilled to see Corene after how long we've been apart. I've longed for her bright blue eyes like the sea. Every night I've thought of the lemon-and-lavender scent of her perfume and fantasized about our last night together, her legs wrapped around my hips.

She was my reason for returning to this damned castle, my reason for inventing the squork-brained idea that's ruined everything. I reach out to take her hand, because it's what I'm supposed to do. Maybe the feel of her will transport me back to that time and place.

Her flesh is as cold as Harged's body. I feel nothing.

"Bayled." She throws her arms around me, and the stench of the sewer drains is overwhelming. She backs away, sniffing herself. "It's awful, isn't it? I'd better take a bath when Thelia's done."

"I'm sorry about your father," I say, trying to think of anything but Harged. Except I keep reliving the moment—the elf's smile, the sword sliding in and out. Cruel, and meant only to punish me.

Corene nods. "Dad's declining quickly. Those bastards let me see him for a moment just to extort me for a full surrender."

"He's *alive*?" It feels like I've been punched.

"What did you think?"

I shake my head. Sasel told me the King was gone, and I accepted it as truth. In a way it was easier. It meant I'd never have to confront him.

But wait—that message came from Forgren. Why would the court wizard lie? It didn't serve him, only Nul se Lan.

"Bayled?" Corene asks. "Can I ask you something?"

I feel so tired. "Of course."

"Where's Nul?"

The way she says it, I know it's the question she's been holding in since the moment she saw us. Rage blossoms in me at her mention of the man who stole everything, who tried to have me murdered.

"I don't know gobble about him," I snarl. Corene's eyes go wide. I've grown angry so quickly that I'm trembling. "He left.

He took the entire King's army and sent his guard after me to kill me."

Thelia's voice cuts in. "The cratertooth did what?" She stands in the doorway, short wet hair tousled around her head. "Melidia be damned. If Parsifal had told me what he'd heard sooner, maybe—"

I hold up a hand. "There wasn't anything more you could've done."

Corene looks at Thelia, stunned. "You didn't tell *me*."

"We didn't want to upset you. We had Priestess Ilisa send Bayled a warning."

"I can't believe it." Corene breathes heavily a few times. "I . . . I never trusted the Southerner."

"Oh, really?" Thelia's eyes turn to slits. "You were all over him."

Am I really hearing Thelia stand up for me? She suddenly reminds me of Harged—fierce and loyal. I've never seen her like this.

Corene glares at her. "As if I had a choice. I had to pretend to like him for the Kingdom, and so Dad wouldn't feel terrible about sending me away."

Thelia rolls her eyes. "I'm sure."

"Theels—" Corene starts.

"Look, it makes no difference to me. But Bayled came back for you—the least you can do is be honest with him." Thelia stalks back into the main room.

Corene squeezes my arm. "You know it's you I love, not Nul. Right, Bayled?"

"Of course." But what should I believe? This castle is full of lies.

We should've been grateful for the meals Sapphire made for us while we had the luxury. When dinner arrives, it's mush that's not even pretending to be real food. My nose is still filled with the stench of sewage, but my stomach hasn't seen a meal in days, so I manage to eat some lumpy gruel. Duke Finegarden doesn't touch any, and his face looks ghastly.

As much as I don't want to go anywhere near Morgaun, I find myself next to him at the dinner table. Luckily, he doesn't look up from his reading.

"Have they taken you yet?" Duke Finegarden asks us.

"Taken us where?" I ask. We've been taken a lot of places.

"The procedure."

Morgaun spits something into his dirty mug. "A *procedure*? You mean, a personal invasion."

"What's he talking about?" Thelia asks the Duke.

He sighs. "Once a week they bring us all to the banquet hall for dinner. We've heard stories about the long ears taking people, one at a time, to a room downstairs. And doing . . ." He lets out a long, troubled breath. "Nobody knows."

Morgaun leans perilously far back in his chair. "I bet they take you apart, piece by piece."

He must be wrong. Sapphire said, *wash, relocate*.

The Duke sighs at his son. "They go one at a time. Others have seen them through the windows and they have no hair anywhere. They don't come back."

"I told you," Morgaun says, looking at Thelia and me. "Boiling us. Cleansing us for mass sacrifice."

Corene's head jolts up, and she looks at him for only a moment before looking away. I remember what she said: I know how these things go. Invasions end in blood.

Duke Finegarden turns to Bayled. "What about the King's army? We assumed they had defeated you when the elven host appeared."

"I lost contact when Nul se Lan left with them," he says.

Duke Finegarden scowls. "He left? Why?"

"He thought we stood no chance against the long ears. He wasn't wrong. But when the Baron didn't arrive at the Crossing, and I took a detour to—"

"You what?" the Duke sits up. "Why would you abandon your own force?"

Bayled holds up a hand to silence him. It's the boldest thing I've ever seen him do, and Duke Finegarden's face curdles. "There were no good options, so I made the best choice I could. I won't apologize for that."

The Duke *hmms*. "And how did you end up back here, General Vasha, without an army, in the company of a deserter?"

"We heard the King was dead," Bayled says, face impassive. "Baron Durnhal helped me return to Melidihan and committed his force to my cause. He's more than made amends."

I'm impressed with Bayled. Only a few moons ago, he'd have frozen up facing Thelia's father. Now his face is hard and his voice is firm. No more nervous energy—it's been replaced by a sort of soul-deep irritation.

I look at him thoughtfully. "With Nul se Lan committing high treason, I suppose that makes you the King's heir again, doesn't it?"

He just stares at me.

"Not that it matters," Thelia says. "There's nothing left to be king of. There's nobody to tell what to do." What a Thelia view of the world.

Bayled rolls his eyes. "Ruling is about more than telling someone what to do."

"I suppose out of anyone here," I say, "you would know."

THELIA

I've never been more eager for a meal to end. Parsifal heads into the other room to begin sorting through his parents' belongings. Daddy lies down on the daybed and seems to instantly fall asleep. Bayled sits by the window and looks out absently, while Morgaun remains at the table reading a book.

Corene leans over him. "What are you reading?"

"Nothing." He tucks the book into his lap and hunches over it so she can't see it. The craggon is clearly hiding something.

She sighs sadly. "I miss reading. It was my escape for so long. I'd just returned all my books to Forgren before everything happened, and I'll never see them again."

Morgaun looks up slightly. "I got these from Forgren."

"You've found him?" Corene whispers back.

She has the audacity to titter around with Morgaun, right in front of us? She knows how he's tormented me, and continues even when everything has collapsed around us. She must be angry that I exposed her lies to Bayled, and this is her revenge.

I feel the shuddering, consuming fury rising up in me again. My breath starts to catch in my throat, and I'm suddenly so angry. I could kill her without regretting a single thing.

"Theels?" I hear Parsifal say. He squeezes my shoulder, and I know he's seeing what I'm seeing.

I close my eyes and take long, deep breaths. I won't give them the satisfaction of seeing me fall apart. Bayled glances at them, but nothing registers on his face.

As evening approaches, Bayled locates a pillow, lies down on the floor, and looks ready to go to bed there. It's like nothing matters to him anymore.

"This is silly." I kneel by him. "You're going to sleep here?"

Bayled yawns. "Why not? I've been sleeping on the rocky ground since I left. I'm used to it. Your bed's yours, and Parsifal's is Parsifal's."

Corene sits up at the table. "What about me? Where do I sleep?"

I shoot Bayled a look, but he says nothing. So I whisper to Parsifal, "Do you want to sleep in my room? Give Bayled and Corene yours?"

His eyes search mine for what feels like an eternity. I rub my hands together, feeling like I've made a mistake. We left what happened behind, back in North Hall. When Sapphire abandoned us . . . Perhaps those were desperate acts, quiet things meant to be left in shadow.

"Absolutely." Parsifal clears his throat. "You two lovebirds," he says, glancing at Corene and Bayled, "can have my room. I'm small and so is Thelia, so as much as I'd like to share a bed with you—" he waggles his eyebrows suggestively at Bayled, who just sighs, "—I can sleep in her room."

"Thanks," Bayled says. "It'll be the first time I've slept in a real bed in a while."

To not draw attention, I go to bed before Parsifal does. We're just cousins. We've grown up together. Sleeping in the same bed when there aren't any other options isn't suspicious. Right?

As I crawl under the blankets of my old bed, Sapphire's face clings to my memory—their diamond-shaped face, those purposeful eyes. The lips that look like stiff metal, but feel like velvet on mine. The musical sound of their voice.

When we escaped, were they blamed? I sit up in bed, my heart pounding. Maybe Sapphire was thrown in the dungeon and left to die in the dark because they trusted us. Because they liked me. Because they believed I liked them back.

I think Sapphire would be right about that.

I'm not asleep yet when Parsifal slips in. He drops a pillow and a thin blanket on the floor next to the bed. I lean over the side. "What are you doing?"

"Going to sleep."

"Down there?"

He sits back on his heels. "What would you have me do?"

I lift the blanket up and pat the bed next to me. Eyes crinkling in the dim moonlight, Parsifal slides under the blanket. I don't know who puts their hands into whose clothes first, but when we're finally together, it's just what I need.

BAYLED

One single bed sits in the middle of the tiny room—a bed that everyone expects Corene and me to share. The happy couple, reunited.

But the gap between us is a canyon. This war has changed us. I'm more weary. More suspicious. And she's . . . bitter. Sharp-edged. She has so many different faces now.

The soft mounds of pillows and blankets make me think of Red and Captain Tarkness, swimming in their own filth somewhere far below us. I feel sick to my stomach as I lie under the blankets, waiting for Corene.

When she comes in, she sets her candle on the small table and begins to undress. I'm wearing my clothes, hoping that we'd just sleep after the enormity of this day. She pulls up the blankets and climbs in next to me. Her cold hand finds its way over my stomach, running from my chest to my groin, and prickles sprout all across me. "I'm so glad to see you again," she whispers, burying her face in my neck. "I thought I'd lost you forever. It tore me open inside, Bayled."

The words roll over me like water, vaporizing into air. She was happy enough to pretend to like Nul se Lan and dance to the tune of *duty*, to ask about his well-being before anything else.

I say, "I'm happy to see you too." It's enough for her. Her hand ducks under the fabric of the pants Parsifal lent me and I close my eyes. When we kiss, her lips are harder than I remember. I go through the motions—touch her chest, let her slide on top of me. A long time passes before I'm useful to her. I claim that it's not her, I'm just tired.

We try not to make a sound, not that we have to worry. Our one remaining job is to conceive an heir, to continue the Hindermark line, like a pair of breeding horses. But I'd feel even more humiliated if we were overheard.

We've lit no candles, and that saves me from having to see. Only Corene's swinging hair appears in fits when the moonlight touches it. As she moves, Corene whimpers, until I realize that what I thought were sounds of pleasure are quiet sobs. I stop. "Corene?"

She collapses to my chest. "I'm sorry, Bayled. I'm sorry. I'm so worried about Dad." She cries into me and that's the end of this.

I've never been more thankful.

SAPPHIRE

The bowls and plates on the tray will not cease rattling. They are like squorks in a cage, trying to claw their way out. A misbehaving pot left a black scorch mark on my arm. Soon we will not be able to cook anymore, because open flames allowed to burn for more than a few seconds start to sizzle and spark.

The sour, cinnamon scent of Magic is so thick and dense it fills every spare stretch of air. It is heavy, like fog. It is in every inhale of breath, clogging up my lungs. Even in the High Seer's cavern in Viteos, where liquid Magic bubbles up from the ground—vibrating green and blue—it is not like this. A volatile second skin, waiting to ignite.

I hold the bowls and plates down on the tray just long enough to get into the dungeon. It is empty now besides the two new prisoners. We did a decent job cleaning out the remains, and it does not smell quite as terrible.

The woman sits on the floor, impassive. The man gasps when he glimpses me. He has bushy hair on his upper lip, styled in a curve on each side. Humans do such creative things with their facial hair.

"Why not just kill us?" he asks. I say nothing and slide him his food. He leans forward against the cell door. "Tell me if

Thelia Finegarden is all right." Recognition must show on my face. "You know her!" He rattles the bars. "Where have you taken her?"

I sigh, taking his old bowls. "She is fine." When I stand up, I find myself looking into hopeless, desperate eyes.

"What can you tell me? I came here for her."

I should not make conversation and get drawn into their complications. But I need to know. "What does she mean to you?"

"I'll answer one of your questions if you answer one of mine," he says, one bushy eyebrow rising.

The Commander would have me stop, not give them anything they can use. But these two are isolated here with me as their only caretaker—whatever I tell them, they cannot repeat. And maybe I can learn something. "One question for one question," I agree.

"Where is Thelia?"

"South Hall with her family. My turn. How do you know her?"

"I'm a friend of the late King's. Baron Durnhal, by the way—pleasure to meet you. This is Captain Tarkness." The woman barely raises her head. "I met Thelia while visiting Four Halls, and I almost married her." When I fail to control my snap reaction to this, he lets out a chuckle. "She's something, isn't she? How do *you* know her?"

"I kept watch," I say carefully. "Same as I do for you."

"So you're a prison guard?"

"One question at a time. Now me. Why did you come to Four Halls?"

"We tried to rescue them—Thelia and the others." A cynical laugh. "I knew it was a flawed plan, but I had to try."

I am grateful, though. Had they not arrived, my charges would have escaped. Parsifal, covered in Magic but with no training on using it, would have hurt himself—or Thelia.

"What about you?" the Baron asks. "Why are you here, caring for us?"

"I am being punished."

I should not have said it. I have given him an opening.

"For what? Oh, I know, one question at a time." He peers through the bars at me. "Whatever you did, I'm sure you did it for the right reasons. You know, what's being done here—it's wrong. I can tell you think so too."

I pick up the bowls and head for the stairs.

"You could leave," he calls after me. "Maybe we could help each other escape this place." I cannot even let myself listen. "Hey, come back! We weren't finished."

"I am finished," I say, and let the dungeon door fall closed.

I'm about to ask him to explain when Lady Harmouth leans toward me. "General Vasha, how did you survive battle with the long ears?"

"There wasn't a battle." I look her right in the eyes. "Nul se Lan is a traitor. He tried to have me killed, and then the coward took off into the woods with the army."

Gasps ripple down the table.

"We're so sorry to hear it, General," the Count says. He scowls. "That Southerner is no King of mine. Never was, never will be."

The table echoes it. "No King of mine."

I try to put on a smile, but the words are hollow. At least he wanted to be King. What happens when old Hindermark really does kick off? For a few weeks, I was spared that future—the endless, impossible responsibility of ruling.

"Doesn't that make General Vasha the King?" says Lady Harmouth.

"I believe you're right." The Count hits the table with his fist. "After that traitor Nul se Lan, Vasha is the rightful heir."

Corene clears her throat. "I think determining succession is a little beyond us at the moment, isn't it?" she asks, as a bowl of gravy pours itself onto her plate. "My father is still alive. Who are we to choose who will succeed him? For all we know, he could decide that I am best suited to be Queen."

Next to me, Parsifal elbows Thelia in the side.

"Perhaps, Princess," the Count says, measuring his words. "As you say, we will leave it to the King to decide such matters."

"What is most important right now is to restore the Kingdom," I say. "Not choose kings and queens."

Corene glares at me, but I ignore her. Where was all this

certainty, all this confidence, when she refused to fight for me? When she put the Kingdom before me, and before our love?

Because it was never about the Kingdom for her. I have to wonder, now—has it ever been about the Kingdom for me? Or did I do it all simply to earn my place at Corene's side?

At the end of the table, I notice a dark cloaked shape take a seat beside Morgaun. It's the court wizard, Forgren. His many necklaces—the jewels that allowed him to harness Magic—have all vanished. Probably seized by the elves. He's the one who told Sasel, *The King is dead.*

Forgren whispers something to Morgaun, removes an object wrapped in paper from his pocket, and sets it down on the table. Without his Magic to hold it in place, his hood starts to slip, and I brace myself to see what he's been hiding underneath—wrinkles as deep as canyons, heavy purple bags under his eyes, drooping jowls, and scars scattered across him like puzzle pieces.

The hood slides right off his head and underneath . . . he has faded blond hair, long and tied back. Smooth, young skin. Bright green eyes with long lashes and dark eyebrows that are handsome, yet severe. He's barely as old as we are.

Next to me, Thelia covers her mouth. She saw too. "Melidia be damned," she says. "Doesn't he look like someone we know?"

Forgren looks so much like a hillman, he could practically be Nul se Lan's brother. Now I think I understand his false message to Sasel. A traitor in our midst this whole time.

My stomach lurches as Forgren whispers something else in Morgaun's ear. After the transaction's complete, the court wizard rises from the table, adjusts his hood, and finds a different seat.

Thelia whispers in Parsifal's ear, and I glare at them. "All right, what am I missing?" I demand. They remind me of two squeaking mice, plotting and gossiping and hoarding secrets like they always have—and shutting me out.

Thelia meets my eyes and for once, she lets me in. "Morgaun said he was going to burn everything down," she says. "I think he means it."

SAPPHIRE

I've been summoned out to the castle courtyard, where I find Zylion kneeling, digging gray bones out of the ground like weeds. All across the courtyard, wriggling white fingers protrude from the cold mud, trying to escape from the earth.

Zylion looks up at me. He holds out a spade and it leaps into my hand, ready to work. If only I were so ready. "The humans must have buried their dead here long ago," he says, hacking at skeletal arms. "Now, they have all reanimated."

First it was the undead in the dungeon. Now this? At the nearest hand squirming for purchase in the dirt, I begin to dig. First the bony arm comes out, attached to the body by threads of ligament. Magic keeps it functioning.

When Ferah's cart is full of wriggling, exhumed corpses, we take it beyond the city gates and unload the skeletons onto the bare ground. We take a step back while Ferah explodes them, and then we begin again.

Upon returning to the castle, I find Ellze waiting for me on the bridge. "I have been looking for you," he says, flicking some of his green hair over one shoulder. He shouts up to the two elves on the wall. "Open it for us, will you? Today?"

He is growing more and more overbearing. He loves to tell the soldiers what to do, and he loves even more when they obey. I barely recognize him. Something is changing among The People the longer we remain here.

As I follow him inside, he gives me a disingenuous smile. "You are quiet."

"Nothing to say."

"Are you dissatisfied with something?"

He wants me to say yes, to expose my displeasure with my role. Has he always been this way, or has this place changed him?

The floor under my feet suddenly starts to shake. The sound travels down the halls toward us—a rumbling *boom*, coming from the other side of the castle.

"What was that?" Ellze asks, eyes narrowing. Instead of conjecturing, I run toward the sound.

We weave through the halls to the set of stairs closest to the source. Smoke funnels down toward us. Screams. Soldiers stamp down the stairs. "An explosion!" they yell. "Stay away from West Hall!"

"I should tell the Commander immediately," Ellze says. *I*, not *we*.

By the time we reach the temple, the other Jaguars have arrived in the Commander's chambers. We all felt it. Commander Valya rises slowly from his scattered piles of papers, armor, and weapons, as if his joints ache. His quarters are a mess I have never seen. Even his usually liquid hair looks tangled and dry.

"What have you learned?" he asks.

"A fire in one of the rooms caught," Ferah says. Thus the explosion. "A section of West Hall is gone."

The Commander's face is devoid of color. "It seems Magic is spilling out of the well faster, and in greater quantity, than any of us expected." He sighs. "No more fires, anywhere in the castle. We cannot afford for the Magic to catch."

I gape at him. "Commander, it is the middle of winter."

"We will be fine," Ellze says. "Have you never been cold before, little Sapphire?" A few of the other Jaguars laugh at me. But it is not us I worry about. Humans are fragile.

"We have other concerns," Commander Valya says. "The human King, despite our best efforts, died this morning. His body could not withstand being without wine any longer."

The Commander should have told me this hours ago. When I visited the King with breakfast, he was alive.

"It will be much harder to control the humans once they suspect the worst," he continues. "The sworn Lords of the Kingdom may move on the castle. If that happens, we will be forced to defend ourselves."

Not that it would be much of a fight. If humans gathered what remained of their forces and tried to advance on Melidi-han, every last one of them would die. Ellze's mouth tips up on one side, as if he hopes for exactly this to happen.

"I want everyone to be prepared," Commander Valya says. "Continue the operation as usual. But should the Magic grow too volatile to control any longer, we may have to abandon those humans we have not cleaned yet and collapse the castle anyway, so we can build the new hold and contain this catastrophe."

The rest of the Jaguars nod and clear out of the Commander's quarters, but I stand outside the door, unable to move.

Collapse the castle . . . with all of them still in it? Thelia and Parsifal are not scheduled to be cleaned for some time. They would certainly be among those left behind.

This is not what we came here to do. *Do no harm*—that has been the backbone of The People for as long as I have been alive. What is becoming of us here? What has Commander Valya been thinking?

I realize Ellze has not left yet when I hear him on the other side of the closed door. "We should fell the castle now. With such an abundance of Magic at our disposal, this new hold could be even stronger than Viteos."

Commander Valya's voice is weak. "Indeed. But we must still contain it, which will be harder than ever now. We cannot rush things, nephew, or we could anger the High Seer."

"Even the High Seer will want to relocate to our beautiful new capital once we have the well contained and the hold built. Then, certainly, she will agree to our plan to reclaim what the humans have taken from everyone else."

The Commander sighs. "And you will take charge of building this capital, will you not?"

I can hear the smile in Ellze's voice. "Of course."

So Ellze has bigger plans now—plans that no longer align with the mission the High Seer gave us. I could send her a smoke message, tell her what I have heard. But what could she do from so far away?

What chews at my insides is what this means for my humans. Parsifal's grip on Magic is erratic and dangerous, certainly—like a toddler with a sword.

But now I fear far more what will become of them should they remain in Four Halls.

THELIA

Sapphire said we wouldn't be harmed. That we'd be treated for Magic, then released. So why are they letting us freeze to death?

Every fire was extinguished after that dinner in the banquet hall, and the temperature's crept lower and lower until our breath comes out as smoke. We wrap ourselves in blankets and talk as little as possible.

They've left us to die.

Daddy handles it the worst of all of us. During the day, he curls up under his blankets until only his forehead shows. I bring him food whenever it comes and cajole him to try something, even a bite, but he barely eats. Morgaun does nothing to help.

At least Parsifal and I have our room where we can lock the door and huddle under the blankets to chase the cold away. Every night we struggle to get to sleep. When will it be our turn? When will The People come for us and take us to their strange, secret room and decide that it's our turn to go? Perhaps it would be a relief to be free of this nightmare.

But I have too selfish a grip on living. I've worked too hard for it. When Parsifal lies next to me, hand wrapped in mine, I know I must keep fighting. The only cure for wondering whether we're still even here is to turn to each other. Once we're satiated, we're finally able to sleep—but it is cold and restless.

I'm drifting off when a tiny, pink light appears under the door. I sit up, freeing myself from Parsifal's arms. I tap his shoulder as it starts to drift upward, weightless.

"Wake up. Look."

Sapphire's wisp floats toward us, chittering. Parsifal reaches out to grab it but it ducks, loops around me, and flies toward the door.

"It's telling us something." Parsifal climbs out of bed. "What is it, little guy?"

The pink ball of light spins around the door handle again. I follow him as he pushes the door open. "What are you thinking?" I whisper, but he ignores me.

Everyone's asleep. The wisp stays close to the ground, dodging behind furniture to hide its light. I follow it to the suite's main door and it bobs around the handle, urging us to go through.

"Don't listen," I tell Parsifal. "We can't get out. It's trying to trick you."

Parsifal reaches for the handle anyway, and I expect the Magic seal to bounce him back like it did to me. But the door opens without complaint, and the wisp bounces out into the dark hallway, unrestrained.

I peer out. The guard who's usually posted here is gone and the hallway is empty. We slip out, following the bobbing pink light. A few doors down, a familiar head of sky-blue hair appears.

"Sapphire!" I want to hug them, to kiss them again, but after everything that's happened . . .

The wisp lands on their outstretched finger. "Thank you," Sapphire says to it. The glowing bauble spins happily around their hand before ducking back into the open belt pouch.

"I'm sorry," Sapphire and I say at the same time. They shake their head. "No, let me. Please. There is no excuse for what I did."

"I'm sorry if you got in trouble for me," I say.

"It was my idea, Theels," Parsifal says. "I should be sorry."

Sapphire puts a gentle hand on each of our shoulders. It feels like a bolt of lightning. Sapphire feels it too—their eyebrows rise and the sides of their mouth twitch. "It is not important now." They take a long, arduous breath. "I must tell you. The King has died."

About time. "When?"

"This morning. The Commander do-o-oes not want humans to know. But your friend . . . the Princess." Sapphire drops their gaze to the floor. "She should be told."

I feel nothing. Not for the King, not for Corene, not for us. This Kingdom has been sinking into oblivion since the three of us hid in a dark passage, waiting for the screams to subside.

"I'll tell her," Parsifal says. "I speak Corene."

"We're a lot less concerned about the King than we are about freezing to death," I say, taking Sapphire's hand in mine. I bring it to my face and inhale the cool tang of their skin. It's heavy. "My father—he isn't handling it well. I think he may die."

"I am sorry." Sapphire's head drops. "Commander Valya is watching me. But I am designing a plan to help you out of the castle. To be safe. Take this." They hand me a small box. "I know that you may never forgive me for what The People have done to you and your families." They look at Parsifal like they want to touch him, to hold his hand—but they don't move. "I will do everything within my power to ensure your safety. It means . . . more to me than I can say."

They reach forward and wrap us both in a hug. At first, Parsifal's shoulder is crushed into mine, until I put my arm around him. I feel Sapphire's lips, soft and yet also hard, leave a kiss on my forehead.

Sapphire pushes us away. "Take care," they say. Then, looking at Parsifal: "Don't let Thelia be foolish." Sapphire gently touches the back of his neck, ruffling his hair there. Parsifal's eyes go wide.

With that, they're gone down the hall.

Quietly, we step back inside the suite. Everyone's still asleep. In our bedroom, I open the box Sapphire gave us. Inside is a single charcoal smokestick, a small fire striker for lighting it, and a note.

Use in emergency only.
Exercise caution. May explode.

PARSIFAL

We don't sleep much—not that the insomnia matters when there's nothing to do. After a breakfast we hardly eat, Thelia and I retire to the window seat to play pa-chi-chi. Thelia gasps as I skip and take one of her buttons. "I didn't even see you coming!"

I grin. "Don't underestimate me."

Bayled settles on the chair by the window and watches us play in silence. When we finish a game, I ask, "Do you want to play?"

He jolts upright like he'd forgotten he was there. "I'm no good at pa-chi-chi."

"You don't have to be." Thelia places a peanut shell in Bayled's hand. "Learn."

He looks at her a long moment before accepting. I let him take my spot. "I like your hair like this," he tells her.

"Thank you." Thelia sets her first pair of stones. "Parsifal did it when most of my hair got ripped off."

His eyebrows rise. "How?"

"Thelia tried to climb out a window," I say, elbowing her.

"Hey! Don't spill my secrets."

Bayled grows serious. "Can you two do something for me?" he says quietly, leaning toward us.

We both lean in too. "What?" I ask.

"Stop keeping secrets." He sounds sad, like this resentment has been building a long time. "I can tell there's something else. Something important."

"I don't know what you mean." Thelia crosses her arms, but I take pity on Bayled. He's right.

Under my breath I say, "The King's dead."

Bayled sighs, like this doesn't surprise him in the least. "It was just a matter of time." He looks almost relieved—until he looks at Corene, where she sits at the table reading. "But this might be the thing that tips her over the edge."

I don't think I agree. She's been falling for a long time.

"How did you two find out about his passing?" Bayled asks. I look at Thelia and we both wait for the other to speak first. "I thought you were going to be honest with me," he says, with a note of bitterness.

Finally I sigh and say, "We know someone."

"Who?"

Thelia chews on her lip. She still doesn't trust him completely, but how can his knowing the truth possibly hurt us?

I put a long finger next to the side of my face—like an elf ear. Bayled's eyes widen. "You can't be serious. How?"

"It's not a big deal," Thelia whispers urgently. "They were our guard when we were in North Hall."

His eyebrows rise even higher. "Your prison guard?"

"It's not like that." I know how ridiculous we sound.

Corene abruptly stands up and walks over to us. She looks hardened, ready to do something rash. "I can't believe you're all sitting over here *conspiring*, when you could be helping us."

I rise to my feet, and it takes more energy than I have. "Seems like you and Morgaun are perfectly happy plotting on your own. Why do you need us?"

She eyeballs me. "I know what you can do, Percy. You should be using your powers to help, not just sitting there whispering."

Morgaun looks over. "What are you talking about, cousin?"

"That's Your Majesty to you," she snaps. "I'm the Queen now."

I'm stunned into silence.

"See?" says Corene with a bitter laugh. "You think I don't know anything, but I know my dad's dead. I know the elves are planning to destroy us all. And I know it's within Parsifal's power to get us out of here."

I've overestimated Corene. All those times I thought she was playing the good, dutiful, wholesome Princess—letting Bayled believe she'd marry him, kissing Nul se Lan on the stairs—I thought she was lining up her pa-chi-chi stones for the final move, where she'd wipe out all the pawns at once and take the game.

But there's no plan. There's no game. She's chased one hope for happiness after the next, throwing her pieces in whichever barrel looks least likely to roll off the cliff.

Morgaun peers at me. "What can you do, Bellisare?"

Bayled's standing, too, looking angry—that's new. "What's she talking about, Parsifal?"

"He can use Magic," Corene says. Her blue eyes are filled with lightning. "We escaped through a portal he made."

Morgaun's face stitches itself into something terrible. "I get it." He looks at me like he's never seen me before, and my arms erupt in prickles. "You're working with them, aren't you? You licked some long ear cock, got a free room in North Hall, and gave in to the sinful call of Magic."

Duke Finegarden stands up, hurling his blankets to the floor. "You will stop speaking this way at once." His fatigue seems forgotten as he storms to the table and seizes Morgaun by the ear. Morgaun howls, trying to pull his head away, but the Duke's arthritic grip is iron. "Shut up and sit down, son."

Morgaun shoves Duke Finegarden away and stumbles back, laughing. "So angry, Father! Why are you angry at me? You should be angry at Thelia." He grins widely at us. "Given that she's fucking her own cousin while all of you are sleeping."

The Duke's skeletal face contorts with horror.

Thelia lunges at Morgaun, roaring. "You worthless craggon!" Before I can grab her, she lands a punch to his face. He falls to the floor as she bludgeons him. "As if it's any business of yours. You've tormented me, cut me open, and you have the gall to—?" I put my entire body weight behind restraining her arm while blood drips from Morgaun's nose. He laughs as Bayled helps me drag her off. Even after starving, Thelia's far stronger than we are. "Let me go!"

"It's not worth it," I say as we push her to the window seat.

"If Melidia weren't so preoccupied," Morgaun snarls, "she'd strike you both down from the sky. How could you do it with that deformed thing, sister?" He laughs again. "Sick."

I've been called worse.

"Is this true?" the Duke asks me.

I inhale sharply and sit beside Thelia. "Yes, it's true. I love her."

The rage drains out of Thelia's eyes. My uncle sinks into his chair and drops his face in his hands. But Bayled puts his arm around both of us, and I feel him squeeze my shoulder.

I'm not ashamed. After all the lies I've told, this is the one truth I'll keep.

We have split into three camps: Thelia, Bayled, and I at the window, playing pa-chi-chi. Duke Finegarden under his blankets, refusing to look at any of us. Corene and Morgaun at the table, whispering more feverishly than ever.

It's Bayled who speaks first, quietly enough that the others can't overhear. "He's pulled Corene into this plan of his, whatever it is."

Thelia's mouth twists into a grimace. "No kidding."

"Let me try," I say. I know one way to get anyone to open up.

After rifling through my trunks for a while, I plop down across from Corene and Morgaun, a blanket draped over my shoulders. I set a freshly opened bottle of wine and three glasses on the table between us. "Truce?" I say, starting to pour. "I've been saving this."

Morgaun picks up a glass and sips. Corene doesn't take hers.

"Very good, Bellisare," Morgaun says, licking his lips. Behind me, Thelia sits on the window seat, staring out the window. I know she's listening.

"We're all a little—erm—tense right now," I say lightly. "So we'll all make mistakes while we cope." Morgaun's eyes narrow. "But of course I want to do whatever I can to get us out of here. Why don't you tell me how I can help?"

Morgaun gives me an appraising look. "You know, those long-eared monsters think they're so much better than us. Treating us like cattle. But you're proof that humans could use Magic just as well as they can, if Melidia permitted it."

It's the closest Morgaun will ever come to complimenting me. "So what's your plan?"

Morgaun says nothing. I top off his glass of wine. I haven't made a dent in mine but he hasn't noticed. Corene, on the other hand, reaches past Morgaun for a book. He puts a hand on her wrist. "What are you doing?"

"I'm telling him. We could use his help." Corene opens the book to a page of diagrams that look like flames scattered among lines of rippling wind.

"Forgren gave this to us," she says, turning the book to face me. "Magic is flammable. That's what we think happened in West Hall—the Magic in the room caught fire and exploded. And that's why the long ears banned fires." The page is written in an older script I can't read, but I understand the depictions of fire. "It's not flammable like paper, where it will catch fire and keep burning as long as there's fuel."

"How is it different?" I ask. Morgaun looks at me suspiciously.

"It consumes whatever Magic is immediately available in a space and detonates on the spot. It won't spread."

Morgaun pulls something out of his lap and sets it on top of the book: it's a small lump of a dark gray mineral I don't recognize. "This is a conductor," he says. "Forgren's had it on his shelf for years. Whereas a fire will simply burn out the Magic nearest and then dissipate, this taps into the entire *line* of Magic."

"Line?" I ask.

"I don't completely understand it," Corene says, pointing to the squiggly lines on the next page, some larger and fatter. They cross a map of Helyanda—the lines thicker and more numerous on the elves' side of the Great Mountains, and thinner and sparser on our side. "But basically, Magic travels in interconnected threads all across the world." She flips a few pages to show me more diagrams. "If we could get our hands on some fire and tap into a whole thread with this," she holds up the lump of rock, "we could send an entire line into flames. It would hit the elves where it hurts, back home."

"How does that help us?"

"It does Melidia's bidding," Morgaun says. "By destroying them. The long ears rely on Magic to survive—it's why they can live forever, why they can't be hurt. They are her enemies because they dare to use what isn't theirs." He glances up at the ceiling and shakes his head, like the Goddess has said something only to him. "Thanks to Melidia's grace, we don't need Magic, and we can continue along fine without it when it's gone."

"Wouldn't destroying them destroy us, too?" I ask. "We're all in the castle together."

Morgaun just smiles as he drinks. "The ultimate sacrifice, yes. And Melidia will reward us greatly for it."

My eyes dart to Corene, to see if she finds this as nonsensical as I do. But she's gazing upward, beyond the ceiling, beyond Four Halls, to some imaginary destination in the sky.

Her final blind leap at happiness.

It is late that night when I return from dumping our chamberpot out the window in the main suite.

"Why are you working with Morgaun?" I hear Bayled whisper under the door. I stop and listen—I can't help myself. "How could you do that to Thelia?"

"You mean my cousin who left me to die?" snaps Corene.

"We've all suffered and done regrettable things," Bayled says. "But Morgaun . . . he's a wretch, Corene. And he's only going farther up the parapets. You heard him. *The ultimate sacrifice?* He wants us all dead, even you."

"Maybe I'm a wretch too," she retorts. "Is that what you think? Is that what you're saying?"

There's a long pause. Then the door opens and Bayled comes out, carrying a pillow and a blanket. He stops and stares when he sees me, and closes the door behind him.

"I give up," he whispers.

I put down the chamberpot and touch his shoulder, just for a moment. Then he makes his bed on the floor and I leave him to sleep.

In our room, I pull out the smokesticks and the fire starter. Only priestesses can send smoke messages—they have the focus needed to find their target, and just enough Magical prowess to carry the smoke to its destination. But I have a feeling . . .

I rouse Thelia and tell her what I've overheard. "We can't stop them on our own," I say. "We have to tell Sapphire."

SAPPHIRE

I awake to the tang of smoke. Sitting up in bed, I expect to find a candle in the cool darkness, or maybe a fire. What I find are words written in the air with strands of thin smoke.

> *Parsifal and Thelia here.*
> *Help.*
> *Morgaun has a plan to end all of us.*
> *Boom.*

I blink as the final words start to dissipate. I was right that Parsifal's newfound ability to harness Magic would allow him to use the smokesticks. I did not expect to receive a message so soon, though.

Boom?

I am shivering as I descend to the rooms where we keep the priestesses. Even The People feel cold eventually. Today we begin transporting humans to the settlement in greater numbers. Previous groups have proven resistant, so the Commander has decided to send priestesses along to ensure their cooperation.

I was worrying enough about Thelia and Parsifal even before their message. Even if I could get them cleaned and transported to the new settlement . . . what becomes of that settlement when Ellze gains command of the new fortress?

Ilisa jumps up when I enter the room. The other priestesses barely rise from their sleep.

"Come with me," I whisper to her. My wisp glides up to settle on her shoulder.

She glances back at her sisters. "What about them?"

"Only you this time." I gesture to the open door. She has no reason to trust me, but she follows me out anyway.

We walk in silence for a while, the wisp riding along in her hair, until she finally asks, "Where are you taking me, Sapphire?"

I glance down. "To be cleansed of Magic. If you were to leave the castle as you are, you might be a danger to yourself and others." I look away from her. "I am sorry. This is the only way to ensure your safety."

"I get to leave?" she asks.

I nod. "Do you remember what you said you wanted the first time we met?" I ask.

"I wanted to keep my people safe."

"I do not know what will happen after our mission here is complete—but my brethren . . ." I lower my head. "They are corrupt. You may need to protect your own again soon."

I stop outside the cleaning room, a cellar reinforced with Magic. I hear the sound of screaming inside. It is in use. Ilisa has a horrified look on her face. "It's going to be painful, isn't it?"

"Yes," I say. I try not to imagine Ilisa inside, the Magicker's controlled flames burning off every last bit of Magic still attached to her body. It will be purged from the pores in her skin, between her teeth, the creases between her fingers. She will not emerge the same.

"It will be over soon."

Her eyes search mine. They are not like Thelia or Parsifal's—they are old and strange. "What will you do to stop this?" she asks me.

Me? "There is little I can do," I say. "But I want to free two humans I care about."

She leans close and whispers solemnly, "There are hidden tunnels for servants. I doubt your people have found them. Look near stairs."

I am surprised—and grateful. "Thank you."

The door opens and a Magicker steps out. "Healthy?" he asks me, pointing at the Priestess. "I cannot work on anyone who is ill." I already know—the intensity of the procedure can be too much for the weak.

"She shows no sign of sickness," I say.

He ushers Ilisa inside and closes the door. While my insides churn with apprehension for her, it gives me an idea.

I must get my humans completely out of the Commander's hands—and I know only one way.

I rush down the stairs into the dungeon so quickly, I almost spill two bowls of food. The Baron rises from the floor where he has been sleeping.

"I received a message last night," I say as I slip him his dinner. "Thelia says they need assistance, now. Something about her brother . . . having a plan. A dangerous one."

Baron Durnhal scowls through the bars. "Morgaun. She was always so guarded with what she'd tell me about him. But I heard plenty of rumors."

"What would you do to help her escape?"

He crosses his arms. "Not much I can do from here. I have soldiers waiting in the woods, but they won't move if I can't contact them." He exchanges a look with the Captain. "Why do you ask?"

The Baron loves Thelia—and he will ensure she reaches

freedom safely, since I cannot. "I can get all of you out of here," I say. "I will bring supplies. Meanwhile, you must act sick. When others come to check on you—and they will—lie on the floor. Look like you are dying."

The Captain's eyebrows climb into her hair. "I see what you're thinking."

"You brought it in with you." I make a gagging sound. "Mysterious human illness. Very contagious. Spreading fast."

CHAPTER 18

SAPPHIRE

News of the King's death has traveled quickly through the castle. Desperation is spreading like a sickness. Two humans hung themselves, and one argument turned into a murder. Luckily, no explosions followed.

The Commander ordered a stop to group meals in the banquet hall, "to contain the contagion." What he does not understand is that humans are not animals, and what ails them is not a disease.

We have done this to them by trapping them in rooms without any heat, without exercise or proper food or contact with others, and we expected them to survive. I could offer so many solutions, but Commander Valya would never listen. The People regard me from the sides of their eyes; never talking to my face, but around me and behind me. I grew too close to the humans. I allowed them to escape. I have developed *unnatural affinities*.

In South Hall, the soldier guarding the door to Thelia and Parsifal's suite eyes me. I do not know if she recognizes me. I have only one chance to do what needs to be done before word travels to Ellze and Commander Valya and I become a traitor.

"The Commander sent me," I say. "There have been signs of contagion in this room."

The soldier does not move, but she raises one eyebrow. "Yes, they are all depressed. They fight often, but nobody in here has died."

I shake my head. "No. Some of these prisoners came from the outside. They are potentially carrying an illness that is communicable to The People. I need to observe them for signs."

Her expression sinks. "That cannot be."

"I need proof of infection in order to get an evacuation approval to remove the diseased—before it spreads." I wave her away. "I would leave here if I were you. To limit your exposure."

She starts retreating down the hall. "I will close up this room when I am finished. If they are ill, I will have to remove them, and you do not want to be here when I do."

PARSIFAL

Thelia, Bayled, and I sit by the window, trying to soak up the sunlight, when the suite door opens. Sapphire enters with their gold mask pulled down over their face, eyes lost in deep crevices. The big black cloak billows up around their sharp frame, making seven feet of height feel more like eight.

Morgaun stalks forward. "What are you doing here? What do you want?"

Sapphire ignores him, looking around the room like they're searching for an escaped convict. Their gaze settles on me.

"Yo-o-o-ou," they say, forcing as much of that rolling, musical accent into it as possible. "The Commander wants to see yo-o-ou." Then they point at Thelia. "You come, too."

We both jump up. "You can't take them like this!" Morgaun shouts. Without even glancing at him, Sapphire ties our hands behind our backs and shoves us out the door.

We follow their billowing cloak down the hall, toward the staircase. Right before the big pillar, Sapphire leans down and bangs the wall with one fist. A squat door I've never seen before pops open.

The tunnel inside is dark and windowless. The air smells like it hasn't been used since the invasion. When the door closes behind us, everything vanishes into darkness.

This must be a special servants' entrance. Derk was holding out on me.

"Sapphire?" I ask, surprised by the nervousness in my own voice.

"One moment." The small pink wisp crawls out of Sapphire's waist pouch, bathing us in mauve light. "Please forgive me for not coming sooner." Sapphire unties our hands. "We must get you two out. Now."

I peer at them in the darkness. "What haven't you told us?"

"The Commander may make a decision I cannot stop."

"What kind of decision?" Thelia asks, her voice low.

"There is too much Magic, more than we can siphon off. Unlike anything we have seen. It is volatile and the operation is taking too long. Commander Valya wants to end it now, without seeking the High Seer's permission."

"End it?" I ask.

"Give up on cleaning and evacuating everyone." Sapphire exhales a shuddering breath. "We cannot reach the Magic well with the castle on it, and so we cannot contain it. The Commander wants to destroy the castle to begin building the new hold—and filter this powerful Magic into something he can use."

"Destroy it," Thelia repeats, her face contorting. "With us inside."

Sapphire nods. "I will try to stop him, if I can. But I must make sure you are both safe first."

I snort. "So much for all that not wanting to hurt anyone stuff, huh?"

Sapphire shakes their head and a ghost of a smile graces their lips. "Parsifal. This is merely one of the many reasons I enjoy you so much."

"Only one?" I ask, allowing myself a mischievous smirk in return. "What else?"

Sapphire brings my hand to their chest and the air changes. "You made me consider the meaning of days, when my life was a blur of years." Their tone is grave. "You take every single moment and make something, whether it's drinking wine or playing pa-chi-chi. And I promise—I will protect those moments. I will not let the castle fall without getting you out first."

We both startle when we hear Thelia hiccup. I turn to see her eyes bright with tears. "Theels?" I say. Sapphire and I both reach for her at the same moment, and our hands collide. Sapphire pulls their hand back, looking embarrassed. Thelia hiccups again and turns away.

"Sorry. I just need a moment." She rubs her face with her arm. "That was just really nice, Sapphire."

"It was." I take Sapphire's hand again just to feel their skin under mine, to reclaim the rush I get when we're this close together. I want even more of it. "So what were you saying again, about how great I am?"

Their laugh is like a wind chime. "You are so much more clever, more charming, more beautiful than I ever expected," they whisper to me, dragging one hand up my arm, my neck, to my chin. Sapphire's sunset eyes—icy blue at the top and golden brown at the bottom—peel away my layers, seeing past my strange face, my protruding eyes and flat nose. "You are always surprising me, Parsifal."

My name is a summons. I rise onto my toes and even then, my eyes barely reach Sapphire's chin. Melidia be damned—too short. But they wrap a hand around the nape of my neck and lean down, their breath running across my upper lip. I always thought the long ears didn't smell, probably because of that metal skin; but the scent of Sapphire's breath is surprisingly human.

Suddenly I remember that Thelia's here with us. I stumble back, embarrassed for being swallowed by my lust. I search the dimness for Thelia's face, for her betrayal.

But she's staring at me like I'm a total doorknob. "Why did you stop?"

Why indeed? Whole mountains of complication—doors and walls and cell bars—lie between Sapphire and me. "Can I?" I ask no one in particular. The only thing I've ever wanted as much as this . . . is Thelia.

Sapphire smiles, and it's not the awkward one I'm accustomed to seeing. It's big and real and full. They swoop down in one motion and capture my lips.

The height difference doesn't make it easy, even when I stand on my toes, but Sapphire smoothly wraps a hand around my waist and stoops to even us out. Their lips are soft as silk and their tongue is . . . talented. Kissing Melidia would be like this. My hands find their way up Sapphire's slick, metallic arms to their powerful shoulders, up a slender neck corded with muscle.

When I finally step away, I'm gasping for air. Thelia's hand reaches out to steady me. She presses my palm—*Isn't it amazing?* I pull her against me, my other arm still wrapped tight around Sapphire. I'm so full of the two of them that I might burst.

"Look," Thelia says, breaking the silence. "Sapphire, I . . . I was taught not to be emotional." Her voice breaks. "Not to let anyone really see me." Sapphire takes her hand in theirs and the look they give her, it is love and admiration and something even more profound, something I can't place. "But I don't want to die. I don't want to lose Percy. And I don't want to lose . . . you." She's crying again. So much for Delia's training. I'm proud of her.

Thelia rises up on her strong calves and stares into Sapphire's eyes. Something passes between them, something fierce and hungry, before Thelia presses her lips to Sapphire's. She pours everything into it, all the uncertainty and fear and pain that has followed us like hounds. They are both so beautiful. Thelia hasn't let me go, and I know she won't ever.

"Now, now," I say as they continue on. "I'm feeling a little cold here." Sapphire grabs me hard around the waist and pulls me against them. Thelia releases Sapphire's mouth and takes my chin in her hand.

"Then it's your turn," she says, and her lips seize mine. I have always longed to be ravaged by her. A circle has finally, perfectly, been completed.

I pull away from them both and lean against the cool wall. Whatever this is, whatever we are . . . this world can't bear us.

"Parsifal?" I hear Thelia ask. I just shake my head, knowing I'll break if I try to talk.

Sapphire pulls us both to their chest, tucking our heads under their sharp chin. The wisp flutters around our faces. "I will get you two out of Four Halls," they say. "You must be ready to go when I say."

"What's your grand plan, then?" I ask.

"You need to get very sick."

THELIA

It's simple enough: once we show enough signs of illness, we're rounded up and quarantined. Then we will be put in a wagon and sent as far from Four Halls as possible. The elves won't dream of coming near us if we're contaminated, and we'll be free of this city forever.

"It'll be obvious we're faking it," Parsifal says, using his reason-and-logic voice.

"You underestimate how much The People fear filth," Sapphire says. "Disease, sickness. Any bodily fluid. Our kind has never existed in the same place as humans—we have no bodily systems to prevent cross-infection."

It makes perfect sense to me. I put my hand on Parsifal's arm. "It's the best chance we have." Not just the best chance, but the only chance.

"All right," Parsifal says. "But don't say I didn't warn you if that big silver trit throws us in the moat."

I roll my eyes. "I'll be too dead to say anything."

Sapphire wraps us in an embrace. "All I need is to know you two are out and free."

I suddenly understand: Sapphire doesn't plan to come with us. "No!" I grab their arms. "You can't send us off alone."

Sapphire kisses the tops of our heads fervently. I gasp when a tear lands on my head. "Sapphire?"

"I haven't cried since I was a child." There's a sniffling sound and an embarrassed laugh. "I wish this all had been different and I had met you both under better circumstances."

Parsifal tries to smile. He holds out one finger and the pink wisp lands on it, chattering softly. "This life is long and full of chance meetings, if we're lucky."

At the door of the suite there are no guards in sight. Sapphire was right—the idea of disease was enough.

"It will not be me returning for you," Sapphire says, pulling the gold mask back down over their face. Their blue eyes vanish into empty eye sockets. "Appear as sick as possible. Convince your family to do the same, if you want them to go with you. Boils, blisters—"

"I understand," Thelia says.

Sapphire leans down and delivers one last kiss to each of our foreheads, through the gold mask. They go stiff and intimidating once again as they open the door.

Morgaun, Daddy, and Bayled all surge out of their chairs as we enter. Daddy hobbles toward me, looking me over from head to toe. He glares at Sapphire. "Where did you take my daughter?"

Sapphire says nothing. They leave the room in a swish of

their black cloak, sealing the door with Magic once again. Morgaun opens his mouth, but I don't give him a chance to speak. I feel like I'm on fire.

"We have a plan—and it doesn't involve burning the world to the ground."

BAYLED

I'm the only one who isn't surprised to see Thelia and Parsifal return, unharmed. But I'm also the first to volunteer for their plan. Thelia kneels in front of me, opening a wooden box to reveal four colors of clay.

"Close your eyes," she commands. I obey, and she works on my face for what feels like ages.

Corene peers down at me. "What are you doing to his beautiful skin?" Something about the way she says it makes me feel dirty, as if she thinks this skin belongs to her.

"I'm making him sickly." Thelia scrubs my cheek with a stick of purple kohl. "Good welt there, Bayled. Looks like something's trying to crawl out of your skin." While she gets to work on Parsifal next, I take her hand mirror and examine myself.

Dark pustules and boils decorate my forehead, face, and collar. Upon close inspection, they're clearly fake—but Thelia and Parsifal are certain the long ears won't risk getting close enough. I reach to touch one when Corene says, "You'll smear it."

She drops her chin onto my shoulder, her strawberry hair dripping down my chest. She tries to smile but it doesn't reach her eyes. "Actually, you look good all diseased like that," she says, winking, as if we never argued the other night. She squeezes me around the middle and I close my eyes, wishing myself far from Four Halls. If I'd never come back for her, Harged would still be alive.

Duke Finegarden, who hasn't said a word about our plan yet, evaluates his daughter's riddled face. "It's rather unbecoming."

Thelia smiles. "Thank you. Can I do yours next, Daddy?"

Morgaun sits at the table, fitting the piece of conductive ore into a wooden box he's built. "This plan is idiocy."

Thelia shrugs. "It's better than yours."

I'm tired of this back-and-forth, just like I'm tired of Morgaun seizing Corene's desperation and wielding it against us. And I hate that I still want to make excuses for her.

I slam myself into the chair across from Morgaun. "Do what you want, you rat-faced craggon." I lean in close so he's forced to lean back. "But you are not taking us down with you. When we're gone, you can blow this place to the demon plane for all I care. But we will escape first. Understood?"

Morgaun's jaw flexes, but he says nothing. He fiddles with the device in his hand. Biding his time.

SAPPHIRE

In the morning, I go to see the Commander. I have not slept. The only thought inside me is of Parsifal and Thelia, their smell, their hands tangled in my hair, the rapid beating of their tiny human hearts.

In the temple atrium, the plants have all wilted to brown and gray stalks. Papery petals scattered from dead flowers cover the floors. When Commander Valya answers his door, his face is drawn. Lines like canyons crisscross his gray, dull skin, deepening his eyes and his mouth. As if centuries have passed in only a few days.

"Mahove, friend Sapphire." He returns to his chair slowly, like he is in pain.

"Commander, I have an urgent matter," I say. "My prisoners are sick."

His face turns hard and dark. "How did that happen?"

I have withheld information from the Commander before, but never have I lied to him. "I believe it came with the new prisoners—those who arrived with the King's ward."

"Ah." He gives a slow nod.

"It should only have affected those in the dungeons, and those with whom the King's ward has come into contact. Like the Princess—and any others kept with her."

The Commander's eyes narrow. "I will have Ellze deal with them."

My Magic heart freezes. Ellze cannot be in charge of Parsifal and Thelia's fates, or they will not make it out of Four Halls alive.

"Commander, would it not be better to—"

"Sapphire." My name hangs in the air while the Commander inhales, wobbling the skin under his eyes. "Do you know why I brought you into the Jaguars?"

Once, I had ideas. Perhaps he was attracted to me; but that was vain. Perhaps he was impressed by my speed and diligence in battle; but that was proud. I am certain now that my only attribute was being Ellze's friend, and Ellze asked for the favor.

I shake my head.

"You showed so much promise," the Commander says, his voice thin. "Young, quick, smart. And above all . . ." He takes a breath. "You are dedicated, Sapphire."

I sense the turn coming, the multitudinous ways in which I have failed to live up to expectations.

"I thought that in a new place, under uncertain conditions, that dedication would make you a rock. The one who would work hardest, while remaining honest." He leans forward so his face is very near mine. I do not lean away—it is no time to show weakness.

"I will still always do that," I say.

He sits back again and breathes as if just moving is taxing. "Is what Ellze told me the truth?" he asks. "That your concern for the humans in South Hall is . . . personal? That you are attached?"

I must stay in control. Not let my surprise and fear show on my face. "E-Ellze only wants an excuse to destroy it all, to eliminate the rest of the humans and hurry on the operation. He wants to become King of the new—"

"Sapphire." Commander Valya sounds so tired. "You are going to great lengths to protect them, aren't you?"

"They do not deserve death."

"No? Not for the centuries of warring and conquering? What about butchering animals and consuming trees? Who will stop them from stealing even more land?"

"They are too temporal, Commander!" I find my voice rising. "They forget their agreements with us from centuries ago. You underestimate how much they can learn and grow and feel in such short lives. They are not all the evil things you paint them to be."

Commander Valya considers me, and for the first time, it

feels as if he might actually see what is in front of him. "Nevertheless, you lied to a soldier in order to gain entry to one of the human rooms."

I cannot deny this. The Commander's eyes close, and for a moment, it looks as if he has fallen asleep. Why doesn't he sleep? Why won't he eat? With a great sigh, his eyes open once more. "I think you know what comes next."

I do. In some ways, it is a relief. I can leave this place. I can forget Parsifal and Thelia, and all the pain that came alongside caring for them.

The Commander's mouth widens, exposing his teeth—no longer straight and white and perfect, but yellowed and pointed. "As your Commander, I strip you of your post as Jaguar."

The words carry no sting. At one time, this mask and this cloak meant so much. Now they fill me with remorse. The Commander holds out his hands and I remove the gold mask—heavy now that its enchantment has released me—and return it. He rises laboriously to unclasp the cloak. I remember how his hands felt like Magic when he put it on, but now all I feel in his fingertips is a seething hatred. It has crippled him, filled him, until there is very little left that is The People.

It is eating him alive.

I face the commander who once gave me so much hope for the future. "I will return to Viteos and tell the High Seer everything," I say. "She will not allow this to continue. Ellze will not get his palace."

Commander Valya turns away. "We will already be done by then. The High Seer will find that we have successfully contained the well and harnessed the most powerful source of Magic ever known. She will have nothing but appreciation for my nephew's work here."

There is nothing left for me to say. As I exit his room, I know one thing.

Ellze is going to kill everyone I care about unless I stop him.

PARSIFAL

Duke Finegarden has given in and sits before Thelia's brush. The suite's filled with the sound of a knife whittling down wood. Morgaun fits one piece into another, sealing up his small box. The long wick of a candle protrudes through a misshapen hole in the top. I don't know how he intends to light it. Does he know it functions, or does he simply believe it does because Melidia's willed it?

I suppose it's fitting that what I hate most about the Holy Kingdom will be the thing that kills me. Where will Melidia be when Morgaun sends a spark of flame into the very heart and soul of Magic and blows us all to ashes? Maybe she'll die too. One can only hope that the Goddess will suffer at the hands of what she created.

"All right, everyone," Thelia says. "Who knows when they'll arrive—lie low and fake it."

Morgaun sneers, gets up, and leaves the room. After a moment Corene follows. I lie on the floor by Thelia's feet, looking as pathetic as I can manage, trying not to imagine what they're doing. Bayled shows no interest in them whatsoever, lying like a corpse against the window seat. I'm proud of him.

After many candlestick-hours of thinking and then trying not to think, a familiar sound echoes in the suite: the *tsssssssszit* of the Magic seal around the door releasing. When it opens, three elves stride in—including the elf with the green hair, his face hidden behind a gold mask.

He surveys us silently. I hear Duke Finegarden's breath pick up. The green elf stops near me and pushes me back. I let myself fall, as if I have no control left over my own body. Pretty good acting, I'd say.

After circling the room, the elf pulls up his mask and grins at us. "What has befallen you?" His gaze stops on Bayled. "Where is your Princess?"

"Hiding," he says blandly. "She's not infected yet." He protects her, even now. I suppose no amount of abuse could kill his decency.

"Then we must remove you at once. You will be cleansed, then tossed from these walls to die alone, far away from here." I let my head fall forward, as if devastated. Thelia lets out a sob.

"Tragic end for the King's heir," the green elf says to Bayled with a keen smile. "I will return shortly."

With that, the elves leave, sealing up the door behind them. Thelia falls backward onto the floor next to me. "That went well," she says with a great sigh.

"Where do we go once they set us free?" I ask, starting to believe that Sapphire's plan just might work, that another life lies ahead of us. "I don't care how cold it is, I'm going straight for a wash."

Bayled shakes his head. "Don't be stupid." He sits up, his brown eyes narrowed. "That elf is going to kill us."

CHAPTER 19

BAYLED

My great mistake was trusting. I won't make it again.

"Sapphire said they would let us go," Thelia insists.

I scoff. "Do you really believe that? After all this?" I gesture at the frozen windows, at the Bellisares' scattered belongings, at the skeletal Duke under his blanket with his eyes closed.

By the stunned way that Thelia's staring at me, I'm sure we're thinking the same thing—we have crossed each other's paths and taken it up as our own. She trusts and believes, because she loves that elf with the blue hair, maybe as much as she loves Parsifal. Her feelings hide the truth from her, as my feelings for Corene hid the truth from me.

I quickly cross the room and begin to rifle through Morgaun's trunk. "Be prepared to fight. They won't come back peacefully."

The door to our room opens and Corene steps out, her face shifting when she sees me. "What are you doing?"

"Defending us." I find what I'm looking for: Morgaun's dagger. The same one that cut open Thelia's face years ago. I wrap it up in a shirt and shove it into the belt of my trousers.

Morgaun appears in the doorway. "What are you doing with my stuff?" He grabs my arm. I wheel around, landing my fist in his nose. Morgaun howls and stumbles backward.

"Bayled!" Corene gasps. "How could you—?"

"Oh please," I interrupt her, just wishing she would stop. "I followed you around like a chick for so long, you thought I always would. But I do have a mind of my own, and I'm tired of being used by you." Corene stutters with fury, and I turn to Thelia and Parsifal. "Prepare yourselves. Find whatever you can use as a weapon."

Thelia grins at me and grabs a poker out of the fireplace. "Ready."

This is our last stand. We'll be ready when the Green Demon returns.

I'm unsurprised when the point of a sword tears through the door like it's paper. The wood splinters to pieces. Two elves rush in, faces covered, hands tucked into thick, heavy gloves—led by the green one with the cheetah-fur cloak and the gold mask. My target.

The first soldier runs at the Duke, sword out. The most frail and defenseless among us. "Daddy!" Thelia shouts.

The blade punctures the only part of him exposed by his blanket—the throat. His eyes bulge, and blood springs from his lips with a squawking, gurgling sound.

A scream of rage fills the suite as Thelia lunges at her father's murderer. She aims the poker to impale the elf's chest, but it bounces off metal armor. "Horsefish," she says, leaping backward. The elf spins around and charges.

"Here," Parsifal chirps, putting a foot out. "Let me step in." The elf stumbles right over it and careens into the wall head-first.

The second elf rushes me, thinking me unarmed. One hand inside my belt and I've ripped the dagger free. I duck and sidestep, just like Harged would have done—and bury Morgaun's dagger right where the gap between his greaves and his chestplate leave exposed silver skin.

He slides to the ground, blue blood boiling all over my hands. Thelia's expression is surprised—and impressed.

Wild laughter streams out of the Green Demon. "They fight back!"

The elf who got her head knocked around tries to move, so Thelia stomps down on her back with one foot. Holding the wriggling body still, she grabs the fallen sword and points it at the Green Demon. "Come on. Come get me, since you want it so bad."

He grins and pounces. Thelia swings, but he seizes the blade with one hand and bits of blue blood spatter across Parsifal's face. Thelia flips backward—a kroga move—out of the way.

A howl of mad laughter. "Quick little critter!" he sneers. "No wonder Sapphire likes you."

The door to Corene's room flies open with a *bang!* Morgaun stumbles out, face flushed. In his hand is the small wooden box with its white wick.

"I'm ending this!" he roars. "I'm going to destroy every last one of you perverted monsters!"

Even the Green Demon is momentarily distracted. Thelia spins and kicks, delivering a blow to his abdomen. He stumbles back against the wall.

"How do you plan to light it, you rusty nail?" Parsifal asks.

Morgaun grins. "I found your note, your smokestick, and this." He holds up the fire striker. "Your long-eared lover left it for you, but it's mine now. Isn't it beautiful that it will be the thing that kills them all?"

"End it!" Corene shouts behind him. "Free us from this!"

I stare at her but speak to Morgaun. "If you tap into that thread of Magic, you destroy everything. All of us. All humanity."

The Green Demon's getting up, and though I can't see his face through the mask, I don't think we're the only ones afraid of what comes next. Morgaun looks at Corene. "Ready?"

Corene breaks eye contact with me. "Yes."

His face contorts into a wild smile. "Perfect." With a flick of his hand, the fire starter lights. The tiny flame surges upward, spitting and lapping at the air, fueled by Magic all around us. He lowers the machine so the flame touches the tip of the wick. Behind Thelia, the Green Demon charges.

A blaze of fire roars up into Morgaun's face, burning his hair and skin. His screech of agony is lost in an unearthly howl as the machine ignites.

PARSIFAL

I turn to Thelia and her frightened black eyes find mine. I hold them like that, searching them for the part of myself I need to do what has to be done.

There. The warm heart of Magic, pulsing in my chest. It surges up, hot and full of light, when the box explodes.

Everything slows down. The flame swells like an overfull stomach, the curling tips reaching the far corners of the room. I lean down and press my hand to the stone floor. *Please, Four Halls.* Even my breaths are slowed. *You helped us before. Help me now.*

When I look up, the world is changed. Shimmering blue, white, and yellow strands—some thick, some thin; some wavy, some straight—flow through the air around me, pulsing with energy. It's Magic, making up the fabric of everything.

And one of the threads has caught fire. Forgren's conductor worked. In slow motion, the flame that began in Morgaun's hand grows at lightning speed, ripping along the top of the fat thread. Magic itself is screaming—a noise like no human, or elf, would ever make. Wailing as it's consumed. I feel it in the warm center of my chest.

And the castle answers.

The stones beneath my feet shift, like I'm standing on water. The gaps widen and lips appear. Then teeth and a tongue.

"Wider!" I demand. "Don't you want your snack?" The mouth grins at me and suddenly, it's as wide as Morgaun. As wide as the expanding explosion that's already burned off half his arm. Morgaun's horrified face contorts into an inhuman shape as the tongue wraps around his feet. It yanks him down, between two long rows of teeth—and the burst of flame that would eat the world and leave it simmering ash is swallowed up with him.

Everything speeds back up—Corene screaming. The

green elf's roar as the rippling stones throw him and his soldier backward. The mouth's great lips closing, cutting off Morgaun's howl of fury.

The stones slide back into place. Beneath our feet is the sound of a muffled explosion. The whole castle shakes. Smoke bursts through the gaps between stones.

And it's gone.

THELIA

Parsifal did it. The castle ate Morgaun and whatever horrible thing he'd created. Only the window shattered. Corene drops to her knees on top of the spot where he was, running her hands over the stone like it might open back up again.

The green elf lying on the floor moans, dragging himself along the stone, clutching his gold mask.

The remaining soldier kneels down to help him up. But I'm faster, and I bury the point of the sword I've stolen into the slender space between her helmet and chest armor. She tumbles to the ground, and I finish it.

The green elf slithers out from under me and rushes Bayled. His gigantic cloak billowing behind him, the elf raises his sword to slice Bayled in half.

"No you don't." He's exposed his bronze underarm. As far away as I am, all I can do is spin and slash as hard as I can, hoping to puncture the metal skin.

The elf roars in pain, but my sword has punctured him— and now it's stuck. "Go!" I shout at Parsifal.

He rushes to the door, but it's still sealed with a Magic barrier. The green-haired elf laughs at me and rips the sword from his arm, throwing it to the floor.

"Can you open it?" I shout to Parsifal.

"Oh, you mean with all those Magic powers I just used up?"

The green elf pivots to face me. I step to one side of him, and he isn't ready to guard when I jump quickly back the other way. "You're a much worse fighter than Sapphire," I whisper to him and slam two fingers into his chest, in the crease right on his pectoral. He stares at me open-mouthed for a few heartbeats before his knees give out.

He won't be down forever. Parsifal's trying to get through the Magic barrier, so I run over to help. "I've got nothing," he says.

I throw myself at the doorway with my forearm protecting my face—and crash into a barrier. "Damn it!" I pound the invisible barricade again with one fist. "Let us out!" I can't fight off the green elf forever, and more of them will arrive soon.

"Step back." I know that voice. I look up to find Sapphire standing on the other side, half smiling. They wave a hand, and the familiar blue crackle of Magic ripples. I stumble out into the hall. We're free.

Bayled emerges behind me, dragging a screaming Corene. He just can't let go, can he?

"We must move," Sapphire says. The wisp circles them, clearly agitated. "Now."

We trudge through the dark servants' tunnels behind Sapphire for what feels like an eternity. We'll take a turn, or go down some stairs, only to find more pitch-black darkness. The wisp floats on ahead, casting the walls in pink.

The hallway abruptly ends in a door. Sapphire opens it slowly and peeks out to look. "Safe."

We emerge into a room of broken stone walls and rotting tapestries. I know this place—we're near the dungeon. Around the next corner is the door I've had many nightmares about. But there's light shining on the wall, so we all stop and go silent as we turn down the hall.

A man leans against the stones, with an overgrown mustache that I recognize immediately. "Red!" I cry. Captain Tarkness rises from her spot on the floor, covered in bruises and boils.

"About time," she says.

"Everyone hurry," Sapphire hisses. "Now's not the time. To the wagon."

We move quickly to the livery, and thankfully, we don't come across anyone. "The horses are not a frequent attraction for The People," Sapphire says as we slip into the stable. "You'll be happy to know, Thelia, I've made sure they are exercised."

"Parlor Trick?" I rush over to the white horse hitched to the front of the wagon.

"Halrendar!" Bayled pets his own horse's face. "I'm so glad you're okay."

"Everyone in the wagon," Sapphire says. "Now."

Nobody speaks as we're laid on top of each other like sausages in a dish—Parsifal next to me, Red under me. I can't imagine anything more awkward.

"Come now, Parlor Trick," I hear Sapphire say to the horse, and the wagon starts to move.

SAPPHIRE

To my vast surprise, we make it out of the stable without incident. But this is only the beginning. At any moment, any of The People could stop to question us. Thankfully, they are all occupied. Soldiers rush about the wide open courtyard. A Magicker tends to her worried orkuk.

Smoke rises from South Hall, and confusion has spread through the force. Still, for now, we are ahead of the news. But we still have to stop at the front gates.

As we make our way around soldiers' tents, I call out, "Diseased. Move aside! Diseased!" The People clear away from us, horrified as they catch sight of the bodies in the wagon. They whisper, but no one approaches.

When we finally reach the portcullis, my heart of Magic is blazing hot. Everything could end here. A squad leader approaches us but I shout, "Stop!" She freezes, and I stay near the wagon. "They are plagued."

"Who are you?" she asks, not recognizing me without my long cloak and gold mask.

I ignore the question. "The Commander asked me to remove these bodies and destroy them. I must ensure no one comes near them or me, as I may also be infected."

The squad leader gives a deferential nod and backs away even farther. "Bring up the gate!" She waves at the two soldiers on top of the wall. "Let them out."

Every moment we stand there waiting is a moment someone could notice the humans in the wagon are still breathing. The gate rolls up and we are ushered through.

The horses' hooves clack on iron-studded timbers as we cross the bridge. Then we make our way down through the

Upper City without confronting a single other living thing. We will emerge from the city walls intact.

And after that? As much as I would prefer to run away with my humans, I must hasten to Viteos and tell the High Seer everything I have witnessed here. How Ellze has seized command, how the Commander deteriorates. How corruption has eaten through us.

I worry about my humans out there—Magic infused in their hair, their skin, their breaths of air—but there is nothing I can do for them now. I must trust that Parsifal and Thelia can handle themselves.

The wagon descends into the Lower City, past collapsing roofs and crumbling stone. Someone in the cart moans as it hits a pothole. Now the rolling green hills of Melidihan sprawl out before us. The Low Road, muddy with melted snow, winds up to meet the white wall of the city—and the closed iron gates.

A wagon sits on the other side. Ferah wipes her hands off on her cloak, and Zylion stands beside her. The air is full of smoke. One more load of corpses exploded.

They turn our direction when our wagon approaches. "Stand back," I call out, walking in front of the horses. "I have diseased bodies."

"Mahove, friend Sapphire. I will take care of it." Ferah forms a ball of Magic in her palms. "Put the wagon there. I need a clear shot."

"Wait," I say. "They—"

A guffaw echoes on the stone walls behind us. I spin around to find Ellze following us down the street, blood dripping from his arm. "Ferah, this is not what you think it is."

"Come no closer, Ellze," I say, holding up both hands. "I could be infected, too."

But Ellze does not stop until he is right in front of me. He grabs both sides of my face and yanks me in like I am a dog, not one of The People. "You disappoint me, Sapphire." His eyes, which once reflected the light like emeralds, are as dull as Commander Valya's—and filled with hatred. "This lie is bad, even for you, who has kept so many secrets poorly."

Someone in the cart sits up. "They are reanimating!" Ferah shouts.

Ellze's awful grin widens. "You thought you could sneak them out, Sapphire?" Everyone in the cart is wriggling and gasping for air.

"I had to try." I clench my fist over the hilt of my sword. "Before you could finish poisoning the Magic well, kill off the Commander, and blow the castle to pieces."

Ferah steps between us, one hand raised. "If the humans are sick, we should destroy them quickly."

I cannot waste time—the longer we are delayed, the sooner reinforcements arrive. I rip my sword out of its sheath and leap at Ellze.

"Sapphire!" Zylion shouts, horrified.

Ellze just sidesteps me and laughs again. "The Commander did not bring you because you were a good fighter."

"At least I can fight," I say. "You only became a Jaguar because you asked your uncle for a favor." While everyone focuses on me, Thelia has climbed out of the wagon, Bayled close on her heels. When Ellze spins around to slash at me, Thelia raises a sword and charges him.

Zylion steps in her way, parrying the blow. She roars at him and begins to hack with furious speed.

When he sees her, Ellze bursts out laughing again. "You," he growls in Thelia's language, sneering. "Who gave me this nice wound." He pats the big gash in his arm.

"I'll give you another one!" Thelia kicks Zylion in the stomach, sending him off-balance.

"Come get me." Ellze raises his sword. "I can take you both at once."

I swing at him to distract him from Thelia. "Don't worry, Ellze," Ferah says. "I will deal with the human." She raises her hands, and the ball of Magic in her palms swells.

"Thelia!" I shout.

But the Prince is there. He shoves Thelia out of the way as a ball of blue Magic sails past them. It hits the ground right behind the wagon, making the horses rear up in fear—and Parlor Trick's yoke snaps in half. She leaps away, throwing her head.

"Get out of here!" I shout at the humans still in the cart. The Baron, who seems to understand they are far outmatched, climbs into the driver's seat and seizes the remaining horse's reins. In the corner of my eye, Ferah prepares another projectile—and aims for the wagon.

"Kill them!" Ellze commands gleefully. "Sapphire will hate it."

Thelia goes for Ferah, sliding across the ground and knocking her legs out from under her. But I have been distracted too long—Ellze stumbles toward me, swinging his sword.

The blade entering me hurts worse than anything I've ever felt. I look down to find it buried in my hip, a dribble of blue blood seeping out. I jerk backward to free myself and blood sprays across Ellze's neck and face. He licks it off his lips, his face overtaken by a feral smile.

"You've become a monster." I raise my sword once more and step toward him, but pain lances through my right leg. I stumble forward.

"Me, old friend?" Ellze asks. "I think the monster is you." He towers over me where I kneel on the ground and raises his sword over his head.

THELIA

I'll be no match against the Magic user if she has time to summon another Magic projectile—so I can't give her time. Before either of us can get up off the ground, I slam my elbow into the side of her head. She squawks and falls back, giving me the chance to get on my feet again.

She needs distance and space to use Magic, so when she swipes at me, I step closer and lift my sword high up over my head. She's wearing no armor—only robes—so my elven blade sinks easily into the flesh at her throat, and she topples forward into the mud.

When I get to my feet again, Sapphire is crouched on the ground, bleeding. The green elf stands over them, sword raised, ready to murder the love of my life. Well, one of them.

I'm too far away to slug him, so I swing at his sword with mine, hoping to set him off-course just enough. It works— and we're both sent careening into the mud. I get up first, my reflexes still honed despite weeks of captivity.

"Thelia!" Bayled shouts. "Behind you!"

I spin as a blur of purple and bronze blazes toward me. I bring my sword up just in time to block the elf, but the force of it knocks the sword right out of my hand. I stumble back, blinded by a flash of steel. Surely, this is my end.

CLANG! Instead, the purple elf's sword collides with another blade. It's Bayled, barely parrying him with Morgaun's dagger. "Don't look," Bayled says as he dodges another strike.

So I turn around and look.

Behind the city gate come one-headed bears. Raptors. Lions. Soldiers. All streaming down the main street, straight toward us. We only have moments left before they're on top of us.

The green elf is back on his feet. He cackles wildly as his eyes dart to Sapphire, still on the ground, and back to me. *Come at me*, I will him, but he knows that's exactly what I want.

He charges with the point of his blade at Sapphire instead.

I square my shoulder like I did on those stairs ages ago, the first time I laid my eyes on Sapphire's beautiful face—and I lunge. With the entire force of my body, I hurl myself into the green elf. The impact of his armor knocks the wind out of me, and we go down together—me on top of him. And the point of his blade plunges deep into my belly.

A surge of agony rips through me, toes to head. Sapphire screams, "Thelia!"

The green elf shoves me off him, into the mud. But I'm not finished. That's what Mother always said: *You're not finished until you're dead.* While he struggles to get up, his sword still buried in my flesh and his feet slipping in the mud, I raise myself up just enough that I'm level with his stomach. When I smile, his face twists in confusion.

I reel my arm back, closing my fist except for my middle and index finger. With two fingers, I slam him right in the exposed abdomen. His face contorts in horror as his vital organs implode.

I've always wanted to try that.

Halrendar pulls the wagon down the muddy Low Road, away from the city gates. I saw Thelia leap fearlessly from the wagon. I've watched her take on two of the long ears already and win. Each time it's a gamble—her skill and desperation against their size and speed and training. At some point, she's going to lose the wager.

At least she has Bayled to back her up.

"We have to wait for her," I tell the Baron. For both of them.

Captain Tarkness shakes her head. "Don't be a brave fool and end up a stupid corpse."

Can't really argue with that. I clench my fists and settle back into the wagon as we slip into the dark woods. All I can think of is how outmatched they are, and how awful it would be to not see them again.

The wagon wheels slow as they stick in the mud, but Halrendar's strong. I check back over my shoulder, hoping that Thelia and Sapphire will appear.

Corene lets out the first sound she's made since we left the castle behind. "It's them!" she shouts. "Long ears!"

Figures emerge from the trees ahead, their dark leather clothes studded with pine branches, their faces scrubbed in deep green to hide among the foliage. "Keep it down, Princess," says the Baron. "These are my soldiers."

The Baron and Captain Tarkness are the first out, reuniting with the force as they swarm around the wagon. Red starts to point out a team among them. "We're going back," he says, shifting his gaze pointedly to me. "To find Thelia."

Captain Tarkness gapes at him. "You saw the size of the

long ears' force. By the time you got back, you'd get your head bitten off by a raptor before you could swing your sword."

"She's right," I say. "We don't have the numbers. I've spent a long time inside that castle—and we simply can't take them."

The Captain crosses her arms. "Thank you."

There's a distant crash through the trees. We all spin, swords at the ready. The soldiers form a line as the tearing of branches and pounding of hooves grows nearer. "The People have found us," Captain Tarkness hisses.

If they have, that's the end.

A great white shape emerges between two trees. I shout over the din, "Parlor Trick!" On her back is Bayled—with a body draped across his lap.

He reins the horse to a halt. "Someone come get her." I catch sight of Thelia's dark hair and a trickle of blood streaming down Parlor Trick's snow-white side. *No.* I can't lose both Sapphire *and* Thelia.

I sprint over to the horse and together, Bayled and I get Thelia down to the ground. "Sasel!" he shouts. "I need your help."

A priestess emerges from the band of soldiers. She nudges me out of the way to kneel beside Thelia. "She's unconscious but breathing. Step back." I take one step back, but no more. Sasel puts a finger to Thelia's throat. "She doesn't have long. She's bleeding out."

Captain Tarkness kneels next to her and examines the gushing wound. Part of her is missing—on the same side as the scar on her face. The world has chipped away at Thelia Finegarden, piece by piece.

Sasel raises her hands as the soldiers stand around,

murmuring. "We need silence!" the Captain roars, and everyone goes quiet. My eyes never stray from Thelia's face as Sasel and the Captain begin their work. Bayled sits down next to me.

Their four hands form a circle over Thelia, and under their fingers, light begins to gather. Sasel's fingers comb the air, pulling, gathering. The light takes shape. Soon, resting in her palms are a shining, glowing needle and a spool of thread.

"Magic thread?" I ask, feeling a familiar place in my chest growing warm.

"The best kind," the Captain says, as Sasel guides the needle through the flesh around Thelia's open wound. Thelia moans but doesn't open her eyes. I am grateful she isn't conscious.

I turn to Bayled. "Where's Sapphire . . . ?"

He shakes his head. "I don't know. They were injured. Thelia took this blow to save them and killed that green one. When Parlor Trick came back for her, Sapphire demanded we get to safety. I saw long ears coming so I didn't want to wait around."

If Sapphire was already wounded . . . I doubt the elven force will forgive them for all this. Thelia sacrificed herself for Sapphire—and it might be in vain.

I drop my head into my hands and a sob bursts out of me. What was the point of saving the world from Morgaun if neither Thelia nor Sapphire are in it?

Someone puts an arm around my shoulders as I hiccup. Bayled? Well, demons be fucked, I actually appreciate it.

When the sewing is finished, Sasel ties off the glowing thread. The stitch pulls itself tighter, bringing the edges of Thelia's healthy skin together. She doesn't wake up.

SAPPHIRE

Two soldiers grab me, and I am in too much pain to consider fighting back. Thankfully, the Prince listened to me and rode away with Thelia to safety. Our force could follow the tracks, but they may never catch up. And the Baron's men are out there, ready to defend them to the death.

"Seize them!" roars Zylion. "The Commander must know what happened here today." Two soldiers tie me up, and we start the slow march back to the castle.

I don't fear my judgment. There is nothing left for Commander Valya to take from me except my life. If he wants to sentence me, he will have to send me home to Viteos first or risk the High Seer's wrath. She will discover the truth sooner or later.

Behind us, soldiers carry Ellze's and Ferah's bodies like something sacred. I've committed a sin beyond sins: abetted the murder of two of The People. My own brethren. I will never forget the way that Ellze's face turned to horror, and his body contorted like something possessed, when Thelia dealt her final blow.

My limp slows us down. I catch Zylion shaking his head. "Sapphire," he says. He sounds confused. "Why did you put your life on the line—betray us all—to rescue those humans? They are beetles to an orkuk. You will live for one hundred of their lifetimes. And we are so close to ending all this."

"By bringing the castle down and killing all these innocents?" I shake my head. "I could never have called myself one of The People if I let them perish. Especially those I love."

Zylion sighs. "The Commander will decide what to do with you."

I wonder which Commander we will find when we get there. The one with gray, sallow skin, and broken, pointed teeth? Or the one who once led us with grace and strength?

Not that it matters. Even if I spend the rest of my days locked up in the High Seer's hold, I will never regret a moment.

CHAPTER 20

PARSIFAL

When we reach my family's estate, we get Thelia settled in my room upstairs. Sasel and the Captain take turns attending to her wounds. We can't stay long, but we can let Thelia rest and heal for a little while.

I hover outside the door until I work up the nerve to ask how she's doing. "I don't know," Sasel says. "She's taken extensive internal damage. That monster carved her up."

I remember the green elf's wild, opaque eyes. Something had gone very wrong there.

I put a hand over my warm chest, which hasn't returned to normal since I called for Four Halls to swallow Morgaun. We're still coated in Magic, swimming in it. It crackles around me as I move out here in the regular world.

It could be the end of me, or the beginning.

THELIA

There's a hole in me. Even as I travel through brightly-colored fever dreams, I know a piece of me has gone missing. When the nightmares finally grind to a finish and I float up to the surface, I don't want to open my eyes. If I do, I acknowledge that I may never fight again—not to mention ride a horse. Or walk.

I'll always have this hole in me where Sapphire should be.

Fingers run up and down my arm. I'm sure it's Parsifal, reminding me he's there with feather touches. It's the kind of lover that he is—knowing that's all it takes. I suppose I can face anything as long as Parsifal's waiting.

When I open my eyes and the world drifts into focus, I find a face with a bushy mustache smiling down at me, pity wrinkling the corners of his eyes. " . . . Red?" I ask, my voice a crackling whisper. There's more silver in his hair than there used to be.

He leans forward and draws a lock of hair away from my face. "It's so good to see you. I've missed you ever since I left Four Halls."

I frown at him and it makes the dull ache in my side flare. I can tell my sense for pain has been numbed, probably by Magic. "But you left." I sound so . . . emotionless. I was never angry at Red for leaving, only at Corene for saying what made him leave. But now it occurs to me: what kind of person would listen to her? Not someone I would choose now.

He lowers his head like a dog that's been chastised. "I was going to ask you to marry me, until Corene said you were in love with Bayled."

My mind, still foggy from sleep, struggles to take this in.

The idea of marrying Bayled, of wanting nothing more than to be Queen of the Holy Kingdom, seems ridiculous now—the way a child imagines becoming a dragon or a cloud.

"Corene lied to you."

The Baron sighs. "I know. I'm sorry I left. I didn't want to."

"It's fine," I say, and take the effort to pat his hand—hoping that if I make him feel good enough, he'll go away. I want to go back to sleep and be left alone in my mourning.

"Thelia." Red picks my hand up and rubs the back. It makes me itch. "You know how I feel about you. That hasn't changed."

Once upon a time, I liked this touch. Baron Durnhal's still handsome and kind. But I pull my hand back. "Please," Red says, his eyes boring into mine. "You're hurt. You'll need time to rest and recover. Come back to the Crimson Woods with me. Live in my home. Let Captain Tarkness take care of you." He stops and turns his head away for a moment, like he's trying to get back his courage. "There may be nothing left of the Holy Kingdom, and the title may be meaningless, but please—be my Baronness?"

It feels like the world's tipping sideways. Soon the paintings and the tapestries and the furniture will start to slide across the floor, taking us with them, until we're all falling into the ceiling. Once, this would've meant the world to me.

I shake my head. "No," I say, leaving it at that single word. I look away as his face breaks apart. I won't apologize for refusing a request that I made no indication of wanting.

"You're right." He stands up suddenly. "I believed the lie so easily. I never thought to simply ask you if it was true."

I sigh. "There are so many wonderful people in the world who could make you happy. But it's not me."

He rubs his eyes with one hand. "I hope you don't mind

if I . . . leave. Right now. I'm just . . ." I nod and he walks out. I wonder if I'll ever see him again, but I'm too tired to worry. Too tired to care about the barony I could've ruled, the castle I could've lived in. I never want to see a castle again as long as I live unless Sapphire and Parsifal are in it.

PARSIFAL

Bayled goes with me to see Thelia, and Corene insists she come along. We find Thelia staring at the ceiling, exhausted. When she describes her conversation with Red, I want to kiss her all over. She didn't even attach an "I'm sorry" when she rejected him. I love her even more.

"So where do we go from here?" Bayled says, sitting on the other side of her bed.

"I'm not moving for a while."

I look down at her, combing my fingers through her black hair. "We can't stay at the mansion. We've only stayed this long so you can heal."

She sighs. "Yeah. We can't let *them* find us."

"Sasel is returning with Red and his army back to the Crimson Woods," Bayled says. "It sounds like you won't be going that way."

"All the more reason you should come with me!" Corene claps her hands together.

"Go where with you?" Bayled asks, his voice flat.

"To the Klissen, of course! Bayled, you and I will build a new Kingdom there."

Thelia stares at her. "With the traitor?" She lets out a laugh. It clearly hurts her and she starts to cough. "The same cratertooth who sent a wizard to Four Halls to help the long ears take over? The same one who tried to have Bayled murdered?"

Corene's eyes narrow. "It makes the most sense strategically, *Theels*. The Southerners are our best chance of restoring what we've lost." She's always had a contingency plan.

"And who says I want that?" Thelia shuts her eyes and sighs. "Please, just go. Your last hog-brained plan almost killed us all."

"Well, I'm going to be Queen of the Holy Kingdom no matter what you do," Corene says, getting off the bed.

"There's nothing left to be queen of," I tell her. "You'd rule over ghosts and broken stones."

"And for that," she snarls, her face transformed, "I will get my revenge." She turns to Bayled, and her very eyes seem to cackle with energy. "This is your chance, Bayled, to be King."

"I never wanted to be King, Corene," Bayled says with a sigh. "If you knew me, you'd know that. I only wanted you."

She scours each of us with her eyes. "Fine. Good luck trying to survive out there on your own." She leaves the room, slamming the door closed behind her.

BAYLED

I know Corene suffered, living the dark—but that doesn't excuse what she's become now. Maybe she's always been this way. Maybe when we wanted the same thing, when we idolized being together, I chose not to see her for what she was: selfish, unmoored, desperately searching for herself.

"Never mind her," Parsifal says impatiently. "What about us, Bayled? We only survived this long because we've stuck together. You and Thelia took down, what, four elves together?"

I'm aghast. "You were the one who convinced Four Halls to eat Morgaun whole! I'm the one who completely ruined your escape plan." And got Harged killed.

Parsifal claps me on the back. "Nobody was calling you a master strategist, Bayled."

Thelia covers her side as she laughs. "Percy, stop!"

"You're as brave as either of us, though," Parsival says. For the first time in our lives, he might actually respect me. "Definitely braver than I am when it comes to hitting people with pointy things. I know we haven't always been the best of friends to you . . ." That's an understatement. "But I think we're better off together than apart."

I take a deep breath and smile, just a little. "Well, in that case—what if we went north?" If we're going to stick together, well, I'm going to commit. I need a team to play for.

"Go to the Northern Republic?" Thelia *hmms*. "But that's so far. In the shape I'm in . . ."

"We'll help you get there," I say brightly. "We can do it together." I had completely written off the Northern Republic, but in the end, maybe it really is my home. The Kingdom never wanted me anyway. I feel almost excited.

"And you're fine with Corene leaving—?" Parsifal begins.

"*Yes.*" I inhale sharply, stuffing my anger back down. That's a new feeling for me. "I'm done."

"Finally," Thelia says, rolling her eyes.

Parsifal takes her hand. "Then it's settled. I'll make sure you get there safe, Theels. Just think—a new life. It won't matter where we're from, or what we were, in the Republic."

"We'd all just be normal citizens," I say. "Rising or falling on our own merits."

Her eyes close, and she lets out a relieved sigh. "Sounds nice."

CHAPTER 21

THELIA

After three moons of trekking across the hills of my ancestors, through their abandoned cities and ruins, we spot the glittering metal roofs of Dezha on the horizon. We're tired and thirsty and starving.

Thanks to the thick coating of Magic around me, I've healed far more quickly than anyone expected; instead of riding in the wagon, I get to approach the city walls on Parlor Trick's back. I may never be my old self again, but I'm a new Thelia Finegarden—with one handsome scar down my face to remind me of where I came from, and another down my side to remind me of someone I loved.

There's no wall around the city, as if the Northern Republic doesn't fear outsiders the way the Holy Kingdom did. Dirt becomes neat cobblestone. The houses are squat, their walls made of hardened clay, their roofs reflective metal.

Every street corner has a market stall, and people seem happy. Well-fed. Children play with their pets, and older people chase loose chickens around. I wonder, as we often did around a campfire, what Melidihan looks like now.

Abandoned? A new elven hub, bustling with life?

I don't want to think about whether anyone else made it out. My cracked soul can't handle the possibility that they didn't.

A few people stop to stare as we pass through with our shabby wagon. "You're taking us to the Prime Minister, right?" I ask Bayled.

He laughs. "No, we won't meet the Prime Minister. We're only ordinary citizens, remember?" We stop in front of an unremarkable large building. As we enter, a woman in a long blue coat rimmed with gold tassels approaches us.

"How can we help you at the Ministry of Records and Licensing?" I'm glad that Bayled taught us some Keshar on the way so I understand some of what she says.

"I need to look up my family records," Bayled says. He nods to us. "They're foreigners, so they'll need citizenship paperwork."

I end up with a tiny booklet containing my name and birthplace and a small medal I can pin to my chest showing that I'm now a Citizen. It's simpler than I'd thought for us to sell off the majority of the Bellisares' valuables at the market. By nightfall, we've had a marvelous dinner of foods I've never imagined, and we're ready to turn in.

We take rooms in a small inn. The owner looks at us curiously but doesn't comment on our clearly foreign appearance.

Bayled, Parsifal, and I huddle in the common room for wine and dessert. "I learned something surprising in Records today," Bayled says, pulling something out of his new coat. He looks just like every other Citizen—it's as if he never left. "You remember my father's merchant business, before my mother was called away to serve as a diplomat?"

"He did pretty well before he and your mother came to the Holy Kingdom, right?" I say, sipping a strange, spicy wine with ice cubes in it.

"Right. It turns out the business still exists, and it's run by his old partner. We should visit her and see about work."

I choke on my wine. "Work?"

Parsifal laughs at me and I scowl at him. Bayled's also grinning, but he's too kind to mock me, even if I deserve it. "That's how we'll get on here. We should use the money we made today to find a place to live. Then maybe we can start rebuilding the family business."

I sigh into the glass. I knew all this when I agreed to come here, but it still feels as if some part of me—the part of me that Mother raised and trained into wanting only one thing—is disappearing into dust.

When we're done talking and drinking, Parsifal helps me to our room. We lie on top of the sheets because it's much too hot. "I don't know that I'll ever get used to this," I say.

"Within a cycle, you won't even notice." Parsifal leans over and lightly kisses my cheek. We have our clothes off before I notice the small pink light hovering outside at the window.

"Percy?"

He looks up and gasps. "I'll let it in!" He thrusts his hand up in the air, and the window opens on its own. The tiny pink wisp flies in, circling the room once, then twice, as if getting a feel for us. It drifts down to the small table beside the bed, where our oil lamp burns. It must have found us by the coating of Magic we still carry. My heart surges, beating a thousand times a second. Hoping.

"Is Sapphire with you?" I ask it. Parsifal kneels beside the table. The wisp doesn't speak, but it settles down at the base of the lamp like a cat finding a comfortable spot to sleep. I look out the window again, begging Melidia that I'll see Sapphire's unmistakeable head of blue hair.

There's nothing except for the late-night dock workers, and a few drunk women kissing and walking home together. Parsifal returns to the bed and wraps his arm around me. We lie there, watching the wisp sleep, its light slowly fading.

I know that Sapphire is alive. That's enough for me.

ACKNOWLEDGMENTS

Since this book was so long-winded, I'll try to keep the next part short.

A huge thank you to my good friend Eddy Rivas (going on two decades!) for telling me years ago this was a fun idea, for gasping and laughing at the right parts, and for always asking me, "When do I get more?" Thank you for being my writing partner for all these years, and telling me the fetus of this weird book was worth it.

Thanks to my dad for raising me with a love of fantasy and sci-fi, for cheering this project on from the beginning . . . and for saying you wanted to read it despite its content.

As always, thank you to my best writing buddy, the Adam to my Becky—Amber Keyser. You're literally the reason I finished drafting this. And of course, Kate and Sione, for all of your insightful thoughts and critiques. You both always take the time for me and I love you.

Huge thanks to my agent, Fiona Kenshole, for championing this from the outset and pushing for it to be real. To Alix Reid for acquiring the not-yet-finished manuscript. And to Amy Fitzgerald, my editor, who picked up the mantle brilliantly, helped me make sense of this weird, wild thing, and who really made all this possible.

And of course, my partner in life, Danny—you are so many multitudes, and I hope this queer little book captured some of them.

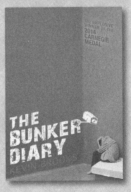

ABOUT THE AUTHOR

Kiersi Burkhart always wanted a high fantasy novel with gobs of kissing, intrigue, and magic. She travels around in an RV with her two dogs, playing tabletop games with her power lifter spouse. A macaron-making master, Kiersi goes on sprees watching Miyazaki movies and *The Great British Bake Off*. She is also the author of the YA novel *Honor Code* and the coauthor of the Quartz Creek Ranch series.